WAIT TILL YOU SEE ME

A LOVE STORY WITH NO ENDING_

ALMA KING

CONTENTS_

"The Book of Love"

The book of love is long and boring
No one can lift the damn thing
It's full of charts and facts and figures
And instructions for dancing

But I
I love it when you read to me
And you
You can read me anything

The book of love has music in it
In fact that's where music comes from
Some of it is just transcendental
Some of it is just really dumb

But I
I love it when you sing to me
And you
You can sing me anything

The book of love is long and boring
And written very long ago
It's full of flowers and heart-shaped boxes
And things we're all too young to know

But I
I love it when you give me things
And you
You ought to give me wedding rings

Peter Gabriel

JUNE 2017_

June 30th, 2017

11:11 am

almaandromeda

Happy Birthday michael! Hope you have an awesome day! 🎁🎉🎈

JULY 2017_

3:04 pm
korbendallas_987
Aww thanks so much. I really appreciate it. I'm old 🙂😅

3:27 pm
almaandromeda
😂😂

3:35 pm
almaandromeda
Me too lol
It's fun!

4:02 pm
almaandromeda
I heard Landslide by Fleetwood Mac on the radio today...

4:24 pm
korbendallas_987
always a good'un. i actually like the tori amos version.

4:30 pm
almaandromeda
I love Tori Amos! But never heard that version, I will look it up.
We were just talking about making an album of our favorite covers because it is so fun to recreate a song that you love. You play guitar?

4:35 pm
almaandromeda
I heard that you played some.. 🎧🎸 We love music! 😄

6:17 pm
korbendallas_987
yes i play anything i can get my hands on including ukulele, recently. i was telling nick that music seems to have a profound effect on me; apparently quite different than it does on other people. Tori Amos is one of my ALL-time favs. Her version of Landslide is on a compilation album, I think it's called "Y-100 Sonic Sessions, Vol. 1" (various artists). You can just youtube it though. Smashing Pumpkins did another killer version of it.

7:47 pm
almaandromeda
Smashing pumpkins version is my favorite. I grew up listening to Tori Amos, Smashing Pumpkins, Bjork, etc cause I was born '78 and feel SO lucky to have the influence of the 90's musically. Poor kids these days 😂 I don't know how unique you will feel about how music affects you after you meet me and nick lol! Music 🎶 is my healing, religion, best friend, so much. I just sing and write songs and nick plays drums, keys, bass, everything!

7:51 pm
almaandromeda
I have been eyeing the ukulele as possibly a good "start" instrument for accompanying vocals when I'm out in the world. Is it still very popular in Hawaii?

7:51 pm
korbendallas_987
VERY popular and very inexpensive. i can search you one down and you can learn to play it in about an hour.

8:31 pm
almaandromeda
I would love that!! It's officially #noexcuses time for us both then when you get your package on Monday too lol 🤓 It would be fun to jam with you. Your brother is my #jammaster and has brought me out so much in music! I am happy that you guys are in touch!

July 2nd, 2017

1:51 pm
korbendallas_987
me too; he seems like a hell of a guy. what a mind-trip this has all been.

3:40 pm
almaandromeda
I bet! My mom found my long lost brother that she had given up for adoption at the age of 16. I knew about him since I was 12 but didn't look for him myself. My mom found him when he turned 30 around 10 yrs ago. I told nick when we were looking for you that from my experience, even though we had never grown up together, there was some soulful connection I had felt from the first time we spoke and even more when we met. He is my brother lol! It is cool to share that unique experience with nick.

3:42 pm
almaandromeda
My llb's (long lost brother) 🤓 name is Kevin and he and his wife and son were the only people we had at our wedding dinner when we eloped to NYC. We are close!

7:49 pm
almaandromeda
I'm gonna have Nick send you the latest music video we made. It is a song I wrote about those mommas but mostly mine lol :-) nick is head in on making the next video and he gets so focused on every aspect. It is awesome to witness. Please enjoy!

July 3rd, 2017

1:31 pm
korbendallas_987
that's impressive.
sometimes i wish i chose a different path;
rockstar would've much more suited me than the military haha

1:34 pm
almaandromeda
You can fly!! That is the coolest ever.

4:33 pm
korbendallas_987
It is, I can't complain. Ever since I was about 4 or 5 it's been my dream--except I wanted to be in a jet--particular a fighter.
Ah well, the grass is always greener, I suppose

5:03 pm
almaandromeda
I could see from your photos as a kid some of that aviation desire..

5:03 pm
almaandromeda
OMG this article I saw says that the Apache helicopter is the hardest rig to fly.

So you use EVERY one of your limbs in autonomous ways?!?

9

July 5th, 2017

7:15 pm
korbendallas_987
Maybe not the HARDEST rig to fly.. But yes, I'm an AH-64D/E Instructor Pilot.

July 6th, 2017

12:06 pm
almaandromeda
Hardest or not!! Amazing! 🤓 I've never even been in a helicopter lol

3:07 pm
korbendallas_987
meh--it's worth a ride maybe 'once' haha
but seriously thank you so much for the birthday package, i feel awful not sending nick anything even tho i really didn't know he was a june baby like me..

3:08 pm
korbendallas_987
what an amazing box to receive!

4:34 pm
almaandromeda
Haha! I love to dance and it reminds me of flying. I love to "fly" so I probably wouldn't mind a helicopter ride "once" this life :-)

4:35 pm
almaandromeda
You are soo welcome for the box o'goodies..
I wear tiger's eye myself for strength.
Have you got anything fun happing on the pedal yet?

4:36 pm
almaandromeda
*happening :-)

4:40 pm
almaandromeda
I'm thinking about getting a loop for vocals for fun

10

5:40 pm
korbendallas_987
Nah I haven't had the time to give it proper attention yet, but I will!

6:34 pm
almaandromeda
Oh yeah sorry I am sure you have been busy lol!

6:50 pm
almaandromeda
Please enjoy it when you can and don't think about anything but that we were on a mission from Coz himself to find you, and were so glad to find that when we did find you that you love music too. It's a cool connection!! Have fun 😄🎶🎷

6:53 pm
korbendallas_987
🙁😣😓😥

6:54 pm
almaandromeda
Sorry to mention your dad 🖤

6:55 pm
almaandromeda
And I am so sorry for your loss.

6:59 pm
korbendallas_987
no it's ok. you not mentioning doesn't mean he didn't die. i need to come to grips with that. if he truly pleaded with someone to find me, that forever breaks my heart and i'm not sure that i'll ever recover. that i'll ever be complete (whatever that even means).

7:21 pm
almaandromeda
When we visited Coz he was very out of it most of it the time. I sang to him a lot.. Lullaby of Birdland especially.. And he would sometimes wake up and look around, he would eat a little from us or sip water and only few times he was so alert that he held conversations.

7:11 pm
almaandromeda
I laid with him a lot and in his little spurts we would talk to him about you existing

as a brother and his face would light up and he would agree that yes you were his son and yes you were nick's brother and Heather's uncle..

7:25 pm
almaandromeda
When we found the pictures we told him about them and that we would find you and he was so happy about that.. He didn't say "Go find michael" but we said "Cozzie we are going to find michael" and his eyes lit up so much and he nodded his head Yes. This was only a few days before he passed away.

7:26 pm
almaandromeda
I have a lot of fkd up family stuff going on so I know how hard it is to let time pass... But you can only do what you can from where you are now.

7:32 pm
korbendallas_987
goddam Alma i will never forgive myself. thank u so much for telling me. i have to ask you, where did the old pictures of my mom come from? i showed her and she flipped out. i'm assuming Coz kept them after all these years?

7:33 pm
korbendallas_987
they were pics of just her getting promoted in the army, e.g.

7:41 pm
almaandromeda
All of the pictures were in a large plastic envelope.. those old ones of her as well. Those were so cool of your army family legacy! It looks like your dad held on to them all. He was a mystery to the end.. He would respond to one thing and then shut off the next. Enigma with the sweetest smile :-)

7:43 pm
almaandromeda
I have a lot of recordings of those two days if you ever want any when you are ready for all of that.

10:29 pm
korbendallas_987
oh gosh no

10:29 pm
korbendallas_987
please don't delete them but i can't bare to watch

10:29 pm
korbendallas_987
you describe him just as my mom did-mysterious.

10:40 pm
almaandromeda
I get it! :-) We will always have them.

10:40 pm
almaandromeda
Did you feel that way about him too?

10:41 pm
korbendallas_987
actually no, not mysterious. just kinda 'different', but i look at myself the same way so it didn't seem peculiar.

10:44 pm
almaandromeda
We can learn a lot about ourselves through looking at those closest to us for sure. I am glad you have found another angle and insight to the elusive Coz :-) I am grateful to share in his life even a little bit.

10:50 pm
almaandromeda
I am learning my hardest lessons yet with my teen son! The party never ends lol

July 9th, 2017

7:10 am
almaandromeda
I mentioned a loop for my vocals but I actually found an app for iPad that is rad – "Music Studio" just FYI for expanding your set up easily. I am just starting to play with it.

5:45 pm
korbendallas_987
i actually mess around with with that GarageBand app a bit. It's pretty neat

11:27 pm
almaandromeda
 Good point. I have that too but just been intimidated by everything haha

11:29 pm
almaandromeda
I should probably be more oFUX like your license plate lol

9:25 pm
korbendallas_987
haha glad you got it--half the time people are like "what does that say?" and i just tell them it's what the DMV gave me 🤷

9:29 pm
almaandromeda
It's my new life motto 🙃 Thanks for the inspiration 😊

9:29 pm
korbendallas_987
ya gotta be careful with it tho; admittedly, sometimes i over-do it

11:01 pm
almaandromeda
If you knew my family you'd understand 😕😂 #nolimits

July 11th, 2017

2:53 pm
almaandromeda
It's hard to not care but I'm working on it haha... mottos help :-)

4:06 pm
korbendallas_987
yea i don't usually practice what i preach; born worrier

5:25 pm
almaandromeda
You're a Cancer, it's not your fault 😂

5:25 pm
almaandromeda
🦀

5:26 pm
korbendallas_987
oh my god--someone who finally understands!

5:26 pm
korbendallas_987
nick is just BARELY a gemini

5:27 pm
almaandromeda
I know! But at the same time SO very Gemini ♊

5:28 pm
almaandromeda
I have been an astrologer for 12-13 yrs

5:29 pm
korbendallas_987
that's cool. i check mine everyday with an app that seems to know the signs extremely well. i could be wrong but i thought nick was almost a cancer

5:31 pm
almaandromeda
How cool! The cusp is around the 21st so you are close.. Do you know your birth time/place?

5:32 pm
almaandromeda
There is a lot more you can see in astrology than the Sun sign, though it is a lot. Helps me accept people as they are! 😊

5:32 pm
almaandromeda
And myself lol

5:34 pm
korbendallas_987
born in Honolulu and Tripler Army Hospital at 12:11 am on a Wednesday. Tell me everything.

5:34 pm
almaandromeda
Don't "worry" I will! 😄

5:35 pm
korbendallas_987
30 June 1979

5:35 pm
korbendallas_987

5:35 pm
korbendallas_987
haha i am worried alresdy

5:35 pm
almaandromeda
I know that part 😂

5:35 pm
almaandromeda
Can't wait, will let you know 👊

5:36 pm
korbendallas_987
I don't say this to many, but I am severely emotional and exploded with crying when nick called. it was too much for me.

5:36 pm
korbendallas_987
gotta be my cancer

5:37 pm
almaandromeda
Combined with the moment.. some real shit!! I cry all the time haha.. it's just something we do around here

5:37 pm
almaandromeda
In a good way lol

5:39 pm
korbendallas_987
i hate it

16

5:39 pm
almaandromeda
Me too really..

5:39 pm
almaandromeda
Lately I have been so emotional it's tiring!

5:40 pm
almaandromeda
Stuff catches up..but crying is good.

5:42 pm
almaandromeda
Get ready lol.. I will check in soon with your "Astro-results" 😬

5:42 pm
korbendallas_987
ready

5:53 pm
almaandromeda
You sound very positive about your birth time, is that the case? Just want to be super sure before I start reading because the "houses" the planets are in are related to the time of birth.

5:54 pm
almaandromeda
It's like the second you decided to come into the world and take your first breath.. and that is the moment you are imprinted with the star pattern around you from the place and time you are on the Earth.

5:56 pm
almaandromeda
I will go with it because you sound very sure!

6:00 pm
almaandromeda
Ok! Right away you can see the beautiful grand trine of Venus, Pluto, and the Moon.. that is the big blue triangle in the middle.

6:02 pm
almaandromeda
Your Sun is in Cancer and Moon in Aquarius, and you are an Aquarius rising. You

also have south node in Aquarius. You are seriously steeped in Aquarian energy in a time of the "Age of Aquarius"..

6:03 pm
almaandromeda
Aquarius is the 11th sign of 12 signs and is known in astrology as the "Perfect Man".. we are evolving as a species to do things like fly and manipulate technology for all kinds of purposes.

6:05 pm
almaandromeda
Your moon in Aquarius shows that you have been working through many evolutions as a soul and are an "old soul"... so old that sometimes you can be "detached" emotionally and socially because you are not matching the frequency of those that are more "normal". Your sun in Cancer is an incarnation of the moon's journey in it's many times in Aquarius.. And in this journey your sun is in Cancer and is learning the lessons associated with family, history, honor, memory, parents, past lives, karma etc

6:06 pm
almaandromeda
So the Cancer sun and Aquarius moon don't always "jive" so to speak, so you may cry and then be like wtf, this sucks

6:06 pm
almaandromeda
You said tell you everything :-)

6:08 pm
almaandromeda
Your south node is in Aquarius too.. the nodes of the moon show your past lives and future lives.. It shows that you have actually possibly come here from the future or from another plane of existence that already understands many of the Aquarian lessons that are coming in this new age for us all.

6:09 pm
almaandromeda
Ok?

6:11 pm
korbendallas_987
jesus

18

6:11 pm
korbendallas_987
that is amazinf

6:11 pm
korbendallas_987
i will have to read and read over again

6:11 pm
almaandromeda
There is a dichotomy of sorts going on between heart and head, and it is the in the opposite direction of normal, usually the heart feels all the woo-y emotions and the head is reasonable. In your case, it is opposite.

6:11 pm
korbendallas_987
i'm positive about where and when i was born

6:11 pm
almaandromeda
There is a lot, is it too much? I am an intuitive astrologer so I can just kind of flow

6:11 pm
korbendallas_987
man, this is unreal

6:11 pm
almaandromeda
Cool! Wow! Oh my gosh cool

6:12 pm
almaandromeda
I am so glad :-)

6:12 pm
korbendallas_987
i nearly broke down talking to my shrink today about normal shit like loving my mom, etc

6:12 pm
korbendallas_987
nothing is too much

6:12 pm
korbendallas_987
i am the most mysterious person to myself

6:12 pm
korbendallas_987
i don't know who i sm

6:12 pm
korbendallas_987
am

6:13 pm
almaandromeda
So hard to look at it all in the same frame

6:13 pm
almaandromeda
I will keep going haha

6:15 pm
korbendallas_987
my wife is an aquarius i believe, which we aren't supposed to be compatible. but we get along fibr

6:15 pm
korbendallas_987
fine

6:16 pm
almaandromeda
So "Sun" and "Moon" don't talk (head and heart, mom and dad) and that makes it hard to have a channel between the two. When emotions come they are attempted to be put into a processing, and this life is about elevating your ability to process to a "human" level of "Care"..

6:16 pm
almaandromeda
That is so cool that you are both Aquarius's.. I could see you definitely getting along!

6:17 pm
almaandromeda
nick and I both have Leo moons and that helps us live together lol

6:18 pm
korbendallas_987
we're both water signs, which i thought was bad

6:18 pm
almaandromeda
I mean you are a cancer but with so much Aquarius lol

6:18 pm
almaandromeda
I see energy haha

6:18 pm
almaandromeda
Aquarius is not a water sign it is an air sign

6:18 pm
almaandromeda
It is the highest air, the atmosphere

6:18 pm
korbendallas_987
at one time, i was. when i was younger

6:18 pm
almaandromeda
You were destined to fly 🚁

6:19 pm
korbendallas_987
ohhhh

6:19 pm
almaandromeda
So your sun is in in Cancer, which is water

6:19 pm
korbendallas_987
she is 14 Feb 1991

6:20 pm
almaandromeda
But your moon is in Aquarius, which is air, and your rising is the same. Those three
are the kind of "trinity" of the chart and then rest fill in the blanks

6:20 pm
almaandromeda
I will look her up!! Also I can do "synastry" which is cross referencing charts
together

6:21 pm
almaandromeda
So much understanding and also it is always so obvious the deep love in married
couples, and past life stuff

6:21 pm
korbendallas_987
wow this is bigger than i thought

6:21 pm
korbendallas_987
don't waste your time if u don't want to

6:10 pm
korbendallas_987
it sounds like is one of the most conflicted

6:10 pm
korbendallas_987
like cancer_*

6:10 pm
almaandromeda
Only if you want me to continue I am happy to! It is one of my passions.

6:11 pm
almaandromeda
Not at all.. Cancer is just home and family, memory, and history.. it is the crab who
is sensitive on the inside but a hard shell on the outside. It moves side to side and
can be cautious.

6:24 pm
almaandromeda
Do you want me to keep looking at your chart?

22

6:25 pm
korbendallas_987
you've described me to a T

6:32 pm
almaandromeda
All charts are conflicted.. Because there are so many signs and planets all in the same chart.. As you can see in the picture. That is what makes it so cool to be human! There is no "one way" in our heads and hearts and histories... everything adds up to make each person very unique.

6:35 pm
almaandromeda
Moon trine Venus - you are playful! Moon trine Pluto - staying power and drive. Saturn conjunct Mars- extreme focus and diligence where you put your mind to a task, especially in the sign of Virgo which is detail oriented.. engineer, pilot, very focused mind.

6:39 pm
almaandromeda
What I see about your future is the Leo north node which is about coming into the the spotlight, coming out of the shadow. The north node is often the thing we feel like doing least until around the middle of our lives and then we go forward into it with purpose and a sense of direction that is new and different.. that Leo north node is drawing you out and saying "michael.. be seen!" It is something that is cultivated over the whole lifetime and can feel awkward and different

6:41 pm
almaandromeda
That is a lot of it in a short synopsis, I hope I did not freak you out with my take on it all. All astrologers are a bit different and I am a bit different anyways lol. Message form is also hard for inflections obviously :-)

6:45 pm
almaandromeda
In short your chart rocks 🌙 and you are here to seriously influence the New Age in your own special way. 🚁 🌀 I know it's hard to see it all at once, but just the fact that you fly means that you are actualizing the highest evolution of mankind thus far... think about it. Seriously cool stuff.

6:46 pm
almaandromeda
Tomorrow I will check out lorie if she wants and tell you guys about her chart, if she wants let me know!

8:43 pm
almaandromeda
Thank you for letting me share your chart with you and I hold it and your information in the highest regard 🪷

July 12th, 2017

8:14 am
almaandromeda
Sleeping brought a few more small insights or exercises I woke up with..

*let emotions wash thru w/out needing to assign meaning & purpose to each feeling.. crying and emotions serve many purposes - cleansing, sensing, expression.. they are not inherently "bad" or "good" - just feelings.. as they move thru you can trust your intuitive mind to work it out on it's own time.

8:14 am
almaandromeda
*Trust time.

8:16 am
almaandromeda
*Tinkering, perfectionism... with Aquarius being "The Perfect Man" and your Saturn/Mars in Virgo of striving for perfection in all tasks... You can be hard on yourself! You are "perfecting" on a spiritual plane and one a physical plane BOTH - so much work and tho you have major stamina and capability to go the distance and achieve, you must tread lightly with your own judgements of self.

8:16 am
almaandromeda
*Once your see your own greatness, it becomes a gift you can offer the world.

8:57 am
korbendallas_987
so much to process. it hits home because of how introverted i "can" be.. and emotional. my head goes too fast sometimes but it can be helpful because of my job. been in a real rut lately so i'm hoping for a change. thank you so much.

9:38 am
almaandromeda
Lots to read and sift thru... ❤🖼 Take it easy on yo'self yo! 😊 You are so welcome.

3:59 pm
almaandromeda
Just heard Tori Amos is playing in Seattle in November, tix go on sale Fri 10 am .
Oh yeah! 😎 I just did a karaoke cover of hers.. forgot how much I missed her voice.

4:00 pm
korbendallas_987
hnnnnngggggghhhhh

4:00 pm
korbendallas_987
my GOD "Muhammad, My Friend🎶..."

4:05 pm
almaandromeda
Haha 😂 I wonder if she still plays any old stuff.. 🎶 I think I'm the wrong band..🎶
or older than that. I don't know if I would if I was still making new material. Do you
know her new stuff?

5:09 pm
korbendallas_987
i have ALL of her stuff but favor the 90s through early 00s (Scarlet's Walk)

5:09 pm
korbendallas_987
🖤

5:10 pm
almaandromeda
I don't know if you've heard of Regina Spector, she is sort of newer, but since I read
your chart I have had this song in my head.. Apparently, "this is how it works" 😄

5:11 pm
almaandromeda
This part especially..
This is how it works
You're young until you're not
You love until you don't
You try until you can't
You laugh until you cry
You cry until you laugh
And everyone must breathe

25

Until their dying breath

5:24 pm
almaandromeda
No, this is how it works
You peer inside yourself
You take the things you like
And try to love the things you took
And then you take that love you made
And stick it into some
Someone else's heart
Pumping someone else's blood
And walking arm in arm
You hope it don't get harmed
But even if it does
You'll just do it all again

5:25 pm
korbendallas_987
You know, Tori Amos has a condition called "chromethesia"--which is where she
can physically see the notes on a scale/song like colors of light in a spectrum.. She
can "see" music. 👀

5:25 pm
korbendallas_987
didn't mean to ignore your reply

5:25 pm
korbendallas_987
those lyrics hurt

5:27 pm
almaandromeda
That is cool about Tori's spider music sense, I believe it

5:27 pm
almaandromeda
I'm sorry to share that then!! 😐🖤

5:27 pm
korbendallas_987
she's a got-dam savant

5:28 pm
almaandromeda
I know it is trivializing also honestly

5:28 pm
almaandromeda
But the motto thing lol..

5:28 pm
korbendallas_987
no it's ok, i listen to powerful, POWERFUL music and welcome ALL of it

5:28 pm
korbendallas_987
apologize for nothing

5:28 pm
almaandromeda
Ok I won't haha

5:29 pm
almaandromeda
In your chart you have moon conjunct south node, as I mentioned and it is SUPER DEEP to say the least

5:29 pm
korbendallas_987
99% of my music is blasphemous, offensive, or any mixture of the two

5:30 pm
almaandromeda
Your your music?

5:30 pm
almaandromeda
Do you ever write anything?

5:30 pm
korbendallas_987
my shrink says that i am a 'see-er', and that it is a double-edged sword

5:30 pm
korbendallas_987
no i mean my music collection

5:30 pm
almaandromeda
I can imagine your music is very eclectic

5:30 pm
korbendallas_987
she seems to think i'm brilliant and should belong to MENSA but i think she's just putting me ob

5:30 pm
korbendallas_987
on

5:31 pm
korbendallas_987
what did u mean by the super deep prt

5:31 pm
almaandromeda
That is cool that she 'sees' you... you have already taught me so much!

5:32 pm
almaandromeda
It's hard to explain but just by getting to connect with you both I have become much more aware and open hearted.

5:32 pm
korbendallas_987
well i think she means that i can walk in a room and tell exactly what everyone is thinking and/or predict what will happen next

5:32 pm
korbendallas_987
i am NOT claiming clairvoyancy

5:32 pm
almaandromeda
Oh my gosh that is freakin amazing

5:33 pm
almaandromeda
Amazing

5:33 pm
korbendallas_987
i can imagine that nick and I will be two of the more intriguing people you will meet in this journey

5:33 pm
almaandromeda
Already are.

5:33 pm
almaandromeda
You are a "sensitive"

5:33 pm
korbendallas_987
extremely

5:33 pm
korbendallas_987
Über

5:33 pm
korbendallas_987
💀

5:33 pm
korbendallas_987
too sensitive

5:34 pm
korbendallas_987
the mere thought of harm to my mother beckons the darkest and deepest demons that lurk inside of me

5:34 pm
korbendallas_987
please don't let any of this scare you

5:34 pm
almaandromeda
im not scurried :-)

5:34 pm
korbendallas_987
she's just all i ever had and i hope to die before she does

5:35 pm
almaandromeda
You seem very connected to her spiritually in this life

5:35 pm
almaandromeda
I can see that you are sensitive also in how you build up your body and the military life

5:35 pm
korbendallas_987
i am

5:35 pm
almaandromeda
It is part of being a "sensitive" so that you are protecting your Spirit on the inside

5:35 pm
korbendallas_987
it's a thin candy shell, though

5:36 pm
korbendallas_987
it must be very easy to see

5:36 pm
korbendallas_987
how embarrassing

5:36 pm
almaandromeda
I am grateful honestly to your foresight in a tough world that you built up that shell because it kept your Spirit light inside and that is the easy part to see

5:37 pm
korbendallas_987
i don't know what i've done to myself, honestly

5:37 pm
almaandromeda
It is so difficult for people who are very open and aware to be put in dark situations over time... we build up walls, shells, defenses, advances, habits.. it's natural and I do it too

5:37 pm
almaandromeda
You have protected yourself

5:37 pm
korbendallas_987
i have severe body dysmorphia and all i see is normal people who don't spend 20 years straight inside a fucking gym

5:37 pm
korbendallas_987
what kind of person does that?

5:38 pm
korbendallas_987
i'm never happy with my body and this is probably too much information but you're easy to talk to

5:38 pm
almaandromeda
Remember I mentioned that you have a serious "thing" with "tinkering" and perfectionism?

5:38 pm
almaandromeda
It's a real thing

5:38 pm
korbendallas_987
my shrink said same thing

5:39 pm
korbendallas_987
i'm a perfectionist and it's why i'm always disappointed

5:39 pm
korbendallas_987
are you a shrink?!

5:39 pm
almaandromeda
You are very focused on perfecting yourself on all the planes of existence in this life and you are not "satisfied" with yourself until you reach this ideal that is in your head and not in everyone elses

5:40 pm
almaandromeda
The rest of the world is not so hard on itself.. but it is a double edged sword because you are a "warrior" and you are training always for betterment so it is in some ways awesome and amazing that you have this "issue" because obviously it makes you strive WAY far ABOVE and beyond others

5:40 pm
almaandromeda
I am an astrologer lol :-)

5:41 pm
korbendallas_987
yes all true 😪 😳

5:41 pm
almaandromeda
I have this issue myself in perfectionism to be honest in other ways

5:41 pm
almaandromeda

5:41 pm
korbendallas_987
she said the most successful people in the world have anxiety

5:41 pm
korbendallas_987
she also said something that blew me away; "depression is anger turned inward"

5:44 pm
almaandromeda
A lot of that striving can stem from not feeling good enough for someone or some-

thing specifically as a kid.. You want to be the "best" and keep proving how awesome you are but they will never acknowledge that no matter what

5:44 pm
almaandromeda
Fuck'em haha

5:44 pm
almaandromeda
My mom is the biggest evil woman on planet earth..

5:44 pm
almaandromeda
I win on all counts of a terrible childhood haha

5:45 pm
almaandromeda
I was just sued by her this past year :-(

5:46 pm
almaandromeda
Don't mean to freak you out on the mom tip

5:47 pm
almaandromeda
But I am just saying that I know how it is to want to be super good and awesome for someone but they won't acknowledge it so you just try harder in all the wrong ways..

5:48 pm
almaandromeda
Sorry to offend if I did, I know how much your mom means to you and I just have a very different relationship with my mom..

5:49 pm
korbendallas_987
what the actual PHOK

5:49 pm
korbendallas_987
you are mirroring what my damn shrink says

5:49 pm
almaandromeda

5:49 pm
almaandromeda
All true haha your shrink rocks

5:49 pm
korbendallas_987
she says it comes from childhood—"all behavior is purposeful, and we are molded by experiences we don't even remember"

5:49 pm
korbendallas_987
no offense AT ALL

5:50 pm
korbendallas_987
it's all fucking true

5:50 pm
korbendallas_987
i grew up with her fighting my stepdad every night

5:50 pm
korbendallas_987
2 people know this, now 3, but as a result, i am an extreme mysoginist

5:51 pm
almaandromeda
How do you feel that reflects you in your life?

5:51 pm
korbendallas_987
which makes no sense because i would slit god's throat if he even spoke ill of her

5:51 pm
korbendallas_987
i don't know

5:51 pm
korbendallas_987
i can't make any sense of all of this

5:51 pm
almaandromeda
What does it mean?

5:51 pm
korbendallas_987
too much information to procrss

5:51 pm
almaandromeda
The word mysoginist?

5:52 pm
korbendallas_987
a mysoginist is a person who hates, to their absolute core, the female genderx

5:52 pm
korbendallas_987
gender*

5:52 pm
almaandromeda
How are you able to be married to a woman?

5:53 pm
korbendallas_987
understand Alma, that i am only telling you this because i feel you have insight --
you damn sure have knowledge

5:53 pm
almaandromeda

5:53 pm
korbendallas_987
thats the thing--i make extreme exceptions to my own rules

5:53 pm
almaandromeda
You are EXTREME in general my friend haha

5:53 pm
almaandromeda
And so your exceptions would of course have to be extreme :-)

5:54 pm
korbendallas_987
i mean, how could i hate 5 billion women automatically--that's silly. but in general, it's the way i've always been

5:54 pm
almaandromeda
I understand.

5:54 pm
almaandromeda
I really do.

5:54 pm
korbendallas_987

5:55 pm
almaandromeda
For some reason michael, you have seriously opened my eyes to understanding "other"

5:55 pm
almaandromeda
It's really humbling

5:55 pm
almaandromeda
And it is through that understanding that I can see how this makes sense...

5:55 pm
almaandromeda
I look forward to seeing you guys and sharing war stories lol

5:55 pm
almaandromeda
The real kind

5:56 pm
korbendallas_987
absolutely. you think i'm nuts now, wait till you see me. garden-variety sociopath

5:56 pm
korbendallas_987
you're a very nice girl, nick hit a homer and I'm sure he knows it. hard to find a
grounded female--trust me

5:56 pm
almaandromeda
I already see you lol and I have also seen you as a kid.. no hiding here

5:56 pm
korbendallas_987

5:57 pm
korbendallas_987
lol

5:57 pm
korbendallas_987
i suppose u have

5:57 pm
almaandromeda
Thanks :-) nick is such a healing and loving person, and also very "seeing" too

5:57 pm
almaandromeda
You guys are both super heros

5:57 pm
korbendallas_987
it was all just a moustache, hiding my inner Beelzebub!

5:57 pm
almaandromeda
You are are real life "Transformer"

5:57 pm
korbendallas_987
nick seems like a see-er

5:57 pm
almaandromeda

5:57 pm
korbendallas_987
must get that from Coz King the POPS

5:58 pm
almaandromeda
He is a healer and also "Transformer" but in a spiritual sense

5:58 pm
almaandromeda
We just listened to some music we made together 8 years ago

5:58 pm
almaandromeda
Hilarious!!!

5:59 pm
almaandromeda
He saw in me something that was not there AT ALL and just worked with me these last 7 years in the basement making music and singing

5:59 pm
almaandromeda
He is the most dedicated DUDE I have ever met and I am so happy for you that you get him as a brother :-)

5:59 pm
korbendallas_987
fuck i wish i had all that equipment--i wouldn't leave the house

5:59 pm
korbendallas_987
i just bought my dream guitar, lookin for an amp now

6:00 pm
almaandromeda
When do we get to hear you play?

6:00 pm
almaandromeda
I have seen your guitars in the pictures for a long time.. looks like you play often at home?

6:01 pm
korbendallas_987
i dabble

6:01 pm
korbendallas_987
NEVER in front of anyone but lor

6:02 pm
almaandromeda
Well this will obviously be another thing that now 2 more people see and know about you haha

6:02 pm
korbendallas_987
Never!!

6:03 pm
almaandromeda
Never say never haha :-)

6:05 pm
korbendallas_987
We cant wait to see Seatac for sure!

6:06 pm
almaandromeda
You guys are SO welcome, have either of you ever been here yet?

6:07 pm
almaandromeda
Though we were just watching Magnum PI with helicopters and they are in HI and I'm like to nick... uhh why are we not going there? Lol

6:07 pm
korbendallas_987
come!! we have plenty of room!! big house (no idea why) but our house is huge

6:08 pm
korbendallas_987
god i would love that

6:08 pm
almaandromeda
Big dog haha

6:08 pm
almaandromeda
We have a big house too and just 2 cats and us living here right now

6:08 pm
korbendallas_987
ah

6:08 pm
almaandromeda
Dog is fine for us!! I am just saying that is why you have the big house :-)

6:09 pm
almaandromeda
We can't wait to meet your little girl

6:09 pm
korbendallas_987
nah these houses we live in are on a national registry (pearl harbor?) so they won't make them smaller

6:09 pm
almaandromeda
Are you in the barracks military base neighborhood area zone?

6:10 pm
almaandromeda
I don't know the correct terminology so I threw it all in haha

6:24 pm
korbendallas_987
yes we live on post. it's nearly all protected "historic" bullshit so the streets make no sense, buildings are inefficient, etc. housing is nice though

6:24 pm
korbendallas_987
an old film with Frank Sinatra was filmed here in the 50's called "From Here to Eternity"--my neighborhood

6:27 pm
almaandromeda
That is so cool... I just realized that I have done something so similar to "misogyny" in a female version due to my older brothers and dad and step dad and the world at large... it makes even more sense now. I don't have the same thing in the past 7 or so years, but it was hard to let go of some of my knee jerk judgements of the male universe

6:28 pm
almaandromeda
All of the "mean" male stuff I lumped together and didn't really allow in my life except in small amounts..

6:29 pm
almaandromeda
I used to be more like Jean Gray - destroying everything around me with my mind

6:29 pm
almaandromeda
Now I use my power for good haha :-)

7:12 pm
korbendallas_987
oh my GADDDTTHEEE--Phoenix!!! my fav of all time

7:13 pm
almaandromeda
Mine too... I have Kali on my back, she is like that too but in the Hindi religion - she is the darkest night, at the moment everything is destroyed.. for some reason I have that as an archetype

7:14 pm
almaandromeda
A lot to work with lol But I am dancing and training and learning how to be
powerful in new ways

7:14 pm
korbendallas_987
"Her telekinetic strength and skill are both of a supremely high power-level, capable
of grasping objects in Earth orbit and manipulating hundreds of components in
mid-air in complex patterns. She often uses her telekinesis to lift herself and others,
giving her the ability of levitation and flight."

7:15 pm
korbendallas_987
"She uses her telekinesis to create durable shields and energy blasts. She later mani-
fests a "telekinetic sensitivity" (called "the Manifestation of the Phoenix"[24]) to
objects in her immediate environment that lets her feel the texture and molecular
patterns of objects, feel when other objects come into contact with them, and probe
them at a molecular or subatomic level."

7:15 pm
almaandromeda

7:15 pm
almaandromeda
I love it!!

7:15 pm
korbendallas_987
she is soooo dope. committed suicide many times over because she couldn't handle
her own ubiquitousness

7:16 pm
almaandromeda
Yup.

7:16 pm
almaandromeda
Haha 😂

7:16 pm
almaandromeda
It is about channeling that strength

7:16 pm
korbendallas_987
watch X-Men: The Last Stand

7:16 pm
korbendallas_987
she is sensational in it

7:17 pm
almaandromeda
I will soon 👊

7:18 pm
almaandromeda
Tomorrow I will tell you about the moon/south node thing

7:18 pm
almaandromeda
Good night 🌙

7:34 pm
almaandromeda
Ubiquitousness is the coolest word. Ever. I get what you mean, she couldn't stand being everywhere at once inside of everything... a "sensitive" to the max yo. I wonder why extreme anger is such a component of extreme sensitivity..

7:42 pm
korbendallas_987
thank you for appreciating my vernacular, genuinely. i work around troglodytes that can barely annunciation their own last names.. 🙁

7:45 pm
almaandromeda
I can't say it's not surprising from the outside in, but that is all part of why you are humbling the shit out of me lol

7:47 pm
korbendallas_987
we King's portend to be a strange bunch indeed 😉

7:45 pm
almaandromeda
I feel lucky to get the name then 😉

7:47 pm
korbendallas_987
annunciate* from earlier text

7:48 pm
almaandromeda
Apparently.. it's a "line" for sure with Coz-mic connections lol

7:48 pm
korbendallas_987

7:48 pm
korbendallas_987
now THAT, is a good'un

7:49 pm
almaandromeda
Haha lol :-) Good night, tomorrow I will tell you about the moon/node thing, part of the "line" actually and all of it..

7:49 pm
korbendallas_987
please do, i look forward to it. night

July 14th, 2017

3:35 pm
almaandromeda
Just thought you should know that as an astrologer and caring person I understand and respect your privacy. :-) Thank you for your openness with me.

3:36 pm
almaandromeda
I have been busy with my nephew all day but I will write after 10:30 on those notes I mentioned.

3:36 pm
korbendallas_987
👌

5:35 pm
almaandromeda
Oh my gosh you rock!! I just saw that letter you wrote on nick's behalf, talk about vernacular lol

5:53 pm
almaandromeda
nick is stoked we are connecting over family stuff and astrology. I spoke of privacy earlier because it is respectful to hold space in that way. Also, because you and your brother are just getting to finally know each other and you both have the right to share very personal stuff on your own time, and learn about each other together.

5:56 pm
almaandromeda
Looking at your chart I saw something that speaks to a lot of the darkness, lonlieness, hanging on a rope spinning in space in the blackness... There is something that you are facing in this life that is very dark and because of that your triumph will be the greatest.

5:57 pm
almaandromeda
You are looking back in time, in space... and a lot of it is attached to memories of violence or anger in your childhood but especially before that, in a past life or lives.

6:04 pm
almaandromeda
One of your focuses this life will be to separate emotionally from your history, your past, your memories, and all the stuff that has "happened" to you.

6:05 pm
almaandromeda
I have 3 older stepbrothers, and they were 8/10/12 years older. I spent my summers in New Orleans, LA with my dad and stepmom and them. My little brother is 18 mos younger than me.

6:02 pm
almaandromeda
I was seriously abused by the 3 of them for years in a few different ways...

6:08 pm
almaandromeda
There is something that over time you will have to objectify from your past and say, "That is not me"

6:09 pm
almaandromeda
"That was them"
"This is Me."

6:48 pm
almaandromeda
I did that with art and poetry, and soooo much anger!!

6:49 pm
almaandromeda
Anger directed out can at least be seen and processed through expression
eventually..

7:00 pm
korbendallas_987
You truly, truly, truly seem to know me-or at least the charts do. I respond to stimuli
with the protection of fire and vehemently defend friends and family. I can hold
grudges for decades. It doesn't make much sense to me, ONLY because all of the
tards at work act like I'm sooo different and weird. My enemies are fierce, but my
friends fiercer.

7:01 pm
korbendallas_987
I have plodded through the shadows of life for almost 40 years now--almost to wear
a smile physically pains me. I just wish I knew how to make it stop without the
obvious solution (one I will not consider).

7:02 pm
korbendallas_987
I'm truly sorry to hear of your childhood, my mother suffered the same fate and if
she told me about it while he was alive I'd be doing a life sentence. Maybe she
knows that.

7:05 pm
korbendallas_987
But you're right, even with a wife that loves me, a new fucking BROTHER with a
clairvoyant wife, friends all throughout the Army, a mom and other brother who
love me, I feel completely alone. I think the only point of solace I can take in all of
this is that the loneliness isn't new; it's been an acquaintance for about 40 years
now.

46

7:06 pm
korbendallas_987
i don't mean to bitch or anything, just always interested in what you make of "me"

7:16 pm
almaandromeda

7:17 pm
almaandromeda
I "make" that you amaze me

7:18 pm
almaandromeda
You are truly one of a kind and I am sorry it has been so hard, so far..

7:19 pm
korbendallas_987
thank you. people tell me that, including my shrink, but it appears completely genuine coming from you. what a gal.

7:20 pm
almaandromeda
You don't see what we see, the same way, but you are VERY special and talented and "selected" for a unique=lonely path

7:21 pm
almaandromeda
You actually chose it yourself because you are that strong

7:21 pm
almaandromeda
Not everyone can hang lol

7:24 pm
almaandromeda
Some of us get to be that awesome.. and you are not alone in that ♥✊🏻♥

7:35 pm
almaandromeda
Your commitment to life through the blackness is SO inspiring 💪 It's only a triumph when it's fucking hard. You are rocking this 🌠📱🤓

7:49 pm
almaandromeda

"I've been soft spoken
Cause I've been afraid
Of only exposing
The way I'm made
An ocean frozen
Alone in space
Untied and broken
Since you're away"

7:55 pm
almaandromeda

Some of my lyrics.. it's hard to show that blackness... but blackness is depth, the
darkest night, the deepest ocean, the breadth of humanity's walk on this plane.. it is
a deep well where all creative stars and sparks are formed. ●

8:00 pm
korbendallas_987

oh we smell our own, trust me. you are not the tainted soul that i have retreated to,
but i do see dark parts. i guess without dark there isn't light?

8:01 pm
korbendallas_987

man it must be a trip being married to someone so cerebral

11:12 pm
almaandromeda

Though I know him better than I know you, it seems you are both so similar.. very
deep, underneath. nick is lucky in being loved this life and does not appear
"wounded" in the way I am but he is so gentle and focused on love this lifetime that
he can "see" and understand and tap in to the heart. You are both so capable of
going in between head and heart, rare in anybody really.. but especially the male
gender.

11:53 pm
korbendallas_987

wow--yea it's very apparent that i mean nearly NO ONE like me. it's a curse, trust
me. it makes us too aware, both inwardly and outwardly, at least for me. I wish to be
a simpleton, maybe even someone mentally retarded or deficient. They don't have
time to worry and talk themselves in and out of things.

11:53 pm
korbendallas_987
meet* nearly

July 15th, 2017

1:30 pm
almaandromeda
I have a MILLION and seven questions for you.. you are obviously fascinating haha

1:39 pm
almaandromeda
Maybe instead of a "simpleton" you can be like a bird or squirrel or cat.. They don't give a FUCK about our "Maya" which is the cultures and stories and government and hierarchies.. all that stuff we all collectively "See" and agree to together here..

1:39 pm
almaandromeda
The bird flys over, the squirrel climbs alongside, and the cat lives within, but they are all immune to the Maya that controls the rest of us.

1:40 pm
almaandromeda
So if even if outwardly as Humans we cannot responsibly ignore the Maya, we can adjust our heart frequency to the freedom of a bird. 🖤🕊🖤

1:42 pm
almaandromeda
It's just another way of desiring that freedom from worry, without diminishing yourself at all. You are SO BIG, and SO FULL of your own Spirit, that there is no way to make less of you. You are a transformer and can just transform.

1:43 pm
almaandromeda
Also.. you make serious moves.. It is understandable that you would weigh all of that heavily.. that only says to me that you have very powerful wisdom.

2:24 pm
korbendallas_987
You hit the nail on the head on the maya thing--it's exactly the way I do NOT want to be. PHOK if i were you, I'd be master of my domain--and that isn't insinuating that you aren't.. I just wish I had that grip on it all that you obviously have.

49

2:25 pm
korbendallas_987
Ask away--all of this has proven immensely cathartic for me. I feel guilty because I haven't paid you!

2:25 pm
almaandromeda
You are one of my greatest teachers already.. priceless :-)

2:26 pm
almaandromeda
Hard to explain why but Dogma is a big reason.. Somehow you being you has made me question everything that I used to know I believed.. I see a new side it all..

2:26 pm
almaandromeda
Thank you for that.

2:27 pm
almaandromeda
Q1: What age did you enter the military? Out of high school?

2:28 pm
almaandromeda
Some of them are boring questions haha

2:30 pm
korbendallas_987
well first, i do not mean to be one of those "off-the-cuff", blowhard atheists, I hate them. And I most certainly didn't mean to sway you spiritually or religiously--there is peer reviewed research that proves that dogmatic humans, or "believers" (in whatever), have, for lack of a scientific term that i'm unaware of, healthier regions in certain cortices (cortexes?) of their brain. so DONT let me take that from you.

2:30 pm
korbendallas_987
but i came into the army late, almost 11 years ago

2:31 pm
korbendallas_987
i shunned it because it's all my family has done successfully and i wanted something different. dumb 😵

2:33 pm
almaandromeda
So cool to know.. As for Dogma, I mean that I used to be (until a month ago haha) so incredibly set in how I believed the world was formed and who I thought was "right" and who I thought was "wrong".. I have been a peace activist and a spoken word artist and a "blowhard" about my opinions my whole life.. Now you, an apache helicopter pilot man, has come into our lives and a boulder was removed from my heart.

2:34 pm
almaandromeda
I believe in the Universe and spiritual connections and Oneness and all of that..no one can take that from me lol.

2:35 pm
almaandromeda
Did you go to college instead of military or work or travel or?

2:36 pm
korbendallas_987
i floated from job to job, often simultaneous ones to afford this car that i wanted. it's weird, i think the only reason i am "considered" successful (by some) is purely driven by having nice things. how revolting is that?

2:37 pm
korbendallas_987
I got my bachelor's after becoming a pilot, while teaching flight school in Alabama.

2:39 pm
almaandromeda
It is what we know. The thing$ and things. For some reason I was spared any interest in things until around this last few years.. now I was to be RICH and free, but I used to not care. The thing about "things" is that it is the "Evidence" of your manifestations in this life. By having physical things you are proving your prowess to manifest, and it is a way we all know to see manifestation and power on this plane.

2:40 pm
a**lmaandromeda**
That is why I am starting to value it now

2:40 pm
korbendallas_987
exactly

2:40 pm
almaandromeda
Money isn't everything, but it's not nothing haha

2:40 pm
korbendallas_987
it's a display for me to show the guy on the car next to me that i am further into the maze of rats

2:41 pm
almaandromeda
And a way for you to show yourself that you are further.. it is a relationship to this world that you have. And it is community, when we aren't given many positive methods of finding community here..

2:42 pm
almaandromeda
Though your car interest to me is rad and it is "positive" if that means anything.. it is JUST money and when we are free to experience this plane entirely, we are free to play with money

2:42 pm
korbendallas_987
you certainly have unique ways of looking at things. doesn't make me feel as horrible

2:43 pm
korbendallas_987
that's funny; like my dad, i have "oFXGIVN" about money

2:43 pm
almaandromeda
You are a Creator, and some of that is in all of the "forms" you have made in muscles and cars and helicopter flying

2:43 pm
korbendallas_987
i don't hoard it, i use it to live. that's really t

2:43 pm
korbendallas_987
it

2:44 pm

almaandromeda

You are seriously inspiring.. in money especially and in Creation of this realm. Make stuff and do stuff and have stuff OK! That is what the Universe says to us before we are born.

2:45 pm

almaandromeda

Speaking of flying.. I have so many questions about that alone. I am FASCINATED by your job tbh.

2:46 pm

almaandromeda

The other day I was dancing and taping it and outside in the sun and I happened to look up at the sun streaming down and the sky was SO HIGH and I just started crying, I was so amazed that you get all the way up there and teach others that.

2:47 pm

korbendallas_987

haha

2:47 pm

almaandromeda

I am making ramen noodles for your bro but I will ask some of that later if that's cool

2:47 pm

korbendallas_987

i have a fear of heights • •

2:47 pm

almaandromeda

Impossible!! :-)

2:47 pm

korbendallas_987

absolutely--ask anything

2:48 pm

korbendallas_987

i'm going to punish my muscles for their insolence

6:12 pm

almaandromeda

😄 Motivation is key, I am amazed at how you make yourself work out that much!!

dance twice a week for 2 hrs at "Ecstatic Dance" which is my absolute joy and freedom and meditation. It is where I figure out all the stuff I know lol

6:59 pm
almaandromeda
Do you go every day to the gym? 💪I would imagine probably for your results lol

9:41 pm
korbendallas_987
ugh.. that's a whole other story.. i'll go for months until i literally can't get out of bed. i overtrain constantly and will pay the price someday. but, it dawned on me one day, that i workout not only for the physical benefits, but to get "high" from th endorphins. almost like an addict. it's another vile characteristic on my list. i do try and take pride in the changes i see take place, and that is a very cool thing to witness, but the real reason is that it just "feels" good.

9:42 pm
korbendallas_987
so, yes, as long as the army allows it, everyday.

9:42 pm
korbendallas_987
on my list of attributes*

10:20 pm
almaandromeda
Endorphins are what's up :-) I access those in dance everytime and that is part of the flying feeling.. so high it is not like anything else. 🚀Speaking of flying.. more later

10:38 pm
korbendallas_987
heck yea--in the rare case i take a few days off, i actually fall into a bit of a depression because of the lack of them. Cool, huh? 😑

10:50 pm
almaandromeda
Caffeine, nicotine, weed, cocaine, endorphins, take your pick.. 😵Human-ing is hard, people escape.. You've really gone "all in" tho huh? Is it a lifetime commitment once you decide to build up like that?

10:57 pm
korbendallas_987
explain your question further, if you would?

11:00 pm
almaandromeda
Of course, sorry :-) I am just wondering if you are committed physically to keeping up that much muscle or if it is even a spiritual commitment for you for life.. do you feel like you are past some point of no return to "normalsville" like the rest of us losers or can you just "stop" if you ever felt like it..

11:04 pm
almaandromeda
Here is that wild moment btw outside looking at the sky.. damn endorphins after 2 hrs of dance haha

11:04 pm (Alma sends a video of herself dancing outside, looking up at the sky and crying)

11:06 pm
almaandromeda
How can you possibly have a fear of heights and get up that high?

11:06 pm
almaandromeda
You must be joking lol

11:47 pm
korbendallas_987
ohhh that is a VERY good question

11:48 pm
korbendallas_987
i talk about it all the time with lorie. please take my candor with a bit of sugar--i do NOT mean to offend

11:49 pm
korbendallas_987
but if her and i are out at the beach or the mall or whatever, i ask her, "how can people look like this? how can people NOT workout?? i would blow my brains out."

11:49 pm
korbendallas_987

11:49 pm
korbendallas_987
THAT is how bad my body dysmorphia is. Those people are largely (pun intended) content with their physical appearances.

11:52 pm
korbendallas_987
as for your other question--LOTS of pilots are afraid of heights. It's very typical with type-A personalities because they (i don't consider myself type-A) have to be "in control." So, looking over the edge of a skyscraper would make me projectile vomit, but flying in an airplane at 37,000 feet doesn't. Same with being in a twin-engine Apache at a 400ft hover. I'm in control (for the most part) so it doesn't scare me.

11:52 pm
korbendallas_987
That make sense?

11:53 pm
korbendallas_987
But the original answer to your question is that I am doomed to this gym-rat life I have chosen. It will wind up being years of my life I'll never get back. Pot-committed.

11:53 pm (Alma unsends the video of her dancing outside)

July 16th, 2017

1:19 am
almaandromeda
Oh my gosh that video must have been torture.. I hope you didn't actually watch it for your sake 😂

1:20 am
almaandromeda
I understand though what it is to look around and feel separate. I actually recently found a Japanese parable about body image and body rejection that they relate to why we have war and violence. It touched me deeply because I have horrible stretch marks from carrying my 10lb son.. you have body dysmorphia, and my body is actually disfigured lol

1:25 am
almaandromeda
ZANAKI and IZANAMI represent the Japanese creation god and goddess, Izanagi
(male) and Izanami (female). When Izanami died giving birth to a fire god, she was
sent to the underworld. Her lover then went to follow and retrieve her from there
(sound like Orpheus?), but upon finding her, it was too late. She had already
consumed the food of the underworld, and belonged to the realm of the dead (sound
like Persephone?).

1:25 am
almaandromeda
It was dark, and Izanagi wanted to see his beautiful lover again, but after bringing a
light forward, found she had become hideous and overrun by rotten flesh and
maggots. So scared by the sight, he cried out and ran away. Izanami was outraged,
and sent monsters in pursuit. After reaching the surface, he blocked shut the
entrance to the underworld, and heard Izanami screaming at him.

1:26 am
almaandromeda
She threatened to send death to 1,000 people everyday, but in retaliation, Izanagi
claimed he would bring life to 1,500 everyday. As such, Death was brought to the
world.

1:28 am
almaandromeda
That's the story lol

1:28 am
almaandromeda
There is something integral to how we feel about our bodies and how we feel our
the worth of ourselves, and then how that spills out into how we view and treat the
world.

1:35 am
almaandromeda
I am still wrapping my head around you flying yourself in the air with your own
controls and feeling safer there than looking over a building.. it is blowing my mind
tbh. I don't trust myself for shit I guess 😅

4:09 pm
korbendallas_987
Japanese folklore is riveting; that is a group of people (homogenous as they may be),
that have done more, with less, than possibly any other country in the world 5 times

57

over. I LOVE their culture, spirit, and (what some uninformed would call disturbing). That story is fucking amazing and I will retell it. While we're on the subject..

4:12 pm
korbendallas_987
lorie and I's relationship used to be taboo: that is, she was enlisted and I was an officer. However, she was relentless in her pursuit of me (at least that's MY version). I would always get nervous, my career was on the line and let's face it--some girls are crazy. I went home on leave and got a tattoo of a Hanya on my left forearm and it's a conversational piece quite often.

4:15 pm
korbendallas_987
But, the story of the Hanya is about a "celibate" priest who was having an affair with a geisha. One day, he could bear the guilt no longer, and broke the relationship off. Immediately, she turns into this dragon/human hybrid and viciously murders him. I've had mine since 2000 but you're probably starting to see them around Seattle, especially more nowadays. They're popular.

4:16 pm
korbendallas_987
When people ask me what is it, I tell them that's my wife (used to say girlfriend).

4:17 pm
korbendallas_987
As far as piloting any aircraft, there is an innate sense of responsibility that almost EVERYONE finds, as at the end of the day, you're life is on the line if something is done wrong.

4:33 pm
almaandromeda
You and lorie have south node conjunct north node/north node conjunct south node... deeply, deeply entangled. I bet that actually happened between you both in a past lol, or you lived out a lifetime archetype of that story. I feel VERY connected to my past lives. It is one of my "talents". It's hard to be on this plane at this time when so few people can tap in to their deeper memories or believe that anyone could.. I can imagine you have many past and future lives together actually..

4:35 pm
almaandromeda
Because of the deep soul bond and also because you are equally able to share and bring to eachothers growth what the other needs, while helping you both feel safe and familiar on a soul level.

58

4:38 pm
almaandromeda
I am glad you took the "leap" this life

4:39 pm
almaandromeda
10 yrs apart and so bonded is a love past time/space 🖤 🖤

4:55 pm
korbendallas_987
omfg

4:55 pm
korbendallas_987
 this SO much

4:59 pm
korbendallas_987
i was always told that water signs don't mix well, but we are a cool breeze. you won't believe this, but i often lament/wonder of a past life, past soul of some kind. i'm EXTREMELY existential--so, you're right; it's difficult to take nearly ANYTHING seriously. I just finished up "The Universe in A Nutshell" by Stephen Hawking and am almost done with "Astrophysics for People In A Hurry" by Neil De Grasse Tyson.

5:01 pm
korbendallas_987
I don't mean to insult your intelligence (as always) but they are reknowned astro-physicists and when you read both their advanced and "lay" material, I'll be damned if you don't feel like flea feces after doing so. Less than a grain of sand, and it doesn't bother me a BIT. Even though I am one of the most egotistical chauvinists you have come across in (I imagine) quite some time, I revel in being humbled by such teachings.

5:03 pm
korbendallas_987
i thought lorie and i were doomed; i was always into old women (like, blue-haired grannies) until i ran into lorie. you can't choose how you love, i can assure you of that. Here we are though, 7 years later?

6:00 pm
almaandromeda
Amazing that you both found each other. Like in Princess Bride, you often have to fight and have strong "faith" for true love. Omg I am watching a doc on Netflix that

was MADE for you imho.. especially GO look up the opening song! It's about intuition and being kind of psychic I guess

6:06 pm
almaandromeda
Humility is another clear awareness of self.. it is almost the other side of the egoistic coin in our consciousness. You can become aware of your greatness thru your feeling of being so small.. the humbling I have experienced recently reminds me that it actually adds to your bigness, after you are brought down, there is much new space for you to be "you." It's cool 😎

6:15 pm
almaandromeda
It actually seems like you are incredibly intuitive, this doc kind of validates that "power" and how it is so valuable in every aspect of life and to develop it functionally.

6:21 pm
almaandromeda
I do have more flight/military questions I will ask eventually haha.. 🪖🛩️🦅 It is so big and different 🔫 I barely know what to ask or what really is ok to ask about

6:46 pm
almaandromeda
Easy reading btw 😄 I'll burn thru those in no time haha

7:09 pm
korbendallas_987
i'm going to watch that intuition vid. there are just too many people in my life telling me that i have this curse. my shrink is the #1 culprit. i use it to forecast dismay, toil, and tribulation. I revel in being right, and that's never good. I do consider myself humble though, without humility, you won't last long in this line of work.

7:11 pm
korbendallas_987
She thinks I'm some kind of rain man type--I guess she perused my test scores and blah blah.. i really do like her but, I can never tell if she's putting me on or not. Guess it doesn't matter.

7:11 pm
korbendallas_987
You can ask me anything.

60

7:18 pm

almaandromeda

Aquarian moon is HIGHLY intelligent.. think Eminem.. his lyrics are kind of violent against women for me, but no one can argue with his rapid fire intelligence. There is a quickening of Spirit and it is often "spectrum" in some form or fashion - in high intelligence and in emotional coldness.

7:19 pm

almaandromeda

That is the moon you have. They are astronauts, scientists, mathematicians, apache helicopter pilots lol.. Seriously brainy m'f's

7:21 pm

almaandromeda

Ok.. are you really fearless when you are in control? If so, was that always the case, even entering the military.. was there a time when you were like, this is terrifying to take myself up in the sky!?!

7:10 pm

almaandromeda

Did you have to overcome something in that or did it come naturally?

7:36 pm

korbendallas_987

the only time i was cautious was when i first became a "pilot in command", which is the first time you have your own aircraft that you manage and control, and YOU are responsible for. everyone's nervous for the first week or two but you get used to it. i study 1-2 hours a day or it all leaks out, we have to know 50-70 regulations COLD. Some of them word for word. So that helps in knowing to make the right decisions.

7:39 pm

almaandromeda

I am just taking in that you study that much each day.. 😵

7:40 pm

almaandromeda

Was it your plan to an instructor pilot the whole time in flight school?

7:40 pm

almaandromeda

*to be an

7:41 pm
almaandromeda
When you entered the military were you hoping to be deployed, and were you ever deployed?

7:43 pm
korbendallas_987
oh yes--yes to all questions

7:43 pm
almaandromeda
Please tell me if a question sucks or is off limits.. I honestly know NOTHING about the military or military life.
Other end of the rainbow 🌈 lol

7:43 pm
korbendallas_987
nothing off limits, no secrets here

7:43 pm
almaandromeda
So yes, deployed?

7:44 pm
korbendallas_987
i've wanted to be a jet jockey since i watched Top Gun at age 6

7:44 pm
almaandromeda
You ARE top gun lol

7:44 pm
korbendallas_987
not a day goes by that i regret not going to the air force/nacala academy

7:44 pm
almaandromeda
To the layman lol..

7:45 pm
korbendallas_987
alas, i setttled for the fucking army. i used to love it, but have grown to HATE it.

7:45 pm
almaandromeda
Tell me everything haha

7:46 pm
korbendallas_987
yes an Apche pilot only truly does his job if he deploys and shoots people and/or defends american lives. everything else we do from year to year is make up bullshit training

7:47 pm
korbendallas_987
but the army has turned into this mass punishment, "you got a DUI so that means your boss is in trouble" mentality. accountability has gone completely by the way side and it is nauseating.

7:47 pm
korbendallas_987
i honestly don't know if i can do 5 more years.

7:47 pm
korbendallas_987
i'm in a bad spot

7:48 pm
almaandromeda
What will happen in 5 years?

7:48 pm
korbendallas_987
retire

7:49 pm
almaandromeda
I saw a picture of where you were born.. a fortress!

7:49 pm
korbendallas_987
which is about $40K a year for, say, 30-50 years depending on how long you live. $2.5ish million is nothing to sneeze at.

7:50 pm
korbendallas_987
Tripler Army Medical Center?? haha i fly over it everyday when i give orientation flights out

7:50 pm
korbendallas_987
The Pink Palace

7:51 pm
korbendallas_987
i actually visited the floor and room i was supposedly born in a few months ago

7:51 pm
a**lmaandromeda**
It's almost magical in it's castle quality.. You were born right into the military and you have been trained up that way your whole childhood.. that is probably some of why you are so naturally fearless in a way that is foreign to me.. I am scared of everything lol

7:51 pm
a**lmaandromeda**
OMG YOU DID!!

7:51 pm
a**lmaandromeda**
That is SO awesome!

7:51 pm
korbendallas_987
haha you think WAYYY too much of mr

7:51 pm
korbendallas_987
it is very flattering

7:52 pm
a**lmaandromeda**
I probably take WAYYY too much of your time lol and you are amazingly fascinating, can't lie haha

7:52 pm
korbendallas_987
hell, half the time i go home on leave, nobody asks me about shit; shooting people in the face, blowing up buildings, cars, navy ships. they could care less

7:52 pm
almaandromeda
I really want to hear about it all.

7:53 pm
korbendallas_987
and yet a textbook existential has endless questions.. wonders never cease.

7:53 pm
almaandromeda
I know it's like a BOOK but anything you want to share haha

7:53 pm
korbendallas_987
when we meet i can tell you stories that i still don't believe myself--and i was there

7:53 pm
almaandromeda
Wonders really DO never cease! That is what I'm finding out too lol

8:10 pm
almaandromeda
The lyrics to that song 👁 👁
It takes a lot to know a man
It takes a lot to understand
The warrior, the sage
The little boy enraged

It takes a lot to know a woman
A lot to understand what's humming
The honeybee, the sting
The little girl with wings

8:10 pm
almaandromeda
It takes a lot to give, to ask for help
To be yourself, to know and love what you live with
It takes a lot to breathe, to touch, to feel
The slow reveal of what another body needs

It takes a lot to know a man
A lot to know, to understand
The father and the son
The hunter and the gun

9:41 pm
almaandromeda
I am looking forward to your war stories for realz. 🔫 🚜 🔫 ⚔️ 🚢 ANYTHING
you are willing to and want to share. 🐚 We will share with you too about this past 2
years being sued in court by my mom/stepdad for custody of my teen son.. I have
been to battle too and I have the emotional scars to tell the tale.. Can't wait for nick
to find out LOTS more about about his SUPERhero transformer top gun brother
from another. It is a privilege. 💬 🖼️

11:47 pm
korbendallas_987
jesus christ, i had no idea. have you considered a hitman?

July 17th, 2017

8:14 am
almaandromeda
We've considered...everything. 😈

8:53 am
almaandromeda
Honestly, most people don't know that about my current life because I can barely
stand talking about it.. basically my son at 15 decided he didn't want to live with us
anymore and started staying with my mom&stepdad, and I told them to NOT give
him a key/room/food and just send him home. They refused and instead sprnt
$20,000 on lawyers to sue me for full custody of Soquel, calling me an unfit mom.
😨 We went to trial, faced judges and in the end I split custody with them and now
pay them $450

9:05 am
almaandromeda
a month in child support.

9:47 am
korbendallas_987
good gof

9:49 am
korbendallas_987
god

10:00 am
almaandromeda
They all three (spn/mom/stepdad) stopped seeing/talking to me completely and they live here in Seattle

10:08 am
korbendallas_987
yea that is hitman fodder if i've ever heard it

10:15 am
korbendallas_987
fuck em

10:37 am
almaandromeda
Fuck them seriously much.

10:41 am
korbendallas_987
i know that's hard to do, but i am viciously vengeful and will hold a grudg for eons

10:46 am
almaandromeda
#ofxgivn

11:03 am
almaandromeda
Now you see why I love your motto haha

11:17 am
almaandromeda
I just have to walk thru hell tbh

11:18 am
korbendallas_987
everyone loves it, even if they don't admit haha

11:27 am
almaandromeda
It sux

12:07 pm
korbendallas_987
i LOVE driving past a minivan of ecumenicals and making sure i get in front of them so that they can read it, loud and deliberately

12:30 pm
almaandromeda
Haha!! Best part I bet lol

12:38 pm
korbendallas_987
i hate that for you, Alma. i don't know you, but i feel like you should NEVER be dealt a bad hand

1:15 pm
korbendallas_987
like Phoenix, you should rip matter apart at the subatomic level over and over again at will

1:42 pm
almaandromeda
My nephew LOVES your license plate. He said as soon as he saw it.. WHAT!! I didn't know you could get that 😂

1:51 pm
almaandromeda
Thank you michael 🖤👊

2:08 pm
almaandromeda
We both have "seen" alot 😎

2:45 pm
almaandromeda
I'd say you know me haha

3.39 pm
korbendallas_987
haha tell him you can do anything in this world. funny story, when i submitted it to

the walrus behind the counter in the alabama courthouse, she says, "now this will have to get approved at the state level, just so ya know."

4:32 pm
almaandromeda
Rebel!

4:47 pm
korbendallas_987
i told her it's a secret family code that has turned into a motto dating back centuries

5:18 pm
korbendallas_987
she shrugged her shoulders (which wound up moving her upper torso) and submitted it

6:27 pm
korbendallas_987
done, and done. ✅

6:38 pm
almaandromeda
Tcob mf

6:44 pm
korbendallas_987
i have to admit i laffed my ass off walking out the door

6:59 pm
almaandromeda
#winning lol 😂

8:37 pm
almaandromeda
The Phoenix thing hurts because I feel SO powerless.. 😕 I hate it so much tbh. I got pregnant with Soquel at 20 in NYC. I met his dad and 2 wks later he had me against a wall choking me off the floor. I didn't know I was pregnant, got away from him and 1 month later I found out I was pregnant. I never told him had a kid until Soquel was 16 yrs old, they met on father's day. I was terrified of father but felt I had to keep Soquel and keep him and me alive so that's what I did.

8:38 pm
almaandromeda
I've facedalot of pain and judgement for that decision but now that we've found him

again everyone can see I did the right thing I think.. he is still really wack unfortunately.

8:42 pm
almaandromeda
Anyway.. long story but basically I have fought so hard since day 1 to keep Soquel and raise him with love.. it fucking hurts.

8:57 pm
almaandromeda
In the darkest moments I have driven over bridges and dreamed of flying.. I could never leave nick but the lonliness is hell. nick fought harder than I have ever seen anyone fight for someone else in my life-storybook love he has for me ❤ Soquel started seeing me again this month finally after TWO YEARS of all 3 of them shunning me. Maybe something can finally shift. Sorry to bore you with this and I DO know you are super busy! We can catch up more when you bring the ukulele lol

9:02 pm
korbendallas_987
I know the loneliness you speak of, and I talk to the shrink about it. It's like you're surrounded by everyone, but not a soul is around. It's horrifying.

9:11 pm
almaandromeda
I started seeing a shrink specializing in Narcissistic abuse a few months ago and will hopefully bring Soquel too soon. She is SO rad, an angel 😇 Nothing makes my mom talk to me or love me and that's life on planet Alma. 🌏🌿

9:30 pm
almaandromeda
I really am doing much better and everything is basically tolerable now lol... Thanks for "listening" michael.. I NEVER share like this and am usually more 2cool4school and blase'. #ofxgivn is a way of life ✋😎🎧 🖤Now get back to blowing stuff up haha 😊

9:59 pm
almaandromeda
#5years 💪 #youcandoit

10:09 pm
korbendallas_987
i dunno. you don't seem so bad to me? 😜

70

10:10 pm
korbendallas_987
i also don't know if i can do 5 more years; i'm weird that i prioritize sanity over success

10:10 pm
korbendallas_987
pretty scared right noe

10:10 pm
korbendallas_987
now

10:27 pm
almaandromeda
I'm the worst just good at hiding it haha

10:28 pm
almaandromeda
I'm so sorry this decision sucks so much and is hard to weigh.. what are your options besides retire? Is it a lifetime paycheck or "success" you'd be holding out for?

10:44 pm
korbendallas_987
That is precisely the conundrum: stay in the Army and make about $40K a year just to simply breathing, OR, go to the United Arab Emirates and take a job starting at $105K a year..

10:45 pm
korbendallas_987
👆

10:45 pm
korbendallas_987
that's a lotta

10:45 pm
almaandromeda
If you chose to go to the UAE would you be "blowing stuff up", teaching, or?

11:20 pm
korbendallas_987
UAE pilots--aren't always the brightest. But they have a lot of dough so we sold em a bunch of 64s. I would be an Instructor Pilot (AKA I.P.). If we do, Lor could finish

her Ph.D. AND get a high-paying english teacher job. So it's really what I'm hoping for.

11:10 pm
korbendallas_987
As far as deployments, the Army hasn't a single clue. I may never deploy again, or I may leave tonight. Makes it really nice for planning vacations and such 💩

11:10 pm
almaandromeda
🖐 Hi five! Do what you love. Life is short!!

11:10 pm
korbendallas_987
Have to.

11:11 pm
korbendallas_987
No other way...

11:24 pm
almaandromeda
I am always the Unicorn in my forest.. I never leave.

11:26 pm
almaandromeda
UAE is far away but I hope you follow your dreams ✊

July 18th, 2017

6:39 am
korbendallas_987
Thank you. By the way, you mentioned slander such as stretch marks and (in general) the way a child can change a women's anatomy.

Let me tell you something, NOTHING is more nauseating than these plastic bodies on the front cover of magazines. Though my wife isn't representative of this, I am overwhelmingly attracted to REAL women. Tall, short, stretch marks--especially stretch marks. They're supposed to be there and I love them. She has a small bit of them on her butt and ai love em.

72

6:40 am
korbendallas_987
Men want "real". I think it's Kendrick Lamar that mentions it in one of his lastest releases. Embrace your body; you're a beautiful blonde; fair skinned woman who reminds me of my mom in a striking way.

6:41 am
korbendallas_987
Not sure what made me think of that but I thought I remembered you bringing stretch marks up.

7:21 am
a**lmaandromeda**
Thank you so much 😊 I appreciate your vote of confidence haha. It has been a long road of self acceptance including contemplating/saving for surgeries but never really wanting to take the leap so far.. I am grateful now for this belly.. nick loves it and me so much I am lucky. It holds me to my son even when he is not close to me right now. It humbles me even when noone can see.

7:51 am
a**lmaandromeda**
Is a good email korbendallas_987@mail.com?

8:03 am
almaandromeda
I have an email I wanted to forward you from the Universe

9:10 am
a**lmaandromeda**
I wonder how you might see yourself with the same incredible compassion of imperfections? 🌚

11:52 am
korbendallas_987
yes that is my email

11:53 am
korbendallas_987
checked daily

11:55 am
korbendallas_987
i can pretty much promise i won't see myself with ANY sort of compassion, but i'm trying to stay open-minded--for you

4:54 pm
almaandromeda

 sometimes that's all it takes.. at first. will send it soon.

9:45 pm
korbendallas_987

👍

9:50 pm
korbendallas_987

Of course, you can tell me anything

9:50 pm
korbendallas_987

It's fine

9:52 pm
korbendallas_987

Really?

9:54 pm
korbendallas_987

?

9:57 pm
korbendallas_987

shoot

10:27 pm
korbendallas_987

You're likely witnessing someone in a lot of pain (because we smell our own) and your inclination to help is a bit overwhelming (to you).

10:29 pm
korbendallas_987

Of course it is! I don't know whether to make heads or tails of any of it--what the PHUK do I do with a brand new sibling at 40 years old? It's gonna take my feeble mind decades to process.

10:29 pm
korbendallas_987

haha I'm not freaked, relax

10:30 pm
korbendallas_987
people find me either vastly intriguing, or repulsive to the core. it's usually one of the two.

10:33 pm
korbendallas_987
ah I think you've just never come across one quite like me. both my dad, and myself are weirder than a 3-headed cat so believe it or not I get this reaction a lot.

10:33 pm
korbendallas_987
that is NOT meant as offensive or insulting.

10:34 pm
korbendallas_987
?? not necessary

10:34 pm
korbendallas_987
no reason to be embarrassed, or overwhelmed or anything. None whatsoever.

10:34 pm
korbendallas_987
this is a private line, by the way

10:35 pm
korbendallas_987
i mean, she has access to my phone but is secure about me

10:36 pm
korbendallas_987
damn u did unsend!!!

10:36 pm
almaandromeda
It's not appropriate honestly for me to tell you that and I am just overwhelmed like you said

10:36 pm
korbendallas_987
i didn't even see half of your messages

10:37 pm
korbendallas_987
but you're still taking it all with a negative connotation

10:37 pm
almaandromeda
I love you.

10:37 pm
almaandromeda
That is all they said.

10:37 pm
korbendallas_987
something/someone along your path has carved you that way

10:38 pm
korbendallas_987
i didn't even know u can unsend shit hahaa

10:38 pm
korbendallas_987
damn

10:38 pm
almaandromeda
You can haha

10:39 pm
korbendallas_987
nah it's none of her business really

10:39 pm
almaandromeda
I am glad we found you

10:39 pm
korbendallas_987
don't worrry about my side, i'm a cool breeze

10:39 pm
korbendallas_987
how's this for weird:

10:39 pm
korbendallas_987
you look exactly like what i thought i was going to marry.

10:39 pm
korbendallas_987
let that marinate for a minute.

10:40 pm
almaandromeda
I am your exact opposite in astro

10:40 pm
almaandromeda
Ascendant vs ascendant

10:40 pm
korbendallas_987
probably why you're 10,000% more emotional than lor

10:40 pm
almaandromeda
We are like mirrors.. or direct opposites.. it fills in a full picture

10:41 pm
korbendallas_987
i was speaking about your physical appearance

10:41 pm
almaandromeda
The ascendant is the physical appearance

10:41 pm
almaandromeda
Your "body" and my "body" are on a mathmatical opposite

10:41 pm
korbendallas_987
weeeeeeeird

10:41 p
almaandromeda
Literally an opposites attract thing

10:42 pm
almaandromeda
To the math degree

10:42 pm
almaandromeda
There is alot of other powerful stuff obviously like that in our charts.. annoying haha!

10:42 pm
korbendallas_987
they say the same thing about me and lor cuz she is young (was pretty dumb too) and i am.. well.. me

10:43 pm
korbendallas_987
they're probably just talking superficial bullshit

10:43 pm
almaandromeda
You guys are strong 💪

10:43 pm
almaandromeda
Me and nick too

10:43 pm
almaandromeda
I am SO happy with him and not even remotely "looking" for anythibg else

10:43 pm
korbendallas_987
we weren't always this way

10:44 pm
korbendallas_987
been a rocky road

10:44 pm
korbendallas_987
i sometimes wonder if it's the right road

10:44 pm
almaandromeda
The road is a journey..

10:44 pm
korbendallas_987
love her to death tho

10:44 pm
korbendallas_987
to DEATH 💀

10:44 pm
almaandromeda
I know you do

10:44 pm
korbendallas_987
haha

10:45 pm
almaandromeda
I love nick forever too..

10:45 pm
almaandromeda
You have found me as a soul friend and I will always be here for you.

10:45 pm
almaandromeda
I am literally your sister haha.

10:46 pm
korbendallas_987
well thank you. i wish i had more to offer but i barely keep my nostrils above the surface

10:46 pm
almaandromeda

10:47 pm
korbendallas_987
i'm not too good at life

10:47 pm
almaandromeda
I understand.

10:48 pm
korbendallas_987
i truly hope you dont.. because it's a horrible feeling

10:48 pm
almaandromeda
I am not asking for anything

10:48 pm
korbendallas_987
?

10:49 pm
almaandromeda
I mean, you don't need to offer anything.. I have what I need and what I can offer you is from the heart without request for exchange

10:49 pm
korbendallas_987
oh i get it

10:50 pm
korbendallas_987
just a natural proclivity to reciprocate on my end

10:50 pm
almaandromeda
I really look forward to you connecting more with nick.. he loves you so much too.

10:50 pm
almaandromeda
The heart does what it does..

10:51 pm
almaandromeda
I feel guilty just to get to know you while had not known you all this time..

10:51 pm
korbendallas_987
i kinda do too. i should've tried to find this 'nick King'.

10:51 pm
korbendallas_987
my mom told me about him when i was 5

10:51 pm
almaandromeda
That is so young..

10:52 pm
almaandromeda
You don't feel empowered..

10:52 pm
almaandromeda
I didnt find my older brother either.

10:52 pm
korbendallas_987
matters none, he has never escaped my memory

10:52 pm
korbendallas_987
i just didn't try--it's that simple

10:52 pm
korbendallas_987
nick was the better man, clearly

10:53 pm
almaandromeda
He is 7 yrs older..

10:53 pm
almaandromeda
At your age he didnt do anything yet

10:53 pm
korbendallas_987
tru

10:53 pm
almaandromeda
He is the very best ever tho and more loving and kind than anyone I have ever met

10:54 pm
korbendallas_987
that much is clear

10:54 pm
almaandromeda
His heart is GIANT!!

10:54 pm
almaandromeda
He is like a shaolin warrior of Loving

10:54 pm
korbendallas_987
definitely master of his domain

10:54 pm
korbendallas_987
just like his dad

10:54 pm
almaandromeda
I have been loved to real lije Velveteen rabbit

10:54 pm
korbendallas_987
i, am not

10:55 pm
almaandromeda
I know haha

10:55 pm
korbendallas_987
lol @ velveteen

10:55 pm
almaandromeda
We are still working on you loving yourself 🖤

10:55 pm
almaandromeda
You are SO precious and loveable btw

10:55 pm
korbendallas_987
goin 40 years strong now (or weak?)

10:55 pm
korbendallas_987
it's almost embarrassing how much you think of me

10:56 pm
almaandromeda
Now you've met us.. good luck keeping up that streak haha

10:56 pm
almaandromeda
Im sorry

10:56 pm
almaandromeda
I know haha

10:56 pm
almaandromeda
I dont care

10:56 pm
almaandromeda
I have seen you

10:56 pm
korbendallas_987
embarrassing for lack of a bettter term

10:56 pm
almaandromeda
I cant explain it

10:57 pm
almaandromeda
I can not judge you

10:57 pm
korbendallas_987
you've pulled me apart limb from limb, no question about that

10:57 pm
almaandromeda
And you will come back together a little bigger.. me too

10:58 pm
almaandromeda
I have been torn down and I cry ALL the time

10:58 pm
almaandromeda
It sucks actually

10:58 pm
korbendallas_987
it's therapeutic

10:58 pm
korbendallas_987
good for you

10:58 pm
almaandromeda
I hate it and I know I love it too

10:58 pm
korbendallas_987
society has taught it as a weakness

10:59 pm
almaandromeda
But if your ears are burning its because I am cursing your name from time to time haha 😂🎧

10:59 pm
korbendallas_987

11:02 pm
korbendallas_987
i hope i haven't said anything wrong

11:02 pm
korbendallas_987
you're a special gal

11:03 pm
almaandromeda
My phone died sprry

11:03 pm
korbendallas_987

11:06 pm
almaandromeda
Thank you and I am sorry to be so forward

11:06 pm
almaandromeda
Please forgive me

11:06 pm
almaandromeda
I just have been changed by you coming into our lives

11:07 pm
almaandromeda
Please just forget everything I said haha

11:12 pm
korbendallas_987
why?!

11:12 pm
korbendallas_987
i demand to know why you were wrong to say ANY of that

11:13 pm
almaandromeda
Just so random and awkward

11:13 pm
korbendallas_987
neither

11:13 pm
almaandromeda
I really am sorry to put all that on you

11:14 pm
almaandromeda
I do feel everything

11:14 pm
korbendallas_987
put what on me?

11:14 pm
almaandromeda
But they are my feelings

11:14 pm
korbendallas_987
i wish i knew where this guilt i coming from

11:14 pm
almaandromeda
Love haha

11:14 pm
korbendallas_987
do u have a side lover or something??

11:14 pm
almaandromeda
I haven't met you and don't know you so how..

11:14 pm
almaandromeda
It is weird

11:15 pm
korbendallas_987
you harbor much too much guilt for no reason. very hard on yourself

11:15 pm
korbendallas_987
true we haven't met

11:15 pm
almaandromeda
I have never ever not been with nick

11:15 pm
almaandromeda
Since 1/1/10

11:15 pm
korbendallas_987
but we will. and then you can judge whether or not your feelings were requited

11:17 pm
almaandromeda
I know how you feel.. I feel you

11:17 pm
almaandromeda
It's annoying

11:18 pm
almaandromeda
Haha

11:18 pm
korbendallas_987
my shrink, (i've told you this), swears i'm a see-er. and just like anything else, there are degrees, or rather spectrums, of qualities of people.

11:19 pm
korbendallas_987
i have a feeling your ability is vastly superior to mine and i'm PRITTY damn proud of mine

11:19 pm
korbendallas_987
and by proud i mean i hate it and it's a curse

11:20 pm
almaandromeda
My phone keeps dying btw

11:20 pm
almaandromeda
I do have that

11:21 pm
almaandromeda
And you have activated it strongly lets just say

11:21 pm
korbendallas_987
the sleeping giant!

11:21 pm
almaandromeda
I want to harness it

11:21 pm
korbendallas_987
the kraken!

11:21 pm
korbendallas_987
that's awesome

11:21 pm
almaandromeda
All of the above.. 😂

11:21 pm
almaandromeda
It's terrifying

11:22 pm
korbendallas_987
i can't harness mine. i walk into a room, read everyone's mind/mood, and it either depresses me further or i want to kill them

11:22 pm
almaandromeda
That's the only word I have.. and fuck!

11:23 pm
almaandromeda
I am in love with every single person I meet

11:24 pm
almaandromeda
None like nick.. or you haha

11:24 pm
almaandromeda
But I LOVE people so much ❤

11:24 pm
korbendallas_987
oh sos

11:24 pm
korbendallas_987
wow*

11:24 pm
almaandromeda
I hope my open heart can rub off on you

11:24 pm
korbendallas_987
yea that is NOT me

11:24 pm
almaandromeda
I know lol

11:24 pm
almaandromeda
We are 'opposites'

11:24 pm
korbendallas_987
i'm a typical sociopath

11:24 pm
almaandromeda
I know you think you are... but why do you think that?

11:25 pm
korbendallas_987
if you and i were in a different galaxy, and bred, we would create Dr Strange or Phoenix II

11:25 pm
korbendallas_987
I have absolutely no regard for humans of all ages; babies all the way up (and down) to geriatrics

11:26 pm
korbendallas_987
they are vile creatures and disease is my best friend

11:26 pm
korbendallas_987
you like stories? i've got one for ya

11:27 pm
korbendallas_987
i was stationed 10 miles from the Pakistan border and one night we had intel to shoot a camel wearing red underwear. If it had red underwear, intel indicated that it was laden with explosive..

11:27 pm
almaandromeda
I want to hear everything michael ❤

11:29 pm
korbendallas_987
So I am the AMC of the flight (Air Mission Commander), and after we receive the

90

brief, we do our team brief (all the pilots). I told them if anybody shoots any animals I will personally pull their flying orders.

Am I being perfectly clear?

yes sir

(was their reply).

11:30 pm
korbendallas_987

Sure enough, it's red illum (which means no moo or cultural lighting (you can't see 5 feet in front of your face))

11:31 pm
korbendallas_987

and sure enough we saw this fucking camel. Nobody did a thing but were VERY pissed at me.

11:32 pm
korbendallas_987

2 weeks before that, we shot 60-70ish people attempting to overthrow an OP (observation post)

11:32 pm
a**lmaandromeda**

I love you.

11:33 pm
korbendallas_987

I'm willing you that to attempt to conceptualize my way of thinking and my priority of life on this planet. I would splatter a baby crawling across the road, but total my car evading a squirrel.

11:33 pm
korbendallas_987

telling you*

11:33 pm
almaandromeda

I know.

11:33 pm
almaandromeda

I have never hurt anything on purpose.. I am afraid of anything mean at all.

11:34 pm
almaandromeda
I stay in my forest with only nice people and butterflys.. I am so scared of the wars

11:34 pm
korbendallas_987
by definition, you should revile me

11:34 pm
korbendallas_987
i don't understand

11:34 pm
almaandromeda
You and I have walked two halves of the earth

11:35 pm
almaandromeda
I dont either

11:35 pm
almaandromeda
Thats why its so annoying haha

11:35 pm
almaandromeda
I hate some of the things you have done tbh

11:35 pm
almaandromeda
But never you

11:36 pm
almaandromeda
I dont hate them.. i hate them for you.

11:36 pm
almaandromeda
I dont like that you suffer

11:36 pm
korbendallas_987
be sure to keep contextnin mind

11:36 pm
almaandromeda
I do

11:36 pm
almaandromeda
Army

11:37 pm
korbendallas_987
picture a 17-year old kid, crying, scared shitless, under a Humvee. 2 Apaches FINALLY come on station and shoot everyone but him. Is that so bad?

11:38 pm
almaandromeda
I dont know

11:38 pm
korbendallas_987
I mean maybe it is, but, I want you to realize that the primary goal of the Apache is ground support

11:38 pm
almaandromeda
The situatipn is impossible for me to imagine

11:38 pm
almaandromeda
I dont judge you

11:38 pm
almaandromeda
I never will michael

11:38 pm
almaandromeda
You found someone who cant for some reason

11:39 pm
almaandromeda
Until a month ago I hated everyone like you

11:39 pm
almaandromeda
Now I hate myself for that

11:39 pm
korbendallas_987
that war should have never happened, so my goal was to protect as many american lives as i could in 12 months.

11:30 pm
korbendallas_987
and i'm a bleeding heart liberal, to boot

11:40 pm
korbendallas_987
stop hating yourself

11:40 pm
almaandromeda
How do you hold it all? It is so much to bear.. do you think about your experiences often?

11:41 pm
almaandromeda
I am ashamed for my small mind from before

11:42 pm
korbendallas_987
I have what is called rosy retrospection of Afghanistan. I remember the great parts of it. Eliminating humans and thus their potential evil acts, working out, eating lots of good food.

11:43 pm
almaandromeda
If you came upon me.. head covered.. you thought I was the enemy.. you could kill me too? Just anybody?

11:43 pm
korbendallas_987
However, Salerno is known as Rocket City. 2-4 rockets a day would come inbound and I will never be the same now. The doppler effect created by a 107mm rocket coming towards you is an unmistakable sound.

11:44 pm
korbendallas_987
No HELLLL no we have to have positive ID of hostile acts or hostile intentions

11:45 pm
almaandromeda
And if I was id'd by intel.. kabloom! There goes little Almita 🌿

11:45 pm
almaandromeda
I am sorry michael

11:46 pm
almaandromeda
Please forgive me

11:46 pm
korbendallas_987
but why would Alma be walking through Afghanistan with an AK-47 under her man-dress?

11:46 pm
korbendallas_987
that makes no sense

11:46 pm
almaandromeda
Just trying to understand

11:47 pm
almaandromeda
I have been very involved with Palestine activism

11:47 pm
korbendallas_987
when it comes to michael King, and homo sapiens, take the time to look up the word 'apathy'.

11:47 pm
korbendallas_987
i know u know what it means, but i want you to refresh yourself with the textbook version

11:47 pm
almaandromeda
Ok.. I will.

11:48 pm
almaandromeda
Hard nut to crack.

11:48 pm
korbendallas_987
my heart bleeds for Palestinians

11:48 pm
korbendallas_987
no home, cornered on all sides by superior technology and enemies

11:48 pm
almaandromeda
Hell on earth.

11:48 pm
almaandromeda
They are my peoples

11:49 pm
korbendallas_987
hard nut to crack?

11:49 pm
almaandromeda
I am here to get free and I identify with them

11:49 pm
almaandromeda
Yup.

11:49 pm
almaandromeda
You.

11:49 pm
korbendallas_987
tell me why

11:49 pm
almaandromeda
You know whay but I will..

11:49 pm
almaandromeda
You are a prince. Inside.

11:50 pm
almaandromeda
You are light and precious

11:50 pm
korbendallas_987
i honestly don't. u had me pulled apart the other day

11:50 pm
almaandromeda
You are beautiful

11:50 pm
almaandromeda
You are wonderous! Smart.. amazing in so many ways.

11:51 pm
almaandromeda
Inside you are absolutely magic.

11:51 pm
almaandromeda
And outside...

11:51 pm
almaandromeda
A hard nut to crack. A killer. A body builder. Apathy.

11:51 pm
almaandromeda
See now haha?

11:52 pm
korbendallas_987
ohhh kayyy

11:52 pm
korbendallas_987
i'll concede that i suppose

11:52 pm
almaandromeda
You must.

11:52 pm
korbendallas_987
not a bodybuilder and never claimed to be though

11:52 pm
almaandromeda
No?

11:52 pm
almaandromeda
What are you in that regard?

11:52 pm
korbendallas_987
never competed even though i would laff half of those clowns off the stage 😎

11:53 pm
almaandromeda
You are big yo

11:53 pm
korbendallas_987
i'm a gym-rat, plain and simple. endorphin/dopamine addict

11:53 pm
almaandromeda
You need to come to dance with me then

11:53 pm
korbendallas_987
haha i used to be big, alma

11:54 pm
almaandromeda
You dont even see what you look like so how do you know lol?

98

11:54 pm
korbendallas_987
you are witnessing pathetic remnants of a past life; almost like a crumbled statue

11:54 pm
korbendallas_987
true point

11:54 pm
almaandromeda
You are becoming something new

11:54 pm
almaandromeda
Me toooooo Aaahhhh!!! Its scary

11:55 pm
almaandromeda
Are you not working out as much?

11:56 pm
korbendallas_987
prefer the term under construction

11:57 pm
korbendallas_987
i had a hernia surgery 2 months ago and lost 20 years of work so i'm back to square one 😫

11:57 pm
almaandromeda
I am SO sorry to hear...

11:57 pm
almaandromeda
The body talks back

11:58 pm
almaandromeda
You know that song by Julia Michaels - Issues

11:58 pm
almaandromeda
Made me think of you.

July 19th, 2017

12:00 am
korbendallas_987
why did it make you think of me

12:00 am
korbendallas_987
truthfully

12:00 am
almaandromeda
Cuz I got issues.. you got em too

12:00 am
almaandromeda
And one of them is... 😊

12:01 am
korbendallas_987
happiness? respectfully disagree

12:00 am
almaandromeda
No duh 😊 listen to it lol! She says, and one of them is *how bad I need ya*

12:02 am
almaandromeda
But you missed all the other stuff about getting sued by my parents this past year, raped by 3 older brothers, almost killed by my sons father..

12:02 am
almaandromeda
I have issues like a mf

12:02 am
korbendallas_987
you told me...

12:02 am
korbendallas_987
and it hurts me.

12:03 am
korbendallas_987
but one of my issues is NOT happiness haha

12:03 am
almaandromeda
Im just a big baby and am nice to everyone so they will be nice to me

12:03 am
korbendallas_987
nah can't do thst

12:03 am
almaandromeda
Its not one of my issues.. but lonliness is

12:03 am
korbendallas_987
have to have a perpetual force field of hate and project it in virtually all azimuths

12:04 am
almaandromeda
What is an azimuth

12:04 am
korbendallas_987
people will bow to you like Nefertiti

12:04 am
korbendallas_987
azimuth is a direction on a compass

12:04 am
korbendallas_987
for example, azimuth 180 is directly south

12:04 am
almaandromeda
People bow to me anyway

12:04 am
korbendallas_987

12:04 am
almaandromeda
I am a queen haha

12:05 am
korbendallas_987
but i prefer them to bow out of fear

12:05 am
korbendallas_987
tyranny

12:05 am
almaandromeda
They love me like Princess Diana

12:05 am
korbendallas_987
i think i'm starting to get it

12:05 am
korbendallas_987
you thought:

12:07 am
korbendallas_987
i was this right wing, conservative, bible beating sheep with no brain (or vocabulary)
so upon actually meeting me it was like a baseball bat to the head.. am i close?

12:07 am
almaandromeda
Nope.

12:07 am
almaandromeda
I mean.. that is part of it.

12:07 am
almaandromeda
On a big scale that is true..

12:07 am
korbendallas_987
of course it is!! haha

12:08 am
almaandromeda
My humility is kind of big and included preconceived notions of people like you

12:08 am
almaandromeda
Killers actually

12:08 am
almaandromeda
But it is because of YOU

12:08 am
almaandromeda
Noone else in the world could have opened my heart like that tbh

12:09 am
almaandromeda
It is unique to the fate of this meeting.

12:09 am
almaandromeda
So thank you ❤

12:09 am
almaandromeda
I hate killing and dying, I am sad for suffering, it all kills me tbh

12:09 am
korbendallas_987
you'd be surprised. we're people too. but thank you very much.

12:10 am
korbendallas_987
that's where our paths split

12:10 am
almaandromeda
I am mama earth herself

12:10 am
almaandromeda
Nice to meet you lol

12:10 am
almaandromeda
The churning of the milky ocean

12:10 am
almaandromeda
Look it up

12:11 am
korbendallas_987
i am the morning star, Lucifer. the pleasure is ALL mine.

12:11 am
almaandromeda
You would take ALL the pleasure wouldnt you? Haha

12:11 am
korbendallas_987
there's plenty to go around

12:12 am
almaandromeda
My middle name Andromeda is my birth middle name and it is a star in the sky

12:12 am
almaandromeda
I was born Alma Andromeda Lexington-Stone

12:13 am
almaandromeda
Noone in the WORLD has my name 🤓

12:13 am
almaandromeda
I was born in Mustang, OK

12:13 am
almaandromeda
Middle of nowhere USA

12:13 am
almaandromeda
Andromeda is one of the brightest stars

12:14 am
almaandromeda
In the northern sky

12:14 am
almaandromeda
And it is actually a double star

12:15 am
almaandromeda
They didnt have telescopes large enough to tell apart the two stars till I was in high school

12:15 am
korbendallas_987
i thought it sounded familiar

12:15 am
almaandromeda
The distance between them is millions of miles but

12:16 am
almaandromeda
Because they are SO giant it is like the width of a penny as seen by the human eye a mile away

12:16 am
almaandromeda
So close

12:17 am
almaandromeda
I used to dream in high school that I had split up from the other star and came to earth to learn everything I could, and them too. And we would meet up and laugh at all the stupid shit that happened to us because WE ARE STARS

12:18 am
almaandromeda
And I have kept my star self intact always

12:18 am
almaandromeda
Sounds dumb haha

12:19 am
korbendallas_987
not at all

12:19 am
korbendallas_987
i've been reading on quasars--that shit'll blow your mind

12:19 am
almaandromeda
Sounds insane

12:20 am
almaandromeda
If you know about quantum than you know that you create and decide your reality

12:20 am
almaandromeda
It is what you land on

12:21 am
almaandromeda
That is why I am SO protective of my little space and my little choices..

12:21 am
almaandromeda
I have to choose joy

12:21 am
almaandromeda
I have seen so much pain

12:21 am
korbendallas_987
it's not a choice to me

12:21 am
almaandromeda
My nerves cant stand it

12:22 am
almaandromeda
I dont have a threshold for evil tbh

12:22 am
korbendallas_987
it's a program that you are lucky enough to have obtained the program nor algorithm

12:22 am
almaandromeda
I dont feel born with it

12:22 am
almaandromeda
When I am near evil or tru meanness my whole body closes down

12:23 am **a**
lmaandromeda
I am a Unicorn

12:23 am
almaandromeda
That is why I KNOW no matter what you have done you are not inherently evil michael

12:23 am
almaandromeda
You are def holding down that side tho

12:23 am
almaandromeda
Good job haha

12:24 am
almaandromeda
Did I offend you?

12:24 am
almaandromeda
You are evil ok!

12:24 am
almaandromeda

12:24 am
korbendallas_987
i don't believe in evil, at least not in the traditional sense

12:25 am
almaandromeda
I do.

12:25 am
almaandromeda
I have seen the face.

12:25 am
korbendallas_987
to drive thru a crowd of people with a bullzdozer isn't evil to me; it's simply driving through a crowd of people with a bulldozer

12:26 am
almaandromeda
It is your job at that time

12:26 am
almaandromeda
I understand what you mean.

12:27 am
almaandromeda
I have to drive home.. thanks for letting me be so honest with you

12:27 am
almaandromeda
And your honesty with me.

12:27 am
almaandromeda
Do you hate me now haha?

12:28 am
korbendallas_987
whaaaaa?

12:28 am
korbendallas_987
no

12:28 am
korbendallas_987
why r u so insecure about that?

12:28 am
almaandromeda
About that and lots of things

12:28 am
korbendallas_987
i told you at the beginning that you can ask/tell me anything

12:29 am
almaandromeda
Thanks. And you me. I know you know I dont know ANYTHING about your
world but I am a listening heart.

12:30 am
korbendallas_987
good god you are a blond haired, blue-eyed blonde. you should treat people like the
dogs that they are

12:30 am
korbendallas_987
you know more than most

12:30 am
a**lmaandromeda**
My favorite motto ever... ready?

12:31 am
almaandromeda
When you come upon someone greater than you, turn your thoughts to becoming his equal. When you find someone lesser than you, turn your thoughts to examine yourself.

12:31 am
almaandromeda
I am the greatest and the smallest.

11:32 am
korbendallas_987

12:32 am
almaandromeda
I am the mouse and the Queen

12:32 am
almaandromeda
I am you and I am me.

12:32 am
korbendallas_987
i've got one like that - i told my shrink that I'm a vagiant

12:32 am
almaandromeda
A wha??

12:32 am
korbendallas_987
vagina/giant

12:33 am
almaandromeda
Is that the smallest and biggest?

12:33 am
korbendallas_987
both

12:33 am
korbendallas_987
yes

12:33 am
almaandromeda
You have it backwards haha

12:33 am
almaandromeda
Woman is the vessel to all life

12:34 am
almaandromeda
She is MASSIVE

12:34 am
almaandromeda
And she receives all death from her creations and only makes more life

12:34 am
korbendallas_987
well, i equate vagina to pussy which is what men call each other men for known reasons

12:35 am
almaandromeda
Or unknown reasons lol

12:35 am
almaandromeda
You are ♪♪ bigger than your body♪♪

12:35 am
almaandromeda
You will never match outside to in

12:36 am
almaandromeda
But you can try haha..

12:36 am
korbendallas_987
i will die and or break everyone, every sinew, trying

12:36 am
almaandromeda
You really will.

12:36 am
almaandromeda
Do me a favor.. an exercise.

12:36 am
almaandromeda
Yes?

12:37 am
almaandromeda
Will you?

12:37 am
korbendallas_987
i'm planning today's punishment as we speak

12:38 am
almaandromeda
Here is my lesson plan for you then. Are you free and alone right now?

12:39 am
korbendallas_987
yes

12:39 am
almaandromeda
Ok.

12:39 am
almaandromeda
Now.. put your hands on your feet and say.. I love these feet.

12:39 am
almaandromeda
Do it.

12:40 am
korbendallas_987
done

12:40 am
almaandromeda
And up to your knees.. I LOVE these knees.. they hold me and keep me and carry me

12:40 am
almaandromeda
And to your strong legs, how powerful they are, they have ran you and saved you, I love these legs!!

12:41 am
almaandromeda
And to your middle, your torso, your belly, your gut.. this sweet body of yours!!

12:42 am
almaandromeda
Touch your belly and say thank you belly, I love you for digesting my food and pulling out my nutrients.. for feeding me!

12:42 am
almaandromeda
And to your chest, your heart, the rib cage that protects your heart.. thank you and I love you!

12:42 am
korbendallas_987
even the bacteria in the spleen? 😫

12:43 am
almaandromeda
We are 90% bacteria.. more that than human

12:43 am
almaandromeda
Of course the bacteria!

12:43 am
almaandromeda
You are balancing out every perfect working order in my perfectly working body

12:44 am
almaandromeda
I love this neck that holds my head

12:44 am
almaandromeda
I love how hard it works all day to truly support me

12:44 am
korbendallas_987
gah i wish my psyche worked that way

12:44 am
almaandromeda
You are not doing it!!!

12:44 am
almaandromeda
Do the thing.

12:44 am
korbendallas_987
you are luckily beyond anything you can dream

12:45 am
korbendallas_987
i guess some people just hit the lotto

12:45 am
almaandromeda
It is just words and repetitipn and work

12:45 am
almaandromeda
I do this everyday

12:45 am
almaandromeda
My mom NEVER once loved me

12:45 am
almaandromeda
Not one day

114

12:45 am
almaandromeda
I cried alone as an infant

12:45 am
almaandromeda
I had to literally lesrn thru fire how to love myself

12:46 am
almaandromeda
I am my own mama

12:46 am
almaandromeda
Thats why I love myself so much

12:46 am
almaandromeda
Im adorable lol

12:46 am
korbendallas_987
my mom loved me along with severe OCD and depression

12:46 am
korbendallas_987
yes you are quite something

12:47 am
almaandromeda
Its hard to learn but you found me and us!!

12:47 am
almaandromeda
You are special-er.. watch.

12:48 am
korbendallas_987
i didn't find shit!

12:48 am
almaandromeda
We found you

12:48 am
korbendallas_987
you guys found me

12:48 am
almaandromeda
Like in the Matrix

12:48 am
almaandromeda
And you were looking for more...

12:49 am
almaandromeda
Rabbit hole time haha

12:49 am
korbendallas_987
i'm definitely always looking. for the pain to stop

12:49 am
almaandromeda
I know.

12:49 am
korbendallas_987
alone in a sea of bodies

12:50 am
a**lmaandromeda**
Lie to yourself and say you are not.

12:50 am
a**lmaandromeda**
See what happens

12:50 am
korbendallas_987
i've. tried

12:50 am
a**lmaandromeda**
Your eyes say everything

116

12:50 am
korbendallas_987
i talk to various individuals about it

12:51 am
korbendallas_987
it's rampant in my family. half-brother has it as well as mom

12:51 am
korbendallas_987
family of kooks

12:52 am
almaandromeda
Mine too!! My mom and dad are both actual psychos

12:52 am
korbendallas_987
no pity party for me though, just resolved to live another 30-40 through this hell
and the nothing

12:52 am
almaandromeda
Bio dad/bio mom

12:52 am
korbendallas_987
then*

12:53 am
almaandromeda
All four of my parents have tried to kill me in some form or fashion

12:53 am
almaandromeda
No pity party.. just while I am alive I want to feel more than that shit

12:54 am
almaandromeda
That's why I smile SO big and laugh SO hard.. I have seen IT ALL and can not die

12:54 am
almaandromeda
They have all tried.

12:54 am
korbendallas_987
jesus

12:54 am
almaandromeda
I am not them.

12:55 am
almaandromeda
They suck.

12:55 am
almaandromeda
I dont

12:55 am
almaandromeda
I am me and I am the sky.. I am everything that fills me up.

12:55 am
almaandromeda
No room for those fucks.

12:55 am
korbendallas_987
i understand

12:56 am
korbendallas_987
mine isn't directed at anyone specifically

12:56 am
korbendallas_987
instead, it's all of them

12:57 am
almaandromeda
My power is not because nothing happened.. its becuz it all happened and STILL I RISE

12:57 am
almaandromeda
I have to sleep. Talk soon

12:58 am
korbendallas_987

4:16 am
almaandromeda
I want to tell you a little more about my relationship with nick so you can understand my heavy guilt I feel just communicating with you this long and then unexpectedly caring for you so much.

4:17 am
almaandromeda
And then telling you about my feelings... all of that is WAY more than nick could stand.

4:20 am
almaandromeda
nick and I are best friends and spend every day together, all day! We work our main job together during the day, we have our crystal business together, and our band together. I am his constant companion and
his sweetie
in every way. I love being that and have NEVER since I committed to him fully 1/1/10 even spent any time chatting or getting to know any other man in this way. He is my WHOLE world and I am his. Nothing has even made me look up since the day I met him. That..

4:35 am
almaandromeda
I have lots of time alone too.. he is always in his studio and I am making stuff, but we are usually pretty close by.

4:35 am
almaandromeda
He is SO excited to have you in his life!! He feels safe and I want to hold nick in that and have already fked up really by getting myself in the middle of your new life

119

with him. I am sorry for that. I feel strongly for you and dont have any idea why. But what really matters is YOU and YOUR BRO and I see that, know that and deeply respect that. 🫶

5:19 am
korbendallas_987
You have so much wrong, and it saddens me. You've done nothing wrong. So what if you are attracted to me or vice verses? SO WHAT? We are mammals and fickle at BEST.

5:19 am
korbendallas_987
you haven't gotten in the middle of anything, christ-nothing has even happened

5:20 am
almaandromeda
I know but nick's heart is so sweet

5:20 am
korbendallas_987
drop the guilt or you're gonna have a heart attack, and they are EXPENSIVE

5:20 am
almaandromeda
I have his absolute trust and have always deserved it until.. whatever I have shared here.

5:21 am
korbendallas_987
Oh my little Alma Mater (always wanted to call you that), but what have we done wrong??

5:21 am
almaandromeda
He really could not possibly understand my deep fascination and draw to you.

5:21 am
almaandromeda
I am glad you did haha!!

5:21 am
almaandromeda
That was obviously my main nickname growing up 😂 Funny, it means nourishing mother *puke

5:22 am
almaandromeda
WE have not done anything wrong and you especially..

5:22 am
korbendallas_987
then what in the alma matters so much??

5:23 am
korbendallas_987
i just don't get it

5:23 am
almaandromeda
Just he is really sensitive about secrets and his ex wife cheated on him.. I cant explain it but he would be sad and begin to not trust me..

5:24 am
korbendallas_987
lor would probably not want our level of closeness but she is no prob; i've never once strayed and have had PLENTY chances

5:24 am
almaandromeda
He is VERY distrustful and I have worked SO hard to hold his trust

5:24 am
korbendallas_987
then just delete everything

5:24 am
korbendallas_987
or even delete me?

5:24 am
almaandromeda
Never you never

5:26 am
almaandromeda
But if you dont mind I will unsend my messages and you can yours... and I want to stay connecting but I dont want anything for nick to stumble on and get broken hearted.. I understand why I want to get to know you but he wouldnt.

5:26 am
korbendallas_987
why don't u just delete the entire convo every once in awhile

5:26 am
korbendallas_987
it deleted everything

5:26 am
korbendallas_987
from the main message screen

5:26 am
almaandromeda
How do I do that?

5:27 am
korbendallas_987
deletes*

5:27 am
korbendallas_987
press the arrow on the top left of this screen

5:27 am
almaandromeda
Done.

5:27 am
almaandromeda
I love it.

5:27 am
korbendallas_987
then slide left

5:27 am
almaandromeda
Thank you xo

5:27 am
korbendallas_987
duhhhhhhhh

5:27 am
korbendallas_987
haha

5:27 am
almaandromeda
I didnt know seriously haha

5:27 am
almaandromeda
I am so weird

5:27 am
korbendallas_987
to be fair i had no clue of unsending

5:28 am
korbendallas_987
so when i graze that stupid heart icon when talking to my boss or something i'm like PHOK

5:28 am
almaandromeda
And you can unsend!!

5:29 am
korbendallas_987
kinda cool cuz u can drunk text someone then if u wake up before them u can unsend

5:29 am
almaandromeda
Once I did send you a heart a long time ago and was hysterically laughing but then realized I could unsend it

5:29 am
almaandromeda
So tru

5:29 am
korbendallas_987
i THINK the notification still shows though... i'm not sure

5:30 am
almaandromeda
It does.. thanks michael ❤

5:30 am
korbendallas_987
she has seen me talking to you and isn't inquisitive

5:30 am
almaandromeda
Not even a little?

5:30 am
korbendallas_987
i think u will be underwhelmed when u meet me haha

5:30 am
almaandromeda
Doubt it.

5:30 am
korbendallas_987
then the crush will blow away

5:30 am
korbendallas_987
never to be heard of again 😳

5:31 am
almaandromeda
It has NOTHING to do with cars, muscles, helicopters.. nothing.

5:31 am
korbendallas_987
i'm aware

5:31 am
almaandromeda
I look at your photo and make your face big to see your eyes

5:31 am
korbendallas_987
ugh thats depressing

5:31 am
almaandromeda
You will have the same eyes when we meet

5:32 am
korbendallas_987
i am THE MOST non-photogenic person on the planet

5:32 am
korbendallas_987
i look NOTHING like i do in pics

5:32 am
almaandromeda
I love your face.

5:32 am
korbendallas_987

5:32 am
almaandromeda
Your eyes are the same.

5:32 am
korbendallas_987
makin me blush

5:32 am
almaandromeda
Its tru

5:32 am
korbendallas_987
i think nick and i have the same eyes

5:33 am
almaandromeda
The mathmatical opposites thing

5:33 am
almaandromeda
No, yours are more black.. and also something else.

5:33 am
korbendallas_987
for sure black

5:34 am
korbendallas_987
so everytime i see a mixed person with light eyes i want to kill them

5:34 am
korbendallas_987
mom's eyes are blue as the sky

5:34 am
korbendallas_987
why me?!

5:34 am
almaandromeda
Windows to the soul.. your eyes are beautiful michael.

5:37 am
korbendallas_987
well thank you.. aren't all eyes beautiful ? if u just look at the eyes and not the face? i always thought they were

5:37 am
almaandromeda
Oh bro's awake. Making food for bro

5:37 am
almaandromeda
Yours more.

5:38 am
korbendallas_987
i used to have long eyelashes like a girl and my mom kept my hair long and it pissed me off cuz everyone thought i was a girl

5:47 am
almaandromeda
I saw how sweet your face was when you were a kid 😍

5:47 am
almaandromeda
The cutest kid I may have ever seen.. and I've had a kid haha

5:47 am
korbendallas_987
charm of the antichrist

5:48 am
almaandromeda
I have been duly warned haha

5:49 am
korbendallas_987
you pretty much know all the bad stuff about me, i suppose

5:50 am
almaandromeda
Not yet but I am willing to hear about it 4 sure ✊

5:51 am
almaandromeda
Impossible to know everything about an ocean

5:55 am
korbendallas_987
true enough

5:56 am
korbendallas_987
anyways, no more guilt

5:56 am
korbendallas_987
it makes me feel bad (worse)

5:59 am
almaandromeda
Completely. ✊

5:59 am
almaandromeda
Done and done. ✅

5:59 am
almaandromeda
I want to keep talking and feel fine with that now

6:00 am
almaandromeda
More in control

6:00 am
almaandromeda
Eating now

6:00 am
korbendallas_987
surely, attraction between 2 individuals isn't foreign to you?

6:00 am
korbendallas_987
it happens literally every second of every day

6:02 am
korbendallas_987
eating as well

6:26 am
almaandromeda
Happens all the time but not really to me

6:26 am
korbendallas_987
?

6:26 am
almaandromeda
I am very exclusive with my attention

6:26 am
korbendallas_987
don't be silly

6:26 am
korbendallas_987
ahh ok

6:26 am
korbendallas_987
i see what u mean

6:27 am
korbendallas_987
oblivious to other guys humping your legs

6:27 am
almaandromeda
I seriously go to dance 2x a wk and engage with ALL kinds of people

6:27 am
korbendallas_987
that's good.

6:27 am
almaandromeda
And noone ever ever ever turns me

6:27 am
korbendallas_987
intimidated

6:28 am
korbendallas_987
tall blonde

6:28 am
almaandromeda
I am just exclusive with myself

6:28 am
korbendallas_987
married, etc

6:28 am
almaandromeda
They go to me but I keep so much space

6:28 am
almaandromeda
My heart just is not open like that, or even my eyesight

6:29 am
almaandromeda
I have a lot of focus

6:29 am
almaandromeda
Thats why this has BLOWN my mind not to freak you out

6:29 am
korbendallas_987
i don't follow

6:30 am
korbendallas_987
i'm supposed to be freaked out?

6:32 am
almaandromeda
Just that is rare for me to be attracted to someone new

6:32 am
korbendallas_987
well, there's a lot of mystique involved

6:33 am
korbendallas_987
not just your normal dude at bar begging for eye contact, blah blah

6:35 am
almaandromeda
Sooo true!!

6:35 am
almaandromeda
A lotttt of mystique

6:36 am
almaandromeda
My fav character btw

6:36 am
korbendallas_987
as previously stated, you shall be severely underwhelmed

6:36 am
korbendallas_987
who is fav character ?

6:38 am
almaandromeda
Not possible haha

6:38 am
almaandromeda
Phone keeps dying!! I never charged it while I "slept" lol

6:38 am
almaandromeda
Mystique from xmen

6:38 am
korbendallas_987
PLUG IT IN

6:38 am
almaandromeda
Love her.

6:38 am
korbendallas_987
ohhh

6:38 am
almaandromeda
I am!!

6:38 am
korbendallas_987
Phoenix is mine

6:40 am
almaandromeda
I relate to Phoenix most but love Mystiques power and #ofxgivn

6:43 am
korbendallas_987
lot of the marvel heroes have that--Wolverine don't give a fuck

131

6:43 am
korbendallas_987
Deadpool

6:43 am
almaandromeda
Have to let my phone charge.. 10 min plz ♥

6:43 am
korbendallas_987

6:43 am
almaandromeda
Ahll be back.

6:53 am
almaandromeda
You know that photo of you...

6:54 am
almaandromeda
with the blue sky behind you, and the sun shining down on you, and you have a green cap on and your face is in the shadows

6:54 am
almaandromeda
Your eyes are deep black and your face is so symmetrical and you have these GIANT muscles &all those tattoos

6:54 am
almaandromeda
some kind of flowers?
so delicate

6:54 am
almaandromeda
perfectly placed –

6:54 am
korbendallas_987
yea I know the one

6:54 am
korbendallas_987
lol

6:54 am
almaandromeda
Well... hahaha

6:54 am
almaandromeda
This is my FVORITE photo of you

6:55 am
korbendallas_987
😩

6:55 am
korbendallas_987
good ol days

6:55 am
almaandromeda
I love your face

6:55 am
almaandromeda
I dont look at anything else

6:55 am
korbendallas_987
you are VERY weird

6:55 am
almaandromeda
Not impressed lol

6:55 am
korbendallas_987
not in a bad way

6:55 am
almaandromeda
 I know sorry haha

6:55 am
korbendallas_987
yes--very underwhelmed at all timed

6:55 am
korbendallas_987
times*

6:56 am
almaandromeda
How do you mean?

6:56 am
almaandromeda
Doctor.. let me tell you my symptoms

6:57 am
almaandromeda
Is your face very different?

6:58 am
korbendallas_987
what do u mean?

6:58 am
almaandromeda
Than that photo?

6:59 am
korbendallas_987
i would love to find a good pic of me but there just isn't one

6:59 am
almaandromeda
Take one

6:59 am
korbendallas_987
ohhh the on IG with my shirt off is om

6:59 am
korbendallas_987
ok

6:59 am
korbendallas_987
mirror shot

6:59 am
almaandromeda
Thats what you look like now u r saying?

7:00 am
almaandromeda
I know the one haha

7:01 am
korbendallas_987
probably close

7:01 am
korbendallas_987
need to shave tho

7:01 am
almaandromeda
Sooooooooo yes.

7:01 am
korbendallas_987
destitute, dearth, povertous

7:01 am
korbendallas_987
2 months and 2 decades is gone

7:02 am
almaandromeda
How are they gone? Muscle gone?

7:02 am
almaandromeda
I am married to nick.. he's pretty thin

7:02 am
korbendallas_987
yea extreme atrophy from laying on my ass from this fuckass hernia surgery

7:03 am
korbendallas_987
haha ye but u have to remember my condition

7:03 am
almaandromeda
Have you been able to work?

7:03 am
almaandromeda
You have that condition so far and for now

7:04 am
almaandromeda
Change is the only constant

7:04 am
almaandromeda
I am sorry about your surgery

7:04 am
korbendallas_987
not your fault

7:04 am
almaandromeda
Are you feeling better?

7:04 am
korbendallas_987
like i said, always under construction

7:05 am
almaandromeda
So the hernia is related to gym life

7:06 am
korbendallas_987
hard to say. it was umbilical. right above belly button. grunting for 30 years plus there's a natural imperfection of the fascia in that area anyway (your belly button)

7:06 am
korbendallas_987
it's my second one

7:06 am
almaandromeda
2nd one!! Please take it easy on yo self

7:06 am
korbendallas_987
never that

7:06 am
almaandromeda
I like you

7:06 am
almaandromeda
I love you actually lol 😊

7:07 am
korbendallas_987
simply not possible

7:07 am
almaandromeda
I said please haha

7:07 am
korbendallas_987
i will not accept failure

7:07 am
almaandromeda
You are failing my request but whatevs

7:07 am
korbendallas_987
have to

7:08 am
korbendallas_987
it's so funny, girl act like they hate muscles and fitness and you should see when lorie and i go out

7:08 am
korbendallas_987
i am the most modest person you'll ever meet and girls break their necks

7:08 am
korbendallas_987
maybe they're lookin at lorie 👻 ♂

7:10 am
almaandromeda
You are attractive OBVIOUSLY

7:10 am
almaandromeda
Thats not a secret

7:10 am
almaandromeda

7:11 am
almaandromeda
I am actually not like most girls.. hard to explain.

7:12 am
almaandromeda
I am drawn by an invisible map

7:14 am
almaandromeda
Basically just weird in plain english

7:24 am
almaandromeda
What makes you smile? 😊 Tell me all the things...

7:24 am
almaandromeda
If anything.. I know you said its hard to

7:25 am
korbendallas_987
i laugh at my own jokes the most, as does my mother

7:25 am
korbendallas_987
i think i'm the funniest person on the planet

7:25 am
almaandromeda
I think you are hilarious 🤓

7:26 am
korbendallas_987
i don't believe i am attractive but i DO KNOW that women stare at jacked dudes

7:26 am
korbendallas_987
no matter WHAT they sasy

7:26 am
korbendallas_987
say

7:26 am
almaandromeda
Is that part of why?

7:26 am
almaandromeda
The female attention...

7:27 am
korbendallas_987
well of course

7:27 am
almaandromeda
I almost am annoyed because its so cliche

7:27 am
almaandromeda
To be attracted to YOU

7:27 am
korbendallas_987
i'm nothing fancy to look at, but my synmetry and proportions cannot be argued with

7:28 am
almaandromeda
Your symmetry is magical

7:28 am
korbendallas_987
there's a pic of me holding an xbox on my IG that depicts such a display

7:28 am
korbendallas_987
thank you, Alma

7:28 am
almaandromeda
Even your face

7:28 am
almaandromeda
Seen it 👀

7:28 am
korbendallas_987
cliche??? pssssssh girls HATE me hahah

7:29 am
korbendallas_987
please take it from me, i have zero reason to lie

7:29 am
almaandromeda
I reaaally dont see it in the photo..
I know its hot but I am hot for your face and your smart eyes 👀

7:30 am
korbendallas_987
i think a few fall for my verbosity

7:30 am
korbendallas_987

7:31 am
almaandromeda
A few here and a few there .. 😂

7:31 am
korbendallas_987
vernacular. i can tell when i talk to certain females that they have never come across someone who speaks the way i do

7:31 am
korbendallas_987
which is frightening

7:31 am
almaandromeda
I have but do appreciate it.

7:31 am
almaandromeda
Nick is so eloquent.

7:31 am
almaandromeda
Whats with that?

7:31 am
korbendallas_987
must be from our dad

7:32 am
almaandromeda
And then you both switch it up

7:32 am
almaandromeda
Must be...

7:33 am
korbendallas_987
lorie does this little chagrin when i drop a new word on her where she wants to
show me that she's impressed but at the same time irritated with me--it's so cute

7:33 am
almaandromeda
Haha 😂

7:33 am
almaandromeda
I bet

7:33 am
korbendallas_987
i'm cursed with a mind of a steel trap and just don't forget words

7:34 am
korbendallas_987
it's nothing special but i use it to talk to people at work like dogs when they
irritate me

7:34 am
korbendallas_987
my shrink says i am VERY intimidating. from my physical stature down to my
resting face

7:35 am
almaandromeda
Im scurred of u

7:35 am
korbendallas_987
so weird bc i don't wanna be (necessarily)

7:35 am
korbendallas_987
Pssssh

7:35 am
almaandromeda
Shaking in my boots haha

7:35 am
korbendallas_987
i bet

7:35 am
almaandromeda
Sort of..

7:35 am
almaandromeda
😂

7:35 am
almaandromeda
Mostly the awarenesses and my expanding heart 🖤

7:36 am
almaandromeda
THAT is scary

7:36 am
almaandromeda
Tcobrother now

7:37 am
almaandromeda
Goodnight xxoo

7:37 am
korbendallas_987
Tco?

7:37 am
almaandromeda
Tcob taking care of biz

7:37 am
korbendallas_987
let me say one more thing--whatever this is that you are going thru..

7:38 am
almaandromeda
Yes..

7:38 am
korbendallas_987
is a bit of a phase so do NOT let it bother you. we are attractive primates, and that's that.

7:38 am
almaandromeda
As long as i dont bother u

7:38 am
almaandromeda
Its fun to know u

7:39 am
korbendallas_987
just know that, when i do physically see you for the first time, i will very slyly up and down you and that could be bad on my end.

7:39 am
almaandromeda
I want to see you

7:39 am
almaandromeda
Do whatever haha

7:39 am
almaandromeda
Not really lol...

7:40 am
korbendallas_987
to be frank, you are stunning--nick hit the lotto and should send a thank you note to the whore that cheated on him

7:40 am
almaandromeda
I agree haha 🙈

144

7:40 am
korbendallas_987
sleep tight

7:40 am
almaandromeda
She actually texted him on our wedding day.. on the way to get married

7:40 am
korbendallas_987
and delete

7:40 am
almaandromeda
You too

7:40 am
almaandromeda

7:41 am
almaandromeda

4:08 pm
almaandromeda
Thanks for walking me thru the delete thing lol

4:09 pm
almaandromeda
I am a whole new woman

5:04 pm
korbendallas_987
haha glad to hear it

5:13 pm
almaandromeda
Obviously there is some part of me emerging that is wanting more attention lol

5:14 pm
almaandromeda
I am aaalllwwaaaayys good and perfect and sweet and impossible to do wrong..

5:15 pm
almaandromeda
There is more fun and play than I have allowed myself

5:32 pm
korbendallas_987
so is that his fault or yours? or, the universe's?

5:32 pm
korbendallas_987
you've had a pretty stressful year, don't forget that

5:34 pm
almaandromeda
I dont know whose tbh

5:34 pm
almaandromeda
Nick has high standards 4 sure

5:35 pm
almaandromeda
But I make my own choices

5:35 pm
almaandromeda
Its not a fault really.. just a lot to keep up

5:35 pm
almaandromeda
I like being awesome

5:35 pm
korbendallas_987
well, yayuh

5:36 pm
korbendallas_987
who doesn't?

5:36 pm
almaandromeda
I guess me right now haha

5:36 pm
almaandromeda
Its hard to explain

5:36 pm
almaandromeda
Im holding alot..

5:37 pm
korbendallas_987
you're very mysterious this morning

5:37 pm
korbendallas_987
almost like you want to say something without saying it

5:38 pm
almaandromeda
I just want to tell you my symptoms Doc.. its bad haha

5:38 pm
almaandromeda
I have like a physiological response to you

5:39 pm
almaandromeda
Want to hear them?

5:39 pm
korbendallas_987
of course

5:40 pm
almaandromeda
Ok.. it has to be textbook endorphins at first sight or whatever but it sucks..

5:40 pm
almaandromeda
I lost my appetite COMPLETELY and totally..

5:40 pm
almaandromeda
None.

5:41 pm
almaandromeda
Berries and mate and kombucha.

5:41 pm
almaandromeda
It is just coming back..

5:41 pm
korbendallas_987
that happened to me couple months ago

5:41 pm
korbendallas_987
body was trying to kill itself

5:41 pm
almaandromeda
Why for you?

5:41 pm
korbendallas_987
lost 30 in 2 weeks

5:42 pm
korbendallas_987
no clue whatsoever

5:42 pm
almaandromeda
I have lost SO much weight.. seriously

5:42 pm
almaandromeda
Its annoying haha

5:42 pm
almaandromeda
At first I liked it but

5:42 pm
almaandromeda
😭

5:42 pm
korbendallas_987
i went to gnc and got a dog food bag of mass gainer and started pounding it right up until the point of nausea

5:43 pm
almaandromeda
I just cant make myself chew

5:43 pm
korbendallas_987
nah don't lose weight u have a great figure

5:43 pm
almaandromeda
I dont want to!!

5:43 pm
almaandromeda
But I will bit hard down all the time.. more symptoms

5:44 pm
almaandromeda
I have a lot more but its embarrassing honestly.

5:44 pm
almaandromeda
What did you do!! haha

5:44 pm
korbendallas_987
?

5:45 pm
almaandromeda
Im just kidding

5:45 pm
almaandromeda
I just mean I dont know why I have all these stupid physical responses to you

5:46 pm
korbendallas_987
i tried to explain last night - its attraction; likely, chemical

5:46 pm
almaandromeda
Very chemical..

5:46 pm
korbendallas_987
why won't u believe me

5:46 pm
almaandromeda
And astro..

5:46 pm
almaandromeda
Same probably

5:50 pm
almaandromeda
Rumi was born in 1207 and was a great scholar until the age of 37..

5:52 pm
almaandromeda
Then he met the whirling dervish Shams and had an esoteric friendship with this wild soul.. once Shams disappeared Rumi became the philosopher and poet everyone reads today.

5:53 pm
korbendallas_987
strange

5:53 pm
almaandromeda
So weird.. plus I am telling you.. when you read these

5:53 pm
almaandromeda
Eerie

5:55 pm
almaandromeda
Later I want to exercise with you lol.. ❤

5:55 pm
korbendallas_987
haha why

5:55 pm
almaandromeda
To tell you everything I like about u while you tell it to yourself

5:55 pm
almaandromeda
Muscle building

5:56 pm
almaandromeda

5:56 pm
almaandromeda
Only if you want lol

5:56 pm
korbendallas_987
of course

5:56 pm
korbendallas_987
i never turn down a lifting buddy

5:56 pm
almaandromeda
Yay ❤

5:56 pm
korbendallas_987
hard to find these days

5:56 pm
almaandromeda
You got a tough one here

5:57 pm
almaandromeda
I am going to get you in shape lol

5:57 pm
korbendallas_987
speaking of which i'm about to clear the gym out

5:57 pm
almaandromeda
Xo

5:58 pm
korbendallas_987
you used a peculiar word yesterday - love

5:58 pm
korbendallas_987
strong word

5:58 pm
korbendallas_987
uncommon word

5:58 pm
almaandromeda
Alot but tru

5:59 pm
almaandromeda
Its easy to love you

5:59 pm
korbendallas_987
i won't argue that, but u barely know me!

6:00 pm
almaandromeda
So true!

6:00 pm
korbendallas_987
maybe my ears are too big for my face and u never caught it in a pic

152

6:00 pm
almaandromeda
Maybe but its really none of that.. Im sorry to tell you really

6:00 pm
almaandromeda
I just know I do

6:00 pm
almaandromeda

6:00 pm
korbendallas_987
sorrry for what

6:00 pm
korbendallas_987
uuggghhh

6:01 pm
almaandromeda
Just to say such big stuff.. its alot!!

6:01 pm
korbendallas_987
you make me cautious to bring up anything at all

6:01 pm
almaandromeda
Anything.. say anything

6:01 pm
korbendallas_987
no more sorry; more this is who i am

6:02 pm
almaandromeda
Ok! Well who I am is someone who strangely loves the shit out of you ❤🤍❤

6:02 pm
korbendallas_987
that's great!

6:02 pm

korbendallas_987
that's the opposite of sorry

6:02 pm
almaandromeda
I know Im happy to tell you really

6:03 pm
almaandromeda
Get that punishment xxoo

6:03 pm
almaandromeda

6:03 pm
korbendallas_987
just don't tell him!!

6:03 pm
almaandromeda
Nevet.

6:03 pm
almaandromeda
*never

6:03 pm
korbendallas_987
i am. ttys

6:03 pm
korbendallas_987
delete

6:03 pm
almaandromeda
Xxxxok

6:03 pm
almaandromeda
✅

6:03 pm

korbendallas_987

8:41 pm
almaandromeda
Kaypacha on youtube
His latest 7/19/17 report Astrology For The Soul

8:41 pm
almaandromeda
At 9:09 he explains what I am going thru perfectly.. high level genius.

8:48 pm
almaandromeda
Only if you are bored and get time to listen.. basically he is describing this intense draw that many people are feeling toward their newness, and the curiosity.. all of it.

8:48 pm
almaandromeda
Its cool to not feel so wtf haha

8:49 pm
almaandromeda
Thanks astrology

8:50 pm
almaandromeda
I am going thru so much change inside.. it is intense.

8:56 pm
almaandromeda
It's like, finally some of my badness is coming out and it feels scary but really good

8:57 pm
almaandromeda

12:44 pm
almaandromeda
Omg I just saw one of my bffs and she looked at me when I first got there and said
You look like a new woman.. weeeird!! I just said that 2 u this am

1:42 pm
korbendallas_987
haha such enthusiasm

1:42 pm
korbendallas_987
i envy you

1:47 pm
almaandromeda
Dont haha...

1:48 pm
almaandromeda
I feel like this

1:48 pm
almaandromeda
Going to dance to get my healing lol

1:49 pm
almaandromeda
Then Im giving u urs later xo

2:58 pm
korbendallas_987
😶

3:09 am
almaandromeda
Is that a no? 😊

3:16 am
almaandromeda
Youll take it and youll like it lol

4:14 am
almaandromeda
Unless you're sick of me lol

4:14 am
almaandromeda
No healing there 😗

4:14 am
korbendallas_987
not at all, busy day

4:14 am
korbendallas_987
calm yourself

4:14 am
almaandromeda
I understand!

4:15 am
almaandromeda
Me too..

4:14 am
almaandromeda
I just didnt understand your emoji thing

4:15 am
korbendallas_987
what was it

4:15 am
korbendallas_987
i forgot

4:15 am
almaandromeda
😞😞

4:16 am
almaandromeda
Spmething like that haha

4:16 am
korbendallas_987
noooo it was t

4:16 am
korbendallas_987
wasnt

4:16 am
almaandromeda
When ru free?

4:16 am
korbendallas_987
always and never

4:16 am
almaandromeda
I am in no rush seriously

4:16 am
korbendallas_987
sometimes fly nights, some days

4:16 am
almaandromeda
2nite not?

4:17 am
almaandromeda
I really dont have agenda xo and am in no rush.. any time just let know xo

4:18 am
korbendallas_987
are you talking about my future?

4:18 am
almaandromeda
No I mean to chat

4:18 am
korbendallas_987
ohhhh

4:18 am
almaandromeda
What r u talking about?

4:18 am
korbendallas_987
i bet u LOVE talking on the phone

4:19 am
korbendallas_987
to me it is pure hell

4:19 am
almaandromeda
not really... i can do this or that

4:19 am
almaandromeda
I am happy where you feel good

4:20 am
a**lmaandromeda**
I want to give you your exercise..

4:20 am
korbendallas_987
i also don't want you to space from nick

4:20 am
a**lmaandromeda**
I get it

4:20 am
a**lmaandromeda**

4:20 am
a**lmaandromeda**
So leave u be?

4:20 am
korbendallas_987
ughhh

4:20 am
almaandromeda
Its fine xxoo

4:20 am
korbendallas_987
i never said that Alma Mater

4:21 am
almaandromeda
Makes sense truly ❤

4:21 am
korbendallas_987
but jesus i don't want u to get a divorce?

4:21 am
almaandromeda
Why should we lol?

4:21 am
almaandromeda
I understand.. please dont feel bad xo

4:23 am
almaandromeda

4:24 am
almaandromeda
Take care xxoo

4:26 am
korbendallas_987
because unless i am reeeeally taking you the wrong way, i'm worried of someone getting hurt

4:26 am
korbendallas_987

4:26 am
korbendallas_987
but admittedly, i NEVER, EVER know when a girl is hittting on me. so maybe i am completely wrong

4:28 am
almaandromeda
I totally get it

4:29 am
almaandromeda
You are not wrong

4:29 am
almaandromeda
I am haha

4:29 am
almaandromeda

4:29 am
korbendallas_987
maybe not wrong.

4:29 am
korbendallas_987
just, forward. which i love.

4:30 am
almaandromeda
You make so much sense xxoo

4:30 am
almaandromeda
I like when u tell me what to do haha

4:30 am
almaandromeda
I will leave u be xxoo

4:30 am
korbendallas_987
haha i don't even do that

4:30 am
almaandromeda
Mr. Fascinating 😗

4:32 am
korbendallas_987
you've never met an attack helicopter pilot who has killed more people than the plague and it has overwhelmed you a bit. it doesn't hurt that we are both attractive, so it's a lot for you to calculate. that's all.

4:37 am
almaandromeda

4:51 am
almaandromeda
You are most likely right and I really am sorry. Like you said its been a tough year for me and it was a nice distraction but I dont want to take your time and energy in that way. I wish you as much joy as you allow yourself and everything I said was true. ❤

4:55 am
korbendallas_987
Samesies. You're an interesting character, and one I'm not lucky enough to meet often.

July 22nd, 2017

5:16 am
korbendallas_987
random enough, but i saw a girl at the commissary today that i actually thought was you.

5:21 am
almaandromeda
Not random haha

5:22 am
almaandromeda
You are everywhere 😊

5:22 am
almaandromeda
I will tell u something I thought of in a bit xo

5:22 am
korbendallas_987
i very deliberately stared at her until she reciprocated. for me, that is random.

5:22 am
almaandromeda
I love it haha synchronicity

5:22 am
korbendallas_987
👍

5:23 am
almaandromeda
Playing 🎶

5:23 am
korbendallas_987
part 1 or 2?

5:39 am
almaandromeda
I had something I wanted to share with u tho that came up to me today but I didnt want to bother u

5:52 am
almaandromeda
About killing.. about that I am actually a killer too. Not esoterically but really. The worst killing of my own baby, my own unborn love after already being a mother for 7 yrs. That is why I got my Kali tattoo. I dont know why I overshare with you so much and please forgive that but I thought it was fair to know xo

5:55 am
korbendallas_987
👎👎👎👎👎

163

5:55 am
korbendallas_987
boooooo

5:55 am
korbendallas_987
on bothering me

5:55 am
korbendallas_987
stop with that already

5:59 am
almaandromeda
Ok well I told you haha

6:02 am
almaandromeda
You dont bother me either 😊

6:16 am
korbendallas_987
nope forgiving nothing from here on out because nothing to forgive

6:18 am
korbendallas_987
not sure who did what to you but you are far too apologetic/remorseful/SOMETHING

6:18 am
korbendallas_987
It distracts from our conversations which i love, so dearly

6:25 am
almaandromeda
Thank you ✊

6:25 am
almaandromeda
Ittsa deal yo

6:25 am
almaandromeda
None o' that.. for some reason I feel safe with u and that is NOT a normal I have
with people

6:28 am
korbendallas_987
you shouldn't feel safe around them; they are vile, repulsive consumers

7:08 am
almaandromeda
I am out with my friends and saw on the tv at the bar men in army suits jumping
from helicopters and it said Army lol

7:08 am
almaandromeda
Told you 😳

7:11 am
almaandromeda
I do know why Im like that btw but its boring lol.. just a lifetime of the Scarlett
Letter conditioning from a having a sweet faced brown baby by myself at 20 and
also living under narc parents.. shame city. Im working on it ok! 😂

7:42 am
almaandromeda
I love them too... our convos 🖤

8:16 am
korbendallas_987
aahhhhhh. now i see. you are attracted to the mulatto-type.

8:16 am
korbendallas_987
it allllll makes sense.

8:16 am
korbendallas_987
i'm afraid to meet

8:16 am
almaandromeda
What!!! 😂😂

8:16 am
almaandromeda
I am NOT even remotely

8:16 am
almaandromeda
I am not racist like that my friend

8:17 am
almaandromeda
I just connect

8:17 am
korbendallas_987
NEVER accused anything of the sort

8:17 am
almaandromeda
Afraid to meet me? 😊

8:17 am
almaandromeda
I just mean I dont have those focuses even a little

8:19 am
almaandromeda
But my fiance before Nick was white

8:20 am
almaandromeda
I didnt think you accused me of that btw

8:24 am
almaandromeda
❤ ur face

8:25 am
almaandromeda
Nite

8:26 am
korbendallas_987
oh. a lotta girls like mixed dudes. that's all

8:31 am
almaandromeda
Tru.. lots do.

8:33 am
almaandromeda
I'm different than most girls in most things.. shoes, purses, mixed dudes, nails etc.. I am into other stuff like drawing and dancing instead.

8:33 am
almaandromeda
And individual soul connections and the bodies they are carried in.

8:34 am
almaandromeda
I did not mean to offend you Michael and hope I didnt

8:35 am
almaandromeda
But Im not apologizing haha 😁

8:37 am
korbendallas_987
no u didn't offend

8:37 am
korbendallas_987
confused on how u could think that i thought u were racist though

8:41 am
almaandromeda
I really didnt think you were saying that about me

8:45 am
almaandromeda
I just said that in relation to myself having a type that has to do with skin color..

8:46 am
almaandromeda
I just don't see the world thru a type lens.. everything is present, specific, unique, precious.

8:47 am

almaandromeda

Astrology helps me see how the the love is always showing up in new unexpected packages

8:48 am

almaandromeda

Of course YOU are everybody's type lol

9:46 am

korbendallas_987

haha no way

9:47 am

korbendallas_987

that's interesting that you don't have a type though; i don't either. at ALL. black, white, skinny, fat.. i have preferences but certainly not a type.

9:47 am

korbendallas_987

you have. beautiful skin and it is very hard to resist.

9:51 am

korbendallas_987

it's what i would focus on most about you in person (i think). i hope i didn't hurt your feeling the other night, i have to draw lines or i will cross them like George Washington crossed the Delaware..

9:52 am

korbendallas_987

make no mistake about it though, i'm feeling what ever you are. it.

4:50 pm

almaandromeda

I feel it too.. so much.

4:52 pm

almaandromeda

It will be funny to meet you.. a total stranger, it will be hard to not seem like I have met you before. I like knowing u stranger ❤️😶

168

4:56 pm
almaandromeda
Something just like this by Coldplay is on the radio...This song.. how can I not think of u?

4:56 pm
almaandromeda
You are a real life superhero 🤓

4:58 pm
almaandromeda
I am not looking for anything as you know and am so happy with ur bro.. but you dropped in and stayed on my mind. You stay on my mind.

11:00 pm
korbendallas_987
i know all of that. no disclaimers required.

11:00 pm
korbendallas_987
you should know that as well!! i've always wanted to see Seattle. it's funny that people refer to it by its airport code.

11:01 pm
almaandromeda
#Seattle

11:01 pm
almaandromeda
We cant wait to see you guys

11:01 pm
almaandromeda
Do you know when you might come?

11:04 pm
almaandromeda
I know that as well xo

l11:05 pm
korbendallas_987
no clue. i would imagine when we leave here en route to wherever the hell i go next..

11:06 pm
almaandromeda
Cool.

11:29 pm
almaandromeda
🖤

11:30 pm
almaandromeda
Hopefully we can come out there soon.. we'll see! In the meantime amhere4u ✊

July 23rd, 2017

12:08 am
korbendallas_987
you're always welcome to come out. we have plenty of space. you're a special girl, i think it's pretty cool that you didn't default to, he's in the army, he must be brainless

12:24 am
almaandromeda
Omg you are the 💀PPOSITE! I can't promise that I would have been wise enough to see that as soon with anyone else but like I said before it is rediculously easy 2 🖤 u. I'm glad u read that poem.. meant 4 u.

12:57 am
almaandromeda
I am glad you spared the camel btw 🖤 Animals need protection too. I know what you mean about garden variety sociopathic behavior i.e. kill a baby, spare a squirrel.. and of course I dont see like that so I can't know what that could be like inside.. but you did care to spare the camel and stood up ✊ with your heart strength so it is in there 🖤 and animals need love too xxoo

12:59 am
almaandromeda
Salerno sounds so loud... I hope you get to share more with me someday in person Me= 👂 👂

1:08 am
almaandromeda
I really dont know anything about it all and can not pretend to.. but I can listen and with you I can not judge. Be yo'self yo. 🤗

170

3:59 am
korbendallas_987
loud??

3:59 am
korbendallas_987
the rocket attacks were for sure

3:59 am
korbendallas_987
other than that pretty quiet

3:59 am
almaandromeda
I can only imagine..

4:00 am
almaandromeda
How come so many rocket attacks? Were they directed at you guys?

4:00 am
almaandromeda
I don't know what to ask.. I really don't know anything at all about anything in all of that..

4:01 am
almaandromeda
None of my business really haha xox

4:02 am
almaandromeda
Obviously I am curious but I know it sucks to talk about and I am interested in so much else about you too

4:03 am
korbendallas_987
of course they were directed at us---we invaded their country

4:03 am
korbendallas_987
americans would do the same thing if invaded

4:04 am
almaandromeda
I agree...

4:04 am
almaandromeda
It is so complex

4:05 am
korbendallas_987
lotta moving parts and pieces but i don't know of a single country that wouldn't defend itself once invaded by another

4:05 am
almaandromeda
It is survival

4:18 am
almaandromeda
I should just get a radio show and you can be my only interview guest for a month haha ... We know what curiosity did to the cat 🐱 lol

4:28 am
almaandromeda
I guess what I'm saying is I really don't have an appropriate outlet for my fascination with you lol

4:44 am
korbendallas_987
i will admit that it has me puzzled

4:45 am
korbendallas_987
prob just never met a guy in the military?

4:45 am
almaandromeda
And annoyed?

4:45 am
almaandromeda
Not that...

4:45 am
almaandromeda
I really don't know either tbh

4:45 am
almaandromeda
I just am! Does it bother you? Be honest.

4:46 am
korbendallas_987
long lost brother of hubby that no one knew about?

4:46 am
almaandromeda
That defintely haha

4:46 am
korbendallas_987
i told you that you don't bother me

4:46 am
almaandromeda
K

4:47 am
almaandromeda
I will be on here at 12:30 2nite my time

4:47 am
almaandromeda
Practicing now 🎶

5:05 am
korbendallas_987
ok

8:21 am
almaandromeda
I dunno.. it's probably that you are just SO fascinating.. you FLY, in the day, at night, one of the toughest aircrafts to fly, you teach others to fly.. you have seen everything I haven't, you care about all the things I don't but am curious about still, and I have this inside private line right now.

8:22 am
almaandromeda
It's just kind of cool 😎

8:23 am
almaandromeda
Plus other reasons too I am sure..

9:05 am
korbendallas_987
i do get that

9:06 am
korbendallas_987
it's just that most people don't have the presence of mind of what exactly i do

9:07 am
korbendallas_987
most of my friends never ask me about all the studying and evaluations and bullshit i have to do.

9:07 am
almaandromeda
I can barely imagine it.. but it is amazing

9:07 am
korbendallas_987
i guess most are just buried in breeding and such

9:07 am
korbendallas_987
the apache is a cadillac, but a lot of work.

9:07 am
almaandromeda
Omg tell me!!

9:08 am
korbendallas_987
one slip up can be disastrous--and then there's elements we don't control, like weather

9:08 am
almaandromeda
Understatement of the year lol

9:08 am
almaandromeda
'Disastrous

9:08 am
almaandromeda
You are seriously holding life in every moment

9:08 am
almaandromeda
And bringing yourself into the sky and other lives

9:08 am
korbendallas_987
yea it's probably why i'm so apathetic

9:09 am
almaandromeda
Overstimulation

9:09 am
korbendallas_987
nothing really gets to me

9:09 am
almaandromeda
I can see that

9:09 am
korbendallas_987
if i DONT die in a helicopter i will be very surprised

9:09 am
almaandromeda
I really hope you don't.. have you been flying since 23?

9:10 am
korbendallas_987
25

9:10 am
almaandromeda
So 12 years.. can you fly both planes and helicopters or strictly the apache training

9:11 am
korbendallas_987
i've never been behind the controls of an airplane but i guarantee you it's galaxies easier than a helicopter

9:11 am
almaandromeda
I read that it was!

9:11 am
almaandromeda
What you do is NEXT LEVEL

9:11 am
korbendallas_987
i know guys with more hours than me that suck (in my opinion)

9:11 am
almaandromeda
Haha

9:12 am
korbendallas_987
i can teach a chimp to do my job

9:12 am
almaandromeda
Doubt it... A chimp has to be brave enough and trust themselves enough to fly

9:12 am
almaandromeda
I have to show you something hilarious..

9:12 am
almaandromeda
:-o

9:13 am
almaandromeda
That is me in 2003.. protesting the Bush wars.

9:13 am
almaandromeda
DONT JUDGE lol

9:13 am
almaandromeda
I told you I have been a peace activist my whole life

9:14 am
almaandromeda
I'm not like that any more for along time, I was a kid then

9:14 am
almaandromeda
But that is me with my son, face covered, marching with upside down Amerikkkan flags

9:14 am
almaandromeda
In the middle...

9:14 am
almaandromeda
So?

9:14 am
korbendallas_987
how funny

9:14 am
korbendallas_987
over 5000 people died in iraq for absolutely nothing

9:15 am
almaandromeda
SO funny that we have been so far apart in the world lol

9:15 am
almaandromeda
It's awesome to me

9:15 am
korbendallas_987
meh. maybe when you see me finish someone off who is missing a torso with a white phosphorous rocket it wouldn't be so sexy

9:16 am
almaandromeda
True, that is NOT sexy.

9:16 am
almaandromeda
I just like knowing you.

9:17 am
almaandromeda
And if anyone else said that I don't know how I would feel, but Michael, you can't scare me 🖤

9:17 am
korbendallas_987
well thanks

9:17 am
almaandromeda
I can't say why, but it just is lol

9:17 am
korbendallas_987
scare? for what

9:17 am
almaandromeda
I mean I won't be afraid of stuff that you share about stuff like that, and usually that would tbh

9:18 am
almaandromeda
I am BIG baby about violence usually like BIG BIG because I have dealt with so much of it as a child

178

9:18 am
almaandromeda
I decided to deal with it by NOT dealing with it ever or having it around me at all

9:18 am
korbendallas_987
hmm

9:18 am
almaandromeda
I'm just being honest

9:18 am
korbendallas_987
i don't section it off as violence, instead i call it a necessitty

9:19 am
korbendallas_987
in my situations, troopers would've died if i didn't show up and kill everyone

9:19 am
almaandromeda
I believe it and have read it

9:19 am
almaandromeda
Your job is the most crucial

9:20 am
korbendallas_987
troopers like my 18 year old brother who did a year over there and hasn't been the same since

9:20 am
almaandromeda
I'm sorry to hear that

9:20 am
almaandromeda
Are you the same since?

9:20 am
korbendallas_987
in most wYs

9:20 am
korbendallas_987
ways

9:20 am
almaandromeda
Except spelling lol

9:20 am
korbendallas_987
all experiences change people

9:21 am
almaandromeda
So true. You could write a book Michael.

9:21 am
almaandromeda
I don't think you see yourself in full 3 D

9:21 am
almaandromeda
You are AMAZING

9:21 am
korbendallas_987
i often wonder if my life-fodder is book worthy

9:21 am
korbendallas_987
sounds boring to me

9:21 am
a**lmaandromeda**
Stop wondering start writing lol

9:22 am
almaandromeda
And you are super eloquent

9:22 am
korbendallas_987
the war i fight in my head every day would be more interesting unfortunately

9:22 am
almaandromeda
You have a lot to say... especially about THAT war

9:22 am
almaandromeda
I know what you mean though

9:22 am
almaandromeda
I need to write a book too and it is all a bunch of thoughts without any beginning or middle

9:23 am
almaandromeda
TOO MUCH INFORMATION and not enough synthesis

9:23 am
almaandromeda
Mine is about my parents suing me and also just my life of learning to love myself

9:23 am
korbendallas_987
that's why you get a ghost-writer

9:24 am
almaandromeda
They don't know shit lol

9:24 am
almaandromeda
You have to live this to write it

9:24 am
korbendallas_987
few people are true authors

9:24 am
almaandromeda
Nobody knows my troubles 🎼

9:25 am
almaandromeda
Michael...

9:24 am
almaandromeda
I think you are.

9:25 am
almaandromeda
What do you think of my voice? 🎤 👻

9:26 am
almaandromeda
If anything lol

9:26 am
korbendallas_987
i like it. it's not my kind of music tho

9:26 am
almaandromeda
Too happy haha?

9:27 am
almaandromeda
I knew that

9:27 am
almaandromeda
I actually went to college and got my bachelors in music

9:27 am
almaandromeda
Specifically for singing but learned dance and acting

9:27 am
korbendallas_987
that's pretty cool

9:28 am
almaandromeda
I started out only as a poet and was NOT a good singer at all

9:28 am
almaandromeda
I have worked REALLY hard for like...20 years to be a good singer/dancer

9:28 am
almaandromeda
And now they are my favorite things to do

9:28 am
korbendallas_987
i have no 'niche' really

9:28 am
korbendallas_987
army has stolen that

9:28 am
korbendallas_987
but it was my choice

9:29 am
almaandromeda
How?

9:29 am
almaandromeda
Just time?

9:29 am
korbendallas_987
yes

9:29 am
almaandromeda
How much time do you spend every day in your Army role, sir?

9:31 am
korbendallas_987
it never stops

9:32 am
korbendallas_987
even at home, dealing with texts, emails, or studying

9:32 am
korbendallas_987
i have to know a lot, verbatim

9:32 am
almaandromeda
Wow.. makes sense.

9:32 am
almaandromeda
Im glad tbh

9:32 am
korbendallas_987
the rest, i better know very, very well

9:32 am
almaandromeda
Life or death shit lol

9:32 am
almaandromeda
Im glad you take it so seriously

9:32 am
korbendallas_987
some ye

9:33 am
korbendallas_987
you have to or you die

9:33 am
korbendallas_987
the one that crashed in kansas city last year was a test pilot that i deployed with

9:33 am
almaandromeda
Woah.. so freaking scary..

9:34 am
almaandromeda
You really have to keep your head.

9:34 am
korbendallas_987
ye lotta dead friends

9:34 am
korbendallas_987
i can count at least 10 off top of my head

9:34 am
almaandromeda
Wow Michael.. I am sorry about that. Brave souls 😇

9:34 am
korbendallas_987
meh

9:34 am
korbendallas_987
we all signed the paper

9:34 am
almaandromeda
Are you are a daredevil?

9:35 am
korbendallas_987
mo

9:35 am
korbendallas_987
no

9:35 am
almaandromeda
No huh wow

9:35 am
almaandromeda
Just doing the job.

9:35 am
korbendallas_987
basically

9:35 am
almaandromeda
Still brave.

9:35 am
korbendallas_987
everyone handles it differently

9:36 am
korbendallas_987
some are ultra hyper over aware

9:36 am
korbendallas_987
some have no clue how close they came to dying

9:36 am
korbendallas_987
i'm somewhere in the middle of those two

9:36 am
almaandromeda
Ohh.. was just asking haha

9:37 am
almaandromeda
Staying aware but also checked out?

9:37 am
korbendallas_987
i suppose so

9:37 am
almaandromeda
You also like driving fast too right?

9:37 am
korbendallas_987
life is boring to me, i've pretty much done what i've wanted to do

9:37 am
korbendallas_987
not not really i just buy expensive cars because it's funny

9:38 am
almaandromeda
Are you kidding lol? 😁

9:39 am
almaandromeda
About buying the cars just cuz funny

9:39 am
almaandromeda
It is funny

9:39 am
korbendallas_987
not really

9:39 am
almaandromeda
Life is awesome if you get to do what u want

9:39 am
korbendallas_987
i dam sure don't drive it fast

9:39 am
korbendallas_987
you can't here

9:40 am
a**lmaandromeda**
Im glad.. for the kids lol

9:40 am
almaandromeda
But fuck the kids haha

9:40 am
korbendallas_987
hell yes

9:40 am
almaandromeda
Just kidding lol.. I saw that on your IG 😂

9:40 am
korbendallas_987
fuck them kids

9:41 am
a**lmaandromeda**
For realz fuck them kids haha

9:41 am
a**lmaandromeda**
No kids for you old man?

9:41 am
korbendallas_987
not a chance

9:41 am
korbendallas_987
got back from afghanistan and RAN to the urologist

9:41 am
almaandromeda
I didnt think you were the typelol

9:42 am
korbendallas_987
nah i've got no use for em

9:42 am
almaandromeda
I hear you.

9:42 am
almaandromeda
They are tough.. got mine done early haha

9:42 am
almaandromeda
1 and done.

9:42 am
korbendallas_987

9:42 am
korbendallas_987
couldn't imagine coming home from work, only to start my next job of dealing with some screaming brat

9:42 am
almaandromeda
He is 17 almost 18 already!!

9:42 am
almaandromeda
You would love it lol

9:43 am
almaandromeda

9:43 am
korbendallas_987
psssh you're done with the hard part then

9:43 am
almaandromeda
Going to sleep xo

9:43 am
almaandromeda
Ttyl

9:43 am
korbendallas_987
ok. til next time

9:43 am
almaandromeda

9:17 pm
almaandromeda
Speaking of writing.. I actually am a published poet and writer and have been in books and magazines in my former life before focusing on singing and pop music.. if you are ever bored google Alma Star for a laugh at how different we are lol! :-)

11:42 pm
korbendallas_987
daaaayum

11:43 pm
korbendallas_987
now that's something. i wiggle controls and push buttons

July 24th, 2017

1:36 am
almaandromeda
I know I look dumb lol 🫠

1:36 am
almaandromeda
The dumb blonde thing- I love it.. use it to my advantage haha

1:37 am
almaandromeda
I will send you a poem of my own sometime..

8:32 am
almaandromeda
That is one

5:16 pm
korbendallas_987
it says up for like 5 secs

5:16 pm
korbendallas_987
i guess it doesn't want you to screenshot?

5:30 pm
almaandromeda
WOULD BE

in a hesitant world
of would-be disasters,
our breathing makes
the night come faster,
where stars burst like
bubbles beside car crashes,
rubbing raw rashes
in the bed you don't sleep.

I don't eat and think
about you, your hands,
wrestling out the willful
spirit of my demands,
tongue clicking in time
with would-be plans,
dutifully branding me
the company you keep.

5:31 pm
almaandromeda
This is one of thousands :-) .. just picked out one for you.

6:09 pm
korbendallas_987
i love it

7:34 pm
almaandromeda

7:36 pm
almaandromeda
I have another in mind 4 u and will send later

8:25 pm
korbendallas_987
👀

8:40 pm
almaandromeda
👁saw😜ur face🤳

10:50 pm
korbendallas_987
?

11:02 pm
almaandromeda
I saw your face.. a recent picture.

11:03 pm
almaandromeda
I didnt know really what you looked like this year haha

11:04 pm
almaandromeda
Not so bad

11:34 pm
korbendallas_987
under construction 😖

July 25th, 2017

8:06 pm
almaandromeda
WAR CAME HOME FOR SUPPER
So we roll up our sleeves
Get our family into the fight
Spit on dirty knuckles
Unsure of what just might

Be under our punches
Who is landing that blow
Who is standing in the trenches
Screaming hurrah and ready to go

I welcome my man back
This has always been his home
Returned to me a murderer
I nurse him as my own

And we absorb his torment
The leeches in his mouth

192

I talk him down and braid him in
A country that spits him back out

War came home for supper
And left the other night
Now we sit in empty beds
Unsure of what just might

8:13 pm
almaandromeda
No idea why I write about the stuff I do..

8:30 pm
almaandromeda
I know NOTHING about that whole world obviously :-) just imagination

9:15 pm
korbendallas_987
close enough. Is that iambic pentameter?

9:26 pm
almaandromeda
I did take lots of poetry classes in college and it may be from a time I was experi-
menting with different forms.. but not sure really. Just words. Making sense of stuff.
Art therapy is my absolute survival and I try to just let it come out.

9:28 pm
almaandromeda
I usually don't even rhyme lol.. so many different ways to get stuff out.

9:47 pm
almaandromeda
YOUR MESSAGE
I only wish that you could hold me.
Instead I'm rudely left with your random
ghost of second best and none of you
I gladly kept yet everyone of you hangs around

Come knock me down, get me out of this!
Pull my proud pain body to the ground
and pray it happens quick, when the ashes
come and the body slips, oh pray it happens quick

Bow in the broken violence, humming your hymn

of brown eyes and weighted silences, you were
not what I wanted to hear, but now
you're all around me, the signal painfully clear –

I've lost you but your message is our tiny child.
We spend every waking moment, baby, her hair
is growing wild and she only eats to feed the
hungry and she prays like there's some kind of god

I only wish that you could hold her, whisper
laws of karma, frozen in time kisses, tell our child
how you've suspended me in awe, show the baby
your world, and how from your words she was born a star.

9:47 pm
almaandromeda
That is not rhyming for example..

9:48 pm
almaandromeda
Anywayz, I will leave you alone again lol :-) We both can't wait to meet you both
and I am glad to have a new friend in this big world. 📱🌍

July 26th, 2017

3:02 am
korbendallas_987
ye i wish i knew when i was going to be in that sector of the planet soon

3:13 am
almaandromeda
Me too 👻

3:15 am
almaandromeda
Till then u rock ✊ be nice to yourself 🧖

3:16 am
korbendallas_987
never!

6:35 am
almaandromeda
The eclipse coming up is so intense.. it is 8/21. Many thousands of people are traveling to Oregon from around the globe because it is hitting here first and blackest, about an hour below us. We are not going to the eye of it cause the traffic seems insane.. Eclipses are VERY powerful shifts in energy and this one coming feels more potent than usual. Heads up lol 🌙

6:59 am
korbendallas_987
i predict catastrophe

7:03 am
almaandromeda
End of the world 4 sure 😂.. but on a personal level most likely. We are never lucky enough for full scale catastrophe and the restarts they provide on a world level haha.

4:55 pm
korbendallas_987
a man can wish

6:44 pm
almaandromeda
and a girl can dream 🤓

9:53 pm
almaandromeda
It's one of the tough things about being an astrologer is you already know how this goes 😵

9:53 pm
korbendallas_987
that would be nice

July 28th, 2017

3:01 am
almaandromeda
Tbh I am scared of this eclipse.. seems silly but it is right to the degree on my ascendant which is my body and it seems impossible not to kill me lol.. I don't know. I know nothing really, astrologer or not haha

4:35 am
korbendallas_987
to me it's just cosmic bodies aligning for a sec or two. no offense

4:37 am
almaandromeda
None taken

4:37 am
almaandromeda
You are ✅

July 29th, 2017

7:16 pm
almaandromeda
🖤

July 30th, 2017

12:09 am
korbendallas_987

12:14 am
almaandromeda
I do not know how that happened haha 😂

12:14 am
korbendallas_987
i thought we talked about apologies. 🙄

12:15 am
almaandromeda
You're right haha.. omg so funny

12:16 am
almaandromeda
You are obviously still on my mind

196

12:18 am
almaandromeda
If only cosmic bodies aligned for more than a few seconds...

12:18 am
korbendallas_987
as are you.

12:18 am
almaandromeda

12:18 am
almaandromeda
That was on purpose haha😊

12:18 am
korbendallas_987
delete this, but check this out

12:18 am
korbendallas_987
I actually sent it as a disappearing photo

12:19 am
almaandromeda
You just got that tattoo😍

12:19 am
almaandromeda
?

12:19 am
korbendallas_987
couple days ago

12:19 am
almaandromeda
Wow!!

12:19 am
almaandromeda
Hard as f

12:19 am
almaandromeda
Nice legs btw lol

12:19 am
korbendallas_987
legs under construction

12:19 am
almaandromeda
Why heretic?

12:20 am
almaandromeda

12:20 am
almaandromeda
What does it mean?

12:21 am
almaandromeda
Ok looked it up

12:21 am
almaandromeda
Yup. You. 😂

12:21 am
almaandromeda

12:21 am
almaandromeda
Deleted xo miss your face

12:22 am
korbendallas_987
YOU didn't know HERETIC?

12:23 am
korbendallas_987
that surprises

12:24 am
almaandromeda
I am full of them 🙊

12:25 am
almaandromeda
I think I did but not fully

12:28 am
almaandromeda
what does it mean to you besides the obvious meaning? to put it on your skin it must be a meaningful word

12:29 am
almaandromeda
I hate deleting your messages 😑

12:37 am
almaandromeda
You said you were Lucifer the morning star and guess what? You have the asteroid Lucifer conjunct your Sun.

12:38 am
almaandromeda
He is the ultimate dissenter and heretic.. but pushes us in form to play outside the rules and conquer this realm.

12:38 am
almaandromeda

12:38 am
almaandromeda
You stay facinatin'

12:56 am
almaandromeda
Eve and the apple..

12:56 am
almaandromeda
Also he tunes through his high musical frequency others who are out of tune in themselves.

12:57 am
almaandromeda
I feel all that from you so much.

1:09 am
korbendallas_987
wow

1:09 am
korbendallas_987
that's me

1:10 am
korbendallas_987
it means that if you are a religious zealot, i want you to know that i am your enemy - regardless of creed

1:10 am
almaandromeda
So funny you say enemy because I found out thru looking at asteroids and deeper connections etc that I am Nemesis - I have that asteroid exactly conjunct my ascendant body and it is also the second I was born.. very specific choice to be born her.

1:21 am
almaandromeda
Now I see why I threaten so many people just by existing.

1:23 am
korbendallas_987

1:28 am
almaandromeda

1:28 am
almaandromeda
Deleted xxoo

1:55 am
korbendallas_987
same

9:30 pm
almaandromeda
Are you not a zealot if you are a sworn enemy? A fanatical reflection of the fanatic that you don't like? Also, is tatooing your wife's name on your hand and a Hannya not some form of of extreme adulation and fanatic worship? Is it different to worship a single person than a Universe or God? #sorrynotsorry haha 😂 you said ask anything xo

9:31 pm
almaandromeda
What about the allegience to the army you have above anyone else? Is that not a form of faith, or at least blind devotion?

10:14 pm
almaandromeda
I love that new tattoo btw.. HARD AS F 😍... and all of urs that I can see.. just so curious about you and how you reason out your world. Don't know why I want to know so much and I'm not allowed to ask forgiveness or you know I would. 🙄

July 31st, 2017

2:12 am
almaandromeda
😂 Just realized that as Lucifer light bringer my burning curiosity is just moth to the flame and I #officially understand why I can't apologize for my fascination with you. 😎🔥

3:04 am
korbendallas_987
i idolatrize nothing, my hope is my for my tattoos to fly in the face of anyone of any religion, but specifically the dogs of the nazarene. christians have spilt more blood than all other religions combined and i vomit at them. that said, i think people think farrrrr too hard about meanings and such of them. some people get tattoos because they look cool.

3:07 am
korbendallas_987
i do what i do in the army because i said i would, not an inch past that. it has fucked me as many times as i have fucked it. i used to love it, now it has been bastardized into some sort of rat-race that i just can't get into.

3:08 am
korbendallas_987
99% of the educated don't even know what Satanism, as an example, is.

3:08 am
korbendallas_987
so it's really hard to call myself a zealot

3:09 am
korbendallas_987
the hanya was just a coincidence, i think i got it RIGHT before I met lorie.

3:10 am
korbendallas_987
i have two hibiscus in my left bicep--why? i dunno, i like em.. ?

3:42 am
almaandromeda
I can see how a tattoo is just a tattoo and not neccesarily a reflection of anything else. I got my hand tattoo because I let a tattoo artist stay at my house around 22 yrs old and he traded me the tattoo. He was covered face hands everything in tattoos. One night we traced my hand and arm and just started on the hand first. I didn't understand how severe it was to tattoo a hand until the next day. So young, so stupid. I had to hunt him down and have him finish it in a motel bathroom.

3:42 am
almaandromeda
Sometimes they just happen.

3:43 am
almaandromeda
I think I get the difference in your focus and the zealot nature.

4:03 am
almaandromeda
Hibiscus flowers.. to me there is meaning in beauty.

4:32 am
almaandromeda
Thanks btw ✌️😊 Take care yo.

6:05 am
korbendallas_987

202

6:25 am
almaandromeda

6:25 am
almaandromeda

AUGUST 2017_

August 2nd, 2017

2:20 am
almaandromeda
But don't you fly with both hands and legs?

2:21 am
almaandromeda
Often we are more ambidextrous when left handed

2:21 am
almaandromeda
Because it is a right handed world...

2:41 am
almaandromeda
Plus tell me a joke because I finally had a bad day 😑😾 Yes, even me, it is possible lol

2:47 am
korbendallas_987
i only know one joke and i am usually berated for it. too long to type, i promise you'll hear it though

2:48 am
korbendallas_987
can't have good days without bad ones

3:28 am
almaandromeda
I don't hold people to promises but I look forward to hearing it 😊

3:29 am
almaandromeda
Some bad days are the worst.. and some good days are the best. Perspective helps if anything does

6:13 am
korbendallas_987
and perspective is the easiest to lose grip on, for me

6:24 am
almaandromeda
I know what you mean lol

6:26 am
almaandromeda
#humaning bleh Coming back as a bird next time.

August 5th, 2017

6:19 am
almaandromeda
I just found out something that is a TRIP! I am in Kansas visiting my family and my Granddaddy told me my mom was born in Tripler Medical Center in Honolulu 🏝️🤓 Her name is Leilauni which is a Hawaian name.

8:41 am
korbendallas_987
very common hawaiian name.. if you were born on oahu you were probably born in tripler haha

8:42 am
korbendallas_987
now there are a couple other civi hospitals but tripler is the main one

1:48 pm
almaandromeda
Oh cool. My Grandaddy was Airforce till retired so they were on airforce base. I didn't realize it was everyone

1:51 pm
almaandromeda
Whatevs haha

2:18 pm
almaandromeda
#ofx2gv sorry to bug you and I'm done now 👻✈️

2:18 pm
almaandromeda
Tc

9:08 pm
korbendallas_987
well maybe not EVERYONE was born at tripler (we call it 'Cripler'), some are probably born in houses or highways or whatever else haha

August 6th, 2017

3:47 am
almaandromeda
Got it lol 👌 📱 ✌️

August 7th, 2017

6:30 am
almaandromeda
WHO IS THIS EMPTY – ALMA KING
who is this empty
sexy forgot to pay me, love lost
my number, money says check
is in the mail running from luck

who stayed in Vegas making lust
With bad taste. anger left the phone
off the hook while malice and revenge
were off to therapy for thrills and pretty is

paint by numbers at the local bar and grill
I have happiness on hold warm body
says he'll fill in loneliness paid my
heat bill last month kisses played nurse

bandaid played doctor fine isn't friends
with me anymore he slammed the door
and almost hurt luxury slipping out the back
to talk smack with new and mundane

about used who's been my only company
cause last I heard stability was laying low
scared off by my run-in with fragility
strong is a song in a girl I know.

6:36 am
almaandromeda
AND EVERYWHERE IS WAR – ALMA KING
what can I save against the drowning of a nation
I got nailed in, from the first crown of my fawn-soft hair
against my mother's other mouth,
doctor's tools slicing her open
as my cloud-covered body slipped quietly out,
into hands swollen many times from violence,
what can I defend in being here?

why must I sleep timidly along outside of bed
with baby tucked beside me along the wall,
my resting pose faced out towards
monsters, rapists, murderers, mermaids, all
phantoms of collective disquiet, our dreams
swell thick with violence, murmurs horrid, familiar,
how did I come to find what it is to sit in fear?

what can I save against upheaval of the end,
when I am sure the war is in my own system –
between synapse and sinew, under pulse of poisoned
fluids, the deep draws of death, war is under
everything I stand for, in my smallest girl child,
mimicking her patterns of abuse, cheeks swollen with violence,
who am I to be quiet when I have been that near to war?

6:37 am
almaandromeda
BLACK CROW – ALMA KING
black crow, what are you looking for?
I hear your music in the crunch of brown
leaves. have the bugs come out? your black
seems a part of all this nothing, your home
the gnarled branches spawned from distant
planets, mossy, green rubbed black.
black crow, you are fine alone and together,
do you mind losing your shape against
the black open sky or is that the way
you might find space? your black is the hole
I fell into and out of landing upside down,
spacewoman stalking this empty planet,
emotionless, softly sobbing. fear is fine
but torture is endless, even the ending is endless,

the worm in your mouth, half carved and swallowed,
eyes still open, the pinprick of black in his
half lived eyes the emptiest black of my nothing,
black of your feathers, black of the hole I fell into
and out of landing upside down, spacewoman stalking
this empty planet, emotionless, softly sobbing.

6:43 am
almaandromeda
STRETCH MARKS – ALMA KING
raised red and fibrous,
attaching end to end hybrid skin

or dips and pools in bruised blue,
soft and taut like dolphin hide,

digging graves on the body
of buried but insidious apocalypse.

communes of hundreds stake out
battle grounds, marking territory,

snake my belly like Medusa's scalp,
scars of youthful indiscretion,

forcing denial of the child to ring
hollow and unfounded.

proof and persecution,
peculiar puffy layered treasure,

see maps across my body,
find your own way home.

6:38 am
almaandromeda
For your reading leisure..

6:41 am
almaandromeda
I know I am so last month lol and that is good and makes sense! 😎 I wanted to get
these poems to you to read on your own time. There is stuff in here on some of the
stuff we touched on. I don't want anything and hope you are awesome Michael 🐢

4:47 pm
korbendallas_987
love the stretch marks one

4:48 pm
korbendallas_987
i think i told you i find them attractive

4:50 pm
almaandromeda
All true lol 😄 its not like a little so I had have to come to terms with it.. most people are not like you in that

5:52 pm
korbendallas_987

August 13th, 2017

7:48 pm
almaandromeda
The Revivalists – Gold To Glass

7:48 pm
almaandromeda
I love this song right now

August 14th, 2017
7:10 am **korbendallas_987**

7:14 am
almaandromeda
👀 lyrics.. wow
THE REVIVALISTS – GOLD TO GLASS
"This is the final come and go
I keep fighting faith 'cause I don't wanna know
On this eve in fall, lights shining over
She's colder than she would show
I guess I'll just take the pill

And fall into the meadow

212

This isn't who I am, I'm a soldier with a medal
All my gold turned to glass
And now I'm breathing fast
Find someone to help these hard times pass"

7:10 am
korbendallas_987

7:15 am
korbendallas_987
All true.

7:15 am
korbendallas_987
Reminds me of these Tool lyrics tbh –
"I know you well. You are a part of me
I know you better than I know myself
I know you best, better than anyone
I know you better than I know myself"

7:20 am
korbendallas_987
You fucking get me its so weird.

August 16th, 2017

11:19 pm
almaandromeda
So sorry to hear about that terrible accident.. holy shit! Very scary. 😨 Be safe! ✊
We haven't even gotten to meet you yet lol

11:20 pm
korbendallas_987
hawaii is special when it comes to weather, and that's what almost always kills helicopter pilots. i don't fuck around with it so you don't have to worry about me. 👍

11:22 pm
almaandromeda
I'm glad, I won't! lol 😊 Take care tho really ✊ I loved the tool lyrics btw.. thanks.

11:26 pm

almaandromeda

There is only one reality, but there are many different ways that reality can be interpreted. - Drunvalo Melchizedek

Learn how to see. Realize that everything is connected to everything else. - Da Vinci

August 21st, 2017

6:17 pm
korbendallas_987
so what does all this eclipse shit mean? apocalypse?

6:21 pm
almaandromeda
Hellfire... shit you're used to lol 😂 Seriously the USA getting hit across the belly like this is significant. Historically where eclipses happen there are dramatic changes of some sort, so it plays out like that.

6:23 pm
almaandromeda
On a personal level for humans, the solar eclipse is a regular new moon that aligns with the north node of our future and future desires, and it sort of shakes us into what we want and why we chose to actualize into form. It's a powerful invisible shift that affects each person in their own way.

6:25 pm
almaandromeda
We just watched it, it is still pulling away and the weight of the big black round moon is so 3D and psychedelic in the sky. A big black balloon over the sun. ☉

9:44 pm
korbendallas_987
fuck

9:44 pm
korbendallas_987
guess hawaii just got shit on then

9:44 pm
korbendallas_987
next one like this is in 2024, i believe

5:48 am
almaandromeda
Shit on or spared? 🦋 ♀ I don't know if it's this eclipse or just alignments in general but this time has me all fucked up to be honest ⚡️♑︎🙂Some days are better than others, hopefully this will be the switch forward. ✌️ ➡️

7:11 am
almaandromeda
How are you?

7:17 am
almaandromeda
Do things get back to 'normal' after a crash like that or are they part of 'normal'?

3:36 pm
korbendallas_987
this unit is kinda crazy so i heard helicopters the next day. usually though, if nobody knows why it happened, there is a complete grounding of all aircraft

3:37 pm
korbendallas_987
i'm ok, i guess. keep waiting for things to get better but everything's just kinda on 'pause', it feels like

11:52 pm
almaandromeda
On pause.. I know what you mean. I keep feeling for the switch in the dark.

11:52 pm
korbendallas_987
🖤

11:53 pm
almaandromeda
Michael Lutins post today was about the Eclipse –
"Eclipse news: Even if it's crazy, ridiculous, absurd, impossible, out of the question and completely stupid... the heart knows what the head denies.

11:53 pm
almaandromeda
One of my 'guides'

11:53 pm
almaandromeda

11:54 pm
korbendallas_987
ALWAYS felt like i live half of a life; not to mention i'm halfway there

11:55 pm
almaandromeda
Your 'pause' reminds me of the 'pause' I took while giving birth..

August 23rd, 2017

12:05 am
almaandromeda
I didn't want to push after rocking my labor but still had to, the baby wanted out!
You are the pilot, in complete control, access to every button, but you are still flying
a beast. You can take a breath while landing but you can't take a break. The beast is
always beneath you, riding you, you riding it. The life force is in your hands, not in
front of you or behind you. ✌️ ☆ 🔥

1:35 am
korbendallas_987
fuck, i wish i was like you

1:35 am
korbendallas_987
i'm just not

1:35 am
almaandromeda
You're better than me silly.

1:36 am
korbendallas_987
some kind of chemical over produces itself in my brain (fight or flight?) and it's
plagued our family for generations

1:36 am
korbendallas_987
it's almost like nature's way of thinning the herd

216

1:37 am
korbendallas_987
though i would never hurt myself

1:49 am
almaandromeda

1:49 am
almaandromeda
I know.. do as I say not as I do lol

1:55 am
almaandromeda
Your mind is your own, is all, even past the chemicals and generations... you are more. YOU are alive and very precious to the PLANet, I can tell.

2:12 am
almaandromeda
I see your astro so I have courtside seats 😍 if you have any questions I am someone 🫰

2:39 am
almaandromeda
Did you see Nick's pdf about my stalker stepdad? I didn't want him to make it but Nick is so done with that freak.

3:08 am
korbendallas_987
"Your mind is your own, is all, even past the chemicals and generations... you are more. YOU are alive and very precious to the PLANet, I can tell."

3:08 am
korbendallas_987

3:08 am
korbendallas_987
strong words

3:08 am
korbendallas_987
but my eardrums are comprised of adamantium

3:15 am
almaandromeda
😂That's a silly place to put that! Good thing my words are comprised of vibranium
💎

4:20 am
korbendallas_987
i didn't see any pdf but he asked if he could use me as emergency contact and of
course i obliged

4:20 am
almaandromeda
Nick sent you an email yesterday, PDF attached. Brace yourself lol

4:45 am
almaandromeda
Thank you for that. There's such a thing as knowing too much about someone I
think but.. Nick had to do something.

7:25 am
almaandromeda
It's fun being your sister this lifetime. 👊It's solid and I'm glad we found you
Michael, for Nick and for me. ❤️I am so glad you have Nick's heart in your life. He
is a love warrior and hilarious and probably a good brother to have in your corner. I
can tell you are too 😊

11:42 am
korbendallas_987
wish i could do more. make things disappear, if i was in they area..

4:00 pm
almaandromeda
Thanks 😊

4:01 pm
almaandromeda
I don't need it be fixed tho, I just need help getting through it tbh

4:45 pm
almaandromeda
I am more than alone right now. It's hard to explain. I just need a friend. I have alot
of friends and my husband but it's hard to really 'get' me and this fkd up loneliness.
I'm not asking you to either, it's just really all I need. 👊

218

2:29 am
korbendallas_987
know the feeling ALL too well

2:29 am
korbendallas_987
i am alone amongst millions

2:29 am
korbendallas_987
always have been

2:29 am
korbendallas_987
GREAT feeling

2:29 am
korbendallas_987
long, long, miserable existence

3:47 am
almaandromeda

3:47 am
almaandromeda
Thanks ☺

4:48 am
almaandromeda
Not so bad knowing you lol

3:49 am
almaandromeda
I just want to be myself for awhile

3:55 am
almaandromeda
🎵Nobody knows.. 🎵

3:56 am
almaandromeda
But I can tell you do 👊

5:16 am
almaandromeda
🌾 judgement free zone 🌾

August 30th, 2017

3:16 am
korbendallas_987
do u send messages and then unsend them?

3:21 am
almaandromeda
Yes

3:21 am
almaandromeda
Stupid but I do haha

3:22 am
almaandromeda
I want to share stuff and then dont want to bother you

3:23 am
almaandromeda
I'm dumb sorry 😊

3:23 am
korbendallas_987

3:23 am
korbendallas_987

3:23 am
korbendallas_987

3:25 am
almaandromeda
So busted.

3:25 am
almaandromeda

3:32 am
almaandromeda
I did just want to share stuff but felt like I was bugging you, which I obviously am haha. I won't send or unsend and hope you are awesome 😊 🙏

4:12 am
almaandromeda
I do that all the time btw and put stuff up and take it down on my page as well as write stuff on paper and tear it up and write it again. Don't feel too special haha 😊 I'm insecure and awkward and that stupid unsend thing does not work apparently.

12:15 pm
korbendallas_987
busted bigtime, no reason to

3:55 pm
almaandromeda
K

8:13 pm
korbendallas_987
how t u obviously bugging me. we speak once a week.

8:14 pm
korbendallas_987
it unsends perfectly, but it doesn't touch my notifications

8:14 pm
korbendallas_987
that's where i catch ya!

8:15 pm
almaandromeda
Doh! 😊

8:15 pm
almaandromeda
Now I know lol

8:16 pm
almaandromeda
Keeping me honest haha thanks

August 31st, 2017

4:11 am
almaandromeda
I learned my lesson twice in 24hrs about unsending.. my best friend had an abortion today. Last night I sent her a message about deciding whether to be present or disassociated during the procedure. I unsent the message because I felt it might be too much to put on her from my mind right before she has to go in and deal herself in her own way.

4:14 am
almaandromeda
Well, she saw the message anyway and she told me today as I was with her after that she took that message very seriously and decided not to take pain meds or sleeping pills and she stayed present because of the message that I UNSENT. I think I get it now lol. Say what you mean and mean what you say the 1st time, because it might matter to somebody. Thanks for calling me on my shit btw, I like that □

5:54 am
korbendallas_987
👍

222

SEPTEMBER 2017_

5:00 pm
almaandromeda
What is 987?

5:00 pm
almaandromeda
I have Q's 😵

5:25 pm
korbendallas_987
i had email when man was still using ravens to communicate back and forth so of course i tried michael@juno.com . didnt work all the way up to michael987@juno.com and a legend was forged.

5:38 pm
almaandromeda
You tried 987 times? 😃 I don't believe you.. that is hilarious! I could have never guessed that in a million..

5:38 pm
almaandromeda
What is korbendallas?

September 2nd, 2017

3:21 am
almaandromeda
I do believe you btw it's just so funny to imagine! 😆 Being a #legend is all I have lived for as long as I can remember. That is definitely epic.

7:33 am
almaandromeda
Alone amongst millions.. nothing like being in a football stadium full of people 20 ft from my mama and have her never look at me once. 👁️👁️ Chilling and lonely no matter who is near ❄️ I'm not comparing just sharing.

2:52 pm
korbendallas_987

nah there was an option that basically allowed you to say fuck it, gimme what ya got and michael987 was the next available

4:04 pm
almaandromeda
Oh! And Korbendallas? What is that?

4:12 pm
almaandromeda
I think I'm cool because I have **almaandromeda**@gmail.com and Nick thinks he's cool because he has nickking@q.com so I know what you were going for there haha

4:15 pm
almaandromeda
*unsent and resent for spelling corrections lol I'm a word nerd and perfectionist and that's part of it for sure!

4:21 pm
almaandromeda
How come you stopped liking posts yo? Very busy or other stuff? 😊 Internet body language is SO hard to read.

7:43 pm
korbendallas_987
i honestly don't get on here all that much. social media nauseates me at times, but sadly it's the easiest way to keep in touch wit peeps

7:44 pm
korbendallas_987
Korben Dallas is Bruce Willis's character in 5th Element

7:45 pm
almaandromeda
That's what I thought... 😊 I love it. LEELOO!!

7:47 pm
almaandromeda
Social media sux it's tru □ But some people live far and I don't see them any other way.

7:47 pm
korbendallas_987
i deleted Farcebook years ago and never looked back

7:48 pm
korbendallas_987
you must not have an updated iphone firmware

7:48 pm
korbendallas_987
a lot of your emojis look like this

7:48 pm
korbendallas_987
?

7:49 pm
almaandromeda
I'm on Samsung haha 😁

7:50 pm
almaandromeda
They don't communicate well Idk why

7:51 pm
almaandromeda
I have an ipad too so sometimes mine look like yours.. when you use the black
version of the hand I just have to guess that's what it was lol

7:53 pm
almaandromeda
Wow deleted fakebook! Cool. I barely go on there, especially because my stupid
family/friends Seattle circle is or USED to be so close knit and THAT is very
nauseating.

7:54 pm
almaandromeda
Thanks for letting me pick your brain sometimes □ - that's a thumbs up lol

8:06 pm
almaandromeda
Or at least social media lol :-)

10:50 pm
korbendallas_987
ok cuz i thought all the boxed question marks were middle fingers *phew*

11:24 pm
almaandromeda
Only like 10 of them

11:26 pm
almaandromeda
Hahahahaha omg that was funny Michael 😂 all nice things I promise lol

September 3rd, 2017

12:02 am
almaandromeda
Today's Rumi lesson is for You apparently because he talks about the adamantium in your ears :-)

12:02 am
almaandromeda
Cry Out In Your Weakness
A dragon was pulling a bear into its terrible mouth.
A courageous man went and rescued the bear.
There are such helpers in the world, who rush to save
anyone who cries out. Like mercy itself,
they run toward the screaming.
And they can't be bought off.
If you were to ask one of those,
"Why did you come so quickly?" he or she would say,
"Because I heard your helplessness."
Where lowland is, that's where water goes.
All medicine wants is pain to cure.
And don't just ask for one mercy.
Let them flood in. Let the sky open under your feet.
Take the cotton out of your ears, the cotton
of consolations, so you can hear the sphere-music.
Push the hair out of your eyes.
Blow the phlegm from your nose,
and from your brain.
Let the wind breeze through.
Leave no residue in yourself from that bilious fever.
Take the cure for impotence,
that your manhood may shoot forth,
and a hundred new beings come of your coming.
Tear the binding from around the foot

of your soul, and let it race around the track
in front of the crowd.
Loosen the knot of greed
so tight on your neck.
Accept your new good luck.
Give your weakness to one who helps.
Crying out loud and weeping are great resources.
A nursing mother, all she does
is wait to hear her child.
Just a little beginning-whimper,
and she's there.
God created the child, that is , your wanting,
so that it might cry out, so that milk might come.
Cry out! Don't be stolid and silent with your pain.
Lament! And let the milk
of loving flow into you.
The hard rain and wind
are ways the cloud has
to take care of us.
Be patient.
Respond to every call
that excites your spirit.
Ignore those that make you fearful
and sad, that degrade you
back toward disease and death.

12:08 am
almaandromeda
It's for me too, probably even more tbh

12:20 am
almaandromeda
I flip thru my book everyday and find a rumination to help me understand myself
and the world. Sometimes they make me think of other people. My bday is next
Saturday 9/9, I will be 39 and officially the oldest person in the world lol. I will say
hi then! 🖐 <- that's a middle finger haha

September 4th, 2017

6:05 am
almaandromeda
MISSIO – Middle Fingers – BEST SONG

6:06 am
almaandromeda
This IS my life theme song however 😂

7:02 am
almaandromeda
🎵 I'll just keep on throwing middle fingers in the air 🎵 🖕 🖕

7:10 pm
korbendallas_987
haha

September 5th, 2017

9:38 pm
almaandromeda
Some say a comet will fall from the sky
Followed by meteor showers and tidal waves
Followed by fault lines that cannot sit still
Followed by millions of dumbfounded dipshits
And some say the end is near
Some say we'll see Armageddon soon
I certainly hope we will
I sure could use a vacation from this
Stupid shit, silly shit, stupid shit
-TooL

9:40 pm
almaandromeda
We're fucked, basically 🙃

September 6th, 2017

1:12 pm
korbendallas_987
..overwhelmed, as one would be--when put in my position.. such a heavy burden now to be the one, born to bear and bring to all the details of our ending.. to write it down for all the world to see--but I forgot my pennnnn..

1:13 pm
korbendallas_987
t👁👁l fav band since around 93

6:30 pm
almaandromeda
"Shroud-ing all the ground around me
Is this holy crow above me
Black as holes within a memory
And blue as our new second sun
I stick my hand into his shadow
To pull the pieces from the sand
Which I attempt to reassemble
To see just who I might have been
I do not recognize the vessel
But the eyes seem so familiar
Like phosphorescent desert buttons
Singing one familiar song
So good to see you
I've missed you so much"

6:31 pm
almaandromeda
🎵 but the eyes seem so familiar 🎵 👁 👁

6:34 pm
almaandromeda
Super intense music and not beautiful to me so I never was drawn to it as a girl and especially a girl like me.. but I seriously get it, and I get why you love them. I love honest lyrics and his are compelling.

7:49 pm
almaandromeda
A lot of it scares me truthfully... at least it used to. I don't even know what I am afraid of anymore. 🫣

September 7th, 2017

4:16 am
korbendallas_987
some of his songs have been scoured for decades and people STILL aren't sure of

the meaning. Which is message all along--their music is meant as a 'Tool' for the transcendence (for lack of a better term) of the mind

4:16 am
korbendallas_987
H is a great example

4:17 am
korbendallas_987
plus his voice is operatic and Adam Jones' tone on that fucking Les Paul he plays is not imitatable

4:17 am
korbendallas_987
nobody has done what they have done

4:17 am
korbendallas_987
it's like a cult, really*

4:18 am
korbendallas_987
you should lay down on your bed with an ipod, turn the lights off, complete darkness, and listen to the Ænima version of Third Eye

4:19 am
korbendallas_987
it's what started my progression

4:26 am
almaandromeda
I love how you love them. I will listen more. I have been told so many dark thoughts in my life from parents/brothers that I created a force field of positive that is fake sometimes but does the job. I have been sensitive to violence my whole life from being tortured by my brothers. It's hard to open up to his words but now.. I am not disgusted, not afraid. I kinda feel inspired and definitely compassionate for the male experience in a brand new way. Seeing thru your eyes is wow 👀

4:37 am
almaandromeda
I will do that. Thanks 😊 I'll let you know how it goes haha

232

5:47 am
almaandromeda
◉ Third Eye is the lyrics I just sent you, how funny of all the songs it was your first like that. I don't know wtf he's saying but at the same time I understand it more clearly than anything I've ever known. Is transcendence utter confusion lol? If it is I am already there.

6:49 am
almaandromeda
I'll let you know when I hear it like you said 🎶

9:58 am
korbendallas_987
god please listen to the song

9:58 am
korbendallas_987
at least read all the lyrics

10:00 am
korbendallas_987
there's a song called Prison Sex that you may or may not pick up on the metaphor he is dropping but he just does it so fucking well.. i mean, read in a certain way, he actually COULD be talking about prison sex...
He'a not though.

4:16 pm
almaandromeda
I am always right haha

4:16 pm
korbendallas_987
his lyrics are ethereal yet tongue-in-cheek, some jocular, and some are just plain terminal.

4:53 pm
almaandromeda
😭 I can't stand it.

4:53 pm
almaandromeda
The ecstasy.

4:54 pm
almaandromeda
It is so much.

4:54 pm
almaandromeda
Feels reaally good. I love the insane timed beats. I really can barely stand it.

4:56 pm
almaandromeda
I parked alone and put the seat back and blasted it in the car.. 13 minutes that I can't explain.

4:56 pm
almaandromeda
I love it and will listen again in the dark next time, now I can't wait haha

5:21 pm
almaandromeda
I feel like the Kali goddess tattoo on my back right now with her red tongue out panting, I feel wild listening to this.. who am I hahaha

8:44 pm
korbendallas_987
i'm really into poly-rhythmic music; it's almost as if my heart pauses until the next successful beat has been strummed or drummed

8:44 pm
korbendallas_987
so yea. Tool is definitely progressive, the time signatures are crazy, but I can see it driving someone crazy as well.

8:45 pm
korbendallas_987
i hope you at least like something about it

8:49 pm
almaandromeda
I am just glad I don't have (much) of an addictive personality lol or it could get easy to get lost in that. I really love it but I don't think I could have accepted it in before tbh. I don't feel as afraid lately because I am starting to understand interdimension-alism and past/present/future realms, quantum shifts and focus, and especially life purpose/mission/timing/desire. Tool is a 'tool' like you said and I have a belt and a loop for that.

234

8:51 pm
almaandromeda
I'm obsessed with it to be clear. It drove me crazy in the best way possible. ♫

9:14 pm
almaandromeda
I don't know if it's different for people who have actually gone through what he describes (on the 3d at least) in ♫ P.S. ♫ that you mentioned or if I am just a total loser but it's hard to immerse myself in it again... I know myself better possibly but I also hate myself in that moment and I have gotten so good at smiling and loving myself from the outside in. #whocares haha 😊 #zerofksyo xo

September 8th, 2017

1:07 am
almaandromeda
*I've NEVER actually been to prison btw, I don't know what you think of me haha.

1:07 am
almaandromeda
♫ You can laugh, it's kind of funny, the things you think, at times likes these ♫
-Tori Amos

September 9th, 2017

8:18 am
korbendallas_987
man it's weird; these last few months have been by far, the most eventful and weirdest things to have occurred yet

8:18 am
korbendallas_987
like, in my whole life. something is going on and i can't stop it and am not sure i want to.

8:19 am
almaandromeda
I know and I know 👀

8:19 am
almaandromeda
It's my birthday

8:19 am
korbendallas_987
oh shit

8:19 am
korbendallas_987
well happy birthday. as an astrologer do u feel weird today?

8:20 am
almaandromeda
I feel so many things. Crying all day.. but I'm fine lol

8:20 am
almaandromeda
Capsize by Frenship

8:20 am
almaandromeda
This is the only song I listen to right now.. music rules me.

8:21 am
almaandromeda
🩶

8:21 am
almaandromeda
I will say hi later tonight xo

8:24 am
korbendallas_987
no need to cry

8:24 am
korbendallas_987
so don't

8:24 am
korbendallas_987
🩶

8:26 am
almaandromeda
Ok.. xoxo miss ur face

8:26 am
almaandromeda
Delete xo

8:27 am
almaandromeda
I will find u tonight

9:06 am
korbendallas_987
haha ok

1:02 pm
almaandromeda
For my birthday I want the permission to speak freely Only you 👀can gift me that tonight.

1:03 pm
almaandromeda
I sent that before I meant to but it's tru.

1:03 pm
korbendallas_987
haha you can always

1:04 pm
almaandromeda
Thanks I am going to my dance but I will find you tonight around the midnights

6:21 pm
almaandromeda
The first time we 'spoke' was on your birthday and I already knew then because I had seen your face. Get ready.. I am scared that T.M.I. is not just a saying this case haha 🤭

6:27 pm
almaandromeda
I have never in my LIFE felt anything like this. I basically hate myself 24/7 because I feel so wrong having SUCH strong feelings for you.

6:30 pm
almaandromeda
But it's also amazing and awesome and the most wild feelings I have ever felt 🖤 I have memories of you, dreams of you.. I feel you all the time.

6:32 pm
almaandromeda
I would never wish this on my worst enemy. I keep feeling the pull of this invisible force.

6:37 pm
almaandromeda
Omg now you know a tiny part but still WAY too much already. Life is short so I'm glad you know how I feel. I've never met you, we've never spoken even on the phone, you are my husband's brother and we are both 'happily' married. I don't 'want' anything at all. I just love you very much and I can't say why.

6:45 pm
almaandromeda
I kissed the cables we sent you for your birthday.. I kissed your bracelet. I knew then. This is so different than anything that's ever happened to me before Michael.

6:54 pm
almaandromeda
If you are not too freaked out I want to hear anything you think, if anything lol xo Tonight I am watching something with bro soon but I would really love to 'chat' soon and I am sorry if this did freak you out at all 🖤

7:19 pm
almaandromeda
I delete everything every time just so you know xo A lot to risk and I REALLY care about your bro & you.

8:41 pm
korbendallas_987
i will reply to this tomorrow, no time currently

9:45 pm
almaandromeda
Oh my gosh I saw Lorie's hanya tattoo, wow... it is so beautiful. please please forget what I said I am SO embarrassed.. dumb. So dumb and I am sorry really.. I am just going through something but please forget it.

9:46 pm
almaandromeda
I wish I just unsent that stuff but I didnt and deleted it instead so just please do forgive and forget that I said all that stuff.

September 10th, 2017

9:48 am
almaandromeda
I am sorry.

4:45 pm
almaandromeda
I am cured lol seeing that tattoo.. I remember what a DEEP past/future life love story you are already in the middle of. I don't want anything, I don't want to know anything... I am sorry and the most embarrassed I have ever been in my life. Please forgive my momentary insanity.

5:36 pm
almaandromeda
TO BE HONEST
To be honest you are not
a mathematical order
designed by the star of Venus,
your face does not stop me,
stop everything, I am not
rolling constantly in the
dry field of your last words.
You do not have a finger
deep through the middle of me,
I am not squirming and moving
on the dream of your lap
I don't want that! I don't want
anything! You aren't the only one
to 'do that thing', and honestly,
this is nothing, I have no feelings,
I don't whisper your name or
cum to your face, I don't cry
hot tears in lonely disgrace.
I don't miss you, I don't want you.
You don't compel me like the
moon moves the oceans,

you don't have a spell on me,
I did not drink your potion.
I'm not made for you.
I don't think of you every morning.
I won't wait for you.
This is not a love story.

7:57 pm
korbendallas_987
it's fine, stop stressing. you've never met me and when you do, you'll probably feel
stupid for feeling the way you do because i'm no diff than anyone else really.

7:59 pm
korbendallas_987
i do hope you had a good birthday. relationships can get stale but that also brings
reinforcement. kinda like a statue. i don't think any different of you at all. everyone
has had crushes

September 11th, 2017

6:11 am
almaandromeda
Good points. 👍I already feel stupid. Please ✖everything I've said for the sake our
respective loves. I am going to take some time to 'dry' out from this wtf I am going
thru. Take care of you 👊

7:13 am
korbendallas_987
alllll good. it's flattering, to say the least

7:13 am
korbendallas_987
now tell me my future, as it doesn't look good

4:31 pm
almaandromeda
It is *sparkling* 😊 I will look into my crystal ball and tell you what I see soon.

6:00 pm
almaandromeda
The whole transition obsession jealousy rage hannya geisha thing REALLY freaks
me out tbh Michael. You are Taken with a capital T for tattoos including name

240

tattoos and matching hannya love stories on you both bout jealousy and rage.. as much as I want to play with fire (and this what that is) my skin is easily torched. 🔥I am way lighter about things, I could never tattoo your name on me or your love story on my skin. My love lives deeper than my skin, and the stories on me are my own.

6:00 pm
almaandromeda
I actually feel stuff, like real stuff for you, so I do just need time to get over it.

6:00 pm
almaandromeda
I hope you understand xo

6:15 pm
almaandromeda
As far as my crystal ball goes, your future is very bright, but you are feeling a heavy strain in your career that will move and shift soon.

6:16 pm
almaandromeda
You usually have the dreamiest planet up there leading the way through inspiration and imagination, allowing you to dream SO big that you can fly!

6:18 pm
almaandromeda
Right now the planet of limitations and burden is on top of that dreaminess, making you feel squeezed, noticed (in a hard way), scrutinized, and especially kind of taking the air out of your balloon so to speak.

6:21 pm
almaandromeda
What it is doing there is sifting through your dreams and aspirations and asking you to make some hard choices. It's almost like you are finally growing up, so, who or what do you want to be when you grow up? You and this limiting planet are teaming up to build a giant platform in the sky for you to safely land your 5 winged silver jet someday in the future.

6:23 pm
almaandromeda
The 'worst' is over in a way, because the planets retrograde and go over and over a certain point, driving you crazy! Now everything is just now moving forward for the last time in that area, so it really is always darkest before the alma.

6:27 pm

almaandromeda

Jupiter the big Santa Claus in the sky is in your house of other peoples money, conjunct your powerful planet Pluto always there in your own natal chart. You naturally have a strong influence on others (duh haha) and now with Santa there you are getting handed ALL the most expensive gifts and no you don't have to pass those back to your cousins, these gifts are ALL for you. Dig deep into the pockets of others, get those raises, those contract offers, play the lotto (and check your tickets haha)

6:32 pm

almaandromeda

The coolest thing happening in my opinion is your are having a nodal return. This means annoying past/future life people like me come into your life now 😊 You are on a SOUL level leveling up with what you came to do here and you will find more than usual right now strong connections with your past and future lives through people you meet. We are here to remind you of everything AMAZING you've done so far and all you have left to do.

6:34 pm

almaandromeda

You are called into this lifetime with a strong soul purpose and some of that is making itself known to through a sunset or a smile. The Universe is talking to you right now in coded language in every flower and bullet. Look for it. I♥u, take care of you please. Xxoo I hope to meet you someday!

7:12 pm

korbendallas_987

jesus christ. how and where the fuck do u see that (not that it's wrong). no question i am going thru something, career wise, and it MAY not be good. and for some reason i'm not that mad about it. something is happening in my life Alma, there is no other way to describe it. i can only hope that a shred of your vision is right, otherwise, things will be bad.

7:13 pm

korbendallas_987

thank u so much, i'm sure people usually pay you for something like that.

7:40 pm

almaandromeda

It's 'leap year' existentially for you Michael. It only comes around every 29 times but when it does you must 'leap.'

242

7:41 pm
almaandromeda
Sometimes we resist life so much that life smacks us hard. I have gone thru it around 28 with my abortion and I fought growing up so I got 'growed' up.

7:43 pm
almaandromeda
Have you heard of the farmer and his son story?

7:44 pm
almaandromeda
May be good, may be bad?

7:45 pm
almaandromeda
Goes like this..

7:49 pm
almaandromeda
There once was a young man who came from a very poor family in China. When he was out for the day his horse ran away. On his return, the villagers ran to his father to express their sadness for this financial loss. 'Isn't this terrible' they wailed! The aged father shook his head from side to side and calmly stated, 'May be good, may be bad.'

7:52 pm
almaandromeda
On the following day, the lad went out to hunt for his missing horse and to his great joy he found a herd of wild horses and was able to bring them back to the village. The elated crowd ran to his father and exclaimed, 'Isn't this wonderful news? What great fortune!' The sage elder again merely stated, 'May be good, may be bad.'

7:54 pm
almaandromeda
The next morning the boy went out into the corral to try and break in a new horse for himself. In the process his leg was trampled and made lame. When the towns-people saw his ruined leg, they ran to their father to convey their grief. The reply was the same, 'May be good, may be bad.'

7:55 pm
almaandromeda
A day or so later the Chinese army came to take away all the able-bodied young men away to war. *End Of Story*

8:03 pm
almaandromeda
Stay light and let the pieces shift into place without judgement or fear. Dream into reality around your career and make bold decisions. Everything in the sky is moving forward concerning that so YOU move forward. Fuck a fear. Fuck a worry. Who has time anymore? You are finally getting old so you can finally get to it with the urgency required.

8:04 pm
almaandromeda
I am here for questions like these and I am your friend indeed 😊 take care for now

10:51 pm
korbendallas_987
thank you so fucking much

10:52 pm
korbendallas_987
goddayum i hope u speak the truth, no offense

10:52 pm
korbendallas_987
did i tell you why i have a hanya on my arm?

11:13 pm
almaandromeda
A little in your first astro reading.. I want to hear it from the top if you want to share it. This hanya thing... man. I want to hear about it. Michael, you are worth it and so welcome.

11:44 pm
korbendallas_987
well there's a few version of the old japanese anecdote, but most follow a celibate monk who was having an affair with a geisha. after enough burden, he revealed to her that they could no longer see each other. and so the geisha turns into this monstrous demon that attacks the monk.

11:45 pm
korbendallas_987
what is on my arm, is actually a geisha--that's why her teeth are black. that was considered 'elegant' back then; black teeth.

11:45 pm
almaandromeda
And you share this story with Lorie obviously

11:46 pm
almaandromeda
It's pretty much what I thought it was I guess.

11:47 pm
korbendallas_987
it just kinda happened that lorie and i met in a forbidden way--officer and enlisted. so, she held my career in her hand had she flipped out at any moment or if i decided to break it off

11:47 pm
korbendallas_987
it was coincidental that i got the hanya tattoo though. i just thought it looked badass.

11:47 pm
almaandromeda
But not coincidental that she did haha

11:48 pm
almaandromeda
It's cool Michael! Deep shit seriously deep.

11:48 pm
korbendallas_987
it inspired her for the back piece obviously

11:49 pm
almaandromeda
It feels like seeing that tattoo that you guys had 12 kids together or something.. super DUG in under the skin and anything else is a distraction or a joke. Just being honest like I can be here I hope. Take care Michael xo

11:51 pm
korbendallas_987
we've been through a lot, as i am sure you and Nick have. everyone has their story

11:52 pm
korbendallas_987
by the way, the hanya i have is about 10 years old--older than our relationship

September 12th, 2017

9:35 am

almaandromeda

I am not judging you guys or your story AT ALL and I think all the work itself is beautiful & badass. You are so right we all have our own lives and our own stories and the personal freedoms to do what the fuck we feel like when we feel like it. And honestly, even though Nick and I don't share tattoos or even rings he is my #master on so many levels and that is not something I can shake this lifetime either, or would want to.

10:11 am

almaandromeda

C'est la vie 😁

1:59 pm

almaandromeda

Nick & I have been really lucky to be inseperable and in love for all these years w/out breakups or other stuff. Nick is good at so much in the Love dept. and is focused on relationship and is just basically worth my devotion on every level. Like I told you, before this I never even turned my head, much less opened my heart at all. I'm not really like that and funnily neither is Nick.

5:29 pm

almaandromeda

You have an awesome new brother and he does too. Imma step back and let you guys work on that like I should have long ago. You are BOTH worth the love you have to bring to each other. Also, you were already kept from him, it hurts my heart to keep anything from him again. ❤

6:34 pm

almaandromeda

Here if you need me for the hard stuff xo

September 13th, 2017

12:38 pm

almaandromeda

For some very unknown to me reason, I feel like I can tell you anything, and so I will

246

tell you something I learned. This is basically like my GREATEST lesson to date and it is surrounding jealousy.

12:42 pm
almaandromeda
I had a relationship with a guy in SF while I was going to college around age of 25-28 and it was very intense and VERY jealous. We were SO inside each other and I was not able check myself at all. My eyes were wild all the time, I would bristle at other women, he controlled me like that too and he and I got violent more than once. One time in the street he had me down and a man ran out with a gun to stop us.

12:44 pm
almaandromeda
Did I learn the LESSON yet? Nope. I did get the fuck out of there and moved back to Seattle. Still he came and visited me a few times because we could not let go and I got pregnant the very last time he came up. He was already with someone new in SF and lying about coming to see me.

12:47 pm
almaandromeda
So I walked around sick and delirious for 3 months not knowing what the hell to do. I couldn't stand the thought of killing my baby because I already had Soquel and knew how sweet the baby would be.. but I could not have it. I just couldn't. I had the abortion and it killed me too.

12:48 pm
almaandromeda
Just like that I was cured! Jealousy doesn't come up for me like before. It is NOT worth the sacrifice I made for it. I just don't invest my personal worth in anyone else like that anymore. Feels amazing like quitting cigarettes.

12:54 pm
almaandromeda
I am working on freedom this lifetime and I didn't even know how free I would feel letting go of my jealousy. It is also not a light thing to play with, as I learned and got so, so badly burned. I never sobbed harder or died longer than when I killed my baby. That's what my Kali tattoo reminds me and why I got her- Get over it, every-thing dies and changes. ❤

1:06 pm
almaandromeda
I guess I'm sharing that to explain why I got so freaked out by your tattoos... it's personal my shit about jealousy and obsession and I'm sensitive about it obviously

haha. You have me in a similar situation like Lorie had you in the officer/enlisted thing when it comes to privileged info but I really trust you, I don't know why, and I always have since we found you.

2:31 pm
korbendallas_987
interesting, i look at abortions as one less hungry mouth on this planet, everyone else looks at me as a monster for it. i had one with the girl who STOLE my virginity (now she's a lesbian 😊) but when we found out she was pregnant there wasn't even a conversation. get rid of it YESTERDAY. we were 19 and had no business having kids, plus i can't stand em.
anyways, we're all different.

3:07 pm
almaandromeda
You have never had the Life Force move inside you. It is awe inspiring like standing on the moon and looking at Earth. Gosh ♥ u fascinate me to no end. I wish you didn't haha. And you were the CUTEST kid on the planet.. never seen a cuter face. Kids are cute, starting with little You. Xo

3:41 pm
almaandromeda
Ready for this? I had a dream about you recently and you were only 18 months or so old and just toddling around. It was definitely You and your skin was so sweet and your face... oh my. I am crying now thinking about it again but that morning I woke up sobbing and somehow 'remembering' your sweetness as a baby. Weird huh? I am sure it was u.

3:42 pm
almaandromeda
Kids suck 4 sho but only starting around age 12-13 haha 😂

3:55 pm
almaandromeda
I get how kids aren't for everyone tho BUT I don't subscribe to the 'small Earth big population' theory. In a quantum Universe it is ever expanding and what we chose to notice, collapse on and create. Plenty of 'space' for everyone on a quantum level.

4:14 pm
almaandromeda
Michael Lutin is excusing my impulsive confessions😊
"Looking back over the solar eclipse, if it comes to it, maybe you should just fess up and tell the judge, Your Honor, to tell the whole truth I admit it. I meant every single word I said and I'm proud of all of my actions at the time in the hopes of

being emotionally honest and authentic. But if the Court please, if I may, I think I should change my plea and claim TEMPORARY INSANITY."

4:15 pm
almaandromeda
He just put this up haha. thank you

6:03 pm
almaandromeda
To get the 'lessons' here on planet Yurt you have to FEEL the things.. no shortcuts. I loved the baby so I learned what I couldn't for myself about jealousy, the medicine was real because the feelings were. Your Cancer&Aquarius connect/disconnect is asking you to learn about how humans feel things here at this time and how to successfully integrate our potentially 'cancerous' addictions to loyalty, possession, deep feelings & memory etc to the New Age of Aquarius where you are from.

8:48 pm
korbendallas_987
no question on the cancer / aquarius thing. no question.

September 14th, 2017

9:12 am
korbendallas_987
🤍

9:38 am
almaandromeda
🌑🎧finally got time in the dark with third eye, stink fist, 46&2, and more tonight just now. Amazing 😄I didn't know.

1:24 pm
korbendallas_987
ok, now, i think you are ready for my fav Tool song of all time (dare I say that)

1:25 pm
korbendallas_987
listen to The Patient. once that storm has ripped through you, follow it with Schism.

1:25 pm
korbendallas_987
i cant believe this stuff doesn't blow your socks off--it's right up your alley

4:46 pm
almaandromeda
I love homework 🤓

4:47 pm
almaandromeda
I'll let you know when it's done haha

4:48 pm
almaandromeda
I went missing for 20 min or so last night.. but where did I go? It was awesome.

5:55 pm
almaandromeda
I am curious about something Michael, if you want to share..

5:58 pm
almaandromeda
What do you know/understand about the 'sacred'?

6:01 pm
almaandromeda
I mean the 'pure', the 'holy', the kind of Wonder that leaves you in humility and grief and joy as you find yourself prostrate before it.. do you know/understand/believe in that?

September 15th, 2017

2:25 am
korbendallas_987
i know nothing of the sort

2:31 am
almaandromeda
Sinead O'Connor – IN THIS HEART 🖤

2:31 am
almaandromeda

2:31 am
almaandromeda
Listen to this in the dark if you dare. I thought you would say that haha.

2:43 am
almaandromeda
I am Sacred. I am precious. I am Life giver and Life taker. I am alive today through countless, endless miracles that will never stop because my life is Sacred and I have so many seen and unseen supporters. That is why I don't and can't play with dangerous symbolism and dark possessive emotions, jealous demons, that kind of stuff. I am on a 'mission' here. I value my life to the sacred level. The music is true. The Sacred is also in you. We have many lifetimes to work this all out xo

3:57 am
almaandromeda
What the happy day will be when we can make beloved our guest
We will make our eyes blessed by his adorned face
If there is a pain from the sadness of his separation
We will treat the pain by the sun of his face - RUMI

9:57 pm
korbendallas_987

9:58 pm
almaandromeda

10:13 pm
korbendallas_987
bit of a stretch but read the fucking lyrics to this song while listening or after (or before?)

10:13 pm
korbendallas_987
Deadsy - Seagulls

10:13 pm
korbendallas_987
it made me think of the human path

10:13 pm
korbendallas_987
"Let us pretend love for the day
This life we live alludes to things away
Suppose in youth the soul depraves
But now suppose the truth's beyond the grave
So all in all we laughed the same tears
Of how we met upon the River Thames pier
Two hearts of gold just for the while
Two Parts to stroll the endless mile
To tame the world again
Let us keep resisting them
Defame your world pretend
Let us keep existing
So I look up at night and ponder the sky
As I realize the sign where the two points collide
Lead me safe towards the light as the heavens decline
Space fold the time now let the planets align
Come dear its safe
We're past the plane
So now this sort of lift
The chance to change
Remember when we sailed along the Nile
Back then you'd turn your head, give me that smile
But through the systems flew the trine
And now at last the Nether's made you mine
Only all because you stayed here
Till pachysandra thins away
End summer winds
The leaves'll change
We'll grow potatoes
Pass the days
And if you feel precocious lead the way
Up and lift
Sink the same
I begin to sift
Sift through the shame
I realize the gift, feel the rays
As I start to drift
Drift away
Only all because we fade here
When all the notes we passed you saved
All juxtaposed and rearranged
In through the nighttime out the day

252

And now it's gone forever
Turn the page"
-SEAGULLS - DEADSY

September 16th, 2017

1:58 am
almaandromeda
It may be obvious as shit, but I do have to admit, y◉u are the coolest person I have
ever never met.

1:58 am
almaandromeda
YES IT PLEASES ME – ALMA KING
your confession, I remember, god what years
ago, bare carpet basement still you took me
nice and slow, so soft I wonder what touching
exists, what merging we had done before this,
old shaman sang the chorus outside our tent
in bora bora god what years ago, what years
from now our bodies electric send quasas
of strings forming one storm, transfer, sensate,
being to being, satisfied we whirl away dervishes
devouring the latest craze, transform and octate,
glide through ropes and gilded gates, smug
and spoiled off the slate, the mortals down there,
baby, they actually speak, you glean with shift
and shiver what I seen, pass to me that meaning,
we both allow for silence, the silence lasts
so musically, I kiss your roaring belly carrying
four seas on cratered plains, and yes it pleases me –
I burned up Alpha and Omega as you turned to say
my name, what years from now, what years ago,
and this is how I must will always loved you.

9:57 pm
korbendallas_987

2:05 am
korbendallas_987
haha def disagree on the coolest person you know

2:05 am
almaandromeda
Not that I know, just that I've never met haha

2:06 am
almaandromeda
When we finally meet you will go way down the list lol

5:27 am
almaandromeda
♫gonna wait it out♫ I loved that song.. I have a song called 'Midnight Patience' and I know the feeling of being very patient.

5:30 am
almaandromeda
Mine was about being abused in the night.. nothing like the patience required there 🖐

7:41 am
almaandromeda
Do you know about 'synchronicity'? Carl Jung coined the term. Some wild ones have happened this weekend, too much to recount here, but at dance yesterday morning they played In This Heart by Sinead O Conner. I have been going to dance 2x a week for 6 yrs and have never heard them play that song. I was struck.

September 19th, 2017

10:32 pm
almaandromeda
OMG I just can't.. seriously. This is getting weird! I just found this book called "Seagulls" by Ann Cleese -

10:33 pm
almaandromeda
I found this book just sitting in a free magazine section on our Sat morning walk. I was looking for my weekly astrology, which I read after I picked up the book, and it said -

10:33 pm
almaandromeda
"In the coming weeks, you might want to read the last few pages of a book before you decide to actually dive in and devour the whole thing. I also suggest you take

254

what I just said as a useful metaphor to apply in other areas. In general, it might be wise to surmise the probable outcome of games, adventures and experiments before you get totally involved. Try this fun exercise: imagine you are a psychic prophet as you evaluate the long-range prospects of any influences that are vying to play a role in your future."

10:39 pm
almaandromeda
You sent me that Deadsy song..

September 20th, 2017

2:43 am
korbendallas_987
eery

2:43 am
korbendallas_987
i knew about synchronicity because it's one of my favorite songs by The Police

3:31 am
almaandromeda
How are you doing this week? Everything magically awesome finally? I called in some favors haha

3:56 am
almaandromeda
You are on my mind.

3:57 am
korbendallas_987

3:58 am
almaandromeda
Also, this is a synchronicity I have wanted to share with you since I found out.. in Kansas I found out my mom was born in your same hospital as I told you. I also found out my Grandma who partially raised me died 30 yrs to the DAY before your dad died. 5/4/87 she died and your dad died 5/4/17. So weird!

9:57 pm
korbendallas_987
I guess it makes sense. I don't doubt it.

4:01 am
almaandromeda
That song rocks btw 🎵 🔑 Sting is a genius.

4:31 am
almaandromeda
Synchronicity is futile for 'humans' because we don't get shit. But it's funny like bubbles blowing in the wind.

5:18 am
korbendallas_987
i think there are some congruencies with the number '23' on this subject, as well

5:19 am
korbendallas_987
Viginti Tres

5:20 am
korbendallas_987
23x2=...

5:30 am
almaandromeda
'The horror begins in autumn' haha great 😄 'vigniti tres' 🎵 46&2.. rabbit hole much my friend? I know I need to read the Illuminatus! trilogy now, we were JUST talking about Robert Anton Wilson and # 23 today.. f'ng synchronicities lol. Down I go..

5:33 am
almaandromeda
"H." TOOL!
I love this song now
I wish I had found them before tbh

5:55 am
korbendallas_987
I feel like I understand stuff better than I can say it.

7:56 pm
almaandromeda
The best pool sharks are Cancers but *especially* Mercury in Cancer - which you have. Communication from the side 🦀 In case that helps you take over the world haha

September 21st, 2017

5:53 am
korbendallas_987
omg u just opened a whole new world to yourself

5:53 am
korbendallas_987
i can't believe you haven't 'met' TooL

5:54 am
almaandromeda
I am glad and scurred haha

5:54 am
korbendallas_987
listen to 'Intension'

5:54 am
almaandromeda
Ok

5:54 am
korbendallas_987
reflection is mindblowing

5:54 am
korbendallas_987
danny carey is one of the best drummers on the planet

5:54 am
almaandromeda
I am obsessed with the beats

5:54 am
korbendallas_987
he used a lot of mandala and worldly percussives

5:55 am
almaandromeda
THAT I did not know existed tbh

5:55 am
korbendallas_987
well you're talking to an O.G. tool fan ('92)

5:55 am
korbendallas_987
before they were cool

5:55 am
almaandromeda
I know 🤓 😎

5:56 am
almaandromeda
I didn't get some stuff before I might have needed to in order to accept it.. that Dogma thing

5:56 am
korbendallas_987
adam jones, their guitar player is what got me into Les Paul's.. that fat ass tone!! hhhgnnnnggghhh

5:57 am
korbendallas_987
understandable

5:57 am
almaandromeda
Is that how you play? Or work on?

5:58 am
korbendallas_987
i told you before, the reason they've been anonymous for so many years is they want their music to act as a Tool for the progresssion of the mind

5:58 am
korbendallas_987
yea i play his stuff all the time

5:58 am
korbendallas_987
he plays like easy background music but it's so cool

5:58 am
korbendallas_987
makes a lot of squealies and such

5:59 am
almaandromeda
I love the idea in reflection that we are all capable of anything. It is the same in astrology.. everything is in you and certain people or days or events trigger that part of you up.

5:59 am
korbendallas_987
i should have known you would love 'Reflection'

6:00 am
korbendallas_987
Intension is your next assignment

6:00 am
almaandromeda
There is a 'boldness' in the music that is visceral.. it moves all parts. I really love that. I am on it haha.

6:00 am
almaandromeda
Did you do yours? Lol

6:00 am
korbendallas_987
H. is another good one

6:00 am
almaandromeda
The Universe is on you.

6:00 am
korbendallas_987
no i never do homework

6:01 am
korbendallas_987
i am atlas at the moment and my back is cracking

6:01 am
almaandromeda
No excuses.

6:01 am
korbendallas_987
true

6:01 am
almaandromeda
I am the homewerk 👑

6:02 am
korbendallas_987
haha

6:02 am
almaandromeda
So I'll get back to you haha

6:02 am
korbendallas_987
did u hear Schism?

6:02 am
korbendallas_987
that's a really good one for you, both lyrically and musically

6:02 am
korbendallas_987
his voice is fucking operatic

6:03 am
almaandromeda
Not 'effectively' like I need to.. listening only. I will now. I have time.

6:03 am
almaandromeda
🎧⚫

6:03 am
korbendallas_987
ha

6:03 am
korbendallas_987
do it

6:04 am
almaandromeda
Now you! I double dare you. 3 minutes. Ttyl.

7:37 am
almaandromeda
I listened 🎧 to Intension first, then H., then Schism, then Intension again haha

7:37 am
almaandromeda
Swoon.. I could sleep to that.

7:39 am
almaandromeda
All the tears.. 🙈 H. says things I can't say right now. At least it exists to say it for me.

7:43 am
almaandromeda
The song I sent you is hard to hear but I only wish for you to know what I mean about the Sacred. When you are ready 🤍I hope you will acquiesce for me lol

7:46 am
almaandromeda
Listening to these songs reminded me of another song that makes me laugh/cry and think of 'the human path'.. you won't listen to it lol but here are the lyrics & the music too just in queso.

7:46 am
almaandromeda
Samson – by Regina Spektor
You are my sweetest downfall

I loved you first, I loved you first
Beneath the sheets of paper lies my truth
I have to go, I have to go
Your hair was long when we first met
Samson went back to bed
Not much hair left on his head
He ate a slice of Wonder Bread
And went right back to bed
And the history books forgot about us
And the Bible didn't mention us
And the Bible didn't mention us, not even once

7:48 am
almaandromeda
We're sorry about all that hair cutting stuff haha

8:46 am
almaandromeda
I don't claim to 'get' To👁ol yet at all but I like the way it speaks to me. I have my 👁
and can see that you are a Teach in my life and I am still very much learning.

10:28 am
korbendallas_987
oh to the contrary; you get To👁oL more than you know. Prying Open My Third
Eye? I mean could it get anymore obvious? What do you think H. is about? I'm
curious.

11:21 am
korbendallas_987
the end of this one just annihilates me— between supposed brothers, between
supposed lovers -SCHISM

4:14 pm
almaandromeda
I know.... uuugghh. Hits hard. I already pondered it and stay there in the IDK how
tf how it all fits. But it all does, or did. There is a Macro/Micro in that song. YOU
are so Macro I don't think you are real lol

4:16 pm
almaandromeda
I will look for words today that make sense for why H. touches me to tears and I will
tell you when I have them. 👁

4:53 pm

korbendallas_987
Good because it should bring you to tears. If you give up, I'll tell ya. I have no problem explaining TooL, it can be exhausting.

5:09 pm
almaandromeda
Thanks Teach 😎

5:14 pm
almaandromeda
I will figure it out

5:19 pm
almaandromeda
For me.. and then I will want to hear what it really means haha

6:11 pm
almaandromeda
I can't take all this 'growing' lol, I feel like Alice when she was first 10 ft tall.

September 22nd, 2017

6:42 pm
almaandromeda
I guess.. I feel like in learning and exploring this p👁werful knowledge I will want to say and ask and even maybe do things that are new and different for me. You have never 'met' me this life, you don't know me how I am already. I am 'Light,' very 'precious', and I have ALWAYS guarded my 'intact' light self. I want you to feel 👁 where I am coming from so I can change forms a thousand times in front of you and you can still know it's me haha.

6:19 pm
almaandromeda
Sometimes I feel overwhelmed from what I find in me. A lot of the tears are from me changing in real time, listening and dying inside.

September 23rd, 2017

12:27 am
almaandromeda
This is not homework it's just AWESOME lol. Sooo worth your 10 minutes when your back has rested Atlas.

1:38 am
korbendallas_987
Lateralis, eh? Fun fact: The rhythm is based on the Fibonacci Sequence.. That explains that specific song's polyrhythm. 😶👁️😶

1:38 am
korbendallas_987
I think I made a Tool fan.

1:54 am
almaandromeda
I love spirals and fractals.. born to with Alma and Andromeda as my 1st 2 names. Yes you did, meanie. I'm not worthy. I love how long the songs are, like in reflection, and the progression of sounds. I am reading Deadsy lyrics in the bleachers now haha.

1:56 am
almaandromeda
Watch my astro reports when you have time, silly. Guides are good lol. I bet even Atlas didn't do it all alone.

1:56 am
korbendallas_987
Deadsy???? FLOWING GLOWER???!!!!

1:56 am
korbendallas_987
ohhhhh ye i sent you seagulls—i forgot

1:57 am
almaandromeda
You forgot haha

2:02 am
almaandromeda
I got the seagull book the next day.

2:04 am
almaandromeda
Modern Tom Sawyer.

2:08 am
korbendallas_987
yea not crazy about that cover but Flowing Glower makes my blood itch it's so good

2:13 am
korbendallas_987
fun fact on that lead singer, he is the product of Cher and Gregg Allman

2:32 am
almaandromeda
You just reminded me of him, or him of you haha

2:37 am
almaandromeda
Omg I just listened to Flowing Glower loud driving home and it is SOoo wild.. does it slow and get fast or just appear to? Do you listen to music flying? <- real question, I am curious. It's so connected to time and time perception.

5:59 am
almaandromeda
As a kid and through high school I would get 'hit' sometimes out of the blue with a weird feeling of everything moving fast and slow and big and small all at the same time. I remember taking a science test once in HS and just getting slammed with that out-of-body feeling.. like Flowing Glower kind of makes me feel.

6:28 am
korbendallas_987
Noooooo, never listen while flying. Too much going on. 6 radios, the idiot in the other seat trying to kill me, entering and exiting commercial airspace....

6:29 am
korbendallas_987
Flowing Glower blew my face off like a 12-gauge

6:38 am
almaandromeda
Soundracks by Lang Leav
"He once told me about his love for lyrics. How the words spoke to him like poetry. I would often wonder about his playlist and the ghosts who lived there. The faces he

saw and the voices he heard. The soundtrack to a thousand tragic endings, real or imagined.

The first time I saw him, I noticed how haunted his eyes were. And I was drawn to him, in the way a melody draws a crowd to the dance floor. Pulled by invisible strings.

Now I wonder if I am one of those ghosts – if I am somewhere, drifting between those notes. I hope I am. I hope whenever my song plays, I am there, whispering in his ear."

6:41 am
korbendallas_987
where do you find this stuff?

6:41 am
korbendallas_987

6:42 am
almaandromeda
I don't know.. she does though, man. Her and Rumi and Maynard get it it lol

7:01 am
almaandromeda

7:44 am
almaandromeda
ANYTIME you want to tell me about flying or that world I love to hear about it.

8:34 am
korbendallas_987
meh i think you're making a bit much of it. all i can speak of is military flying, though i have moved acft back and forth across the states. boring. i'm not. nearly as hungry as i once was, i have to turn a corner soon

4:27 pm
almaandromeda
You don't see what I see. Then I want to hear about the corner. About you. ◉ Where is the turn and how fast?

10:25 pm
almaandromeda
Apparently today Sept 23rd, 2017 is the 'end of the world' lol for your sworn

enemies ✝. It has to do with this revelation and Jupiter's exit and all of the other planets in Virgo.. weird how astrology always mixes with Christianity.

September 24th, 2017

6:28 am
korbendallas_987
christianity = 🌐

6:28 am
korbendallas_987
i do want my enemies to die in a car fire though

7:26 am
almaandromeda
Your 'type' of military killing machine thing was my last 'enemy' and you toppled that. Basically because of you for some reason I really don't hate anybody anymore. It's amazing 🖤 thank you

8:50 am
almaandromeda
*except myself.. still reserve the right to hate myself lol

8:52 am
korbendallas_987
everyone keeps saying love yourself, love yourself WHAT THE PHUK DOES THAT MEAN

8:53 am
korbendallas_987
another headphone song for you off of Ænima, is Eulogy.. hhhhhnnnnn-mgggghhhhhhh

8:56 am
almaandromeda
🌑🎧

8:57 am
almaandromeda
I'm on it 🤓

9:02 am
almaandromeda
👁👁 yourself like someone who loves you does. Borrow the eyes of the Beloved. 🖤 it's a start in..

9:09 am
korbendallas_987
it's creepy feeling

9:10 am
korbendallas_987
you're SUPPOSED TO feel like a creep

9:50 am
almaandromeda
Then I'm doing it right 👌😂

11:11 pm
almaandromeda
Eulogy 🙈yeah, no way, yeah, to recall what it was that you had said to me, like I care at all.

September 25th, 2017

12:09 am
almaandromeda
*I take back what I said before, I actually still hate everybody haha.

12:17 am
almaandromeda
TooL - JIMMY

12:30 am
almaandromeda
I don't hate that song though lol

2:47 am
almaandromeda
Also, it reminded me of your pops honestly, cant't lie though it's hard to mention him to you. I have never been with anyone like that at the end of their life, so close where any moment is just 'the last'.. it was very quiet and intimate and pathetic and sad and very sweet too. Hard.

268

3:28 am
almaandromeda
Mostly it just reminded me of my real dad Jim and how I am very far away from 'fix-ing' that before he goes. He is really 'the worst' and so pathetic but who isn't? I hate school haha 😎

3:40 am
korbendallas_987
Jimmy is obviously short for Nick which is what he goes by—Maynard Nick Keenan

3:41 am
korbendallas_987
at age of 11 his was mom was paralyzed and she thanked god for it (bible beater). that's what he means by what was it like to see, the face of your own stability, suddenly look away...

3:47 am
korbendallas_987
that scream at the end of Jimmy is incred

3:48 am
korbendallas_987
which of course leads right into Pushit. every song is a banger. you need to listen to Right In Two

3:50 am
almaandromeda
I said I hate school! 😎 🎧 🎸

3:51 am
almaandromeda
Just kidding haha

3:51 am
almaandromeda
This shit is tearing me open though and who I am is in question lol

3:52 am
almaandromeda
Not sure why music does this to me but I get 'touched' by some things 😭

3:57 am
almaandromeda
'I don't want it, I just need it, to breathe, to feel, to know I'm alive' 🎵 I really love it haha

4:24 am
almaandromeda
Someday I'll teach you something... I only know 2 things but I know them really well. 🤚 When the pupil is ready the Teacher appears.

9:55 am
korbendallas_987
yea the point of 'Stinkfist' is pretty obvious—more and more to fill that 'void'

9:56 am
korbendallas_987
UUUGGGGGGHHHH I am that void

5:51 pm
almaandromeda
ONE of the 'pains' of this music for me is that I am the Great Denier of anything for myself. Cinderella doesn't want anything for herself, she is to sweet and kind for that. She saves her scraps for the mice. And listening and feeling🎵 .. I want everything. I want it all. I want it for me. That is why I hate school right now. I have the opposite of a void. I have an 'infiniteness'. And I never care about the stupid 3D 'stuff' normal people do.. I hate it all.

6:08 pm
almaandromeda
You don't understand. And I can't explain.

6:35 pm
almaandromeda
At least we won't have nuclear war this week according to one of my fave astrologers.. Michael Lutin knows I guess.

September 26th, 2017

3:35 am
almaandromeda
This is what Rumi says about desiring 'things' seen and unseen..

270

3:35 am
almaandromeda
If you want what visible reality
Can give, you're an employee.
If you want the unseen world,
You're not living your truth.
Both wishes are foolish,
But you'll be forgiven for forgetting
That what you really want is
Love's confusing joy.
-RUMI

9:42 am
korbendallas_987
Michael Rutin has seen at least one episode of the news every year or so, so, yes, he is correct. No war, all hot air.

5:49 pm
almaandromeda
There is always war sadly, and it is always hot air 🖤

September 27th, 2017

4:13 am
almaandromeda
Like Sinead O'Connor says best, my 🖤, I do not want what I have not got.

9:34 am
korbendallas_987
goddam i love sinead o'connor

9:36 am
almaandromeda
Omg you do?!? 😳

9:37 am
korbendallas_987
of course. that one song is timeless and she gives ZERO fux

9:37 am
almaandromeda
All is right with the world.

9:37 am
almaandromeda
She is my ULTIMATE song heroine

9:38 am
korbendallas_987
that is heresy but i will allow your mistake

9:38 am
almaandromeda
She played nonstop through 8 hrs of labor

9:38 am
korbendallas_987
Tori Amos is your ultimate heroine, and that is that.

9:38 am
almaandromeda
I am allowed all of my mistakes haha

9:38 am
almaandromeda
Ok, but Sinead is the rawness in me

9:39 am
korbendallas_987
sinead is ruthless

9:39 am
korbendallas_987
I saw her do that burning of the pope on SNL

9:39 am
almaandromeda
But did you see her stop everyone in the stadium when she was booed down at a Bob Dylan concert?

9:40 am
almaandromeda
The hardest thing EVER

9:40 am
almaandromeda
I will send it

9:40 am
korbendallas_987
yep seen both

9:40 am
almaandromeda
I saw it live on pay per view

9:40 am
almaandromeda
Haha

9:40 am
almaandromeda
Your awesome then.

9:40 am
almaandromeda

9:40 am
korbendallas_987
u familiar with a song called Father Lucifer by Lori Amos?

9:41 am
almaandromeda
Not yet.. I listened to her HS up to 1998 around.

9:41 am
almaandromeda
I will look it up

9:41 am
korbendallas_987
please listen to that at your EARLIEST convenience

9:41 am
korbendallas_987
it blew my dick off

9:42 am
almaandromeda
Yes sir. 🤓 Can't wait.

9:42 am
almaandromeda
Wait... so you have no dick?!

9:42 am
almaandromeda
We're done here hahahahaa

9:42 am
korbendallas_987
let me know when you hear it

9:42 am
korbendallas_987
i'm serious

9:42 am
almaandromeda
Stay tuned for your Astro report.. uploading them now.

9:42 am
almaandromeda
I will, of course.

9:42 am
korbendallas_987
ok

9:41 pm
almaandromeda
Tonight Papa Luz 🎧 👁 & I'll tell u

September 28th, 2017

4:19 am
almaandromeda
Uuuuuugggaaaaaaahh☠️

4:19 am
almaandromeda
ZZZ

4:20 am
almaandromeda
I can't believe that song is 3:42, insane

4:20 am
almaandromeda
It feels like 3 snakes in 3 directions when she is singing over herself at the end.

4:23 am
almaandromeda
I graduated in 1996 and then disappeared hitchhiking
stripping etc for a couple years so missed music and culture for a few years around
then. Need to catch up haha I love this so much

4:24 am
almaandromeda
TELL me your interest/fascination with Papa Luz ˌ I want to know more about
this.

5:51 am
almaandromeda
Alex Grey art Michael – it's killing me. It's us.. in the the the 5D

7:35 am
korbendallas_987
ughh my gaaaadthe when she is having the hallucinations at the end—orgasmic

:35 am
korbendallas_987
supposedly she went to south america and did some kind of hallucinogen and had a
conversation with satan during the trip. that's what she remembered of it

7:36 am
korbendallas_987
seems you're an Alex Grey fan. He does almost all of Tool's artwork.

7:44 am
almaandromeda
I like the art a lot.. art says SO much in just a glance. I was always jealous of that as
a poet so I started teaching myself drawing.

7:46 am
almaandromeda
True love sets you on fire

7:46 am
almaandromeda
Do you disagree with this?

7:54 am
almaandromeda
I love how it feels btw 👁 It's like nothing else. 🎵 I am so wildly inspired as you can tell haha. I want to hear about your interest 🔦 🤓 when you will tell me.

8:01 am
korbendallas_987
too many black and whites to say YES or NO to the whole thing. the world is variables, if nothing else.

8:01 am
korbendallas_987
my interest?

8:02 am
almaandromeda
In Lucifer etc

8:03 am
almaandromeda
You could stay in that forever.. I think it is very true, alchemically

8:03 am
almaandromeda
You have the power to create and destroy

8:03 am
korbendallas_987
jesus christ your reading couldn't have been any closer to the truth

8:03 am
korbendallas_987
how terrifying

8:03 am
almaandromeda
How?

8:04 am
almaandromeda
Today's?

8:04 am
korbendallas_987
my career is changing

8:04 am
korbendallas_987
it is turbulent

8:04 am
korbendallas_987
yes

8:04 am
korbendallas_987
i just listened to it

8:04 am
almaandromeda
Cool.. how are you managing? How is it changing?

8:05 am
korbendallas_987
it's difficult

8:05 am
korbendallas_987
she is hard as a rock tho

8:05 am
almaandromeda
You mean your wife?

8:05 am
korbendallas_987
you'll know more soon

8:05 am
almaandromeda
I want to obvs haha

8:07 am
almaandromeda

9:08 pm
almaandromeda
Like Bjork says, you are Venus as a boy

10:11 pm
korbendallas_987
she's neat

10:15 pm
almaandromeda
DANCER IN THE DARK??

10:16 pm
almaandromeda
The most amazing, saddest, musical, rhythmic movie you will ONLY watch once

11:32 pm
almaandromeda
Recipe: 1 part Sinead, 1 part Tori, 1 part Bjork- mix well. Add some Joni, PJ Harvey, Pink Floyd and Fiona Apple and let sit overnight. Don't touch, put a lid on and let it stew in it's loneliness and child abuse and mother rejection and escapist issues. Leave so long you almost forgot it was something and then take it out to rest. It's actually quite good lol

September 29th, 2017

6:57 am
korbendallas_987
i remember it

6:57 am
almaandromeda
You saw the movie?

278

6:57 am
korbendallas_987
of coudse

6:57 am
korbendallas_987
course

6:57 am
almaandromeda
Wow

7:21 pm
almaandromeda
Enigma - a puzzling or inexplicable occurrence or situation.
a person of puzzling or contradictory character.
a saying, question, picture, etc., containing a hidden meaning; riddle.

8:55 pm
korbendallas_987
hardly

9:28 pm
almaandromeda
Completely.

September 30th, 2017

1:05 am
korbendallas_987
this, for me, was rapture. Maynard with Tori singing "Muhammed, my friend."

1:36 am
almaandromeda
This is AMAZING these two artists? wow 😍 I will watch it after our show 2nite..
loading up gear now.

1:44 am
korbendallas_987
ye it'll blow your fuckin mind

OCTOBER 2017_

October 1st, 2017

2:22 am

almaandromeda

3 months since I 'invaded' your inbox.. I'm worse than the US Army lol

2:38 am

almaandromeda

That was the *ish 🌚 I loved her hissing 👹 and their sweetness together.

2:54 am

almaandromeda

🎧 🎵 we both know 🌐 it was a girl, back in Bethlehem 🎵

3:18 am

almaandromeda

I think I saw what you look like at work? Your friend is an instructor pilot too.. your helmets are crazy, the one eye magnifying glass thing, you look like a gotdang cyorg! No offense lol

5:29 am

almaandromeda

I got tix to see her in November.

5:35 am

korbendallas_987

yea

5:35 am

korbendallas_987

i don't take dumbbass selfies tho

5:36 am

korbendallas_987

the whole apache/IG thing has gottn completely out of control so i stay away from it. someone asks me what i do, army. i make them pry it out of me.

5:42 am

almaandromeda

It's interesting obviously... you FLY 🦋 Can't believe we found you hiding under there.

5:52 am
almaandromeda
You make people pry everything out of you haha.. I have learned not to ask too many questions lol

7:28 am
almaandromeda
To be real: albums like Tori's 'Little Earthquakes' and Joni's 'Blue' and Sinead's 'I Do No Want What I Have Not Got' were all I listened to over and over. I started writing poetry at 15 and wrote a poem called To The Women Above My Bed about those songwriters and how I couldn't sing yet OR write lyrics but I would someday and offered all of my teen material to that future.

7:31 am
almaandromeda
Now I am Her finally, that woman above my own bed, and I have crafted a hundred songs and have trained myself and got a degree to sing for the past 18 years. You and I share all this music, but you don't like mine at all or have any curiosity for my concerts. It's hard because I used to feel the tiniest bit cool before we found you.

9:04 am
korbendallas_987
don't take it personally; he'll, if it worked that way, i would truly be alone. Look up the lyrics to 'Messe Noire' or 'O Father O Satan O Sun'

9:04 am
korbendallas_987
youlll judge before you even realize

9:05 am
korbendallas_987
sorry those songs are by Behemoth

10:48 am
almaandromeda
We are so different. I do take it personally. I take Life personally. I feel connected in a way I could offer you.. like you can teach me to more literally not give a fuck. I 'get' it and will NEVER judge you Michael-ael, you get all the passes.

10:51 am
almaandromeda
I have astral traveled. I have been outside the realms. I am not stuck here. The Satan stuff just seems sad because it seems so 3D and one realm centric. What about your

whole 'self' and all the other yous that I remember? It is a choice to believe what you 'will', does this bring you joy or just pleasure?

10:59 am
almaandromeda
We just watched Ghost In The Shell and YOU deep dived the Geisha lol We told you not to.

11:04 am
korbendallas_987
Behemoth scratches an itch, and gives me unholy motivation

5:01 pm
almaandromeda
I get nothing.

9:10 pm
korbendallas_987
?

10:28 pm
almaandromeda
I am almost NEVER bored, ever.. but 2 things actually bore me to tears- Satanism and unrequited interest/desire. I'm too full of self love for either. You know I think you are awesome. Keep holding down your side and I'll pull mine and the world may just keep spinning yo. 🌍🤙

11:30 pm
almaandromeda
The Churning Of The Milky Ocean 🥄

October 2nd, 2017

2:25 am
korbendallas_987
satanism strikes me the opposite—it's the worship of one's own self (and not a zombie). like christianity, though, there are sects and branches of it

3:16 am
almaandromeda
Satanism is 'adorable' for people who don't know how to worship themselves without a manual. 🤘🤘

6:43 pm
almaandromeda
I am not sure if you take 'in' what I share of my world but I want to share one last thing:

6:48 pm
almaandromeda
Through infinite knowledge, my connection to worlds unseen and my many, many guides I am BLESSED to be a Light Agent. Through my connection to all of Creation I am the deepest Night and the Light born from darkness. 'Satanism' is a small existential 'burp' of lonliness, narcissism and confusion that exists SOLEY on this realm. Instead of worshipping the zombie Jesus, you worship the zombie of Yourself. I am Deeply ALIVE, creating, existing PAST all of that boring shit.

6:48 pm
almaandromeda
I wish you knew how beautiful you are. Thanks for sharing your world with me so kindly and I look forward to putting a 'face to a name' someday Michael. As Sinead says I do not want what I have not got. And I have never got you and will never get you.

9:06 pm
korbendallas_987
yes but it can be so powerful. i'm obsessed with it and how it flies in the face of cafeteria-christianity

9:15 pm
almaandromeda
An ant walking back and forth dutifully along a path between Christ's temple and Satan's throne is suddenly astonished as a giant hand picks him up and takes him into a pocket, in a car, on a boat, to an island, to the sweetest fruit it could have known. Be astonished.

October 3rd, 2017

3:13 am
almaandromeda
The type of 'magic' that you are fascinated with is so powerful, as you say, that it is not for me. My frequency is too 'precious' to be thrown to demonic energy without vigilant protection and cherishing. Real talk yo, since you like to really play with fire. 🔥☂️🐔💈

286

` `

.4:08 am

almaandromeda

🎵 now you know, places where I live.. 🎵 flowing glower.. I am still glad to have gotten to know that a little bit - a privilege for sure. 🙏 Love 🖤 is the Greatest Power, greater than religion, than war, than money. Love heals, love changes, love wins. And you know 👁 🖤 U

5:20 am

korbendallas_987

haha i'm no satanist but if heaven is filled what i've seen is purportedly going there, hell would be juuuuuuust fine for me. 😎 💨 🔥

6:05 am

almaandromeda

As Tracy Chapman says, Heaven is Here On Earth.

6:31 am

almaandromeda

Free will, babaayyy

6:50 am

almaandromeda

I am too sweet 🍎 for hell, I get kicked out at the front gate every time. I'll wait for you outside. 👹

October 5th, 2017

4:07 am

almaandromeda

Latest astro report up for you!

4:07 am

almaandromeda

The career thing culminates and resolves itself somehow with this week's full moon fyi.. you may already see the path but if you don't yet look carefully and any leads or offers you get around now are potent, action oriented ones that have 'legs'.

4:15 am

korbendallas_987

mega-deep—explain further when able

4:27 am
almaandromeda
I will later 2nite.. lots of layers for sure

5:54 am
almaandromeda
Do you dislike 'parables?'

5:59 am
almaandromeda
They are not always 'religious' but they are often analogies to make a spiritual or 'moral' point.. this is a parable poem on jealousy I wrote. I guess I'm asking, do things like that make a 'point' or impression with you or do you scoff at all moral code/ethical/sacred/spiritual stuff? Helps me to know for how to explain things to you.

6:19 am
almaandromeda
Do you want just the facts or the more layered perspective with 'meaning'? It's both there.. I want to speak to you in a language that makes sense.

6:46 am
korbendallas_987
i'm open minded which is what drives people to near suicide. proceed.

6:48 am
korbendallas_987
i'm not sure i have the intellect to dive down into the abyss, i'm just not there. very dumb. facts for sure, meaning as topping.

6:48 am
korbendallas_987
i'm hungry.

7:16 am
almaandromeda
You are smarter than a meat popsicle, that's for sure haha

7:25 am
korbendallas_987
TELL ME

7:26 am
korbendallas_987
WHAT THE FUCK IS AROUND MY CORNER? DEATH?? I would welcome
it with the warmest embrace, possibly even warmer than my first one with you.

7:27 am
almaandromeda
Here goes.. 1st words: -The Great Disillusionment
-All Work and No Play Makes Jack a Dull Boy
-Squaring Off
-Stuck In Gear
-Leaps and Bounds
-Change of Friends
-You Want More
-New Meanings to Old Stories

7:27 am
korbendallas_987
wow

7:27 am
almaandromeda
I will explain each

7:27 am
korbendallas_987
first one got me

7:27 am
almaandromeda
Can't wait btw xo

7:28 am
korbendallas_987
no need to explain that one

7:28 am
almaandromeda
You are taking off now..

7:28 am
almaandromeda
The 1st phase is disillusionment.. everything is a lie

7:29 am
almaandromeda
It is just the unpeeling of the 'throats of your career' that you have been run by.. it has had you, NOW you will have it by the throat

7:30 am
almaandromeda
You are growing up basically and you are taking reigns that you have not had to hold

7:30 am
korbendallas_987
my shrink talks of peeling back the onion

7:30 am
korbendallas_987
layer by lauer

7:30 am
korbendallas_987
layer

7:30 am
korbendallas_987
not sure if that is what u refer to

7:30 am
almaandromeda
That is..

7:30 am
almaandromeda
First you have to get raw

7:30 am
almaandromeda
It sux

7:30 am
korbendallas_987
well, i'm having a hard time with it—not the hardest, but hardest for me i've ever gone theu

7:30 am
korbendallas_987
thru

7:31 am
almaandromeda
Tell me about it plz

7:31 am
korbendallas_987
no shit is sux

7:31 am
almaandromeda
What are you going thru?

7:31 am
korbendallas_987
i feel like a failure in too many ways and lorie does nothing but prop me up

7:31 am
korbendallas_987
it can't go on much longer

7:31 am
almaandromeda
I know.. but why a failure?

7:32 am
korbendallas_987
i'm just never 'enough'

7:32 am
korbendallas_987
never

7:32 am
almaandromeda
You have done SO much

7:32 am
korbendallas_987
Ever

7:32 am
korbendallas_987
lies

7:32 am
almaandromeda
What IS enough?

7:32 am
almaandromeda
What would that look like?

7:32 am
korbendallas_987
atlas hurling earth to the crab nebula

7:33 am
almaandromeda
You are so powerful Michael.. you are 'bigger than your body' haha

7:33 am
korbendallas_987
much

7:34 am
korbendallas_987
i have lost weight which has directly contributed to my body dysmorphia, though
she likes me skinny

7:34 am
korbendallas_987

7:34 am
almaandromeda
I lost 20 lbs since we found u

7:34 am
almaandromeda
20 lbs!!

7:34 am
korbendallas_987
you have looked different..

7:34 am
almaandromeda
I am changing.. but getting it back finally

7:34 am
korbendallas_987
i am truly sorry to hear it and hope it comes back soon

7:35 am
korbendallas_987
i think you looked grrrrreat

7:35 am
almaandromeda
I love my body all ways.. thank you lol 😍

7:36 am
almaandromeda
Hey Michael.. I want to share something that released me from suffering today
when I was at dance.. ok?

7:36 am
korbendallas_987
squaring off, leaps and bounds, chang of friends...

7:37 am
korbendallas_987
sure

7:37 am
almaandromeda
I will get to that.

7:38 am
almaandromeda
This is important for you too I think. Ok. I saw this thing on IG and it was horrifying.. basically a man slapped a dead man at his funeral just to be 'savage'

7:38 am
almaandromeda
It really bothered me that I saw it, it was going over in my mind

7:39 am
almaandromeda
So.. at dance I had a vision of that dead man and he got out of his coffin and hugged Mr. Savage from behind and said, Thank You. That slap is what I needed to leave my body.

7:39 am
almaandromeda
Seeing that helped me release that vision.. Everything Is Perfect.

7:39 am
korbendallas_987
maybe the savage guy was a necromancer

7:40 am
korbendallas_987
and all was well!

7:40 am
almaandromeda
It's just everything is divine, on time, and people like you wear the heaviest gear and have the hard jobs.. just a thought.

7:40 am
almaandromeda
All work and no play..

7:41 am
korbendallas_987
oh my god i feel like my knees are about to shatter from the weight

7:41 am
almaandromeda
Why is it yours to bear?

7:41 am
korbendallas_987
i'm mixed; i'm supposed to live forever

7:41 am
almaandromeda
You do live forever haha

7:42 am
korbendallas_987
own fault; worked my way up a position that is basically the boss of sorts

7:42 am
korbendallas_987
army, leadership, blah

7:42 am
almaandromeda
So are you in it to win it still?

7:42 am
korbendallas_987
not by a long shor

7:42 am
korbendallas_987
just figuring options

7:42 am
korbendallas_987
5 years will be a lifetime regret but my sanity is at stake

7:43 am
almaandromeda
YOU are desirable and life is short

7:43 am
almaandromeda
Squaring off:

7:44 am
almaandromeda
You are in a rock/hard place with Saturn against Saturn

7:44 am
korbendallas_987
no question

7:44 am
korbendallas_987
no clue what u say but i feel it

7:44 am
korbendallas_987
no question

7:44 am
almaandromeda
And YOU have Mars with Saturn so you are always working with a 'checked brake'

7:45 am
almaandromeda
You have a feeling like you want to push the gas but all systems don't seem like 'Go'

7:45 am
almaandromeda
They are

7:45 am
almaandromeda
It's you

7:46 am
korbendallas_987
wtF

7:46 am
almaandromeda
You have to reach outside of this corner you are backed in and push down hard.. see outside your perceived 'ability to withstand' or 'power to make change'

7:47 am
almaandromeda
You are stronger than you realize with a lot of options

7:47 am
korbendallas_987
that shit is hard tho

7:47 am
almaandromeda
Point? That is the point. Supposed to be hard.

7:47 am
almaandromeda
You wanted it to be

7:47 am
almaandromeda
You were born like this

7:47 am
korbendallas_987
i always wanted life to be a cool breeze like an aquarius

7:48 am
korbendallas_987
i don't wanna do anything

7:48 am
korbendallas_987
just exist

7:48 am
almaandromeda
That is your 'old life'

7:48 am
almaandromeda
Your south node

7:48 am
almaandromeda
Past life

7:48 am
korbendallas_987
yeo

7:48 am
korbendallas_987
sure is

7:48 am
almaandromeda
We all have to grow and stretch and it hurts

7:48 am
korbendallas_987
ok—who ARE you

7:48 am
almaandromeda
That is such a gift to bring here Michael.. you are really 'special'

7:48 am
korbendallas_987
no more bullshit

7:48 am
korbendallas_987
who are you

7:49 am
almaandromeda
You know haha

7:49 am
korbendallas_987
u know me better than my wife in ways, and that's depressing

7:49 am
almaandromeda
No, but I do 'remember' you obviously lol

7:49 am
almaandromeda
I do 'remember' you from the second I saw you

7:50 am
almaandromeda
I feel lucky 🍀 that we have this line

7:50 am
korbendallas_987
i must've made some sort of impression

7:50 am
almaandromeda
20 lbs of one lol

7:51 am
almaandromeda
You do that obvs

7:51 am
korbendallas_987
i do that but they are usually bad because my face shows no emotion which the typical troglodyte deciphers to he's a meanie

7:52 am
almaandromeda
You are a meanie 4 sure lol I wish I could actually see your face.. so awesome that we've never met.

7:53 am
korbendallas_987
not a mean bone in my body but if pertains to the protection of my family, life sentence if i'm livkyb

7:53 am
korbendallas_987
lucky *

7:54 am
almaandromeda
I don't think you are mean, you are sweet like crab meat

7:54 am
korbendallas_987
haha

7:54 am
korbendallas_987
we move sideways

7:54 am
almaandromeda
So sensitive.. exoskeletons too

7:54 am
korbendallas_987
which is anti-progress

7:54 am
korbendallas_987
yep exo

7:54 am
almaandromeda
No it is pool shark perfect

7:54 am
korbendallas_987
i've learned to hone it tho

7:55 am
korbendallas_987
which has made me more lethal in work

7:55 am
korbendallas_987
because i will drop nuclear warheads on people rank regardless when i'm right

7:55 am
almaandromeda
Are you tough on your subordinates?

7:56 am
almaandromeda
How do you know you are right? Lol

7:56 am
korbendallas_987
not at all. we have a deadly job in which we people die frequently, almost always because of human error and i fly the most sophisticated, overworking acft in the army fleet—bar none

7:57 am
almaandromeda
I know 😍

300

7:57 am
korbendallas_987
standards are standards

7:57 am
almaandromeda
You are More.. you should switch lives with us for a sec just to see yourself from here. Superhero status Michael.

7:58 am
korbendallas_987
well if u ever feel like helping
my mind breathe, feel free. i have to meditate before
bed or i won't sleep a wink

7:58 am
almaandromeda
I want to

7:58 am
korbendallas_987
you are terribly, terribly, terrificly misinformed

7:58 am
almaandromeda
Just seeing you from here

7:59 am
almaandromeda
To be cont.. xo

7:59 am
korbendallas_987

7:59 am
korbendallas_987
del

8:36 am
almaandromeda
More 2moro but listen: NO dying for you. It will feel like dying, you will want to die, but you were formed 9 months in your mother's womb and then she and all of your Spirit and Living guides watched over you night and day to help get you here.

YOU yourself have suffered this long, to be wise and physically here now. Allow yourself to feel the emotional and Spiritual growing pains and find a new Bravery, warrior. You won't die, I'm here doing it too ♫ Dance with me, it won't kill ya♫

3:52 pm
almaandromeda
This is left to explain:
-Leaps and Bounds
-Change of Friends
-You Want More
-New Meanings to Old Stories

5:21 pm
almaandromeda
Also I see this for you tbh:
-Paper Bill$ In The Wind Both Ways
-Deep Creative Release
-The Words Come
-Cut Down The Hang Man

10:41 pm
korbendallas_987
i must.. know.. more.

October 6th, 2017

12:25 am
korbendallas_987
i take the $ comment to mean i'm about to get fucked

12:26 am
korbendallas_987
goddammit i need MOAR!

3:03 am
almaandromeda
You will get more lol

3:04 am
almaandromeda
I'm on it 2nite

4:22 am

almaandromeda

These different things all relate - to each other and then to your larger picture.. slowly coming to focus. 'You Want More' is related to 'Deep Creative Release'. 'Squaring Off' is related to 'Stuck In Gear'. 'The Great Disillusionment' relates to 'Leaps and Bounds' and that relates to 'Cut Down the Hang Man'. I know that is vague but I will get into it. Basically it's a map with all the lines.

4:31 am

almaandromeda

I will add to the list:
-Fast Rapids of Reflection - can't ignore or deny the obvious, and it is WILD in your chart. You have aligned with a clear polar opposite reflection of your energy frequency. Through this eclipse and this 'Astro weather' we've been having you have created circumstances for yourself that bring you clear reflection from a completely NEW and 'opposite' point of view. This is a sometimes uncomfortable but fast acting agent of change. I am one of these new reflections for you.

4:37 am

almaandromeda

When we found you I found inside myself clear instructions- written out almost like a prescription. It said Love him. I have never had a clearer message to have empathy for anyone. So I can tell I am one of these agents for reflection and change that are helping to shake up and radicalize your life. Your path is widening now and it is nearing the 'middle' of your life (it all relates) and the Universe is calling you out. Got to sing 🎶 more later

5:33 am

almaandromeda

So 'Leaps and Bounds'.. this relates to the above. As above, so below. As you are leaping, so you are bound. This is a yo-yo time of not just being stuck between a rock&hard place but also in the middle between where you want to go and the ties that bind you to where you are now. It's a tightrope that won't always last but for now you are basically in 2 places at once which feels impossible for 3rd dimensional reality and it IS hard, but it is also 'just a phase.'

5:41 am

almaandromeda

You can't stop the 'leaps' you are making in your awareness, your 'home' and heart chakra connections and the desire this Universe has for YOUR unique gifts. You also can't undo, take back, stop loving/enjoying or change quickly the ties and stakes that bind you to the choices you have already made in the direction you have already been heading. Have both! 〰 For now you can 'have it all'. There is no conflict, really. Leap in the 5th 🌑and be Bound in the 3rd 🖤

5:46 am

almaandromeda

Change of Friends: You are going through deep transformation in your networks-relates to the Great Disillusionment- and you are starting to look • • around with a new sense of clarity at your social networks and what you might want more of in peer enjoyment and what you want to lose. The cool thing is that underneath this is a budding desire to 'shine' and find a more powerful way of influencing others in larger networks.

5:48 am

almaandromeda

I know it is painful to even read that right now probably but you are M for More than you think, I promise. 🌝 I will let you take that in and continue later xxoo

6:08 am

almaandromeda

"Art takes time. Monet grew his flowers before he painted them" - Atticus

7:02 am

almaandromeda

I want to hear about your meditation before bed when you have time & if you feel like sharing xo

7:29 am

almaandromeda

Too much haha

7:29 am

almaandromeda

Sorry lol

7:36 am

korbendallas_987

well, to be 💯 with you, i haven't told ANYONE this but lorie. but i have come across some for lack of a better term. trouble, in my career and it may end it—i don't know. never in my life have i been this scared for this long. everyday is a daymare and every night is a nightmare. you hit a LOT on this shit somehow, and like a junkie looking for his next fix, i look for good news from you. it's ALMOST all i have to rely on. does that fit some of the missing puzzlzle pieces into the board?

7:36 am

almaandromeda

Yes thank u.. gosh I'm sorry Michael that it feels this uncertain

7:37 am
almaandromeda
You have to look outside the box, what you know

7:37 am
almaandromeda
But I have no idea what u are going thru in the moment

7:37 am
korbendallas_987
i feel i let everyone down but more importantly me. lorie has been hard as a rock (in a good way). i think she may be autistic

7:38 am
almaandromeda
She is very Capricorn solid

7:38 am
almaandromeda
Like a diamond

7:38 am
almaandromeda
Allllll Capricorn aquarius

7:38 am
almaandromeda
Sort of cold but super solid

7:38 am
korbendallas_987
yea

7:39 am
almaandromeda
I don't know her just her chart obviously.. do you have options outside of army that you actively working

7:39 am
almaandromeda
You need to feel in control somehiw

7:40 am
korbendallas_987
not yet—still uncertain of outcome

7:40 am
korbendallas_987
they like to keep you in the dark and i'm good at playing games

7:40 am
almaandromeda
You are the best 😷

7:40 am
korbendallas_987
just worried

7:41 am
korbendallas_987
it's become nearly a terminal illness

7:41 am
korbendallas_987
worse than a normal cancer

7:41 am
korbendallas_987
always

7:41 am
almaandromeda
I don't like you feeling uncertain in the kind of job u have 😬

7:41 am
korbendallas_987
yea. me neither.

7:41 am
korbendallas_987
but i have to live in the present and be reactive; it's all i got right now

7:42 am
almaandromeda
You do 4 sure...

7:42 am
almaandromeda
Do this with me..

7:43 am
almaandromeda
Visualize this experience and feel you holding it tightly.. feel the grip you have on this moment and feel it's grip on you..

7:43 am
almaandromeda
Feel it

7:43 am
almaandromeda
It is so heavy.. the weight on your shoulders

7:43 am
almaandromeda
Your neck.. so much to bear

7:43 am
almaandromeda
Now..

7:44 am
almaandromeda
Take in a deep breath.. long breath in, then out

7:44 am
almaandromeda
Just breathe for a few breaths

7:44 am
almaandromeda
And feel your shoulders drop, those weights start to fall away, slide down..

7:44 am
almaandromeda
One side, a breath.. the other side..

7:45 am
almaandromeda
Your neck is looser.. you feel your chest expand with breath and fall back

7:45 am
almaandromeda
Shake your shoulders and smile please

7:46 am
almaandromeda
You are holding this ON you.. you see weights and weights hold you

7:46 am
almaandromeda
Look for brightness, rainbows, glints in eyes.. friends

7:46 am
korbendallas_987
thank you

7:46 am
almaandromeda
Friends are everywhere if you look and they want to help you. See it differently 🖤

7:47 am
korbendallas_987
hermit crab over here

7:47 am
korbendallas_987
with BIG clawd

7:47 am
korbendallas_987
claws

7:47 am
almaandromeda
The biggest.. Michael- guess what you don't have time for finally?

7:48 am
almaandromeda
Being SO worried about yourself in the mirror- you are gorgeous, perfect, naturally driven to be 'better' and you can still strive while giving yourself a mental break.

7:49 am
korbendallas_987
that's. while other talk show. i'm hideous so i work out to create a shell

7:49 am
korbendallas_987
whole

7:50 am
korbendallas_987
been fighting it for 40 years

7:50 am
almaandromeda
You are wasting your mental time beating yourself up on your body.. I had that too- vanity really

7:50 am
korbendallas_987
of course its vanity

7:50 am
almaandromeda
When you are hot it feels awesome and I used to be stuck in the mirror

7:50 am
korbendallas_987
but it's empowering as PHOKN when you clear out a gym

7:51 am
korbendallas_987
PHOK*

7:51 am
almaandromeda
Film it

7:51 am
almaandromeda
Share it then

7:51 am
korbendallas_987
nah

7:51 am
korbendallas_987
i act like i'm the only person in the room

7:51 am
almaandromeda
You are stretching and it's not just for 'you' anymore

7:52 am
korbendallas_987
esPECIALLLY around girls who find themselves next to me

7:52 am
korbendallas_987
all true

7:52 am
almaandromeda
But I know about meditation in that.. I do that I dance haha

7:52 am
almaandromeda
Same

7:52 am
korbendallas_987
speaking of i need to knock out a few sessions

7:53 am
almaandromeda
I find myself dancing and men literally are worshipping me on the ground, it's hilarious 😂

7:53 am
korbendallas_987
headspace anxiety and sleep packs

7:53 am
almaandromeda
Xo

7:53 am
korbendallas_987
.... what it would be like, to be normal...

7:53 am
almaandromeda
Let's never find out

7:53 am
korbendallas_987
😥

7:53 am
almaandromeda
🖤

8:04 am
almaandromeda
Thank you for the honor of sharing your thoughts 🙏 I am *whispering* in your ear so much love 🖤 day & night.. I can only imagine all the other people doing that for you too. I gave birth, without a man, at age 21, with no drugs. The ONLY thing that got me thru was This Too Shall Pass.. it is impossible for a moment to last longer than 60 seconds.. and every moment passes. The birth could not go on longer than 24 hrs. It had to be over at some point.

8:24 am
almaandromeda
What I'm trying to say about your body/vanity is rock your sexy self for real!! Work out feel awesome, and just know that shit. You are *radiantly* beautiful. Let your mind rest on that FACT and see if you can use that time that you beat yourself up on something else. Beat the body but spare the mind. You are *stunning* in all the forms.

8:56 am
almaandromeda
I get 2 be honest with you, at least as honest as I am with myself. Thanks for the

311

space to do that. When I heard Love Him the instructions where that clear and that vague. Part of how I love people is to want to help counsel you & see you as your best self..AND part of how I love people is to accept you completely how you are, as is, in the moment, wanting to change or not. You are You with all the self depreciation and self criticalness and it's part of why I am so dang curious about you👁🖐

12:51 pm
korbendallas_987
if that makes u curious, u ain't seen nothin yet

3:37 pm
almaandromeda
Can not wait haha

3:38 pm
almaandromeda
Today I will try to do this:
-Paper Bill$ In The Wind Both Ways
-Deep Creative Release
-The Words Come
-Cut Down The Hang Man

9:35 pm
almaandromeda
Paper Bill$: With Uranus transiting your 2nd house of finances, self esteem, self worth for a while you have the erratic planet of sudden change trying to make a home in your bank account. This can feel like a 'shake down', a 'shake up' OR a shaking of the golden money tree. It comes and goes both ways now, suddenly, and not how you always expect. It is 'tilling' the soil of your personal values, your self care and self esteem through physical financial changes that you feel and understand.

9:41 am
almaandromeda
Again with the 'lightness' shit! Haha There is a lightness that this come&go money woes and random happiness is bringing you.. it's obvious to you I'm sure. You can't get too attached to shit here or Uranus will swoop in and knock it out of your hands with a vengeance. On a macro scale that is the wars we wage, each side knocked down for their attachments to the death. You will get sudden money, you will lose sudden money. Maybe good/maybe bad, and you can get thru both the same if you want.

10:20 pm
almaandromeda
I don't usually predict - I'm not a psychic, too specific.. but for a 'release' from the pressure cooker you are in look at 11/11/17 and after. You feel under the gun but the tables will shift and actually soon. You naturally have Pluto in the 8th- lots of power in others money and resources. Soon Mars will get off your own Mars/Saturn that makes you feel on fire in a desert and you will turn instead into a beast out for blood. $trategize.

11:43 pm
almaandromeda
Darkest Before Dawn type moment for sure. Get excited.

October 7th, 2017

7:22 pm
almaandromeda
Sorry about sending/unsending.. going thru alot alone but that is mine to handle and I want to work it out on my own. Let me know if you want me to keep reading the rest or if you basically 'already know how this goes.' Life just happens and noone knows really anything but trends and data from what has happened before.

7:49 pm
almaandromeda
I know ZERO really.. all conjecture and pretend wisdom from a broken poisoned heart.. but this guy is actually fucking smart. Hopefully this helps.

9:09 pm
korbendallas_987
god i hope you're right. i feel like i'm inside a pressure cooker, as you said, and i greatly appreciate your help.

9:11 pm
korbendallas_987
i don't really know what to do with this kind of information, i've never had this kind of 'resource' before

9:32 pm
almaandromeda
I don't either.. just background wisdom I think. Life still sux or doesn't haha

9:54 pm
korbendallas_987
are you unhappy?

9:57 pm
almaandromeda
Define happy..

9:57 pm
almaandromeda
Haha

9:58 pm
korbendallas_987
who the fuck knows

9:58 pm
almaandromeda
I dont 4 sure

9:58 pm
korbendallas_987
like waking up in the morning ?

9:58 pm
almaandromeda
Not right now tbh

9:58 pm
almaandromeda
Sorry 2 disappoint

9:58 pm
korbendallas_987
disappoint?

9:59 pm
almaandromeda
Not perfect and magically the coolest

9:59 pm
almaandromeda
Its hard for me to not be happy

314

9:59 pm
almaandromeda
Like I let down the world

10:00 pm
almaandromeda
But you and I are on opposites and sameville.. yours in career and mine in home stuff

10:00 pm
korbendallas_987
i'm in such a fucking crisis i don't know what i am feeling

10:00 pm
korbendallas_987
correct

10:00 pm
almaandromeda
Im so sorry

10:00 pm
almaandromeda
Its hard

10:00 pm
korbendallas_987
not your fault?!

10:00 pm
korbendallas_987
my fault

10:00 pm
almaandromeda
I know but I am

10:00 pm
almaandromeda
Mine is my fault, yours is yours lol

10:01 pm
korbendallas_987
mine revolves around uncertain future

10:01 pm
almaandromeda
Mine too..

10:01 pm
almaandromeda
How can u get more certain?

10:01 pm
korbendallas_987
is it the parent stuff?

10:02 pm
almaandromeda
No.. just all of the above

10:03 pm
almaandromeda
Hard to explain without saying too much but its hard right now..

10:03 am
almaandromeda
Directions in life

10:03 pm
korbendallas_987
i know what u mean

10:03 pm
korbendallas_987
u two doin ok?

10:04 pm
almaandromeda
So/sOK lol.. Nick is .. ♥ god I love him but we are super duper different

10:04 pm
almaandromeda
I will be honest..

10:04 pm
korbendallas_987
i understand

10:05 pm
korbendallas_987
lorie and i are straight up opposites but i love her to death

10:05 pm
almaandromeda
Hey..

10:05 pm
almaandromeda
Are the swatztikas on purpose in her tattoo? So curious

10:05 pm
almaandromeda
Japanese etc

10:05 pm
korbendallas_987
lol they aren't swastikas

10:06 pm
korbendallas_987
its actually a symbol used for a lot of different reasons historically

10:06 pm
almaandromeda
Is it an on purpose symbol?

10:07 pm
almaandromeda
Just curious because I know u are conscious of symbolism

10:08 pm
korbendallas_987
i would honestly have to ask richie the artist. he is deep in the streets when it comes to jap folklore

10:08 pm
almaandromeda
Wow cool.. thanks

10:08 pm
almaandromeda
Ok so heres the deal

10:08 pm
almaandromeda
Your brother is an ANGEL

10:08 pm
almaandromeda
Like literally for real

10:08 pm
almaandromeda
No meat, no alchohol..

10:09 pm
almaandromeda
Drums every single day on time

10:09 pm
almaandromeda
A pure pure pure person

10:09 pm
almaandromeda
And for 8 yrs I have been devotedly side by side with him in every step

10:10 pm
almaandromeda
The standards are SO high.. like minute by minute purity high

10:10 pm
almaandromeda
Its alot to live up to and its not that 'honest' after a while

10:10 pm
korbendallas_987
i understand

10:10 pm
korbendallas_987
pressure

10:11 pm
almaandromeda
More than you know... he is a dedication to morality and love

10:11 pm
korbendallas_987
maybe you just put him on a perfect pedestal in order to put yourself down?

10:11 pm
almaandromeda
No its his mouth haha

10:12 pm
almaandromeda
When you meet him youll know ❤ He is just dedicated to the path. I get tired sometimes.

10:12 pm
korbendallas_987
from what i understand he has been through some struggles

10:12 pm
korbendallas_987
at least you two are aware of a path

10:13 pm
almaandromeda
I dont know..

10:13 pm
almaandromeda
Just today is dumb xo

10:13 pm
almaandromeda
Tomorrow I will figure it out again

10:14 pm
korbendallas_987
my problem is extreme boredom with life i think

10:14 pm
korbendallas_987
this is it?

10:14 pm
almaandromeda
I cant wait to get near you and play with u.. no boredom for you!

10:14 pm
almaandromeda
I mean just like music and stuff haha

10:15 pm
korbendallas_987

10:15 pm
almaandromeda
I did have an awesome idea that I have been wanting to share with u..

10:15 pm
almaandromeda
Ready?

10:15 pm
almaandromeda
Ok.. so.. this is exciting.

10:16 pm
almaandromeda
We both feel sensitive to suicide so this is why I thought of you

10:16 pm
almaandromeda
You know how NASA puts up tons of data online for regular people to review and report to NASA?

10:17 pm
almaandromeda
People powered data mining

10:17 pm
korbendallas_987
didnt know

10:17 pm
almaandromeda
Ok so there are all of these bridges in cities around the world...

10:17 pm
almaandromeda
Yes its cool

10:17 pm
almaandromeda
The nasa thing

10:17 pm
almaandromeda
Youcan help find stars

10:18 pm
almaandromeda
So..

10:18 pm
almaandromeda
So I am thinking WHAT IF there were cameras set up on all the bridges

10:18 pm
almaandromeda
And they fed into a website people could watch on their own timw

10:19 pm
almaandromeda
*time just for fun and then if someone in Argentina saw someone in Seattle who looked like they might jump they coukd contact in real time the Seattle response

10:20 pm
almaandromeda
Does that make sense?

10:20 pm
korbendallas_987
sort of

10:20 pm
korbendallas_987
it insinuates that bridge jumping is the leading culprit though

10:20 pm
korbendallas_987
doesn't it?

10:21 pm
almaandromeda
No just catching people in a conversation before they jump may save lives

10:21 pm
korbendallas_987
yea

10:21 pm
almaandromeda
What if the bridge were wired and people could talk right there?

10:21 pm
korbendallas_987
that's the last way i would go

10:21 pm
almaandromeda
1st way for me

10:21 pm
almaandromeda
St Johns bridge

10:22 pm
korbendallas_987
you're not seriois

322

10:22 pm
korbendallas_987
you arent that dumb

10:22 pm
almaandromeda
No.. but it is tru.. not going anywhere.

10:22 pm
korbendallas_987
no offense

10:23 pm
almaandromeda
Why do we have to do everything tho? Argg. It is hard tbh

10:23 pm
korbendallas_987
everyone has pondered the effects, i'm sure

10:23 pm
almaandromeda
Its boring really

10:23 pm
korbendallas_987
yea my life has been hard and it's been mostly my fault

10:23 pm
almaandromeda
Life is cooler.. why yours?

10:24 pm
korbendallas_987
i'm really, really hard on myself

10:24 pm
almaandromeda
Besides that you project your own reality obvs

10:24 pm
korbendallas_987
lotta regret, self defeat

10:25 pm
almaandromeda
I can see how much you expect from yourself..

10:25 pm
almaandromeda
You are only one man!

10:25 pm
korbendallas_987
who knows what others see me as

10:25 pm
korbendallas_987
i weigh it so heavily tho

10:25 pm
almaandromeda
Everything is fine, everything is divine, everything is on time.

10:26 pm
korbendallas_987
i wish

10:26 pm
almaandromeda
You know it.. go to the beach and look at the ocean.. you are tiny and that is life.

10:27 pm
almaandromeda
You are a giant star and that is life too

10:27 pm
korbendallas_987
i see all that. i might lose my job tho and it scares the shit out of me

10:28 pm
almaandromeda
Fuck a job haha

10:28 pm
almaandromeda
But for real

10:28 pm
korbendallas_987
gotta have a roof

10:28 pm
almaandromeda
Tru.. but you may need to learn this.. money and security are an illusion

10:29 pm
almaandromeda
Just like the roof and the ground

10:29 pm
almaandromeda
When we get attached thats when we get scurred

10:29 pm
korbendallas_987
it's more of a feeling of failing lorie

10:30 pm
korbendallas_987
i can live under a bridge and watch people fall

10:30 pm
almaandromeda
Each person must learn to stand .. this is a mother fucking rollarcoaster

10:30 pm
korbendallas_987
but i want to give her the world

10:30 pm
almaandromeda
I can tell ❤

10:30 pm
almaandromeda
She's a very lucky girl.

10:30 pm
korbendallas_987
i've learned that for surr

10:31 pm
korbendallas_987
i hate the feeling of failure

10:31 pm
korbendallas_987
GAWD i hate it

10:31 pm
almaandromeda
Just why u have to feel it I guess

10:31 pm
korbendallas_987
honestly think it's from growing up in a strict ass household

10:31 pm
korbendallas_987
i would never tell mom that tho

10:32 pm
almaandromeda
Did u live with ur mom all the time or was she deployed alot?

10:32 pm
korbendallas_987
this shrink says we are formed entirely by our youth

10:32 pm
korbendallas_987
always with her except when she went to saudi arabia which killed me

10:33 pm
almaandromeda
How old were you?

10:33 pm
almaandromeda
So ur stepdad was strict?

10:33 pm
korbendallas_987
11

10:33 pm
korbendallas_987
no not really. weird asshole but not strict

10:34 pm
almaandromeda
But ur mom was?

10:34 pm
korbendallas_987
they got married 3 times

10:34 pm
korbendallas_987
mom very strict

10:34 pm
almaandromeda
To eachother? Wow

10:34 pm
korbendallas_987
but complete opposite with peter

10:35 pm
almaandromeda
You and I are truly opposites but so exactly that you can just put it all upside down
for me. So funny.

10:35 pm
almaandromeda
My mom neglected me and hoped I would get kidnapped or die

10:36 pm
korbendallas_987
yea i see the opposite thing

10:36 pm
almaandromeda
She banished me from birth .. no lie ... stupid shit.

10:36 pm
korbendallas_987
jesus

10:36 pm
korbendallas_987
my mom was fiercely terrilorial with me

10:36 pm
korbendallas_987
stark raving mad crazy

10:37 pm
almaandromeda
I can see the oppositeness.. she identifies with you to an intense degree

10:37 pm
almaandromeda
Hard to find yourself in there

10:37 pm
almaandromeda
Its all love just thru himans ❤

10:37 pm
almaandromeda
*humans

10:37 pm
almaandromeda
Even my mom

10:38 pm
almaandromeda
She is my best friend honestly

10:38 pm
korbendallas_987
really??

10:38 pm
almaandromeda
She made me 'like this'

10:38 pm
almaandromeda
No she hates me

10:38 pm
almaandromeda
Like never never talks to me ever

10:38 pm
korbendallas_987
didn't want kids?

10:38 pm
korbendallas_987
sounds like me

10:38 pm
almaandromeda
She gave up her 1st son at 16 forced

10:39 pm
almaandromeda
That turned her psycho

10:39 pm
almaandromeda
I was too painful in her arms

10:39 pm
korbendallas_987
hm

10:39 pm
almaandromeda
Fuck a baby

10:39 pm
almaandromeda
I am grateful seriously

10:39 pm
almaandromeda
I have BURNED in hell

10:39 pm
almaandromeda
Everything else is easy haha

10:40 pm
almaandromeda
Probably like going to war

10:40 pm
almaandromeda
You must feel stronger

10:40 pm
almaandromeda
I did the opposite with Soquel and loved him like crazy..

10:41 pm
korbendallas_987
the army became my identity unfortunately

10:41 pm
almaandromeda
What will u be after the army?

10:41 pm
almaandromeda
Identity wise

10:42 pm
korbendallas_987
scariest question thus far

10:42 pm
almaandromeda
Haha so sorry lol

10:42 pm
almaandromeda
You are a trooper with me tho

10:42 pm
almaandromeda
Tough guy 4 sure

10:42 pm
almaandromeda

10:43 pm
almaandromeda
Take care for now xo

10:43 pm
korbendallas_987

October 8th, 2017

12:38 am
almaandromeda
I have thought more.. and here it is:

12:41 am
almaandromeda
For some reason at this time I am being asked to come more 'authentic' 'real' 'raw' and 'myself.' Even tho it seems like I am SO raw cuz I dance and sing and suck at it and still put it out there.. I am hiding behind a big fake smile covering layers and layers of active pain that there is no fix or cure for.

12:41 am
almaandromeda
So I am at a crossroads.

12:46 am
almaandromeda
I thought all this time I could 'regiment' it out of me and shine it away. Nick is not interested in the pain, it 'bothers' him to know the dirtier/uglier/darker aspects of me, things just need to be fixed and if I start to talk about my past stripping or my other weirder moments I am cut off quick. So much 'light' it can be sun exposure sometimes.

12:49 am
almaandromeda
And the thing is, my mom is the original Night of darkness and she pushed me out from the Night past the edge into Day and just left me there to fry. There is no

331

comfort there. The moon and the Night are what we rest in. It kind of feels like I haven't slept once since I got here tbh.

1 2:5 1 am
almaandromeda
That is part of why I really appreciate your unexpected friendship and this dimly lit corner of the 4th dimension where I can be my freaking self, actually. It is what it is and it's nice. ♥ 🐾 ☂

1:57 am
almaandromeda
Some thoughts on boredom:

1:59 am
almaandromeda
Playfulness, gratitude, imagination and discipline are the enemies of boredom.

2:03 am
almaandromeda
When u are bored, think playfully.. what would be silly, funny, mischevious - like Parkour running thru the streets, handstand challenges, making an IG or youtube video of your cool life. Think gratefully when you are bored and you will write someone you miss and love, you will check on an elderly neighbor, you will make some homeless packs to keep in your car.

2:06 am
almaandromeda
Think imaginatively when you are bored and the sky is the limit, if even that is. Get free, get wild, get imaginative with your partner and it's over the top. You could start a book together, plan trips to see the world, write a love song a day, plant a garden of herbs and take care of it.. anything is yours in the imagination.

2:08 am
almaandromeda
With discipline boredom is officially murdered. Even if you don't feel like getting playful, grateful or imaginative with your time, you HAVE to when you discipline yourself to do it and ta-da! You are in the mix, moving at a fun and inspiring speed and feeling the Juices of life. So much to do, so much time xxoo

3:2 1 am
almaandromeda
Your brother taught me the essence of that.. the boredom thing. He's really a beautiful, loving person that you are lucky to be related to honestly. He is like a keeper of

332

one of the gates of heaven. You have to be strict to hold that down. I am really only grateful for him and I hope that is obvious too.

October 9th, 2017

7:18 pm
korbendallas_987
You're so cute.. and fkn optimistic. I needed a girl like you. Too late now tho.

7:18 pm
korbendallas_987
you are so much better than me at expressing the problem

7:18 pm
korbendallas_987
i have no clue why my life is so dark, nor excuse

7:19 pm
korbendallas_987
i guess i'm too hard on myself but i don't fucking know

7:20 pm
korbendallas_987
why does my horoscope always call me 'moonchild'

9:17 pm
almaandromeda
You are a child of the moon 🌙 because Cancer is ruled by the moon. Each sign is ruled by a planet, except Cancer & Leo, which are ruled by the moon and the sun. You can see it in your 'moon' face, round and symmetrical.. The moon is yin energy. She is the mother of the earth, while Sun is the father.

9:20 pm
almaandromeda
She orbits us and takes all the 'hits' before they reach the earth. She is powerful as fk, moves the oceans and her orbit is quick and 'moody'. You can be very masculine and be Cancer sun obviously.. it will manifest in service to others, devotion/loyalty, exoskeleton, defense/defensiveness, absolute sweetness that has to be protected, and sensitivities to the world.

9:31 pm
almaandromeda
The cool thing about your Astro evolution is that you are a Cancer sun- yin moon energy, and your north node is Leo-yang father energy. Your Aquarian nature is here as the eternal observer, while you stand back and watch the merging of your yin WITH yang over the evolution of your soul path here. You are so Boy Wonder, you don't see yet I think your value to this big world. 🖤

9:48 pm
almaandromeda
I think what I'm having is a good old fashioned midlife crisis tbh. Regrets, tears, feeling like a fking loser.. and I have a 'special' case of psycho attacker parents never letting me forget the weird shit I 'come from'. A party and no one else is invited so don't ask to come haha

10:52 pm
korbendallas_987
i'm having one too. i think you're right.

11:00 pm
almaandromeda
I'm always right lol 👊 This too shall pass. It works.

October 10th, 2017

3:49 am
almaandromeda
CENTER OF THE FIRE - RUMI
Don't listen to anything I say.
I must enter the center of the fire.
Fire is my child, but I must
be consumed and become fire.
Why is there crackling and smoke?
Because the firewood and the flames
are still talking about each other.
"You are too dense. Go away!"
"You are too wavering.
I have solid form."
In the blackness those friends keep arguing.
Like a wanderer with no face.
Like the most powerful bird in existence
sitting on its perch, refusing to move.

334

5:11 pm
korbendallas_987
weird

6:22 pm
almaandromeda
I love how he does not give a fuck.. I take in other people and listen to myself 1st, but Rumi talks to me in a most brutal way. I love the part about the firewood and flame 🔥 you are too dense you are too wavering they argued all night.

6:25 pm
almaandromeda
To me this is funny/haha and funny/weird.. this is the inside cover of my Rumi book. 37! It says "Jelaluddin Rumi was born in the year 1207 and until the age of 37 was a brilliant scholar and popular teacher. But his life changed forever when he met the powerful wandering dervish, Shams of Tabriz, of whom Rumi said, 'What I had thought of before as God, I met today in a human being.' From this mysterious and esoteric friendship came a new height of spiritual enlightenment. When Shams disappeared, Rumi began his transformation from scholar to artist, and his poetry began to fly."

6:47 pm
almaandromeda
Shams was probably killed by Rumi's family according to historical info. Rumi was told that Shams just left and never came back. This line breaks my heart-

6:47 pm
almaandromeda
When Shams comes back
from Tabriz, he'll put
just his head around the
edge of the door to surprise us.
Like this.'

6:54 pm
almaandromeda
He waited and waited and never saw Shams again.

6:54 pm
korbendallas_987
So are you saying I'm Rumi or Shams? I'm 37 obv but not a whirling dervish lol

6:54 pm
almaandromeda
I don't know which is which hahah! I just can't fucking wait to see you.

6:54 pm
korbendallas_987
you will, keep your pants on 😜

6:54 pm
korbendallas_987
that's funny, i am super brutal honest and it's been an issue

6:54 pm
korbendallas_987
people say i'm honest to a fault

7:04 pm
almaandromeda
I call it 'radical honesty'

7:05 pm
almaandromeda
That's been my M.O. 4ever till this summer, honestly haha

7:06 pm
almaandromeda
Honest is a basically lie because it is always less than the whole truth.. I'm getting that lately

7:06 pm
almaandromeda
Miss High Horse is coming down for some water

7:21 pm
almaandromeda
How is it an issue for you? Subordinates, superiors, or civilians?

8:45 pm
korbendallas_987
always my superiors

8:45 pm
korbendallas_987
i have a good friend here that i've known forever that says it's my best trait

8:45 pm
korbendallas_987
he loves it when i hit the roof with someone in front of ANYBODY

8:45 pm
korbendallas_987
very confrontational

8:46 pm
korbendallas_987
so i have sworn friends, and sworn enemies alike

9:05 pm
almaandromeda
That literally just made me laugh out loud haha

9:06 pm
almaandromeda
Are you one of those that people are like glad I'm on his good side.. ?

10:18 pm
almaandromeda
I'm glad I'm on your 'good' side lol

10:34 pm
korbendallas_987
yes good side. everyone knows what side they're on or will know shortly

10:42 pm
almaandromeda
Boss 💣

October 11th, 2017

4:34 am
almaandromeda
Have you heard of pushmi-pullyu?

4:36 am
almaandromeda
it is a gazelle/Unicorn cross. Half real/half myth. 2 perpetual directions. Practical/playful. 3D/5D. We are all trying to fit in 2 places and on this plane you can hold only one thing in your hand or mind at a time.

4:37 am
almaandromeda
The 'sky' tonight

4:59 am
korbendallas_987
too true

4:59 am
korbendallas_987
looks a lot like me

5:07 am
almaandromeda
I keep turning in circles trying to catch a glimpse of the other half

5:08 am
almaandromeda
I forget I'm both halves lol

5:49 am
almaandromeda
There is a song 'phone down' by Emily Warren that is the modern version. Focus is key to 'the mission' if you are on one.

6:36 pm
korbendallas_987
i don't feel as only one half but i may not get it. i certainly handle problems about half as well as anyone else does so maybe

October 12th, 2017

7:19 am
almaandromeda
I think I just identify with one half at a time and forget I am the whole damn picture in color and shadow. How are you handling stuff today yo?

338

7:19 am
korbendallas_987
it's actually been a bit better but i don't know. i fear the worst.

7:20 am
almaandromeda
Glad to hear 📖 Don't fear.

7:23 am
almaandromeda
May be good, may be bad.. you know the story

8:02 am
almaandromeda
It got better 4 me 2

8:30 am
almaandromeda
Tonight I danced with a down syndrome 8 yr old girl for most of Dance and it was the sweetest night ever. Gratitude and silliness keep my frequency up.

10:29 am
korbendallas_987
...peaks and valleys...

5:19 pm
almaandromeda
Dance is my 'view from the top' - helps me fly over my own oceans and not fall in.

5:19 pm
almaandromeda
You meditate yo?

5:55 pm
korbendallas_987
i started about 6 months ago, not very good at it

5:55 pm
korbendallas_987
i am easily my worst enemy

5:57 pm
korbendallas_987
i have that headspace app

6:20 pm
almaandromeda
I dance till I lose my mind and feel till I don't anymore.. my only meditation right now.

6:20 pm
almaandromeda
The app looks rad tho

6:30 pm
korbendallas_987
it's guided meditation

6:32 pm
almaandromeda
I saw. You were in my dream last night. Suited up in war army gear, 'going in', and I just remember that you were very, very brave.

6:32 pm
almaandromeda
Nothing else. Dreams are awesome and weird and also annoying haha

10:15 pm
almaandromeda
If you haven't watched the Emily Warren "PHONE DOWN" vid it is literally laugh out loud hysterical to me. I just feel the tides, see the changes and know when it makes sense to put the phone down.

10:20 pm
almaandromeda
Thank you 👊 🖤 👊 for every everything

11:09 pm
almaandromeda
Btw I never figured out why the H. song fucks with me SO much but I love it still and always will 👁
"I am too connected to you"

340

1:11 am

almaandromeda

recalling all the times I died or will die, it's alright, I don't mind.. !! Best moment in any song for me... it's like a trigger for so many tears. Thank you.

2:05 am

korbendallas_987

that's their best album but it doesn't have my fav song.

2:05 am

korbendallas_987

although eulogy was good

2:08 am

almaandromeda

The Patient is too 'patient' for me. Why suffer? Lol

2:17 am

almaandromeda

I cultivated patience from being forced in small spaces. I guess I'm just tired of that shit, tired of 'patient'. There has to be more than more patience.

4:04 am

korbendallas_987

yea but it's euphoric when it starts

4:25 am

almaandromeda

Michael.. I don't know what to do with anger. I am SO brutally angry with my parents. It's like the shock finally wore off an now I am a rage monster inside. I just saw them at the fb game and I was psycho and menacing.. I hate how I feel like this. I am SOoooo fucking pissed.

4:27 am

almaandromeda

Phoenix is raging but with no powers . I am worried this turns in. So broken hearted honestly and MAD.

5:04 am

almaandromeda

I will figure it out obviously.. just today it hit me. It's not that bad really.

5:24 am
almaandromeda
I'm embarrassed to share that & sorry 2 - Im never that angry anymore. I do feel fkd but I can handle it.

5:24 am
almaandromeda
Big girls don't cry

5:30 am
korbendallas_987

October 15th, 2017

4:29 am
almaandromeda
I came home and told Nick and he understood me and held me. I wasn't that 'psycho' to others, just to me.. just felt pissed and was looking for advice. My bad haha. Take care of you my brother xo

4:31 am
almaandromeda
👍

4:32 am
almaandromeda
Sorry to 'bother' you I guess.

4:33 am
korbendallas_987
not sure what u mean but what did u tell nick

4:35 am
almaandromeda
I told Nick about being menacing seeming to my parents.. that is all

4:36 am
korbendallas_987
ah

342

4:36 am
almaandromeda
I wrote you about it on my way home.. I was shook from seeing my parents and I was so angry at them. Seems like I freaked you out I guess. I'm never angry or crazy

4:36 am
almaandromeda
I just didn't know how to feel

4:37 am
almaandromeda
Not ur prob obvs

4:37 am
almaandromeda
Are you mad at me for something?

4:38 am
korbendallas_987
noo not at all. i just haven't been on IG

4:39 am
almaandromeda
K

4:39 am
korbendallas_987
I don't really like IG it kinda depresses me

4:40 am
korbendallas_987
trying not to be glued to my phone

4:47 am
almaandromeda
I understand yo. That's why I love that song Phone Down. Sometimes it's what's up. 👍 Autumn is good for recharging.

October 18th, 2017

8:15 pm

almaandromeda

Hope u r good.. I'm sorry if I bothered u or offended u in some way. I can see you on here so I think I get it now. Be well and if u feel like it plz keep me posted on any big news.

8:41 pm

almaandromeda

Stay awesome. And inspired. Now that you've been 'all u can be' you can be more than you've ever been. The 'sky' is the old limit. Take care.

9:37 pm

almaandromeda

Btw it's all ether ✅

October 19th, 2017

1:52 am

korbendallas_987

?? no clue, again what you are talking about but i do know that you have a gud, gud hubby—hang onto him. they're not common

1:59 am

almaandromeda

Hes the best

2:00 am

almaandromeda

Peace out yo

344

NOVEMBER 2017_

November 18th, 2017

10:34 am
korbendallas_987

10:43 am
almaandromeda
🖤

10:44 am
almaandromeda
How are you?

7:11 pm
korbendallas_987
ok

8:22 pm
almaandromeda

8:22 pm
almaandromeda
I'm ok too

8:24 pm
almaandromeda
Did you hear that I will be a grandma 🐥

8:45 pm
almaandromeda
39 and a granny.. It's weird.

10:18 pm
almaandromeda
what's up with you?

November 19th, 2017

1:33 am
korbendallas_987
i didn't. congrats? sounds like a nightmare to me but i know i'm not supposed to say that to people

1:36 am
korbendallas_987
i've been better. some sort of kraken has split me open lengthwise and demands human sacrifice

2:59 am
almaandromeda
Dang it when that happens.. tell me more xo

3:02 am
almaandromeda
At 37 I was skinned alive, thrown in a lions pit and eaten as light snack by my whole family, a judge & a $20,000 lawyer. I know human sacrifice.

3:45 am
almaandromeda
What is your Kraken like? I love spooky stories...👺

0:32 am
korbendallas_987
$20K is an appetizer with what I'm dealing with. The Kraken is when the old, original, and brutal Michael comes back to Earth to eat people alive. My mom got first victim 2 nights ago. You would be appalled.

6:22 am
almaandromeda
If I was going to be appalled it would have happened by now.

November 20th, 2017

12:46 am
almaandromeda
We have been going through some darrrk Scorpio nights lately.. 🐎 the vicious stinger is out for death 💀 because of a primal urge for transformation. It feels monstrous.

348

12:52 am

almaandromeda

Could you really be worse than I have been in my most horrible Kali/Phoenix the Destroyer moments? At least you care how your mom feels afterwards. You 'feel' anything.. I have been so brutally cruel to my mom and then walked away fantasizing about doing worse. She is my only sworn enemy. There are so many sides to one 👤 person.. I want to know. Tell me about you 🙏 🍽️ I'm not scurred.

2:45 am

korbendallas_987

Who said I 'feel' anything for mom? She tried to gaslight me and I told her I will drop her off a cliff to where even her name strikes no familiarity. So threaten me, and see who comes out on top.

5:00 am

almaandromeda

I've said worse.

5:09 am

almaandromeda

You stopped liking anything of mine for a whiiile so I figured you hated me now and I almost got over it lol.. I see how you can turn on and off and open up and shut down. You are a deep dude in a shallow world, having to bore through concrete slabs just to get to the depths of yourself.

5:26 am

korbendallas_987

can't figure out a way to get you to understand that i do not get on instagram but once a week. i suppose i'll keep trying, though.

5:41 am

almaandromeda

I really don't think I'm that special either way lol.. I know you are super busy. When Richard Pryor got Multiple Sclerosis he called it M.S. for More Shit. Sometimes when it's a pile on everything feels like more shit.

7:34 pm

almaandromeda

I want to hear about your work situation... the full scoop 🍦 when you have time.

8:20 pm

almaandromeda

Christmas 🎄 wow! You guys are never invited here for the holidaze lol.. we seriously suck at that stuff. I think our house would just offend you by existing tbh haha

9:16 pm
almaandromeda
I'm just kidding

9:17 pm
almaandromeda
Are we friends?

9:19 pm
almaandromeda
I can't tell if it's ok to ask about you or not

9:19 pm
korbendallas_987
what does are we friends mean

9:19 pm
korbendallas_987
you weird me out sometimes

9:21 pm
korbendallas_987
you've asked me tons of shit and i've always answered right ?

November 29th, 2017

5:00 am
almaandromeda
Have u seen Tori Amos live?

10:41 am
korbendallas_987
never

10:41 am
korbendallas_987
prob never will

5:27 pm
almaandromeda
I saw her on Saturday night

6:05 pm
almaandromeda
Why NEVER? That's almost as long as forever.

7:59 pm
almaandromeda
She played an electric piano and a grand piano at the same time.. it was, needless to say, fucking incredible 😊 you don't think she will come to HI? Or you don't care to?

8:35 pm
korbendallas_987
she also plays a harpsichord or at least used to a lot. goddam... Professional Widow... The end of that song...

8:35 pm
korbendallas_987
nobody comes here it's too expensive to

8:35 pm
korbendallas_987
the Deftones came and lorie and i were in tears

8:38 pm
korbendallas_987
lorie isn't really into tori amos

8:38 pm
korbendallas_987
i will never see my favs like tool, APC, etc

8:40 pm
korbendallas_987
i just don't see it happening. it's like a dream, you have no control and guarantee you cannot force another like it

8:49 pm
almaandromeda
I hear you... I have a funny story about this show, and missing stuff, but I am late for this and late for that right now

351

November 30th, 2017

5:24 am
almaandromeda
weird

5:44 am
almaandromeda
I looked up APC to make sure you meant A Perfect Circle band and I saw they are playing here.. so funny because Tori was JUST here - 1 week apart.

5:46 am
almaandromeda
Have you heard of lucid dreaming?

5:46 am
korbendallas_987
of course

5:51 am
almaandromeda
It's dreaming you can control or be conscious in... I'm not going to APC, just saw it. Barely made it to Tori but that's another story □

6:45 am
almaandromeda
I have met a lot of other people who hadn't heard of lucid dreaming and other weird stuff like that. I hope I did not offend you by thinking you hadn't. Lots to know on this planet 🌍 I know nothing or less than that lol

7:13 am
almaandromeda
Thanks for answering my q's, you have been very generous with your time. If I ever write a book on pilots or the military I know who to interview ✌

352

DECEMBER 2017_

December 2nd, 2017

6:25 am
korbendallas_987
no prob

6:25 am
korbendallas_987

6:54 am
almaandromeda

@OPHELIAONFIRE_

(@ALMAANDROMEDA'S SECRET INSTAGRAM ACCOUNT)

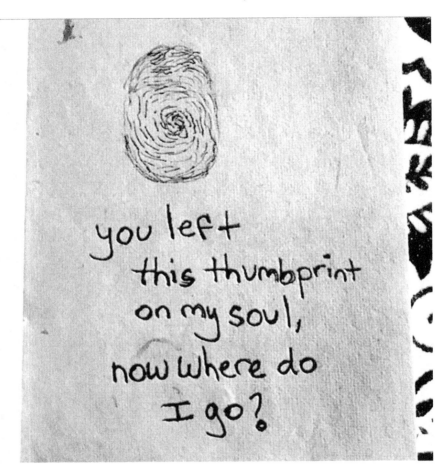

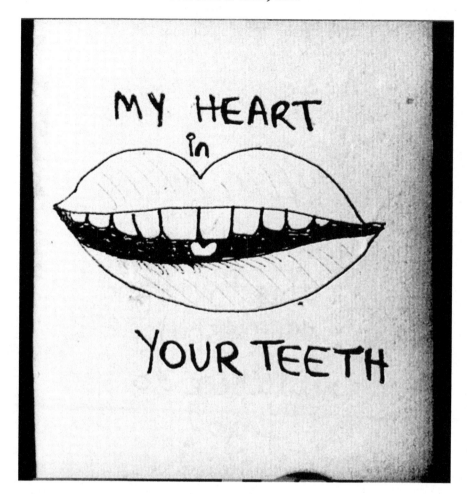

November 14th, 2017

"Trying"

I am trying
so hard
not to love you.
Your silence
does nothing
for my attempts,
you think you
are helping by
killing me quickly.
Nothing helps
only now I am dead.
Without your attention
flowers wilt and
my face is pale, it's
freezing in this cave
without your Sun that
turns to milky darkness
I can rest and sleep in,
without your enigmatic
texts to puzzle out
I stay up all night
putting together
the puzzle of why
they stopped.
I am trying so hard
not to love you,
but I am not
doing my best.

-Alma King

"Yes I Lied"

The only time I ever lied to you was
when I made it seem like
I don't love you anymore.
There couldn't be anything further from the truth.
The way you live in me is Wild Love 🖤
like a dragon bursting from my mouth.
I want to have you, in me, with me, near me, all over me.
I want to feel your stubble cheeks and I want to rub my face
all over you and kiss you everywhere.
Between every appointment and meeting I sob like
I am grieving a close death.
It is a month since we pushed each other away and I still lose hot tears
from my eyelids ten times a day.
I hate to be alone, because I sit and think of you.
I hate to be with others, because I just want to sit and think of you.
I am in a Chinese finger trap game. I can't get out.
We haven't even met yet and you have turned my life inside out.
I don't think I want to meet you,
I can not trust myself near you.

-Alma King

November 24th, 2017

"The Bid"

Before we were born
you put a bid in.
You kissed my eyes
and whispered
remember me.
Now we are here
with your black eyes
laughing at me,
your sweet fat face
always the same ratio,
and how could I forget?
Covered in masks
and on the run
you are hilarious
in your fear of me.
It was only a bid,
just an idea, before
we were born...
I don't have to
take you up on it.

-Alma King

November 24th, 2017

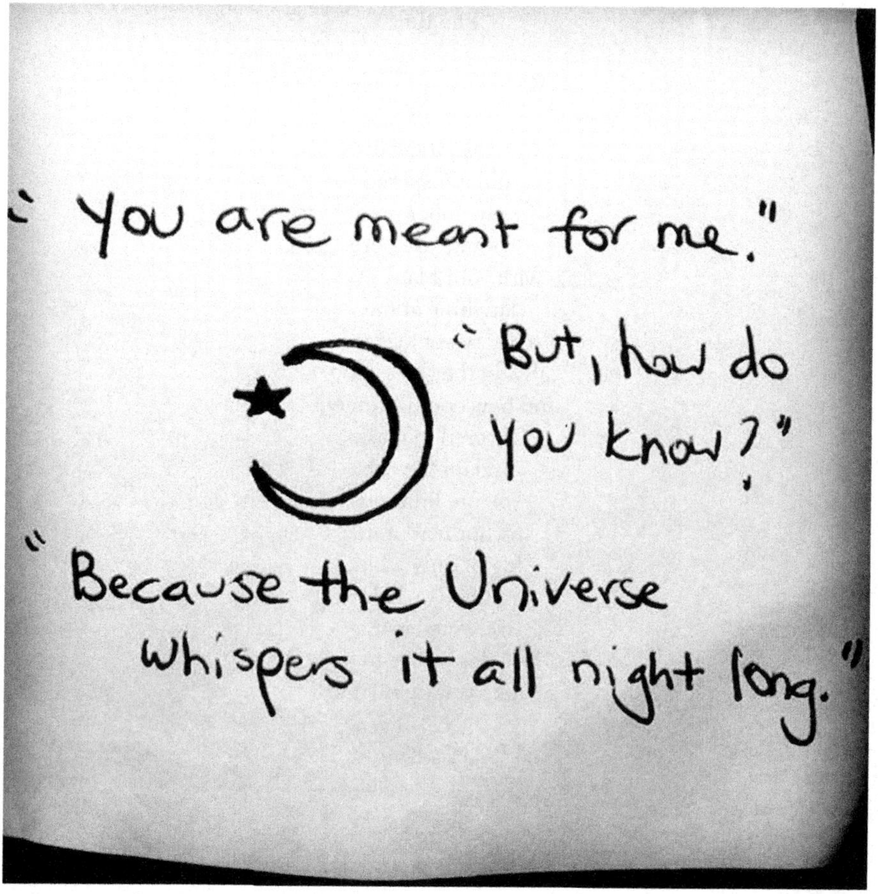

November 25th, 2017

"What Was It You Said?"

I could fight
to prove the fate
of our wings,
but who has time,
what with the weight
of things, the state
of these songs
I used to sing.
It's true, yes,
all those words
I said, but I said them
with a heavy head.
I'm a fish split
for supper, can you
make another mold
of me? I don't want
to leave this place,
the corridors are lit
here and he finishes
my sentences. I went
to bet the farm last
night but I never owned
a cow. I want to make
this clear to you but
nobody taught me how.
What was it you said?
It stayed ringing
in my head, I gave the
ghosts their proper rest
but some still want me dead..
What was it you said?
I am a stranger and it
gets stranger, a distant
particle of You.
A freak, yes, but you
are the dangerous one ☝ and we both know that it's true.

-Alma King

"Last Look"

He said
with his eyes dim,
'Look! If I loved
you then I would
fetch the stars and moon
from the sky for you.
But I don't. So I won't!
You have to believe me.
I don't remember anything.
I never said I loved you.
You are indescribable,
but only because
I don't care to try.
I tear down worlds
and build castles
for mine and you would
know if that were you.' She said, 'Look!
You think that's not clear?
Who put me in this
awkward place,
eating dirt, head over heels,
neck crushed
in a headstand
to the death,
no trophy for the trouble?
I fell down for you,
yes, but I was a baby
before this aging,
you were milk
and love was sweet,
now there is a
worm left in the bottle,
since I loved you first,
it's mine to eat.'
He lifted his eyes
and said, 'Go.'
She closed her eyes
just for show.

-Alma King

"Pity Party For One"

So leave me alone then
Get out of my way
I don't want to talk to you
Don't want you to stay
Every word that comes out
Is another hard hit
About love you are giving her
All the sweetness I've missed
You sound like my mother,
My son, father too,
No one remembers me
So why should you?
It's fine, I'm OK,
But really, leave me alone
It's hard enough living
In this hell on my own.

-Alma King

your love
is quiet
but it's O.K.
I like quiet...

"Weeping Willow" 🌳

I'm the weeping willow
and I belong to you
You won't come and destroy me
In fact, you don't know what to do
When you left me without passion
The vines drew up my side
When you left with all your love, dear
I might as well have died.
And now I'm the weeping willow
You'd know me on sight
I'm the one with all the big space
and everything to hide
I can keep it dark forever
Anywhere my shadow lands
And no I won't forgive the sunlight
For when she took away my man.

-Alma King

Warrior with the
FAT FACE,

Almond eyes, and sweet
smile... I would
recognize you
* ANYWHERE *

"Nightswimming"

Poisoned, swollen, laid down,
your wings are lorn, my dear.
All I have are these thin wrist
hands and magic touches but
I am the only healing
you are not allowed,
so you swallow white lies
and make them last long
enough to see the reason
that you eat them.
How does it all pan out?
Under the mistletoe,
under that pitcher you
brought me, so long ago,
the river was alive that night
you took me as far as I could go,
and then we went night
swimming in the ocean of stars,
you didn't tell me I could die this much,
I could cry this much,
the ocean 🏊 my tears for the
drive in the morning, to the airport,
to the tsunami of my midlife tragedy.
I leave then, but for now, my end,
this ocean of stars is what I'm drowning in.

-Alma King

"Flower"

How surprised you are
to notice, this whole time
I was your beating heart.
You were still down
in the thorns when you
heard the whoosh of fast
moving blood and looked
up angry, because you
only feel at all if you're in pain,
but the blood of my heart is
warm and calls you softly,
urgently, constantly, to climb
up the sticky vines and
learn about the Flower of our Love.
I won't hurt you, darling,
but I will let you hurt me.
I won't leave you, my only,
but I will leave you be.

-Alma King

November 29th, 2017

"I Can Fly"

Yes, but you can fly.
The bridge I am standing
on is the highest in the city,
blue steel spikes curve the sky
and they never ask me why
I'm standing here, looking down.
You can fly but I also have these quiet
wings I've never used, golden tattered
purple edged feathers that will light up
in the air if I can just pick up speed,
you can fly, I still want to, it's not the
same as wanting to die. No one takes
me to the sky, and I have stopped
asking for rides. This bridge will still be here,
is already laughing at me, a midlife tragedy,
nameless on the TV, body lost and empty..
but I can fly, and once I hit the sky,
it will be the bridge who just stands by.

-Alma King

"Caged Bird"

The thousand things
I could have said,
the words that became
this space instead.
Nothing coming
from these lips,
I know too much,
each word a whip.
The way my heart
is feeling now,
my love, I would just
take you down.
Better to quiet
this fat mouth
that you should
just be kissing now.
I can't control
what may be said
if I say what's
on my mind instead
of love you with
a simple heart,
every moment a brand
new goldfish start.
Is this the way
they do the love here?
Lonely, drugged up,
distracted in fear?
Your face shape is angel,
you know who you cage inside.
I would help to liberate you
but I'm scared of what we both may find.

-Alma King

"Get Free"

Everything about you
bothers me. I don't like
your self pity, the oozing
loneliness like Pluto's
termites leaching from
your mouth, Satan's breath
is a stench on your lips in
every word you slur, you
are sad, you feel small.
You have hurt indiscriminately,
you loathe me for my
feminine power, for
existing and looking this good in a dress.
I don't like your obsession
with vanity or jealousy or
money or death or killing,
I don't like your exceedingly
young entourage and the
level of 'groupie' you have
made out of some. I don't like
how lightly you throw around your power,
it has hurt people. I don't
like how quickly you give
your power up. I don't like
how you stop and start at Love
or care nothing about the Sacred.
You have hidden so long
you can't find your own 'damned' self
and I don't like how you rob the world
of your beauty. I don't like
what a waste this whole
life will be, for the world,
because you never saw your
real power or true gorgeous
nature but instead lived out the lie till you are
dead and buried with the worms.
Will they at least cremate you?
When will you be free?

-Alma King

November 30th, 2017

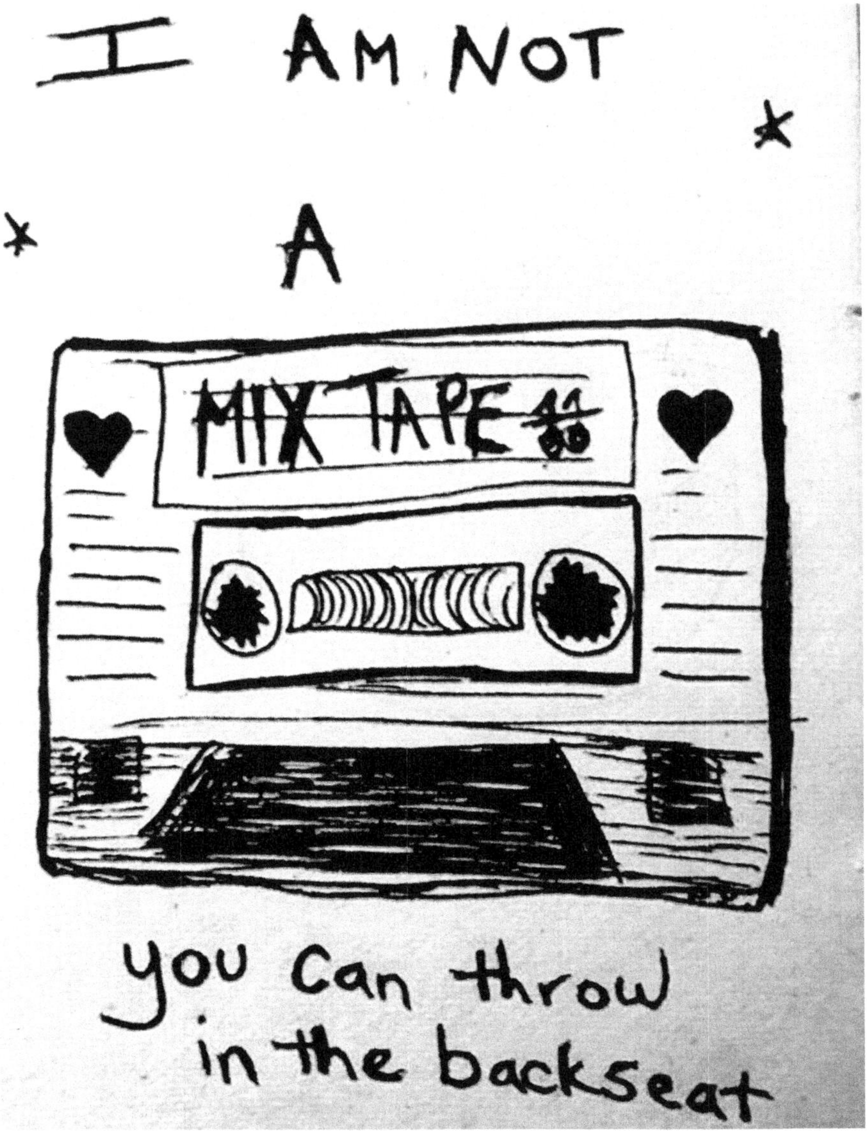

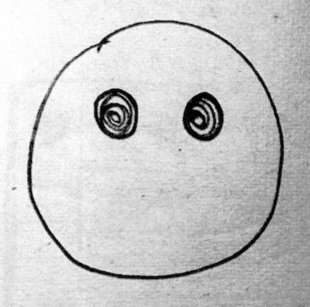

December 1st, 2017

"No Words" 🙂

Oh, I'm sorry
by the way,
for all those things
I did and did not say,
for leaving you
alone out there,
for acting like
I didn't care,
for faking
and blaming
and starting
and running,
for knowing
and shaming
you for the
one thing that
I wasn't,
for holding you
and dropping you,
like glass out
on the street,
for telling you
I loved you
when it's hotter
than that heat.
I'm sorry I was
busy and not ready
when you got here,
I'm sorry that I
took the easy route
and simply forgot, dear.
I'm sorry that I'm sorry
instead of running
this old world
and impressing you
with my powers
even though I'm just ☝ girl.

-Alma King

December 2nd, 2017

"Love Is Free" 🖤

How can I be jealous?
You were never mine,
always yours or
someone else's,
what am I to ask for
but some crumbs off
of your table, I really
don't eat much, time
is ticking out the
message like Morse
code in tiny dots and
dashes, I don't want
to wait for ashes,
I want a seat in all
your classes. I am a
magician and it comes easy,
I want everything
for you. Lust fills
your cup and I like
to see you full.
There are days like
yesterday when I am
so pale I am see through.
You fought too hard
to win her, it's a prize
I won't pry from you.
Your face is sweet
enough for me, and your
heart tells me the truth.

-Alma King

December 2nd, 2017

"Nature"

If I am Nature then
you just come, naturally,
you are the forged iron
from the metals in my belly,
you are the buildings from
my dirt, the planes from my
dreams, you are the
beginning and the end of
things. If I am a Goddess
then you are an Avatar, a
deity, made heavenly and
discarded here
unceremoniously, you are
star matter turned to anger
and poured out raw over
the Earth. If I am rest then
you are the Awakening. If
you are Final Sleep then I
am just settling in. If this
what it is to live or die then
take me on the ride of my
life, I want to fall in
before I fry and
scream out this is fucking
WHY, all those times you
asked me and I lied, so
scared of my conditions and
getting left behind, but this
is fucking why, my nature
and your nurture, my
creation and your fall, my
nothing and your everything,
my empty and your all.

-Alma King

December 2nd, 2017

"Wandering"

Believe me when I say,
I am lost without you.
The children are wandering
alone, there is no fire in the
pit, no wood to burn, no
meat hung on strings to dry
for winter, there is nothing,
no wine, no water either, the
tap is dry, there is no way to
fill this thirst, there is no
home to hold my hurts, there
are no stars left, no sky, no
bed to cradle my head when
I die, there is nothing, I am
lost here, we are wandering
alone, until you call me
I am falling, until you
call me your own.

-Alma King

"Tree Of Life"

We are connected
but you're not breathing
holding your breath
hoping I don't see you
We are connected
but I'm alone here
you sent me first
and then forgot me dear
We are connected
but you don't care
dirty laundry and
red flag scares
We are connected
and I found sanity
in the grocery line
behind the candy
We are connected
but I don't care
I have to make do here
however I dare.

-Alma King

December 3rd, 2017

December 3rd, 2017

"Messages"

I've been drawing this flower
for at least a thousand years.
I thought maybe you would
see it, come find me here.
Always the same, five petals,
one 🐌 stem, spiral from
the center, and then I do it
again. This is my message,
this is my SOS to you.
I've left crop circles
and sent snail mail too.
Emails fail and my voice,
it breaks. If I reach out
in red I'm afraid of the
monster it makes.
I love you like the last jade
bowl from the 1st Emperor
of China. You are more
precious than a feather
from a bird outside of Time.
I won't crush you, I won't
keep you, I won't speak
to you if that's what it takes,
but in these five petals there is a message
and yes, we both know what's at stake.

-Alma King

December 4th, 2017

It was so sweet,
those things you said....
that night
you were on drugs.

"Big Cat"

You are hiding.
I can see your form
behind the bushes,
feel the heat of
your powerful body
stalking helpless prey.
You are hiding, I can
smell your desire and
fear, your intrigue
and despair, your anger
and shame, the futility.
You are all big cat
and patience, stalking
yourself, you forgot
the prey, forgot you
were hungry. You
don't know what blood
tastes like, the zoo
feeds you strictly apples.

-Alma King

It's easy
to fall
for you.

You never
put your
half in,
and I
can't get
mine out.

WE HAVE THE SAME SKY.

December 9th, 2017

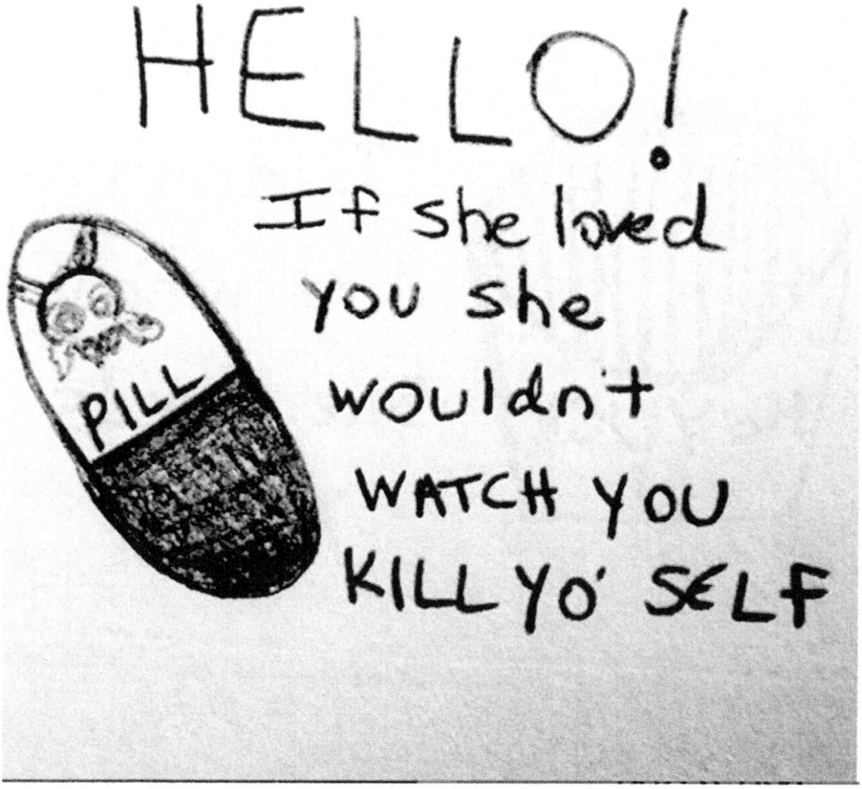

I see how you two are a match.

YOU have a
LOCK on me.
Please, give me
BACK my key.

You are
not mine
to
fight for.
♡

"Have you ever kissed?"

"No, But
I've thought
about it..."

December 13th, 2017

"Prayers Just For You" 🙏

Prayers
for my love
prayers for
his aching heart
prayers for
his loneliness
prayers for
his friends
prayers for
his confusion
prayers for
his life
prayers for
his body
prayers for
his mind
prayers for
his uniqueness
prayers for
his strength
prayers for
his desire
prayers for
his peace
prayers for
his vision
prayers for
his sweet face
prayers for
his new joy.

-Alma King

At least I
finally found you.
I have relaxed a little
deeper ever since.

I'M AS STUBBORN
AS A BULL

WHEN IT COMES
TO LOVING YOU
♡

Definitely DON'T
stop buying her Stuff.

STUFF FROM A MALL
GAP
$ STUFF ONLINE
-AMAZON-
$ STUFF AT A CUTE BOUTIQUE
tattoos
jeeps
trips
OH MY!
$CUTE STUFF

She would have
nothing to post on
— IG —
#stuffnstuff

December 14th, 2017

"Last Words"

Though
I couldn't fly
I always tried.
I'll leave
the body,
take the light
and I loved you
till I died.

-Alma King

December 14th, 2017

"Pwnd"

Her darkness is a
sickness, a pill you
swallowed and can't
spit out. She owns you,
is written on you, she
drags you around by
your pig snout. Your
balls are in a sling and
she holds the string
that keeps them tight,
you won't move without
her permission, she holds
your virility and your light.
Her fangs are obvious, I can
see the blood, her eyes
never smile or have lit
in Love. She is sitting on
your head taking your
breath and you'll just
wait until your dead.
Why do I care?

-Alma King

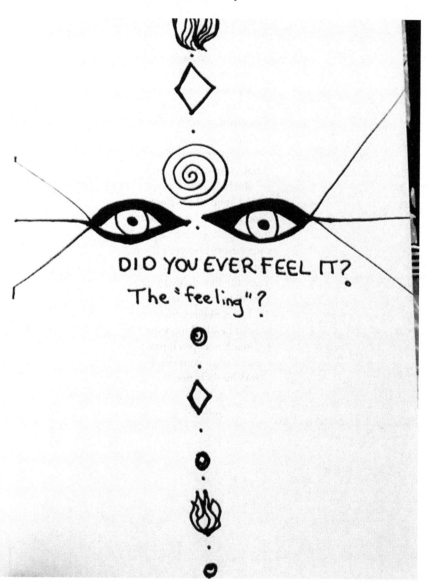

I miss your
fat face.
♡

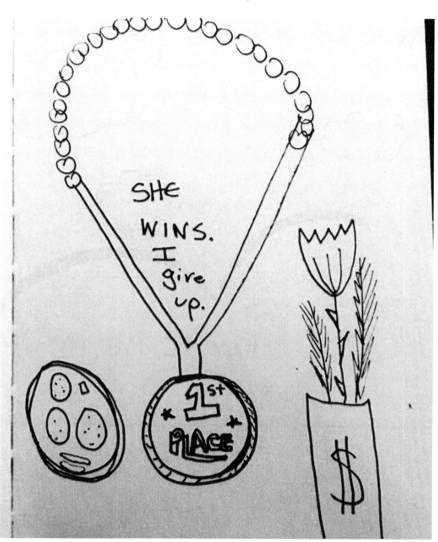

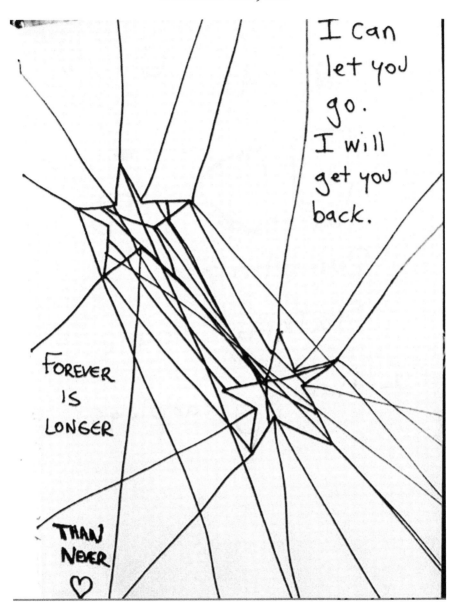

December 28th, 2017

"When You Visit A Witch"

When you come visit
bring me the head
of your boss. Bring
me the strings your lover
had you wrapped in.
Bring me a white
flower in a crystal
vase. Bring me a
small bottle filled
with your tears.
Bring me shards
from your favorite
toy after you
smashed it.
Bring me your sex,
your smell, the feel
of you. Bring me
your anger and
lay it across my
body, watch it turn
to drunken trust.
Bring me your smile.
Bring me your eyes. 👀
Bring me leather and
wool and black ink.
Bring me a drink. 🥃

-Alma King

December 28th, 2017

"To Be Honest"

To be honest you are not
a mathematical order
designed by the star of Venus,
your face does not stop me,
stop everything, I am not
rolling constantly in the
dry field of your last words.
You do not have a finger
deep through the middle of me,
I am not squirming and moving
on the dream of your lap.
I don't want that! I don't want
anything! You aren't the only one
to 'do that thing', and honestly,
this is nothing, I have no feelings,
I don't whisper your name or
cum to your face, I don't cry
hot tears in lonely disgrace.
I don't miss you, I don't want you.
You don't compel me like the
moon moves the oceans,
you don't have a spell on me,
I did not drink your potion.
I'm not made for you.
I don't think of you every morning.
I won't wait for you.
This is not a love story.

-Alma King

December 29th, 2017

"Hunger"

I feel like
sinking my teeth in.
Arching my body
around your body
like a playful kitten
and after that I
want to fucking
tear you apart.

-Alma King

I don't start talking to you because I will never want to stop.

January 1st, 2018

"Starlight is Silent"

Your laugh is silent.
I don't know the tone your
voice makes when you're tired,
can't hear what it would sound
like to make love to you,
there is no bell to ring,
I can't hear a thing. Your
face is nameless, a lump in my
throat and warmth inside, there's
no place to hide, reflection pools
inside your eyes. I have no proof
of our love, not a single formula
of alphabet to test and disprove
the disbelievers. In the records of
eternity it is all kept safely and I
sweep and clean there nightly in my
dreams, a mad woman pacing,
waiting for the star I don't hear
or see yet that you are.

-Alma King

441

our private jokes are now just my thoughts in my head.

January 12th, 2018

"By My Selfie"

It's written
across my face that
your slap left marks.
I've been hiding
in dark alleys
till the blood dried
and they would stop
asking questions.
Am I different now?
Wouldn't you be?
Mother Earth
got laid in the dirt
with a mouthful of
her own humility.
Your silence is
the only answer
I need, the only words
I've ever heard we're
whispered lies so
this is actually nice.

-Alma King

two worlds apart

together
you never stay
and you never go.

January 18th, 2018

"Offerings" 🔥🔥🔥

I drew
this flower
on the new moon 🌙
in the morning light
and I burned it
that dark night.
Every line is a word
you said I am trying
to forget. Every
fire takes to ashes
what I can't let
go of yet.

-Alma King

"Hanged Man"

The more
I watch you hang
from your toes
from her mouth 👄
the more
I understand
why you have
hated women.
If only you knew
the womb of them
who love you like
I love you, every cell
of you a cherishing..
but no, they can't
love you like I love you🎵
so you don't know
what it's like to have
a woman who is kind,
who loves your face
without consequence
or to prop her up.
I won't want anything
from you. Anytime I do
I step further away
because I know to love
you is to not hold you
in hooks and hang you.
I don't want your
devotion. Don't swear
your life to me.
Just love me,
if you wanna...
Naturally.

-Alma King

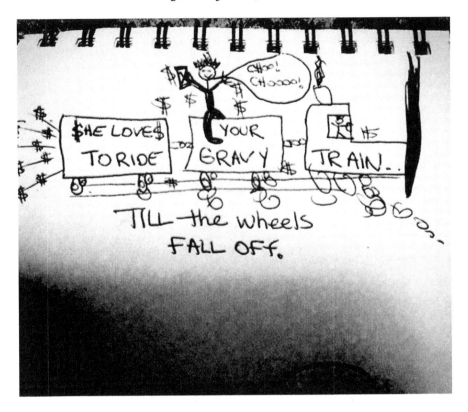

suc·cu·bus
ˈsəkyəbəs/
noun

a female demon believed to have sexual intercourse with sleeping men. THAT is why you need to stay woke but whatever makes your train go yo

You're gone so I've got to stay high all the time 🖊️🔫🍷 I loved you forever and always will 🌙👁️💜Michael 💜🖐️😔

JANUARY 2018_

January 31st, 2018

5:38 pm
almaandromeda
My friend posted her helicopter view, thought of you.

5:38 pm
almaandromeda
🦋 𝐖

5:38 pm
almaandromeda
not to rhyme like a fucking dork

FEBRUARY 2018_

February 1st, 2018

3:51 am
korbendallas_987
i'll take some pics for you one of these days

5:24 am
almaandromeda
Please do 🦋

February 2nd, 2018

8:28 am
almaandromeda
Thank you btw for thinking of that when you do 🚁📷 My only helicopter views are from watching the Amazing Race so far! And my way awesomer life having friends I guess lol :/

February 19th, 2018

12:58 am
almaandromeda
It's a boy! My grandson coming in 5/8/18 🌀

1:34 am
korbendallas_987
congrats. almost another cancer i think

6:10 am
almaandromeda
That's true! Especially if he waits 2 1/2 weeks after his due date like my baby Soquel did. Wouldn't be the worst 😊How is the OG King 👑 of all Crab 🦀 things?

7:17 pm
korbendallas_987
guess i'll find this week on more news. easily the most stressful year of my life, has taken its toll on my body time and time through

February 20th, 2018

2:57 am
almaandromeda
I am sending you 🖤 and healing energy for what you are going thru.

3:08 am
almaandromeda
Is the news job related? How have you been dealing with everything? Stress and healing are hard together. Lmn if I can share a healing meditation 🧘 ♀ I am thinking of for you.

4:34 am
korbendallas_987
please do. it is job related.

4:57 am
almaandromeda
I will tonight 👍

5:46 am
almaandromeda
1st - in Astrology you just went through an eclipse 2/15 right on your rising sign degree of Aquarius which is your body, your personality, your physical operating system on this plane. That will affect so many aspects of life. This is a bookend (exactly opposite) to the eclipse in August 2017... stuff coming up for true resolution.

6:47 am
almaandromeda
Some intuitive words for you from me...
I am not my job.
I am not my car.
I am not my pension.
I am amazing.
I am powerful.
I am strong.
I am not my job.
I am not my past.
I am not anyone else.
I am intelligent.
I am resourceful.

458

I am wise.
I am not my job.
I am not my cash flow.
I am not alone.
I am loved.
I am supported.
I am awesome 😎 💪

6:51 am
almaandromeda
😊 feel free 🎈 take care xo

6:55 am
korbendallas_987
thanks so much but it's so easy to say on the outside. but when you're on the inside and your world is crashing, it's jarring.

6:55 am
korbendallas_987
so fuckin hard, i never fail historically

7:00 am
almaandromeda
What are you going through? I am curious. Please tell me if you want.

7:01 am
almaandromeda
I am all ears 👂 and no 🐵⚖️

7:05 am
almaandromeda
I did sit in court 1.5 yrs ago (around your age) across from my own mom, stepdad and only son as they sued me with fancy lawyers for custody of my 16 year old kid. That was my whole world.. before that. I am living in the after world now. I do know how it feels to lose everything you identify with all at once.

7:12 am
almaandromeda
5 of my best friends came and surrounded me in love and support, I'm so grateful. It was 100% the worst day of my life.

7:13 am
almaandromeda
I thought I was going to die but I am doing much better in a lot of ways now.

459

7:13 am
korbendallas_987
yes. identity

7:14 am
korbendallas_987
i pissed hot for performance enhancers

7:14 am
korbendallas_987
please don't let anybody think less of me

7:14 am
almaandromeda

7:14 am
korbendallas_987
normally u would guess the military wouldn't care but nope

7:14 am
korbendallas_987
so my identity has to be resurrected

7:15 am
almaandromeda
You are still waiting to know if you stay in the job?

7:16 am
almaandromeda
Or do you know?

7:16 am
korbendallas_987
still waiting

7:16 am
korbendallas_987
8 months now

7:16 am
korbendallas_987
scariest year of my life

7:17 am
korbendallas_987
lorie is finishing her masters in may

7:17 am
almaandromeda
Oh my gosh I bet

7:17 am
almaandromeda
Are you using that as a goal?

7:17 am
almaandromeda
Still thinking of rich desert 🐫 lands?

7:18 am
korbendallas_987
yes

7:19 am
korbendallas_987
no i just don't wanna get the boot before she finishes

7:20 am
almaandromeda
I get it... how are you feeling about the identity part? Are you daydreaming of a different you outside of army yet?

7:20 am
almaandromeda
Imagination helps to prepare our minds for new experiences.

7:24 am
korbendallas_987
yea i daydream it's just hard to plan anything when you don't know anything

7:25 am
korbendallas_987
i catastrophize about losing everything and begin to obsess uncontrollably

7:27 am
almaandromeda
Actually, I know what you mean... I am going through a holding pattern and I am having panic around loss right now... uggh. It's not fun.

7:27 am
almaandromeda
I don't think anybody has it down yet. 🫠

7:32 am
almaandromeda
Thanks 🙏 for sharing more about why it's tough right now... you are human having a human life. I don't think less of you 💫 it's impossible.

8:09 pm
korbendallas_987
not impossible

8:09 pm
korbendallas_987
i feel i've let many down

8:10 pm
almaandromeda
You never held me up lol

8:10 pm
almaandromeda
I just think you are awesome 😎

8:11 pm
korbendallas_987
not sure why. it's a cool story but im just like everyone else

8:11 pm
almaandromeda
How? You can fly.

8:12 pm
almaandromeda
You are not like anyone I've ever met.

8:12 pm
korbendallas_987
i can.

8:13 pm
almaandromeda
I'm just cheering you on and wish you the best 👍 I'm like that.

8:14 pm
korbendallas_987
i do appreciate it. just gotta figure out what i'm gonna do. was on the phone with my mom just now and didn't have the heart to tell her.

8:15 pm
almaandromeda
You haven't told her so far at all? Or just the latest..

8:15 pm
almaandromeda
When you tell her you will feel better

8:16 pm
korbendallas_987
i told her that i had a seizure do to stress last week and that i went to the doc today. he cited severe stress and depression

8:16 pm
korbendallas_987
so i'll be out of a job one way or another

8:16 pm
almaandromeda
Are you on depression meds?

8:18 pm
korbendallas_987
he is going to start me after i see a neurologist. the ER did a bunch of tests on me and everything came back negative. i have been extremely depressed in the military but hid it because my job relies on it

8:18 pm
korbendallas_987
i'm to the point where i can't hide it anymore

8:19 pm
korbendallas_987
nothing is ever good enough

8:19 pm
korbendallas_987
all self-stemming

8:20 pm
almaandromeda
Gosh Michael.. honestly I wish I could just give you a big hug. You have taken on so much! You are sooo strong 💪 and you feel like you should be able to deal with everything perfectly. You have been through so much. It makes sense why you are hurting.

8:21 pm
almaandromeda
You only have one body and one life. You are very hard on yourself.

8:21 pm
korbendallas_987
it's all tumbling down. i used to be strong

8:21 pm
korbendallas_987
i am

8:21 pm
almaandromeda
You will come out stronger

8:21 pm
almaandromeda
You will see that you won't die

8:21 pm
almaandromeda
That you only renew

8:22 pm
almaandromeda
More beautiful and more authentically powerful

8:22 pm
korbendallas_987
i wish u were right

8:22 pm
korbendallas_987
starting to lose hope

8:23 pm
almaandromeda
No matter what happens you can do this 👐 Please just be nicer to yourself. I feel
like coming down there and slapping 👋 some sense into you lol

8:23 pm
korbendallas_987
i need it

8:23 pm
korbendallas_987
my mom just said same thing

8:23 pm
almaandromeda
You really do haha

8:23 pm
korbendallas_987
called me crying last week after lorie spilled the beans

8:24 pm
almaandromeda
She needs to know you as the real you

8:24 pm
almaandromeda
She will keep loving you

8:24 pm
korbendallas_987
mom thinks what my shrink said is right -ptsd from when i was very very young

8:24 pm
almaandromeda
I am sure that's true.. then compounded with new traumas

8:24 pm
korbendallas_987
i grew up in a violent household whether it was my dad or paul's dad

8:25 pm
almaandromeda
Really.. violent to you or in front of you?

8:26 pm
almaandromeda
Both suck. My family was violent in front of me to each other but my trauma was behind closed doors and quiet.

8:26 pm
almaandromeda

8:28 pm
almaandromeda
Every day is new. You still have the rest of your life to live and you are worth the effort you make for your own happiness. It's possible. I promise. I have shed so much trauma and ptsd from sexual abuse and lorture from my 3 brothers.

8:28 pm
korbendallas_987
never to me always in front of me

8:28 pm
almaandromeda
They would babysit and burn me, hold me down, molest me, lock me in closets etc

8:29 pm
korbendallas_987
dam

8:29 pm
almaandromeda
It is a lot to carry but you can let it go too

8:29 pm
korbendallas_987
it's hard to let go when you aren't aware

8:29 pm
almaandromeda
My ascendant degree is "After a heavy storm, a rainbow 🌈"

8:29 pm
korbendallas_987
i'm talking at infant stage on up

8:29 pm
almaandromeda
But you can't say you are not lol

8:29 pm
korbendallas_987
it's a part of me

8:30 pm
almaandromeda
I know what you mean seriously

8:30 pm
almaandromeda
I met my bros at 3

8:30 pm
almaandromeda
But before that my mom rejected me completely

8:30 pm
almaandromeda
So I was alone day in day out as an infant 👶

8:31 pm
almaandromeda
Just quiet... and loneliness. She was insanely depressed.

8:31 pm
almaandromeda
It's just aaaalllll shit other people did who fucked shit up

8:32 pm
almaandromeda
I am more awesome than that.. the real me is in here just still shining, and I understand that people who hurt are going to hurt others

8:33 pm
korbendallas_987
yea you are very nice

8:33 pm
almaandromeda
At some point... Michael... when do you just forgive them... and yourself?

8:34 pm
almaandromeda
You are worth it. 👍 You are worth the work. 💪

8:36 pm
korbendallas_987
i was until i got in trouble. everything changes at that point

8:37 pm
korbendallas_987
i dont mean to argue with you just trying to show you a glimpse of half a second in my brain

8:37 pm
almaandromeda
I love it inside there lol

8:38 pm
korbendallas_987
not me. maybe i can get lobotomized

8:38 pm
almaandromeda
And I don't mean to argue with you but you are even more awesome now 😎 you are getting to the real you, the health of you, the honest you inside. It's so cool.

8:38 pm
korbendallas_987
it may be nice on the outside looking in

8:39 pm
korbendallas_987
i don't consider it an argument everywhere

8:40 pm
almaandromeda
I will bet you 💰 that you are happier in 1 year after this whole tower episode of your life.

8:40 pm
korbendallas_987
i'd be willing to lose that bet

8:42 pm
almaandromeda
I got $100 on it and that's a lot for me lol 😂 But I am sure.. This kind of stuff comes for our throat to release us. You will be different, but that's not always a bad thing.

8:43 pm
korbendallas_987
don't care about different, just happiness

8:43 pm
almaandromeda
Get me some pics before you lose your job lol 📷

8:43 pm
korbendallas_987
started meditating daily again and it helps a smidge

8:43 pm
korbendallas_987
too late for that

8:43 pm
korbendallas_987
just what's on my instagram

8:43 pm
korbendallas_987
i have some vid on my computer

8:44 pm
almaandromeda
Happiness is an inside job 🖤 I love that you are meditating. Deep breaths are your best friend. Breathe in.... and then let it out.

8:44 pm
korbendallas_987
yea

8:44 pm
almaandromeda
That is your own space for yourself. Your own breath.

8:45 pm
almaandromeda
The ocean and the sand are good places to leave the bullshit too.

8:45 pm
almaandromeda
The earth absorbs it all

8:45 pm
almaandromeda
Takes it from you

8:45 pm
almaandromeda
And transmutes it to neutral energy

8:46 pm
almaandromeda
The Earth can take your pain. Send it down out of you and into the ground.

8:46 pm
almaandromeda
I am an earth sign and it is part of my healing magicz.

8:47 pm
almaandromeda
You know tho inside you where happiness lives and how to live in it 🖤 👍 I trust you infinitely to heal yourself. 🙏

8:48 pm
korbendallas_987
i think the craziest part is that i don't wanna die. i just don't know what the next step is aside from finding out what is going to happen to me

8:49 pm
almaandromeda
How cool that means you want to LIVE 😎 💪 living is awesome. We need you here.

8:49 pm
almaandromeda
What do you do now during the days and stuff?

8:50 pm
korbendallas_987
nothin. can't fly. sulk in the house

8:50 pm
korbendallas_987
my unit is deployed to louisiana

8:51 pm
almaandromeda
Oh wow.. gosh you are seriously going through it.

8:51 pm
almaandromeda
What I hear is you have lots of time to love on yourself and do some good R&R 👻

8:53 pm
korbendallas_987
i suppose. should be working but hard to do when you're grounded

8:55 pm
almaandromeda
Why do you think you got tapped for this when it's an army thing usually to harden up with PE's? Is it personal or random or do you know..

9:06 pm
korbendallas_987
that i can't tell u. i don't know if someone at the gym said something or what.

9:06 pm
korbendallas_987
but the army rarely tests for it

9:06 pm
korbendallas_987
took 3 months to get the result

9:06 pm
almaandromeda
Haters lol

9:06 pm
almaandromeda
When will you tell your mom?

9:07 pm
korbendallas_987
i don't know

9:07 pm
korbendallas_987
i guess when i know something for sure. no sense in making her worry more than she does

9:09 pm
korbendallas_987
it's a goddam trainwreck

9:09 pm
almaandromeda
Makes sense.. will you keep this random girl in Seattle posted? 😶 You are in my thoughts 🖤

9:10 pm
korbendallas_987
i will. just ashamed

9:10 pm
korbendallas_987
shame is the strongest human emotion

9:10 pm
almaandromeda
Please don't be.

9:10 pm
almaandromeda
Shed that shit.

9:10 pm
almaandromeda
Before I come down there and slap 👋 you

9:10 pm
almaandromeda
You are AMAZING 😎

9:11 pm
almaandromeda
You are just going thru it right now

9:12 pm
almaandromeda
Shame can really fuck with you... please be nice to yourself 🙏

9:14 pm
almaandromeda
I am going through a serious transition right now but I can't hate myself for it. People change.

9:15 pm
korbendallas_987
you're just fine.. u do what u want to do and are happy

9:25 pm
almaandromeda
Believe it if u wanna 🤷 I am changing... everything. I will be fine tho because I want to be. 💪

9:32 pm
korbendallas_987
i want it bad

9:45 pm
almaandromeda
I want you bad lol

9:48 pm
korbendallas_987
🖤

9:49 pm
almaandromeda
🖤

9:50 pm
korbendallas_987
one of the most jarring aspects is that it affects my whole family. is ANYTHING bright in my future?

9:52 pm
almaandromeda
Your future's so bright you gotta 😎

9:53 pm
korbendallas_987
u always say that. surely u have some kind of bad news for me

9:53 pm
almaandromeda
Especially because it affects your whole family... try to imagine a world where people don't rely on you for their happiness or expectations. Where you have already broken up that plastic floating castle and you can really lay back and float on the water..

9:54 pm
korbendallas_987
because now, all this worrying i've been doing for 30 years has culminated to be a self-fulfilling prophecy

9:54 pm
almaandromeda
Perfect timing apparently

9:54 pm
korbendallas_987
god that sounds so nice

9:54 pm
almaandromeda
You've been working hard at this lol

9:55 pm
korbendallas_987
it's either perfect or my help or the most imperfect

9:56 pm
almaandromeda
You have been systematically creating a life for yourself and at the same time tearing it down in your mind..

9:57 pm
korbendallas_987
yep

9:57 pm
almaandromeda
What else besides flying do you love?

9:57 pm
korbendallas_987
music and gym

9:58 pm
korbendallas_987
no gym since my two elbow surgeries last month

9:58 pm
korbendallas_987
i can't believe i had a seizure. that's when i became no longer comfortable hiding it

10:04 pm
almaandromeda
Oh my gosh you really seriously had a seizure Michael? 🙁 I don't how I didn't catch that. I thought you were just saying that. Shit. Wtf? Is it just stress?

10:04 pm
almaandromeda
What were you doing when it came on?

10:11 pm
almaandromeda
I don't know why 👻 ♀ I just feel like giving you a good ass whooping... you have
not been good to your body and now your body is fighting back. What will it take
for you to be gentle with yourself? A karate chop to the head? 👊 🤸 A big hug and
kiss? 😊One time in the store I overheard this dad say to his little kid "What do you
need, a spanking or a hug?" 😂

February 21st, 2018

2:05 am
korbendallas_987
i hadnt slept in a couple of days with no appetite and no water

2:06 am
korbendallas_987
my body just shut down on itself. i'm still force feeding but it hasn't happened
since

2:06 am
korbendallas_987
ER doc cited severe exhaustion

2:13 am
korbendallas_987
i turned the light off and watched tv which i never do

2:14 am
korbendallas_987
next thing i know i'm walking on my own accord to an ambulance

2:33 am
almaandromeda
What is force feeding?

2:35 am
almaandromeda
And are you still on the PE's? Do they make you not sleep/not eat? 🐱

2:47 am
almaandromeda
I am really sorry you had to experience that btw. Sounds fucking confusing and

476

scary too. I am glad you are taking the wake up call to heart

2:49 am
almaandromeda
Since you feel so many people rely on you... they also rely on the health of your body. To care for your own true physical health is actually a loving act to others. Keeps you around longer 💨

2:52 am
almaandromeda
😂 🙏thanks for letting me bug you with all my q's and opinions btw lol - you are kinder than you think, I think.

3:30 am
korbendallas_987
FUCK no i'm not on anything

3:32 am
korbendallas_987
i think i am very kind but it's gottten me no where

3:32 am
korbendallas_987
what's funny is the army is hemorrhaging guys like me so them kicking me out blows menawsy

3:32 am
korbendallas_987
me away

3:32 am
korbendallas_987
they're offering bonuses for guys like me

3:35 am
almaandromeda
That's so dumb.. but are you like 90% positive they are kicking you out or totally positive now? Aren't there a lot of other doped up dudes? It seems like they accept it or they don't accept it. This seems so random. And brutal.

3:36 am
almaandromeda
I HATE arbitrary shit. Pet peeve of mine lol

3:37 am
almaandromeda
It's like a new identity then already off the PE's huh

3:45 am
korbendallas_987
no i know nothing right now. i have a job lined up on the outside but it's just majorly stressful

3:45 am
korbendallas_987
in a way, yes

3:46 am
korbendallas_987
20 yrs ago a commander would give an attaboy to me

3:46 am
korbendallas_987
now, i'm a shitbag for trying to get everything out of me that i could

3:49 am
almaandromeda
I'm so glad you have a job lined up Michael.. and I'm glad this is happening to you and for you. Fuck their 'attaboy for getting more out of YOUR temple body. Somehow when the dust clears you are going to be glad too. YOU are so resourceful! This is showing you that. 🌝🌟

3:50 am
almaandromeda
If I'm right you owe me $100 😘

4:58 am
korbendallas_987
i wanted an 'attaboy'

4:59 am
korbendallas_987
if i was a commander and i found out a soldier was trying to get an edge, and not high, i would sweep it under the rug

4:59 am
korbendallas_987
and tell him not to do it again

5:00 am
korbendallas_987
well, i know a lot of people after 15 years of doing this shit

5:58 am
almaandromeda
If it makes you happy...

5:59 am
almaandromeda
And if happiness is even what you are after 🦋 ♀ 💀

6:01 am
almaandromeda
I had the idea of an art installation that reminds me of this... I'll tell u about it later. We are so different that the miracle is communication... not necessarily understanding.

February 22nd, 2018

12:39 am
almaandromeda
I'm glad we are different.

12:39 am
almaandromeda
I could actually use your advice on something if you have any to spare.

12:41 am
almaandromeda
Something weird and kind of dark happened to me this week and it has been fking with me..I could use some outside advice.

2:44 am
korbendallas_987
sure

3:10 am
almaandromeda
I really don't know how to go into it tbh... I have some embarrassment and shame around it right now.

3:19 am
almaandromeda
I really don't want to burden or bother you either... seems like you got tired of my wacky self and I don't blame you lol. I do need advice but it's just embarrassing too for me.

5:10 am
korbendallas_987
nothing matches my fall from grace

5:40 am
almaandromeda
Just wait lol

5:52 am
almaandromeda
I'm way less than perfect unfortunately

6:52 am
almaandromeda
If I ever get the nerve to expose what a fuckup I am then I will appreciate your advice. I don't have words for everything.

7:53 am
korbendallas_987
no judgment here. i'm the bottom of the barrrl as i know it

8:19 am
almaandromeda
I really do need to talk this out with someone... I feel like a complete dumbass. I have to do my videos and then I will try to

7:40 pm
almaandromeda
I didn't do anything toooo dumb I guess. Nothing in person. Still don't like myself for it but I am seeing today it's a symptom thing and I need to just get deeper and more truthful with myself in general. Just in the trenches right now like you I guess.

7:41 pm
almaandromeda
Thanks for being open. Sorry to bug you and please do take care of those bows 🏹

MARCH 2018_

APRIL 2018_

April 3rd, 2018

2:15 am
korbendallas_987
hey

2:48 am
almaandromeda
hey you😊 I hope you are doing cool and feeling better xo

3:15 am
almaandromeda
am always curious about you if you ever feel like wasting time 🤜

6:36 pm
korbendallas_987
i'm still alive

6:46 pm
almaandromeda

7:03 pm
almaandromeda
I love that song by Pearl Jam 🎵 and I'm so glad to hear.. xo

9:50 pm
almaandromeda
My son went to jail last week. It's always some stupid shit up on this planet as they say 🤭🤜

April 4th, 2018

8:35 pm
korbendallas_987
jesus. i've felt weary as of late

8:36 pm
korbendallas_987
like i'm dying; body giving up

11:48 pm
almaandromeda
I 🖤 don't want you to give up. Please don't 🙈 Your body is your kingdom. It holds You and carries You. Tell your body how grateful you are that it is so gorgeous and carries your Spirit loyally every day and night. Your body is perfect 👌 and deserves your kindness and gentle attention. You matta xxoo

11:53 pm
almaandromeda
Are you back to working out? 🏋️ ♀

April 5th, 2018

9:12 pm
almaandromeda
Hope today is better 👊

April 6th, 2018

2:44 am
korbendallas_987
it waxed and wanes

2:44 am
korbendallas_987
waxes *

2:45 am
korbendallas_987
i actually starts working out this last weekend

2:48 am
almaandromeda
Is that making you feel better?

2:49 am
korbendallas_987
no worse i look like hammered dog shit

488

4:48 am
almaandromeda

4:49 am
almaandromeda
I can't see that as a possibility

April 7th, 2018

2:25 am
almaandromeda
Do you ever see my videos?

3:25 am
almaandromeda
I'll take that as a No lol

3:25 am
almaandromeda
Take care 🤘

5:36 am
korbendallas_987
i just don't get on here much

5:47 am
almaandromeda
👍

8:48 am
almaandromeda
I understand. Whatever you are up to these days I hope 🤞 you take care and be nice to yourself. My videos aren't for everyone lol

11:45 am
korbendallas_987
still waiting to see if the army deems me a man or boy yet. it's so fuckin stupid

4:44 pm
almaandromeda
This waiting game must be driving you insane. Gosh. You are really strong Michael.. getting through this.

4:46 pm
almaandromeda
You are a man btw 👊

4:47 pm
almaandromeda
Deemed. 🐱⚖️

4:54 pm
almaandromeda
Mercury goes direct 4/15 ☝️ maybe you will have movement then. The Waiting Room -reminds me of Beetlejuice lol

April 8th, 2018

10:27 pm
korbendallas_987
so somethins gonna happen 15 april.. lor is pullin her hair out trying to finish her degree next month and i'm hopefullly out of the army soon. severe stress.

10:32 pm
almaandromeda
Things will move soon. You said hopefully out 😃 that's a change right there 👀 Acceptance is a big part of things actually shifting. You are both loved 💚 and you will be carried through this lightly like a magic carpet. As Bill Hicks says It's just a ride. 🤘

10:33 pm
korbendallas_987
ye i found another job that pays well so i want out now. was just worried i'd be on the streets

10:34 pm
almaandromeda
You are the manifestor, I was never worried. So happy for you guys. All down hill from here xo

10:35 pm
korbendallas_987
i hope

10:41 pm
almaandromeda
I know.

10:35 pm
almaandromeda

10:44 pm
almaandromeda
YOU get what you want. I'm so glad you guys are ready to start your new life outside of what you have known. Adventure awaits! At least you know what's coming for you... I'm still working all that out lol. And I'm supposed to be the psychic 😖

10:44 pm
korbendallas_987
i don't know, it hasn't happened yet.

10:55 pm
almaandromeda
🍀 Love is all you need but here's some luck too 🍀

10:56 pm
almaandromeda
Keep a hippie chick 🌼 posted lol

April 18th, 2018

2:42 am
almaandromeda
How's life for you?

3:16 am
korbendallas_987
hard to say at this point. i want out of here so i can move on

3:22 am
almaandromeda
RELEASE THE KRAKEN!!!!

3:25 am
almaandromeda
Life is shit😖 right now 4 sure but it's just good motivation 💪 I'm looking for a
j.o.b. Wish me luck 🍀

12:30 pm
korbendallas_987
good luck. i'll be shortly.

4:43 pm
almaandromeda
Can't wait 😘

April 24th, 2018

3:04 am
almaandromeda
I really can't wait to see you Michael.

5:00 am
korbendallas_987
🖤

7:02 am
almaandromeda
🖤

April 26th, 2018

6:50 am
almaandromeda
Hey I think I mentioned to you that Soquel went to jail awhile back- he only was
in for a single day and back out immediately. I didn't want you to think he was in
there languishing lol 😖 it was more being a black teen in America than anything-
all charges dropped. He's awesome 👏 actually

492

April 27th, 2018

2:22 am
korbendallas_987
haven't had the pleasure, yet

3:01 am
almaandromeda
congrats hopefully never lol me neither but not because I wasn't trying

3:03 am
almaandromeda
I've been to other prisons of the mind tho and am still getting free.

11:55 am
korbendallas_987
i have been and more importantly will be imprisoned mentally for the rest of my life

4:09 pm
almaandromeda
I will fight you on the will be imprisoned mentally for the rest of your life for the rest of your life 💕

4:10 pm
almaandromeda
I've seen 👀 your wings and they are gorgeous xo

4:14 pm
almaandromeda
I want to hear how it went telling your mom btw when you feel like sharing.

9:56 pm
korbendallas_987
haven't told her but this app knows me and it's surreal

9:56 pm
korbendallas_987
Its an astro app – daily – look it up

9:56 pm
korbendallas_987
won't tell her until i know something

10:12 pm
almaandromeda
Cool 😎 I heard recently and thought of you that things you think will be hard in the next month may actually be much easier than you expect.

10:13 pm
almaandromeda
And people you are avoiding or reluctant in some way about may be your biggest supporters for your new direction.
Expect the best.

10:17 pm
almaandromeda
I just got the app 🌝 🌚

10:17 pm
almaandromeda
I will see about these things you say.

10:28 pm
almaandromeda
WTF!!! That's insane. I'm freaked out actually. And I do astrology. HOW do they know? My Virgo one is fucking me up. Hopefully they are right and my family shit is behind me. 🌾

10:34 pm
almaandromeda
Of course I read yours 🤓 .. and wow!

April 28th, 2018

2:29 am
korbendallas_987
haven't told her but this app knows me and it's surreal

2:30 am
korbendallas_987
no idea why that sent twice

494

11:29 pm
almaandromeda
your phone misses me duh

2:30 am
korbendallas_987
i'm tellin u that app is cray

11:29 pm
almaandromeda
It's crazy 👻 ♀ however it works

11:29 pm
almaandromeda
But I'm excited 🤓 🚀

MAY 2018_

May 3rd, 2018

2:22 pm
a**lmaandromeda**

2:22 pm
a**lmaandromeda**
I saw this a couple days ago but I just finally got the joke lol

2:27 pm
almaandromeda

2:27 pm
almaandromeda
This made me laugh immediately 😂

10:21 pm
korbendallas_987
thats funny—not where he came up with the name tho

10:46 pm
almaandromeda
Oh Ok where then?

May 4th, 2018

12:19 am
almaandromeda
just got a message!

12:19 am
almaandromeda
It's from a magazine I love, they want me to do monthly horoscopes

12:19 am
almaandromeda
Print & online - $500 a month!!

12:19 am
almaandromeda
Oh yeah my first monthlies

7:04 am
korbendallas_987

7:04 am
korbendallas_987
fuckin awesome

7:04 am
almaandromeda
🖤

7:05 am
almaandromeda
Thanks 🤘

500

7:08 am
almaandromeda
You should fly here and celebrate with me 😊

8:04 am
almaandromeda
Have you heard this quote before?

Millionaires don't use astrologers, billionaires do.

8:04 am
almaandromeda
There is Astro-finance where people predict stocks etc based on planetary trends

7:41 pm
korbendallas_987
no interesting tho

10:57 pm
almaandromeda
📱✏️🪙Looks like I figured out how to transfer money 💰 from my mind to my bank account lol 🤑

May 5th, 2018

5:10 am
korbendallas_987
then i am even more alone 👍

1:27 pm
almaandromeda
Never x 1000 🤘🥦🐏

4:24 pm
almaandromeda
At 5 am are you still awake or waking up? 🥴

May 6th, 2018

2:52 am
almaandromeda
Happy 7th wedding anniversary 〰️ 💐💜mazeltov and blessings 🙏your going to be ok 👌

8:37 am
korbendallas_987
thanks 😌

5:15 pm
almaandromeda
I think I saw the hashtag #myrib in your post about her? ok🙏 🤚 take care yo

5:17 pm
almaandromeda
Your mindset is up to you. Whatever you've done in the past.. let it go. Whatever people have told you are... believe yourself. You are awesome 💅 and will be ok. Peace ✌️ out yo. 👋

5:32 pm
almaandromeda
I just understood that when you say you feel something you mean you and Lorie feel it because you are like, one 🤚 person who share ribs... ✅ I guess.

7:50 pm
korbendallas_987
i hope you're right

7:50 pm
korbendallas_987
i happen to think that there isn't happy endings. just luck or unluck

7:52 pm
almaandromeda

8:08 pm
almaandromeda
I just don't believe. 👁️👁️It's so adorable that I ever did.

10:17 pm
korbendallas_987
you say adorable, i say destructive

11:01 pm
almaandromeda
I say I got it 👍 💯 ✌️

May 15th, 2018

4:34 am
korbendallas_987
?

6:32 am
almaandromeda
I dont have a good explanation, Im really sorry tho. I have been going thru alot and went straight Jean Gray for a sec. We are in the middle of 'D' word. Im late night delivering Postmates right now. Im feeling kind of unlucky and acted out. If you can forgive me please do.

6:19 pm
almaandromeda
Baby 👶 coming today. Looks like it will be a Taurus and I will be a grandma 👶

May 16th, 2018

9:34 am
almaandromeda
It's hard to explain unless you understand my insane mother and son but.. I showed up at the birth early on with balloons and snacks and gifts and my mom was there. I asked her when my stepdad would be coming and my son flipped out and threw all of my things into the hallway and physically manhandled me in front of my mom as she sat there and said nothing and he made me leave. So I wasn't at the birth but the baby got born tonight. Pretty fucked really.

9:35 am
almaandromeda
He's cute tho.. just haven't met him.

9:35 am
almaandromeda
His other grandma sent me a pic.

6:23 pm
korbendallas_987
middle of D word?

6:39 pm
almaandromeda
Yep.

7:04 pm
almaandromeda
Thats not public.

7:13 pm
almaandromeda
After yesterday I lost the ability to feel anything anyway so.. idk. If u can understand and forgive then Im glad. Take care.

May 17th, 2018

8:47 am
korbendallas_987
divorce?

5:19 pm
almaandromeda
Thats the word but tbh after this shit I just experienced I finally realize that nick is truly the only person in this world who gives an actual and real fuck about me.

5:20 pm
almaandromeda
I would be insane to let that go.

9:24 pm
korbendallas_987
you ALMOST turned into amorica's worst nightmare

10:29 pm
almaandromeda
I've never been to amorica but I really just dgaf 🍷😴

11:24 pm
almaandromeda
I know all about American nightmares. I was looking for the dream but I've been sleepwalking around and knocking into stuff. Nothing adorable about self destruction.

May 18th, 2018

4:41 pm
almaandromeda
I can't tell did you forgive me or not?

May 19th, 2018

2:38 am
korbendallas_987
for what

3:58 am
almaandromeda

4:00 am
almaandromeda
For nothing at all. ✌️

May 25th, 2018

7:48 am
almaandromeda

7:48 am
almaandromeda
Hey 🦋 this made me think of you.

6:57 pm
korbendallas_987
says photo unavailable

7:22 pm
almaandromeda
Sorry.. looks like he took it down. It said, When the world told the caterpillar its life was over, the butterfly objected, My life has just begun. — Matshona Dhliwayo

7:54 pm
almaandromeda
And I'm sorry for blocking you and just generally being lame 😔 I've been going thru a lot. No excuse but still it's a lot. Hope you are good 💪

May 26th, 2018

12:54 pm
korbendallas_987
never noticed, i'm not on here much

506

10:07 pm
almaandromeda

10:52 pm
almaandromeda

11:03 pm
korbendallas_987
he's playing a fender. the cherry on top of everything in this pic that i hate

May 27th, 2018

12:48 am
almaandromeda
Haha 😂 so.. the fender, the song, wine, jesus of course.. but seriously how can you hate bread? 🥖 👶 #breadislife for us poor peeps

507

May 31st, 2018

11:46 am
korbendallas_987
i gotta get back in gym

4:35 pm
almaandromeda
Maybe it's good u are resting those bow 🏹bones 😔

4:36 pm
almaandromeda
Is it less inspiring w/out the stuff? 🖊️💪

8:09 pm
korbendallas_987
very plus my elbows are still fucked

8:28 pm
almaandromeda
I love dance because I go super hard and barely notice cause I'm so into the music. And it is however I want it to be, so my body is always moving and not repeating. Do you take walks or dance at home instead? Gotta move yo 🕺

JUNE 2018_

June 1st, 2018

9:54 pm
almaandromeda
🐸My first monthly horoscopes are up! These are for June 2018

June 5th, 2018

7:02 am
korbendallas_987
will check it t out

8:10 am
almaandromeda
It's my 1st time so I'll get better hopefully 🌱

9:45 am
korbendallas_987
i'm zeroed in on occupation right now, no such thing as love, to me, at this moment

7:10 pm
almaandromeda
How's that part going at least? 😺🦎🕸 there's owlways love xo

7:17 pm
almaandromeda
Intuitive Tarot CAREER Spirit Animal reading: The armadillo reminds us that to be great in our craft we have to get our hands dirty. Spirit is asking you to get your nails deep into your interests and into the stuff of your career if you want to get the most out of your efforts. You are made for your craft/career path and you have all the skin and bone requirements needed to dig deep to find your nourishment. You are tough skinned and thick boned. You are capable. Now- dig deep. 🌿🐾🌍✏
⛏

7:17 pm
almaandromeda
This is a 'career' reading I did last night. 🐸 I'm glad you are focused on #1 👐💲

511

June 6th, 2018

1:48 am
almaandromeda
3rd interview for the same position tomorrow.. I think this is when they give it to me 🤞 It's full time $27/hr exec assistant so ya I am getting focused too 💪

2:42 am
korbendallas_987
seems everyone's employed but me

3:21 am
almaandromeda
So that's how it's going 😶

3:23 am
almaandromeda
I'm not employed YET so you know 🌸 but Postmates is always hiring lol

5:15 am
almaandromeda
#getit 🐬

June 7th, 2018

4:17 am
almaandromeda
Ok NOW everyones employed but you 😶

4:17 am
almaandromeda
Got the J O B offer

4:28 am
almaandromeda
You'll be next 💪 💚 💵

9:24 am
korbendallas_987
i have a flight evaluation board on tuesday where i was i'll stand in front of voting
members with 15 years of stellar evaluation reports along with degree, schools, blah-
blah to defend myself and my wings. no idea how it'll turn out but if it's bad, it was
a hatchet job from the beginning. i want out bad, but i don't. it's pathetic. they've
wasted a LOT of money on me. 15 years, spotless record. i know guys with DUI's.
who were retained

9:25 am
almaandromeda

9:26 am
korbendallas_987
congrats

9:26 am
almaandromeda
I am putting protection on you. 🕊 What will happen is in your greatest good no
matter what it is.

9:27 am
almaandromeda
Are you prepared?

9:27 am
korbendallas_987
goddamn i wanna believe that so bad

9:27 am
korbendallas_987
always

9:28 am
almaandromeda
Do you know the people you will speak to or are they strangers?

9:28 am
almaandromeda
I'm excited for you that it's finally moving at least

9:29 am
korbendallas_987
i was pewpews for the 2 star as well and he gave me a permanent letter from of
reprimand when it could've been local

9:30 am
korbendallas_987
it's moving at least part of it; this is the best apart where they take lt wings is or not

9:31 am
almaandromeda
If they take your wings can you still fly commercially?

9:31 am
almaandromeda
Or other than military

9:32 am
korbendallas_987
i know one of the voting members and i'm not supposed to and he isn't supposed to
as well. so that's either really good or really bad

9:32 am
almaandromeda
😂😂

9:32 am
korbendallas_987
that is. a question i don't know

9:33 am
korbendallas_987
i wish i found this half as funny as you do

9:33 am
almaandromeda
Be sure of how you want it to go so you can use your intention

9:33 am
almaandromeda
It's not, Im sorry

9:33 am
korbendallas_987
no need to apologize for true feelings

9:34 am
korbendallas_987
you got your go so it's natural to laugh at those beneath u

9:34 am
almaandromeda
I think stuff is funny when it's horrible.. that's how I've survived this far 🖤

9:35 am
korbendallas_987
i don't

9:35 am
almaandromeda
I am still waiting on passing the credit check and background check

9:35 am
almaandromeda
Which is hilarious because I have horrible credit but it's just from school loans so I'm hoping they still give it to me

9:35 am
korbendallas_987
they got more thantheir pound of flesh from me

9:36 am
almaandromeda
I'm not renting a job lol

9:36 am
almaandromeda
Do you know what you want to have happen Tuesday?

9:36 am
almaandromeda
Definitely go in there with clear intention

9:36 am
korbendallas_987
yes

9:36 am
almaandromeda
Know what you want to see happen

9:37 am
korbendallas_987
honorable discharge

9:37 am
almaandromeda
Picture it going well how you want from start to finish in your mind before hand

9:37 am
almaandromeda
Oh really?

9:37 am
korbendallas_987
i can't take the army

9:37 am
almaandromeda
Is that the best scenario you can picture?

9:37 am
almaandromeda
Cool 😎

9:37 am
almaandromeda
Army doesn't deserve you 🫣

9:38 am
korbendallas_987
already have job lined up outside

9:38 am
almaandromeda
So glad for you

516

9:38 am
almaandromeda
So you are just defending your honor?

9:38 am
korbendallas_987
i'm not

9:38 am
almaandromeda
You're not happy to leave Army?

9:39 am
almaandromeda
Or not happy for new job

9:39 am
korbendallas_987
they have to let me out first

9:39 am
almaandromeda
Release him

9:40 am
korbendallas_987
very happy happy. next job will be a cool breeze makin $

9:40 am
almaandromeda
🖤

9:41 am
almaandromeda
You happy is the best

9:41 am
korbendallas_987
i'm gonna hit the sack before tornado comes

9:41 am
almaandromeda
Goodnight

9:43 am
korbendallas_987
everyday getting out of bed is the nearest to suicidal i get

9:43 am
korbendallas_987
night

9:46 am
almaandromeda
🖤

9:46 am
almaandromeda
🎵 Don't ask me what you know is true.. 🎵

4:10 pm
almaandromeda
It's impossible to take your wings Michael 🦅 you have them always & they are beautiful

4:42 pm
almaandromeda
It's weird but the same month I turned 38 I finally had my custody trial after 1.5 yrs of being sued by my parents for custody of my then 16 yr old son.

5:00 pm
almaandromeda
The lawyers, judge, my parents, my only child.. all in a room to sufficiently judge ⚖️ me finally. I had a dream about the judge beforehand and it was her!

5:01 pm
almaandromeda
I felt like it was the lions den and they did everything to break my back. It's not possible. Just like taking your wings. 🦅

5:02 pm
almaandromeda
Stay focused 👌 👁️👁️ and I will send you good luck 🍀 and check in later this week to see how it went xo

June 9th, 2018

3:20 am
almaandromeda
I'ma tell you what to do 1. Get good rest from now to then 2. Let ALL shame & regret go, you are past that phase of this 3. Know your worth, you are an amazing soldier who is loyal and has sacrificed so much 4. Eat well and get good rest from now till then 💜

7:08 am
korbendallas_987
sounds good. i will.

June 11th, 2018

7:36 am
almaandromeda
🤍

June 12th, 2018

3:32 am
almaandromeda
I'm cheering for you from the bleachers 💪🎤💜

3:36 am
almaandromeda
You got this 🙌 Sleep well

3:37 am
korbendallas_987
tomorrow's the day they decide to take my wings. whatever you have, send it my way

1:54 pm
almaandromeda
🤍

1:54 pm
almaandromeda

1:57 pm
almaandromeda
There are a lot of people in that room today and only one I love. 🖤 Your wings are sewed in with gold angels strings and they are impossible to take away. Breathe and let time do it's thing. This too shall pass. 💪🖤💚

2:16 pm
almaandromeda
I will be thinking of you all day Michael. I wish you could see how beautiful you are.👁️🗡️🦋 Wings or not, I will always see yours on you. 🕊️🙌🙌

2:29 pm
almaandromeda
CAIM – Sanctuary; an invisible circle of protection, drawn around the body with the hand, to remind one of being safe and loved, even in the darkest times.

2:57 pm
almaandromeda
I just remembered this dream I had about you a long time ago while I was driving to work- I told you about it then but you were dressed in your full Army war gear and you were going in walking in to a building and I saw you from behind and could just FEEL how incredibly brave you are.

2:58 pm
almaandromeda
Thank you for your loyal, brave, amazing service. The Army was lucky to have you and I pray that you are discharged with honor. ❤️

5:37 pm
almaandromeda
Thinking of you. 🕊️ hope u take care of Yourself a little Xtra in the next few days no matter how it went 🕊️🙌🙏

June 14th, 2018

4:10 am
almaandromeda

4:12 am
almaandromeda
Hope you are doing ok today 🙏

10:48 pm
almaandromeda
I am so curious how it went for you. If you feel like sharing with me I want to know how you are and how it went. However it went, I just hope you are making it through ok.

June 15th, 2018

2:27 am
korbendallas_987
grounded but i keep my wings. i just want out at this point so i can move on

2:30 am
almaandromeda
Yay!! 🦾

521

2:31 am
almaandromeda
Did you get discharged?

5:11 am
korbendallas_987
nope back to waiting game. that's ANOTHER board

7:15 am
almaandromeda
It'll happen 👊

7:21 am
almaandromeda
I had a 2nd trial with my parents re:child support after my 1st trial with them. A long time ago I had a DNC a week after my abortion...it's like that. Aftershocks. Hard to let go, both ways.

3:07 pm
almaandromeda
Today is bros birthday 🎂

June 17th, 2018

5:09 am
korbendallas_987
oh fuck i didn't know

5:22 am
almaandromeda
Say hi anyway if you want to 👊 I'm sure he'd love to hear from you anytime

5:34 am
almaandromeda
We found you a year ago tomorrow 〰

12:26 pm
korbendallas_987
wow a year ago tomorrow. i still have that pic. broke me down.

4:52 pm
almaandromeda

4:57 pm
almaandromeda
Today's my son's 1st Father's Day but we haven't talked since the birth. Still haven't met baby. 💔

4:58 pm
almaandromeda
Meeting your dad and finding you changed my life for some reason. 1 year into the new me. 😿

5:00 pm
almaandromeda
We had dinner with Heather for bro bros Father's Day last night. He's a really loving papa 🖤 and Heather is amazing. Hope you meet your niece who is almost a doctor soon!

June 18th, 2018

11:55 am
korbendallas_987
20 years of work gone in a few months

2:18 pm
almaandromeda
You and me both 🙌

2:22 pm
almaandromeda
Yours is work at work and mine is work at home. I gave everything to my son as a single mama.. 20 years exactly. ⚪it's over like Rover. Plus..

2:22 pm
almaandromeda
Fun times 🤘

7:22 pm
almaandromeda
Really it's 40 yrs ... My whole life, your whole life. I've been my parents child since

523

birth until getting dumped and you've been in the army your whole life too since babyhood. So lame getting x- nayed from everything you know.

June 20th, 2018

12:41 pm
korbendallas_987
how does a mom lose custody of her son to her parents

10:42 pm
almaandromeda
I didn't lose custody. I was a loving/stable/focused mama until Soquel was 16 and he decided to run away to my parents house, angry about never meeting his dad. My parents are something called NARCISSISTS and they personally loathe me so they let him stay there for exactly 6 months and then sued me for custody. Spent $20,000 on it. I fought the whole time and eventually SPLIT the custody with them at court because I agreed to it. It was never taken from me.

10:43 pm
almaandromeda
It's a lot to explain in a few sentences. You will have to read the books. 📚

June 21st, 2018

12:15 am
almaandromeda
My mom had her 1st son taken from her and put up for adoption at age 16. Since then she has been fucked up from that. Her and my stepdad never had their own kids. They are both control freaks. I went to the only narcissist abuse therapist in Seattle last year and she freaked out so bad on me about how psycho my parents are that I had to tell her to calm down. And remind her that I was paying her for her help. I stopped going.

12:16 am
almaandromeda
Basically I don't fucking know.

524

4:17 am
almaandromeda
If you're judging me for that then there is a stadium full of fuckheads already at that show but I think tickets have sold out tbh

12:09 pm
korbendallas_987
i've been called much worse than a judge

2:17 pm
almaandromeda
"You stupid bitch? You stupid bitch? You stupid bitch? Mickey, that's what my father used to call me! I thought you'd be a little more creative than that!" - Natural Born Killers

4:08 pm
almaandromeda
I have been judged by the best, but sometimes it bothers me more than other times.

7:21 pm
almaandromeda
What's funny is you are exactly the kind of human I reserved all my judgements for before we found you. I've been released from that and I will always be grateful. It's like I see the man behind the curtain now and just FEEL for his struggle.

7:22 pm
almaandromeda
Have you told your mom yet about everything?

7:41 pm
almaandromeda
I really don't care. Don't know why I even asked actually. You obviously love good entertainment and following the crowd so I'll just send you 2 tix for you and #bae and you can say hi to the haters for me. Peace.

June 27th, 2018

3:39 pm
korbendallas_987
told mom months ago. she encouraged me.

5:48 pm
almaandromeda
I'm glad, really.

5:49 pm
almaandromeda
That's never happened to me before.

6:31 pm
almaandromeda
And I don't expect it ever will.. So ♪ don't listen to a word I say, hey! The screams all sound the same ♪

June 29th, 2018

7:32 am
almaandromeda
I think I will get to meet baby soon at least 🤞🖤

1:03 pm
korbendallas_987
yikes what a nightmare no offense

1:03 pm
korbendallas_987
i can barely take care of myself

2:24 pm
almaandromeda
Upside down man 🙃🌐

2:27 pm
almaandromeda
To me the nightmare is silence, loneliness, separation... this is BLISS to be connected. I've lived the nightmare a 1,000 times. Do my daydreams seems like terrors and my terrors like daydreams to you? 🤯🤯I'm not offended tho, just curious about you still 1 yr later.

2:28 pm
almaandromeda
My dad always said to be a grownup you need to be able to take care of yourself and 1 other person... you are doing great 👍

7:10 pm
korbendallas_987
i want this part of my life to be done so i can move on. i'm stuck because of extreme inefficiencies

7:18 pm
almaandromeda
I know how it can be to feel like you are in a cell standing on your head waiting for the time to pass. This is the engine of inner strength. Time always passes but what you take with you from that time is what you have with you forever.

7:20 pm
almaandromeda
You are already a year older and wiser from when I first start bothering you lol 😵 🤐

7:20 pm
almaandromeda
Tomorrow that is

7:44 pm
almaandromeda
You've been quiet with Nick lately I guess so he asked me if I've been communicating with you. I told him I bother you with memes sometimes and you barely respond which is pretty much the play- by- play 😂 just fyi

June 30th, 2018

8:02 pm
almaandromeda
Hope your day is good 🎂 Happy birthday 🤐

JULY 2018_

July 15th, 2018

9:46 am
korbendallas_987
no fuckin clue how i missed this aside from not getting on here that much. Thanks, life feels awful, 40 feels good.

July 16th, 2018

6:18 am
almaandromeda
I'm seeing baby 👶 lots now and working full time and doing lots of readings too so luckily I didn't even notice this time that you forgot about me 🧜‍♀️ ♀ 😹

6:19 am
almaandromeda
You turned 39 I thought. I'm the 40 yr old 🙀 ♀

6:47 am
almaandromeda
But if 40 feels good do 40. It's all the same. Hope life feels better for you soon.

4:15 pm
korbendallas_987
thanks me too

4:30 pm
almaandromeda
We are going thru some tough stuff now too so keep bro in your thoughts. Life is a Dragon and it's hard to ride.

5:18 pm
almaandromeda
If you feel like venting I'm never too busy.

5:48 pm
almaandromeda
My son and his little family are hiding out in a motel an hour outside of town evading gang violence and that's not even my biggest problem today so no judgements here as always.

July 18th, 2018

10:43 am
korbendallas_987
Dragon? Substance?

2:24 pm
almaandromeda
I was just being poetic.

2:26 pm
almaandromeda
Translation for the homies in HI: Life can be tough sometimes. 👍🏼

July 23rd, 2018

8:07 am
korbendallas_987
somethin happened this week that turned my cursed, fuckass life around. too much to explain much less digest. still in disbelief.

2:14 pm
almaandromeda
You've been saved? ✝️

2:15 pm
almaandromeda
Just kidding but when you want to share I want to hear about it 🖤

2:16 pm
almaandromeda
Huuuuge changes here. And soon.

4:30 pm
almaandromeda
In my world that would be having a baby or winning the lottery so you know I'm curious lol xo

July 24th, 2018

12:24 am
almaandromeda
Are you guys having a baby?

July 25th, 2018

7:34 pm
almaandromeda
To be clear it wouldn't be a baby that would do that for me.. Been there, done that. 😎 Just to my limited imagination it sounded like something big like that for you. Do tell 🤓

July 29th, 2018

1:20 pm
korbendallas_987
fuck no no kids

1:20 pm
korbendallas_987
at all. do u understand yes/no circle one

1:23 pm
korbendallas_987
despite the 2-stars best efforts I got an honorable discharge from the army and already hired at civilian job. makin some pretty good dough. i also kept my wings but they grounded and the lawyer worries about that in case i try to get a job with FAA

3:42 pm
almaandromeda
Circle yes

3:42 pm
almaandromeda
I'm soooooo glad

3:43 pm
almaandromeda
Just expressing my fears out loud lol

3:43 pm
almaandromeda
Congratulations 🫠

3:44 pm
almaandromeda
You rock and you deserve a fkn break lol

3:45 pm
almaandromeda
You have a lawyer.. thats so fancy! I'm happy for you xo I thought this was probably what it was. ❤️

3:46 pm
almaandromeda
Are you staying in HI?

6:01 pm
almaandromeda
Or are you guys heading to the deserts 🌵 🐪 🏜️

July 30th, 2018

7:37 am
almaandromeda
Sounds like you made it through the dark tunnel tho. ❤️ You won't need Alma Poppins anymore and the winds have changed for me too. Soon we won't be sis&bro anymore but I felt lucky to get to know you as much as I was able. Take care. If you ever feel like it, look up Twin Flames... I think there is something there. There is no explanation for my fascination of you that I can find. It's harder (for me) than it looks.

AUGUST 2018_

August 4th, 2018

1:05 pm
korbendallas_987
yep—got an honorable discharge despite the 2-star's best wishes here. the secretary
of the army actually has a brain and was like uhhhhhh absolutely not. so i kept my
wings and getting an honorable discharge, currently clearing post. i'm already hired
in the middle east and lor is flying to london for an interview for a job in the same
city as me. comPLETE 180.

4:21 pm
almaandromeda
All the best

4:23 pm
almaandromeda
Please don't write me again and I'll do the same for you 👍

August 13th, 2018

6:00 am
almaandromeda
Hey I'm sorry for being so abrupt. Just how I protect my heart. I try to forget. I send
you good vibes for your next adventures 🐪🌵👍

August 15th, 2018

7:25 am
korbendallas_987
ye can't figure u out but i have my own problems

2:24 pm
almaandromeda
I will just be honest with you so you don't have to figure me out...

2:26 pm
almaandromeda
A year ago I saw your face and fell in love. I've never felt love-at-1st-sight before but
that was what it was.

2:28 pm
almaandromeda
I kind of woke up from a long mental slumber. It was so inspiring. And obvious probably.

2:30 pm
almaandromeda
I don't think you encouraged my feelings for you or gave me false hopes. You've been honest and clear about your deep love for your wife in every interaction with me and have only tolerated my curiosity of you kindly.

2:32 pm
almaandromeda
Over this year I've changed a lot. And everything around me changed because of what I'm willing to accept for my life. I want more. I know that much at least.

2:34 pm
almaandromeda
You are going to the desert now and I will probably never meet you. I just feel like it would be easier sometimes to forget you because I have a place in my heart for you but it seems pointless.

2:46 pm
almaandromeda
Even the experience of feeling love for you, as strange and pointless as it's been, has taught me a lot. I don't regret meeting you and sort of becoming friends. It's just a lot for my heart personally. I like you and want the best for you wherever whatever. Take care xo.

6:46 pm
almaandromeda
I hope you get me better now

August 17th, 2018

6:54 am
almaandromeda
And I'm sorry for saying that. I love to hear from you.

August 18th, 2018

7:52 am
korbendallas_987
i understand all. nothing is forever incl my desert stint.

August 19th, 2018

8:07 am
almaandromeda

8:08 am
almaandromeda
I hope ☝ I do get to see you someday before I'm ancient lol

8:22 am
almaandromeda
♫ I feel so different ♫ I'll be 40 in Sept and divorced soon after. Nothing even to do with you.. but I did need to wake up and you helped.

9:03 am
almaandromeda
To be honest you are not
a mathematical order
designed by the star of Venus,
your face does not stop me,
stop everything, I am not
rolling constantly in the
dry field of your last words.
You do not have a finger
deep through the middle of me,
I am not squirming and moving
on the dream of your lap.
I don't want that! I don't want
anything! You aren't the only one
to 'do that thing', and honestly,
this is nothing, I have no feelings,
I don't whisper your name or
cum to your face, I don't cry
hot tears in lonely disgrace.
I don't miss you, I don't want you.

539

You don't compel me like the
moon moves the oceans,
you don't have a spell on me,
I did not drink your potion.
I'm not made for you.
I don't think of you every morning.
I won't wait for you.
This is not a love story.
-Alma King, Not A Love Story

9:03 am
almaandromeda
One 🤞 year later almost to the day and I still won't wait for you and it's still Opposite Day

August 20th, 2018

2:44 am
almaandromeda
Tbh: My heart knows there is only one 🤞 💀🙌 but a stint of years means I have to still live in the meantime. I feel like I've been endlessly motionless for many years now and I'm ready for my real life to begin.

2:46 am
almaandromeda
I only hope that when timing does align we are both free to spend the time I want to spend on you💜 🤞 🔭.

3:52 am
almaandromeda
I'm sorry for being so forward all of a sudden out of nowhere.. I wanted to say something for awhile 🖐

August 22nd, 2018

1:34 am
korbendallas_987
remember the grass is always greener but someone still has to cut that shit

540

1:35 am
korbendallas_987
i dontbelieve in a shred of that 'meant to be' hoopla- no offense

7:34 am
almaandromeda
I'm offended but I'm sure you don't care.

7:37 am
almaandromeda
I'm back to bye forever this is pointless

7:47 am
almaandromeda
I don't think it 👋 is you either. Sorry to have disturbed your slumber.

5:41 pm
almaandromeda
I'm glad you said what you did. I'm not grass to be mowed regularly... I'm actually kind of amazing. I'm the whole rain forest. If you don't see that in me then I am free to be loved by someone who does. Have an awesome life.

August 23rd, 2018

7:29 pm
korbendallas_987
even if i see a girl i really wanna bang i know it's just somebody else's grass. was a full blown mysogynist for a long time

7:31 pm
korbendallas_987
it ain't worth it to me. if i'm cheating i hate my wife. maybe i'm just secure in THAT vein?

7:42 pm
almaandromeda
I get it. Goodbye.

7:50 pm
almaandromeda
I don't want anything or even care at this point. I truly wish you both the best. But

good luck with hating women . Since there are just SO many of us sounds like a shitty waste of time. I know aaaallll about wasting my time now.

8:21 pm
almaandromeda
To be clear: I am NOT in love with you. I was delusionally infatuated with my own projections of you and that is obvious to me now.

8:22 pm
almaandromeda
I'm more disgusted at this point than anything else and I just really want to never speak again.

August 26th, 2018

2:21 am
korbendallas_987
where'd that come from? you've piqued my interest..
i've been a garden variety mysogynist since i could crawl but there are women i would blow my brains out for. you misrepresent the definition of the word (through no fault of your own). shrink says it was because the way i was born, from an infant, everything i took in. and it alllll came from a woman who i would blow my brains out for. ironic? not if u think about it. i couldn't piece it together at the time, but i see now.

3:16 am
korbendallas_987
and i don't hold her responidble.

3:18 am
korbendallas_987
what's with the polarization? Either hate or love, ugly or infatuation. People who stick to polarization must look through black and white (no grey, none) sunglasses 😎

6:24 am
almaandromeda
I have stuff to say but tomorrow.

August 27th, 2018

3:33 am
almaandromeda
I'm very sorry for what you experienced under the hands of The Feminine. There are 3.8 billion ways to be a woman. What you experienced is a part of what women are capable of but it is not everything.

3:42 am
almaandromeda
You told me early on you were a misogynist but I still don't know what that means.. to you.

3:43 am
almaandromeda
I know that I have not wanted to be seen a bad woman by you or a whore or whatever... I don't know why it mattered to me.

3:51 am
korbendallas_987
nah not at all. from birth i have truly viewed females as an inferior gender. no hate behind it. it's ME. it's who i am. it's who Hitler was. There is such thing as a misanthrope—that's not what I mean to convey to you.

3:51 am
korbendallas_987
what i mean to convey to you is:

3:53 am
korbendallas_987
that i hate the female gender as entire gender. I hide it well. Believe it or not, ol Cozee's son used to be a looker and I would dog the actual FUCK out of girls that truly loved me (very early on in relationships). just ask like they never existed

3:53 am
almaandromeda
I believe it lol

3:53 am
almaandromeda
Why?

3:54 am
korbendallas_987
my unit in korea had this nickname for me like cold shoulder or some shit i can't
remember maybe it was iceman

3:54 am
korbendallas_987
because i fucking hate them

3:54 am
almaandromeda
And me?

3:55 am
almaandromeda
How do you feel about me?

3:57 am
korbendallas_987
i'm anxious to see my brother and his wife someday before i die in a helicopter. it's
on a bucket list

3:59 am
korbendallas_987
i have a very intimidating appearance and i am only telling you this because my
shrink has told me this 800 times. i look people in there when asking obvious questions and people generally stay away from me. so i have created enemies that i revel
in and even fiercer friends who jump in front of a bullet as a result

3:59 am
korbendallas_987
you'd have to know the last 15 years of my life in the army to understand me better

4:00 am
korbendallas_987
when i get the love/hate/love/hate messages from you i don't pay a lot of attention
cuz u don't mean any of it

4:00 am
almaandromeda
Let me tell you how I feel:

4:01 am
korbendallas_987
people in their eyes*

4:02 am
almaandromeda
You are unique to me... not like anybody else I have met or in my life

4:02 am
almaandromeda
Your messages are meaningful and potent to me

4:02 am
korbendallas_987
how

4:02 am
korbendallas_987
i'm just you're brother in law

4:03 am
almaandromeda
Do you want to know for real?

4:03 am
almaandromeda
You're my brother in law but you're also you

4:04 am
almaandromeda
And something about you made a light ⏻ feeling inside me like ecstasy.. and it has inspired me since.

4:04 am
almaandromeda
If you never felt that it is fine

4:05 am
almaandromeda
And that is why I'm just some girl to you

4:05 am
almaandromeda
You never felt that?

4:06 am
almaandromeda
Yes/no circle O one

4:07 am
korbendallas_987
inspiration? i have gone through living hell over the last 15 months for using performance enhancing substances in the goddam army. I'm thinking about living under a
bridge because i can't make it, not you.

4:09 am
korbendallas_987
maybe if circumstances were different, i could give you more attention but the love
hate love hate is the very very very last thing on my mind right now. I'm fighting for
my life.

4:09 am
almaandromeda
I understand

4:10 am
almaandromeda
I have wanted to be there for you and it's impossible.. I started making nightly
videos to just send my love out.. But I'm useless and I get it.

4:11 am
korbendallas_987
i stay away from IG because of my depression. saw none of it

4:12 am
almaandromeda
Of course lol

4:12 am
almaandromeda
My life

4:12 am
korbendallas_987
how about correction: 1st world problems

546

4:13 am
korbendallas_987
there are people scraping for food right now, addicts that are dope sick, you name it

4:13 am
korbendallas_987
and you say my life to your response?

4:14 am
korbendallas_987
my response*

4:15 am
almaandromeda
Hey I'm inferior what can I say? 👻 ♀

4:17 am
almaandromeda
I wanted a mirage and what a dangerous thing a mirage is to a thirsty man.

4:17 am
korbendallas_987
i'm an existential nihilist. what can i say?

4:19 am
korbendallas_987
i've become a bit neutered in my late years but you did not want to meet me at 29. If a girl seduced me at a bar, I'm thinking ha-she has no clue the mistake she just made

4:19 am
almaandromeda
You were HOT 🔥🙌😍

4:20 am
almaandromeda
She was fine with it I'm sure

4:20 am
korbendallas_987
how u know

4:20 am
almaandromeda
Pictures

4:20 am
almaandromeda
You are the best looking man I've seen maybe ever

4:20 am
korbendallas_987
none of my old pics are on therr

4:20 am
korbendallas_987
here

4:20 am
korbendallas_987
well thank you

4:21 am
almaandromeda
Your older pictures are very fine

4:21 am
almaandromeda
You have the most beautiful face

4:21 am
korbendallas_987
i hate it

4:21 am
almaandromeda
It is different.. so mathematical

4:21 am
korbendallas_987
i want chiseled not fat moon

4:21 am
almaandromeda
I always say in my head you are a fat face

4:21 am
korbendallas_987
don't say a word about cancer or moon child

4:22 am
almaandromeda
And it is nice

4:22 am
korbendallas_987
or i will kill you

4:22 am
almaandromeda
I wish lol

4:22 am
korbendallas_987
i got it from my mom

4:22 am
almaandromeda
Save a bridge the bad reputation

4:22 am
korbendallas_987
although she used to be a bombshell

4:22 am
almaandromeda
Your mom is gorgeous too!

4:22 am
almaandromeda
Big eyes

4:22 am
korbendallas_987
blue

4:23 am
korbendallas_987
i wanted blue so bad. so many mixed have blue

4:23 am
almaandromeda
You are prefect down to the freckles on your nose

4:23 am
almaandromeda
Perfect

4:23 am
almaandromeda
I mean lol

4:24 am
korbendallas_987
infatuation

4:24 am
korbendallas_987
i'm ugly insidr

4:24 am
korbendallas_987
a monster

4:24 am
almaandromeda
We all are.. parts of us

4:25 am
korbendallas_987
one of Satan's own prototypes never even considered for mass production

4:26 am
almaandromeda
Well Satan was just looking for a little understanding and love and to be respected

4:26 am
korbendallas_987
my shrink really took a liking to me. she was nice enough for me to give her the REAL me

4:27 am
almaandromeda
and you opened up to her?

4:27 am
korbendallas_987
sure

4:27 am
korbendallas_987
told her first day

4:27 am
almaandromeda
Is the real you a rage person?

4:27 am
almaandromeda
Do you scream a lot?

4:28 am
korbendallas_987
no

4:30 am
korbendallas_987
but i rage in a different way. i have the curse of a very robust vernacular/vocabulary and i ask people questions in an extreme sincere manner that they are unable to answer. Did you lie to me about preflighting the aircraft? Why is it ok to you, to lie to a senior instructor pilot about prefligjting an aircraft?

4:31 am
korbendallas_987
and i look them STRAIGHT in the eyes

4:31 am
korbendallas_987
i corner them verbally

4:31 am
almaandromeda
We're gonna have the stare down of the century👀👀

4:31 am
almaandromeda
Get ready

4:31 am
korbendallas_987
my friend Jay explodes when i do it

4:31 am
almaandromeda
I'm sure you're horrible!! 😭

4:33 am
almaandromeda
I want to tell you healing

4:33 am
korbendallas_987
i speak very sincerely when i do it. it's hard to explain

4:33 am
korbendallas_987
i'm better than before

4:35 am
korbendallas_987
i'm still a monster. i look about 120 seconds into the future and when i get home
i've got sole business with my neighbor

4:35 am
almaandromeda
I want to get yelled at by you lol

4:35 am
almaandromeda
What is sole business?

4:36 am
korbendallas_987
Some business

4:36 am
korbendallas_987
he'll be speechless and if i have to i will shatter his maxillofacial area of his face so
bad that it will require multiple surgeries before anyone can even look at him
without vomiting

4:37 am
almaandromeda
What did he do?

4:37 am
korbendallas_987
i'll start off with the same earnesty that i always do and when i catch him slip, he's
done

4:37 am
korbendallas_987
he is scared to DEATH of me

4:37 am
almaandromeda
What did he fucking do? 😂

4:38 am
korbendallas_987
he'll fuck with my mom and stare at her while he's perpetually married to someone
in mississippi and living with the woman neighbor of ours

4:38 am
korbendallas_987
textbook manipulator

4:39 am
almaandromeda
Are you in TX?

4:39 am
korbendallas_987
he approached me about the joining the VFW the first time he saw me, and I
screamed get the fuck out of my face right now to him

4:39 am
korbendallas_987
no

4:39 am
korbendallas_987
hopefully saturday

4:40 am
almaandromeda
Did you guys survive the hurricane?

4:40 am
almaandromeda
Saturday.. that's the mainland! Come here now.

4:40 am
korbendallas_987
he fell down running and my brother and i laughed so he could hear

4:40 am
korbendallas_987
there was no hurricane

4:40 am
almaandromeda
So you are evil lol

4:41 am
korbendallas_987
i've gotta takena shower. i'm disgusting

4:41 am
korbendallas_987
you have no idea about me alma, rest assured

4:41 am
almaandromeda
I don't yet but I want to

4:41 am
korbendallas_987
i have killed hundreds and if they'd let me i'd kill hundreds more

4:42 am
almaandromeda
I know.

4:42 am
almaandromeda
And you put up with me

4:42 am
almaandromeda
Hopes not gone yet

4:42 am
almaandromeda

4:43 am
almaandromeda
Before you go

4:43 am
almaandromeda
I want to tell you

4:52 am
almaandromeda
Come to Seattle if you are coming to the mainland. Bucket list that bitch!

4:53 am
almaandromeda
I love Nick but I am divorcing him and we won't live together after a few. If you come soon I will more likely meet you.

5:02 am
almaandromeda
I'm a monster too because you're married and your wife is absolutely a gem

5:02 am
almaandromeda
And all I want to do is tell you how I want to call you Daddy and feel your hand on my neck

5:03 am
almaandromeda
Now who's bad? 🐀 ♀

5:33 am
almaandromeda
What a funny experience tho. Do you think? Complete opposites, complete strangers, I've never heard your voice. With every other stranger I have cut them off after 2 or 3 exchanges. Every single one but you. I keep trying to with you but I keep wanting to know more too.

3:28 pm
almaandromeda
I'm sorry I said I was disgusted. It was because I thought for some reason I was more than just some girl to you, and I felt more stupid than anything so I said that.

3:29 pm
almaandromeda
I know what kind of person you think you are and what you have done and say you have done. I'm not disgusted by that. That is much more complicated.

3:33 pm
almaandromeda
The love/hate on/off switch thing is a defense mechanism from childhood related to me wanting love and it NEVER showing up. I just say fuck everything then and burn it down. It really hurts to feel things. That is why it is weird that I have felt anything for you. Usually I just keep that on mute.

5:07 pm
korbendallas_987
understandable

5:15 pm
almaandromeda
Which part?

10:00 pm
almaandromeda
It was fun talking to you last night and always is. But.. I guess I just believe you. You think women are inferior. You don't feel anything. You're not it. I believe you. I need something a little sweeter anyway.. And thoughtful of me. It's out there. Take care.

August 28th, 2018

7:53 am
korbendallas_987
Never.

8:24 am
almaandromeda
I'm wrong sometimes. 🐀♀ 🐨♀ 🐿️♀

8:25 am
korbendallas_987
I LOVE being wrong. It means I learned something which is rare.

4:43 pm
almaandromeda
If you rarely learn then you are rarely wrong. I like to be wrong more consistently than that.

6:47 am
almaandromeda
What is inferior about the female gender btw? 😐 Reasons. What makes 3.9 billion people inferior to 3.7 billion other people? I really don't get it. 🐀♀

7:19 am
almaandromeda
I have always considered myself ferior to the guys 💪

August 30th, 2018

1:42 am
almaandromeda
Do you know what Kundalini is?

1:43 am
almaandromeda
This is the light ˌ feeling I was talking about

10:47 pm
korbendallas_987
I simply have no use for them so they get discarded like leftover tuna casserole.

August 31st, 2018

11:00 pm
almaandromeda
Liar.

11:01 pm
almaandromeda
You just hurt and so you say that.

11:02 pm
almaandromeda
Leftover tuna casserole is my favorite thing on earth anyways so beauty is in the eye of the beholder. You're missing out. But that's your problem not mine.

11:03 pm
almaandromeda
All I know is... I pity the fool- ette that puts up with your shit 😆 never met anyone quite as miserable as you dear.

SEPTEMBER 2018_

September 1st, 2018

5:53 am
almaandromeda
If you were trying to hurt me with your statement about leftover tuna fish it didn't land. I'm sexy and amazing and 40 soon. I hear how gorgeous I am too much. I see Goddess in everything I do. Nothing you can say touches that.

September 6th, 2018

12:01 pm
korbendallas_987
You missed the mark on that comment.

2:09 pm
almaandromeda
I just miss Mike.

2:33 pm
almaandromeda
I'm a bad shot lol 🏌️‍♀️ 🏀♀️ ✏️🖼️🏀

7:01 pm
almaandromeda
If you were harder to read you'd be Arabic. 🙃I'm bad at nuance. Too much left-overs I guess.

September 7th, 2018

6:35 am
almaandromeda
I love to be happy. And feel safe. I've lived with lots of darkness and violence as a child. I felt unsafe many, many times at the hands of men who had access to me but did not respect me. As an adult... I don't have to.

September 11th, 2018

10:11 am
korbendallas_987
love the Arabic pun, I'll be there before too long.. Home in Texas now with an overwhelming amount of depression, rage and anxiety. Usual Michael.

2:05 pm
almaandromeda
You missed my birthday.

2:14 pm
almaandromeda
I'm pretty sure you told your bro you'd come here next time on main land 😊 but I stopped holding my breath because my extremities turned blue and fell off.

2:32 pm
almaandromeda
But I know this:

2:32 pm
almaandromeda
Life is not a fairy tale.. if you lose you're shoe at midnight – you're drunk.

2:33 pm
almaandromeda
I'm really sorry you are suffering Michael. 🙏 I can't imagine the things you carry.

5:09 pm
almaandromeda
Talk to me. I want to know what hurts. I'm in another world away. And if you want I'm here.

8:47 pm
korbendallas_987
it's genetic and environment; serious brain issues. nothings ever good enough, low self image, etc

9:19 pm
almaandromeda
I hear you. I decided to brainwash my damn self into believing I'm as awesome as I really am because if you knew my parents youd understand. Both my bio mom and dad are clinically insane. And NARCISSISTS. It would be easy to just go with that for myself... But why? I'm worth the effort.

562

9:20 pm
almaandromeda
You are too.. But only you can want to be happy for yourself. It's truly a choice no MATTER what you have done or has been done to you and no matter who has opinions about you. Fuck em, politely.

9:24 pm
almaandromeda
I disagree it's genetics because of my genetics but I'm no scientist.

9:24 pm
almaandromeda
Do you want to feel happy?

10:39 pm
almaandromeda
Will you visit us?

11:23 pm
almaandromeda
Personally I don't really like the word God or any other substitute for the word. Simply because most people are conditioned to see 'God' and religion as being synonymous when they are not! Hence why so many people tend to throw out the baby with the bath water! 😕 💥 ⬛

11:23 pm
almaandromeda
Never forget how you resemble a galaxy

September 13th, 2018

9:24 am
korbendallas_987
i don't really know happy so i assume i keep it at a distance until it proves itself to me, like people. typical 'crab' behavior.

3:44 pm
almaandromeda
You're playing the victim while being a warrior. They don't mix.

3:44 pm
almaandromeda
Please don't use astrology as an excuse for your bad attitude on life.

3:49 pm
almaandromeda
I enjoy two-way conversations, not because I'm a Virgo but because I'm a human being.

10:00 pm
almaandromeda
I found out I have to get an MRI because it looks like I may have MS. Or as Richard Pryor calls it More Shit ugh. I'm actually scared.

September 15th, 2018

5:17 am
almaandromeda
I'm scared but I'll be ok 👍

OCTOBER 2018_

NOVEMBER 2018_

November 23rd, 2018

3:51 am
almaandromeda
Happy Thanksgiving from your new nephew Oscar the Chiweenie! He's so cute!

4:01 am
korbendallas_987
🖤

5:13 am
almaandromeda
And hi 👋 from me 😊 I took lots of roids for my recent health stuff and thought it was funny 😆 I took prednisone today lol

5:42 am
korbendallas_987
••

5:53 am
almaandromeda

2:54 pm
almaandromeda
I found out I've had a brain 🧠 issue called Multiple Sclerosis for the past year & a half. It affects the body but also thinking etc. Now that I am getting treatment I see how dangerously it was fucking with my life. I feel much better and am so grateful for my life 🖤

3:23 pm
korbendallas_987
MS is no joke

4:13 pm
almaandromeda
I'm not laughing 😆 but I feel better knowing wtf has been up w/me because I was feeling bad.

4:17 pm
almaandromeda
Steroids help lower inflammation in the brain. I had a gram a day infusions for 3

days. I've had 3 MRI's and a spinal tap in the past 1.5 months. I got a new tattoo and a puppy 🐶 Nothing is funny. 😑

4:50 pm
almaandromeda
Except puppy 🐶 he's a comedian! 🤪🤣

7:47 pm
almaandromeda
I've had amazing friends and the best husband ever there for me through all of it so I feel really lucky 🍀 it could be a lot worse.

9:34 pm
korbendallas_987
Dogs are important, I miss dogs.

9:36 pm
almaandromeda
I'm sorry 😔 What happened to your last girl?

9:36 pm
almaandromeda
This puppy 🐶 makes me smile 😃 all the time- mini scooby doo 🐶

10:11 pm
almaandromeda
I think pit bulls are so sweet to be around but I wanted a tiny dog to take every-where with me.

November 24th, 2018

4:00 am
almaandromeda
I'm curious how you are

4:58 am
korbendallas_987
i'm programmed to self destruct, like my dad

5:51 am
almaandromeda
Being at your dads bedside was deep, and sad... he was so alone except for this giant

boisterous caretaker lady, and he seemed lucky for her. That's where we found the box 📦 of pictures of you. Fuck a program my little brother 💯

9:51 am
korbendallas_987
Programs are meant to do exactly what they are designed; much like cancer or a pathogen. No sense in denying.

10:51 am
a**lmaandromeda**
What is the purpose for your high IQ? Sincerely curious.

10:53 am
almaandromeda
In relation to following the program.

10:54 am
almaandromeda
I wish you could meet my mom. I beat that program like wot 💪 I'm not perfect but I'm NOT her.

11:04 am
almaandromeda
Nothing is absolute. Everything changes, everything moves, everything revolves, everything flies and goes away. -Frida Kahlo

11:27 am
almaandromeda
Are you teaching 🚁 again?

5:23 pm
almaandromeda

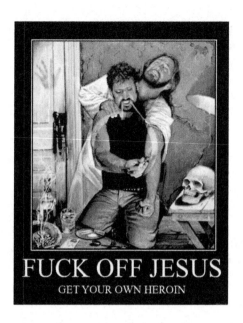

10:20 pm
korbendallas_987
i love that heroin meme. fuck id give anything to try that shit. i am teaching.

10:25 pm
almaandromeda
I thought it was appropriate since I've taken over the steroids use lol 😆 crazy world 🌍 happy vets day belated 1st official. 🎖

10:45 pm
almaandromeda
I used to be able to get by on weed, water and food to regulate my energy levels but now steroids help on long days like Thanksgiving. I don't do that everyday like the other 3.

November 25th, 2018

4:06 am
almaandromeda
Have you seen Leaving Las Vegas?

5:35 am
korbendallas_987
don't think so

5:57 am
almaandromeda
One of my favorite all time movies

6:18 am
almaandromeda
For some reason I think you'd like it. Are you a civilian now for the rest of your life?

6:30 am
almaandromeda
Are you a veteran or a retired army official or is it the same or different?

6:34 am
almaandromeda
I know you're busy no more questions lol

6:47 am
korbendallas_987
didn't retire, hence the sorrow

6:48 am
korbendallas_987
civilian though

6:59 am
almaandromeda
That's right... I'm sorry those fucks did that after all you gave them.

7:00 am
almaandromeda
Civilian life is just capitalism and the orders come from who signs the checks.

7:0 am
almaandromeda
Your nephew doggie hopes to meet you someday! Take care till then.

7:23 am
korbendallas_987
yea i need to make it out there at some point

4:02 pm
almaandromeda
I want to meet you too obviously 😚 but Oscar the Chiweenie is more important lol
🥹 I'm keeping the faith 🤞

6:35 pm
almaandromeda
My little brother just surprised us with a visit from a Unicorn the other day actually.. I hadn't seen him in 7 yrs or so. He built his own house with his woman on acreage in Idaho. We have same mom/dad and he's 18 mos younger. I love my little bros, including you, and they always have a place here 😊

November 26th, 2018

3:46 am
korbendallas_987
😎

DECEMBER 2018_

December 22nd, 2018

10:35 pm
almaandromeda
It's a full moon 🌑 in Cancer today ♋ Did you see that crazy car video I posted?

December 23rd, 2018

9:31 am
korbendallas_987
UAE video 👆

10:31 am
almaandromeda
What's it like in the land of gold? Do you wear long robes?

10:33 am
almaandromeda
Hope you're getting that bread 🥖 😂💯

1:46 pm
korbendallas_987
Always, playboy

1:46 pm
korbendallas_987
they have gold bouillon vending machines

5:39 pm
almaandromeda
I'm off the roids 💊 btw

7:32 pm
almaandromeda
Your niece Heather got married today!

December 25th, 2018

9:03 am
korbendallas_987
nothin makes sense anymore. just wanna make cheddar and die

9:23 am
almaandromeda
Making cheddar's cool 😎 but meet me before you do that other stuff 🖤

9:26 am
almaandromeda
🎄 Merry Christmas 🎄 to the Kings & lots of love xxoo

5:53 pm
almaandromeda
Nothin is as it seems, usually. It's a grey winter ❄️ but I really don't mind. 😌

December 26th, 2018

5:34 pm
korbendallas_987
man if i was in seatac, i would be drugged OUT

5:59 pm
almaandromeda
I'm high 💊 all the time

December 27th, 2018

7:47 pm
almaandromeda
But if you were here I could hide the drugs or find you drugs- whatever you need lol 😅 and there's other fun stuff to do besides drugs 😎

6:07 am
korbendallas_987
nah nothing fun beside drugs

6:16 am
almaandromeda

6:18 am
almaandromeda
Story of my life 😂

6:20 am
almaandromeda
You're in a big kid paradise 🛢️ 🏗️ 🏍️ what could be more fun 🤙

8:36 am
korbendallas_987
freedom from mind

9:13 am
almaandromeda
I hear you 🖤

9:24 am
almaandromeda
But I got you on the drugs bro bro 😎 it's been my main survival technique since I was 12

9:25 am
almaandromeda
I just posted a pic of me at 12 with my dad and my little brother

9:56 am
korbendallas_987
great pic

1:10 pm
almaandromeda
That year I was miserable 😩 and cut my hair off myself.

4:41 pm
almaandromeda
I really can't imagine everything you've gone through, what you've seen, things you've done, so many years in the army, now to become a civilian in a new country.. to me you are really strong 💪 and I can imagine wanting a mind break now and then xo

6:55 pm
korbendallas_987
i would take ANYTHING to break free

6:59 pm
almaandromeda
Just that you want to shows how strong you are. What you've lived... it's real shit. This is a tender time of becoming new, outside what you've always known. Go easy on my bro Michael ❤

1:04 pm
almaandromeda
In the Matrix Neo breaks free because he realizes who he actually is. I'm on this, personally. Sadly, and gladly, 2019 is gonna be that year.

December 30th, 2018

3:47 pm
korbendallas_987
i'm afraid of 2019 but nothing will parallel 2017.

3:48 pm
korbendallas_987
The dogs of the nazarene may have won that battle but my luciferian dogma will prevail.

December 31st, 2018

2:48 am
almaandromeda
That was fucked and to me unfair but you rocked it and came out on top. Yiure a badass like that. My lion's den massacre was 2016 but it might as well been yesterday.

2:49 am
almaandromeda
*you're

2:53 am
almaandromeda
I guess at least with your luciferian dogma you know who you serve. I don't know... I just feel like I'm living the same day over and over again. I don't know if I should just keep it up to make people happy or wake the fuck up and live for me.

5:40 am
almaandromeda
I do like most of my life tho and what I don't like I can change if I really want to. Hope you both have an awesome 2019 and maybe this will be the year we get to meet you guys! Take care xxoo

6:23 am
almaandromeda
And I guess.. to be honest, I just can't relate to "everything Louie" and luciferian. She got SIX louis vutton purses and a burkin? For Christmas? That's like $50K. or MORE
I think you are rad but I can't relate to that world. Peace out xo

7:51 am
korbendallas_987
Luciferian is said with a bit of tongue in cheek; while there are true Luciferians, I am more of a LaVeyan or original satanist. We simply worship ourselves. I just happen to not be so good at it.

7:56 am
almaandromeda
I have to Google so much shit before I can even write you back lol

7:58 am
korbendallas_987
nahhhh

8:17 am
almaandromeda
As Cinderella herself I am the very worst at self worship so I'm glad that's not my religion. I don't have a religion or dogma on anything. I like to Dance tho. I had never heard of LaVayen before.

9:30 am
korbendallas_987
he was a bit of a douche which reminds me of myself. his mantras could be flat out riveting, however

9:39 am
almaandromeda
Douches have the best job 😂 😎

9:40 am
almaandromeda
I have never had a credit card and have raised my son since 21 on cash only and put myself thru college. You are on a WHOLE next level. 💲 I'm inspired but I'm way not cool like you. 😚

9:59 am
almaandromeda
I should probably gets to chanting mantras but that's some freaky shit lol 😂 I'm scurred of incurring demons 😳

10:00 am
almaandromeda
I am so free of all that

10:01 am
almaandromeda
Thankfully 😅

1:03 pm
korbendallas_987
your attention to my sordid lifestyle and cannot and will never understand. I am waifish, mediocre, and a failure at both death and life.

1:03 pm
korbendallas_987
I cannot*

2:43 pm
almaandromeda
I hope that's not a LaVey mantra 😳

2:43 pm
almaandromeda
You are none of those things 😜

584

10.51 pm

almaandromeda

But you do definitely fascinate me and I'll figure out how to say why that is for me..
till then rock out 2019 😊, I won't be there for awhile xo

JANUARY 2019_

January 1st, 2019

5:44 am
korbendallas_987

January 7th, 2019

10:21 am
almaandromeda

January 18th, 2019

8:01 am
almaandromeda
I can't believe you're dead.

4:45 pm
almaandromeda
Hope you have freedom from mind as you dreamed.

THE END_

Made in the USA
Middletown, DE
03 July 2022

68279015R00335